A SUDDEN SUN

Judy MacNeill

A SUDDEN SUN

A NOVEL

TRUDY J. MORGAN-COLE

WWW.BREAKWATERBOOKS.COM

Breakwater Books is committed to choosing papers and materials for our books
that help to protect our environment. To this end, this book is printed on a
recycled paper that is certified by the Forest Stewardship Council of Canada.

LIBRARY AND ARCHIVES CANADA CATALOGUING IN PUBLICATION
Morgan-Cole, Trudy J., 1965-, author
A sudden sun / Trudy J. Morgan-Cole.
ISBN 978-1-55081-559-7 (bound)
I. Title.
PS8626.O747S83 2014   C813'.6   C2014-901924-6

 Canada Council   Conseil des Arts   Canadä   Newfoundland
for the Arts   du Canada   Labrador

We acknowledge the support of the Canada Council for the Arts, which last year invested
$157 million to bring the arts to Canadians throughout the country. We acknowledge the
financial support of the Government of Canada through the Canada Book Fund (CBF)
and the Government of Newfoundland and Labrador through the Department of Tourism,
Culture and Recreation for our publishing activities.

PRINTED AND BOUND IN CANADA.

FOR MY MOTHER

JOAN G. (SUE) ELLIS MORGAN

In loving memory

Prologue

LILY, 1892

_L_ILY HUNT SAT on the front bridge of her family's home, drinking ginger beer and fanning herself, reading Mrs. Gaskell's _North and South_ in the hazy grey-gold light of an early July evening, when she heard the first screams.

It had been hot all day, for days and days in a row—not at all the usual St. John's summer when cool breezes, fog, and rain could be expected to punctuate the warmer weather. When St. John's did have warm weather, the skies tended to be clear blue, free of fog, but all this week there had been heat with smoky haze from the brush fires and forest fires burning outside the city, fires that licked up grass and trees with no rain to slow their progress. She had heard the fire bell an hour ago: no doubt another house or barn up in flames. A tang of smoke flavoured the air and it was so hazy Lily could stare directly at the sun. It looked like the face of a woman wearing a veil.

The heat tired her out, though it didn't strike Lily as hard as it did poor Mother. The benefit came in the evenings when temperatures dropped a little but it was still warm enough to go walking or sit out of doors. Mother was lying down upstairs with a cool cloth on her brow—she had gotten up for supper and gone immediately back to bed—so Lily was alone on the bridge when she heard a man shouting at the top of his lungs.

She stepped off the verandah and looked up the road, hoping to see the cause of the commotion. A knot of people gathered at the end of the street, down by the corner of Garrison Hill, but she couldn't tell what kind of group it might be. Perhaps she ought to go inside and bar the door just in case some young hooligans were looking for trouble. She wouldn't wake Mother, of course, but it might be prudent to take refuge inside and perhaps she could tell Sally to send a boy to the print shop with a message for Papa.

She was just turning to go inside when she saw someone coming—not a threatening crowd but a single man running, stopping to shout at windows or pound on the doors of houses as he passed. Lily stepped down into the front garden, out towards the gate. Though the man was still three houses away, running past the Temples' front door, she could hear that he was shouting, "Fire! Fire!"

"Where's the fire?" she called. The stranger was in the front garden of the house next door now, talking to Mrs. English's cook, and Lily hiked up her skirt with one hand and hurried to join them. "Where is the fire?"

The man turned to her and lifted his cap. "Started at O'Brien's Farm, Miss, but it's sweeping downtown in all directions. We're warning people to get out of their houses in case it comes this way."

"But…all the way up there? Freshwater Road? It wouldn't spread this far," Lily said. Fires were nothing unusual in this town of crowded wooden houses; just a few days ago a blaze had left twenty poor souls homeless. But the fire station lay between here and O'Brien's Farm— Lily remembered the clang of the great bell earlier. Surely even a big fire couldn't travel all the way down to Queen's Road.

"Miss Hunt, the Mister sent me up to tell you and the Missus,

Miss, told me I should get you both out of the house, it's not safe."
It was John Evans, who worked for Papa at the shop and was their
man-of-all-work about the house. When Lily turned to Evans, the
stranger took off at a run, down the road to bring the word to other
families. She had only a quick impression of him—sandy hair under
a flat cap, a smudge of ash on a cheekbone. Had he been that
close to the fire? Looking west towards the site of the fire she saw
the sky was darker there, smokier than the general haze of the sky.
She turned back to Evans. "Papa really believes we need to leave the
house?"

"Yes, Miss. Is the Missus lying down?"

"I'll go wake her." Evans was accustomed to all their habits,
including her mother's mid-afternoon rests and frequent headaches.
It embarrassed Lily that her mother's weakness was so apparent
even the servants took it into account. She hurried into the house and
up the stairs as John Evans continued talking below. "Me and Sal,
we'll just get the little handcart, and you and the Missus can tell us
what things you wants put in it. The Mister said not to take nothing
bigger than a handcart, and I should get you all up to Bannerman
Park."

Lily crossed the upstairs hall to her mother's door. Below, she
could hear the reassuring rumble of Evans's voice and the higher
shrill of Sally, the housemaid, taking in news of the fire.

Eleanor Hunt was in deep sleep, her drapes drawn, her room
gloomy as an underwater cave. The air itself felt thicker in here, an
element to swim through rather than breathe. One of Lily's earliest
childhood memories was of standing in this doorway, teetering
on the threshold, wanting her mother but not wanting to breach the
solitude of that room, of the afternoon rest.

Lily shook her mother awake. By the time she had managed to
wake her enough to convince her there really was a fire sweeping
through the town and Father wanted them to leave the shelter of the

house for the open spaces of the new park, Evans was in the doorway, cap pressed to the front of his shirt. "Miss, Ma'am, sorry to trouble you but did you have any thought about what you might want to put on the cart?"

"Cart?" Eleanor echoed, still not fully awake. "I'm not riding up to the park on a cart."

"No, Ma'am, a handcart. The Mister said we should take a little cart, me and Sally only needs to know what to put in, like. Things you might want to save if—well, if the house were to go, God forbid."

Eleanor's eyes widened. "It won't come to that, surely? Why, we'd have to take—"

Lily stepped forward to forestall the image of her mother loading everything in the house, from her wardrobe full of dresses to the grandfather clock downstairs, onto a handcart. At nineteen she was more the woman of the house than her mother was, and a crisis like this required firm decision, a quality Eleanor had always lacked. "We should take a few of the nice blankets, I suppose, in case we're out long and it gets cool this evening." She couldn't imagine being gone longer than that: surely they would be back in the house by nightfall, the danger past. "The...the silver, in the box downstairs," she said. "Sally will know about that." She took her mother's family Bible from the nightstand, the one with years of careful annotations, with the Hunt and Stone family trees lovingly inscribed in the front, and handed it to Evans. "Take this, and—and Father's strongbox, I'll bring that. Mother, take your pearls."

"The clock!" her mother said, and for a mad moment Lily did think she meant the grandfather clock, until she pointed at the fine old mantel clock above the bedroom fireplace. "That painting—the one downstairs—it was a gift from my mother! Oh, and my furs..."

As Lily had feared, her mother trailed off, unable to stop listing things she could not live without, and as she wandered vaguely about the room picking up a scarf, a fan, a silver letter-opener, Lily met Evans's eyes and nodded. "Just those things, the things I told you," she said.

Half an hour later they made a little procession down Queen's Road to Prescott Street, where they joined a larger group crossing Military Road towards Bannerman Park. The streets had been transformed in that half hour, from quiet residential streets on a summer afternoon to a crowded scene of people straggling north and east, toward the park or the lake. Women, children, and servants mostly, the men still being at business down on Water Street or, Lily thought, probably helping to fight the fire. The acrid smell of smoke was stronger.

"It's gone downtown, towards the harbour now," someone said, and "I heard tell all of Long's Hill is on fire," another added. All around were voices, people sharing news or rumour, advising each other of the best place to take shelter. Ahead of them, Evans pulled the handcart while Sally walked beside, making sure the little pile of worldly goods didn't topple. Lily took her mother's arm and made soft soothing noises while trying to catch snatches of conversation from the people passing by.

"The Missus said she wouldn't leave the house without the barrel of flour because she just bought a whole new barrel and she wouldn't have it go to waste," said a man nearby to a companion, "and I couldn't get her out of the house without it, so I dumped it all into a clean pair of long johns and took it with me." Lily took a second glance at the man and saw that over his shoulder, like the bottom half of a ghost, he did indeed carry a stuffed pair of men's long underwear, tied off at the ankles and waist. He moved in a cloud of flour dust.

"We brought all our furniture, all our good pieces, to Gower Street church, you know," a woman said as they moved into the park itself. "I mean, the churches are stone and brick, they'll never burn. I saw the Church of England bishop himself—well, his men, you

11

Trudy J. Morgan-Cole

know, but he was there—moving trunks of clothing and books into the cathedral."

Eleanor tugged at Lily's sleeve. "Send Evans back—he could take our good furniture to the Congregational church." The Hunts attended Cochrane Street Methodist, but surely in a crisis the Congregationalists wouldn't bar Methodist neighbours from storing things in their Stone Chapel, Lily thought.

"Wait 'til Papa comes," she said. "He'll know what to do about our things. All he wants is for us to get to safety ourselves."

In the park, Eleanor stared at the throngs of people—every sort of person, from well-dressed ladies like themselves to beggars and street urchins. It was as if the sight of so much humanity overwhelmed her, robbed her even of the power of speech.

"Over there," Lily said, pointing at a patch of grass. "Bring the cart over there, Evans. Sally, spread out the blanket, the blue one, on the grass. It'll be like a picnic, Mother. Only without anything to eat."

"Oh no, Miss, I packed you a lunch," Sally said, as Eleanor protested faintly, "Not my good blanket—on the bare grass!"

How clever of Sally, Lily thought, to think of packing a lunch. That was the mark of a good servant—to realize what one needed before one thought to give the order. Cold chicken, hard cheese, and some of the light fruit cake. There was even a jar of pickles and another of tea wrapped in a towel both to protect the glass and hold in a little heat.

The evening was still warm, not yet near sunset. People laid down blankets or sat on the bare grass nearby, everyone crowding closer as more people poured into the park. A girl of about ten in a ragged dress sat very close by and stared with wide, longing eyes at their supper. Lily cut a slice of fruit cake and handed it to her.

The sky grew slate-grey. Every breath tasted of smoke. The babble of voices all around swelled with every group of new arrivals. Now people were fleeing the fire itself rather than just leaving their homes as a precaution. Around their little island of blanket Lily caught snatches of talk.

"It's down to the harbour…Job's premises are burning."

"We was barely clear of it before the roof fell in."

"There's people stealin' stuff right out of shop windows, brazen as brass."

"I saw the windows of the Cathedral—them big stained-glass windows? Blew out like someone heaved a rock through 'em."

So much for the Bishop's furniture, thought Lily. Around her she could hear every kind of voice to be heard in St. John's: the cultured accents of the educated, the rough accents of the poor, the heavy brogue of fishermen.

Lily imagined rain. Thought of cold, wet St. John's afternoons, of rainy mornings and chilly nights. This summer had been so hot and dry, but every other summer of her life she could remember picnics ruined by rain, walks along Rennie's River that had ended with sopping skirts and umbrellas turned inside out by the wind. Rain was the one thing St. John's was never short of. And today barns, houses, whole streets burned, and not a drop of water fell to help the men fighting the blaze.

There were few adult men in the park: only the very old. Every able-bodied man was out at the fire. "You should go," Lily said to Evans, who had just gone around the park to hear the latest news and report back to them.

"No, Miss. Your father told me to look out for you and your mother."

"He told you to get us safely out of the house and to the park." Across the street, on the other side of Military Road, houses were in flames. The street was filled with men, hoses, barrels, and buckets, but nothing seemed to slake the hungry fire. People pressed together at the edges of the park to watch the houses burn. Every few minutes there was a crash and a shout as another roof caved in. Lily craned

13

her neck to see past the crowds as if she could look past the bend in the road and see whether the flames had reached her own house.

A soot-stained man ran up to Evans, grabbed him by the arm. "Come on, b'y," he shouted, "They want men down on Cochrane Street. The fire's going up towards Rendell's big house on the corner, but if we tear down the one next door, it might stop there."

"Oh my God, if Rendell's burns then the flankers might go across the street—" On the other side of Military Road was not only the wooden Anglican church but a school and orphanage, all ready to go up in flames.

"Go, John," she urged Evans, and he fled with the other man, pushing through the crowds of watching women and children.

It grew dark. The light that illuminated the faces around her turned sickly and strange. The sky changed colour again: gunmetal grey overlaid with an eerie orange glow. Lily paced the grass: her mother had finally fallen into a fitful, uneasy sleep curled on the blanket, with Sally watching over her.

"The wind is carrying flankers from one street to another," their neighbour, Mrs. English, said when Lily found her amid the crowd gathered to watch the houses on Military Road burn. "Mr. English is gone down with a crew of men trying to save Gower Street church. I heard the roof was on fire already."

"It's down at the harbour now, down to the wharves," said another woman. "I heard Harvey's wharf is burning."

There was no place to lie down, no possibility of sleep. Back at their blanket she found Sally dozing and Eleanor restless. Lily put an arm around her mother and Eleanor slumped against her. Lily wondered had she ever done this before—put her arms around her mother, held her as Eleanor had held her when Lily was a child. She couldn't remember.

Her eyes stung. She sat with her mother as long as she could then wandered the park again, listening for news, looking for faces of her

friends and neighbours.

By the time the sky lightened to a dull grey, men had returned to the park. Exhausted, soot-stained, coughing men, telling tales of houses gutted, families homeless, wharves and shops and even the churches that were thought to be invincible, gutted by flames. There was still a glow in the sky; smoke was rising, though the weary, dirty men said the fire was no longer spreading. Only the buildings that had already been devastated smoldered like kitchen stoves banked for the night.

Then, out of the grey mist her father appeared, tall and bearded, his suit jacket gone and shirtsleeves rolled up. His face was nearly black with soot. He put out his arms and Lily stumbled into them. "Papa!" she sobbed. "You're alive, thank God! We were praying—"

With the words came the thought that they were not precisely true—she had been worrying about her father and had remembered that she ought to pray, but had been too caught up in the troubles of the moment, even in the long watches of the night, to form the words of a prayer. Her father's shirt smelled even more strongly of smoke than the air around them did. "The building, Papa? The press? Did you save it?"

"It's gone, Lily, all gone." His voice broke on the second "gone" and she thought he might be crying—she had never seen her father cry—but then he coughed. "The press is gone, everything," he repeated, as if he had to say it over and over to make himself believe.

She didn't ask if he had been to see their house yet. She wasn't ready to know.

She was hungry; her limbs were stiff and sore. And she longed to use a privy, but she didn't know where to find one and how could she even ask? Surely her mother, too, must be desperate to relieve herself, but in such a scene, how could one delicately find a place? It was impossible to even think about, and at the moment it seemed more pressing than finding food or bed or a roof over their heads.

Trudy J. Morgan-Cole

When she led her father back to their picnic spot, her mother was talking to another woman, looking more animated than she had all day and night. "Lily, love, you've met Mrs. Ohman, of course," she said, and with the introduction out of the way she turned to her husband's arms.

Lily was left with Mrs. Ohman, whom she had not met, though she had heard her speak once at a meeting of the Women's Missionary Society. She was a neat, trim little woman fond of feathers, beading, and embroidery on her clothing, and she looked tidy and pretty even after spending all night in the park. Wisps of hair escaped from under her hat, and her skirt was stained with grass and dirt, but she still carried herself as if she were Queen Victoria. Lily was almost breathless, for she admired Mrs. Ohman very much. She was a leader in the Women's Christian Temperance Union and the editor of the *Water Lily*, a lady's paper that Lily devoured as soon as it went on sale every month. "I—I'm so very pleased—I've wanted to say how much I…"

"Yes, of course, thank you, dear. You'll be wondering about breakfast and the other necessities. Well, there are no privies yet, of course, but some men have dug latrines down there by the trees and we have people watching them to make sure ladies are given a little privacy—as much as is possible. We've set up some tables with porridge and bread and tea—not very much, among so many people, but we'll get better organized as the day goes on. Come with me now, Lily. You can find a latrine and then I'll get you some water to wash up and you can help some of the girls serve tea and bread. We need to make sure it's distributed fairly, you know, so it doesn't all go to those who are strong enough to push to the front of the lines."

Mrs. Ohman was a whirlwind, and Lily was carried along, happy to bob in her wake now that Papa was here to take care of Mother.

Mrs. Ohman stationed Lily behind a long table—a sheet of

board lying over a line of sawhorses—and put a ladle in her hand. Several large iron pots filled with porridge were placed on the table as volunteers organized a mass of people into lines. As they reached the table each person thrust out a bowl, or a plate, or a cup—whatever they had managed to salvage from home or borrow from a neighbour—to be filled. Every few minutes someone brought another pot, swaddled in towels, to replace an empty one. Most of the people proffering empty bowls were poor, but Lily saw some better-dressed folk among them. She was glad to have work to do, but the ache in her stomach reminded her that she hadn't yet had anything to eat. Sally came to the table with an assortment of the crockery they'd used for last night's picnic, wiped out rather than washed, and Lily filled bowls to bring back to her parents.

"Where is the food coming from?" Lily asked the girl next to her, as someone brought a new pot of porridge. Martha Withycombe was a year or two older than Lily herself. She attended Gower Street Church, her father was a schoolmaster, and there was talk she was going to be engaged to some young lawyer whose name Lily couldn't recall.

Martha nodded her head off in the direction of Circular Road. "Some big houses that escaped the fire—and I think some of it may be coming from the kitchen at Government House. How did your house fare?"

"I—I don't know yet. When I saw Papa he had come from trying to fight the fire at the print shop—he hadn't even been to see our house yet."

On the other side of Martha, a familiar head popped forward, crowned with a flowered hat that still managed to look jaunty. The curls beneath the hat belonged to Lily's friend Abby Hayward. Lily hadn't seen her in the park during the night.

"I'm sure you'll be fine, Lily. Father says we are," Abby assured her. "He says Cochrane Street Church and everything on the west

17

side of the street is still standing, and so is St. Thomas's." Abby lived on Cochrane Street, much further east than Lily's home on Queen's Road. Lily had already heard that the Congregational chapel, just west of their house, had succumbed as rapidly as the other brick and stone churches that were supposed to be invulnerable.

What if our house is gone? Lily wondered. She had already handed bowls of porridge to her own housemaid to feed her parents—surely the first time in their lives her mother or her father had to take a handout from anyone. Father was well-off enough to rebuild his house and business, but where would they live until that happened? The sun was not yet fully up in the sky and already policemen were arriving with tents, temporary shelters for people who did not expect to sleep indoors tonight—or for many nights to come.

"Any more gruel left in that pot?" said a vaguely familiar male voice, as another bowl appeared in front of her.

She looked at the young man holding out the bowl and wondered where she had met him before. He wasn't a neighbour nor did he attend Cochrane Street Church. His sooty clothes were slightly better than those of a working man but neither his suit nor his accent suggested he was a gentleman.

She filled his bowl, still looking at the keen eyes under a shock of ginger hair, trying to place him. "So, did your house survive, or are you taking refuge here in the park as well?" he asked, showing no inclination to move away once he had his bowl filled.

"I don't—I am sorry, I don't think we've been introduced," Lily confessed.

His face broke into a grin. "No, we haven't, not a bit." He stuck out a hand for her to shake, just as if someone had presented him, which of course no one had. After a moment, Lily took it, giving his fingers the briefest shake possible. "David Reid, newsman," he said. "We met yesterday when I was giving the alarm about the fire down by your house. But it's hardly the time to stand on ceremony, is it?"

"An emergency is no excuse for impertinence, Mr. Reid, and Miss Hunt has work to do." Mrs. Ohman appeared by Mr. Reid's elbow. Mrs. Ohman had a high, fluting little voice that led some people to take her less than seriously, but she could sound stern when she wished, and now she wished to.

Mr. Reid touched the brim of his hat and smiled. "I'll leave you to your work, Miss Hunt—now that Mrs. Ohman's told me your name," he said, and sauntered off. Mrs. Ohman was already scurrying in the opposite direction, rolling up her sleeves to cut some of the loaves of bread that had just arrived.

"What a very odd fellow!" Abby giggled. She was a giggler, had been the silliest girl in their class at school. "He certainly likes you, Lily."

"He's very impertinent, is what he is," said Martha. "You oughtn't to have spoken to him without being introduced—and nobody would introduce you to such a person."

"You know who he is, then?"

"He was a pressman or some such thing at the *Evening Herald* who started writing bits of copy and now imagines he's a newspaperman. Trying to strike up conversation with a lady he hasn't met is beyond rude."

"Mrs. Ohman seems to know him…"

"Oh, Mrs. Ohman!" Martha rolled her eyes. "*She* knows all sorts of people—and has all sorts of queer ideas." The line of people coming to have their bowls filled had slowed to a scattered few, and most of the porridge pots were empty. Martha began collecting the pots, moving with brisk efficiency.

"I think Mrs. Ohman is marvellous," Lily said. It was hard to attempt a dissenting opinion in the face of Martha's confidence, but she couldn't stand by and hear her heroine disparaged. "Don't you read the *Water Lily*?"

Trudy J. Morgan-Cole

"Mother reads it first and clips any articles she thinks are appropriate for me to read," Martha said, "There are things in there she doesn't agree with." That surprised Lily, since Martha's mother served along with Mrs. Ohman in the WCTU and the *Water Lily* was, if not the official WCTU paper, certainly a mouthpiece for that organization. Martha turned from the pots to give Lily a measuring glance that took her in from top to toe, then said almost kindly, "But of course your mother's not well, is she? Perhaps she hasn't the time or energy to be aware of all that goes on."

"My mother is well aware of everything I read," Lily said, though she doubted that was true, "and she admires Mrs. Ohman too."

"I love the *Water Lily* nearly as much as the *Ladies Home Companion*," Abby chimed in. "Did you read the latest instalment of Alida's story, Lily? I can't bear to wait for the next issue!"

"It's a temperance paper," Lily said to Martha. "Our family have always been temperance people."

"Of course we are for temperance," Martha said. She handed a stack of pots to a girl in a maid's uniform, who was presumably taking them back to her mistress's kitchen to clean, and Lily passed hers to a similarly garbed older woman. "The WCTU does good work, and so does Mrs. Ohman herself. But if you think the *Water Lily* is just a temperance paper, you're deceived. Mrs. Ohman uses it to promote the idea of votes for women. Father says too many men let their wives and daughters read all sorts of books and papers, not even realizing they are introducing radical ideas. But as your father is a printer, I thought he'd be more aware of such things."

There was little to say to this, since Lily was fairly certain her father had never picked up a copy of the *Water Lily* despite the fact that each month's issue was on the parlour table as soon as Lily could get hold of it. He would be no more likely to read it than he would the *Ladies Home Companion*. But what if Papa heard that Martha's parents had forbidden it, and wouldn't let her read any more of it?

Like Abby, Lily was caught up at the moment in reading Mrs. Ohman's serial story *Alida*, which had been going on for months showing no sign of an easy resolution. Lily secretly tried to model herself after Alida, a girl of her own age and class living right here in St. John's. Alida was so pure, so perfect, so full of high ideals and good works. She had refused to marry the man she loved because he wouldn't take the temperance pledge, and now her wicked younger sister was set to steal his affections. If she didn't find out how the story ended, Lily thought she might die of curiosity.

It would be wonderful to be like Alida, or Mrs. Gaskell's heroine Margaret in *North and South*, or like Mrs. Ohman herself—to fight for good causes and care for the destitute, to be a shining light in the community. Perhaps, Lily thought, the fire, this strange night and day in the park, might mark a turning point in her life.

When the supply of food ran out—which happened before the supply of hungry people did—and all the pots and pans had been sent off, Lily walked back to where she had last seen her parents. Her clothes, worn since yesterday morning, were dirty and smelled of smoke—but then, everything did—and she wondered if she still owned anything else to put on. Little clusters of people camped out on the grass. The wretched poor huddled together in rags, while people like her own family, well-to-do folks suddenly made destitute by unlucky chance, looked far more shocked than the poor at this turn in their fortunes.

Back at the blanket where she had left her family, Papa paced restlessly. "Come with me, Lily," he said when he saw her. "Walk with me down to the house and we'll see what's still standing. I've heard tell that whole row of houses is gone but I won't believe it 'til I see it for myself. Sally's caring for Mother—I don't think she could stand the strain of seeing the place if it has been burned down."

Lily took her father's arm and they made their way through the crowds, out of the park. Military Road was full of people doing the

Trudy J. Morgan-Cole

same thing they were doing: venturing out to see the devastation, to see what remained of homes and businesses.

The dull grey light of the smoky morning showed a road that had become impassable, strewn with the rubble of fallen houses. Across from the park where hundreds of people had sheltered during the night, the fire had ripped through the wooden row houses, leaving only the brick chimneys standing so the street looked like a graveyard with gigantic brick tombstones. Between each lay the debris of what had been a home, a life.

"No matter what condition the house is in, you and Mother are not to worry, now, Lily," Father said, the tremble in his voice betraying him. He and Lily picked their way through the huddled knots of people and the debris in the road, up Military Road, down Prescott Street, down to Queen's Road. "We will be able to rebuild. You may have to go stay with your mother's people out in Harbour Grace until we have a roof over our heads again. It may be only a matter of minor repairs…."

His voice trailed off as they reached the spot that, until last night, had been their home. It had been an imposing three-storey house, not grand but solid, attached to the house next to it. All that remained now were the blackened chimneys, towering above a heap of fallen interior walls, shattered windows, burned possessions that had been their furniture, clothes, china dishes, and shelves and shelves of books.

"Don't, Lily," her father said as she let go his arm and began to walk into the rubble. "Your skirt—your shoes—"

It was a feeble protest and even he recognized it, for he was doing the same, moving into the debris of their home, their lives, as if looking for one miraculously unburnt thing that would be a talisman, a sign of hope. Lily looked in the ashes for a gleam of silver or gold, a face still peering from the frame of a painting, a book whose pages, inside charred covers, might still be intact. The sharp smell of ash almost choked her. And wherever she looked on the ground at her feet, she saw nothing but trash and soot.

Despite the devastation, despite the way her father was rubbing his face with a handkerchief as if he could erase the devastation he saw all around him, Lily couldn't suppress a quiver of excitement, a small winged thing inside her. With everything destroyed, there was always the possibility of beginning again.

She knew better than to mention the phoenix to her father—that was overly dramatic even for her. Papa would be concerned, man-like, with the practical details of insurance and rebuilding. She kept hope folded inside herself, a phoenix in a cage, as she and her father wandered, arm in arm, around the edges of the ash-heap that had been their home.

Trudy J. Morgan-Cole

Part One

1917–1919

CHAPTER ONE

A SEALED ENVELOPE addressed to Reverend Obadiah Collins, Catalina, Trinity Bay, Newfoundland, lay on the kitchen table. When Grace came home she found her mother sitting at the table, her hands folded, about eighteen inches from the envelope. Her gaze was fixed on it.

Grace didn't know, as she crossed the kitchen, that it was a telegram. She came through the door telling her mother that Mrs. Snelgrove had stopped by the school to pick up the little ones and told Grace to tell her mother she couldn't be at the WPA executive meeting this evening. "She said to say she was sorry, hoped it wasn't too much of an inconvenience—" Grace stopped short of trying to convey the undercurrent of nervousness in Mrs. Snelgrove's tone: the women of Catalina did not lightly tell Mrs. Reverend Collins that they could not attend a meeting. Then she realized her mother wasn't listening, saw what she was staring at.

"When did it come?"

"An hour ago."

Grace drew her fingers over the unopened white envelope as if she could break a spell by touching it. She wondered how long her mother had sat here looking at the envelope. She would never have admitted to needing her daughter or her husband with her when she opened and read the telegram. But she had not opened it herself.

"Should we wait for the Reverend?" Grace asked. She and Charley, when very young, had picked up their mother's habit of referring to their father by his title: Mother never called him Obadiah, only the Reverend, and his children said Papa or Father only when speaking directly to him. In the third person he was always the Reverend.

Her mother said nothing. She had not even looked up to meet Grace's eyes; it was as if by looking at the envelope she could will the news inside to be something other than what it must be. Good news never came by telegram, not in the spring of 1917. Not to a family with a boy overseas. The best you could hope for was wounded but recovering in an army hospital in England. Out of harm's way. Some perfect injury, severe enough to send him home for the duration of the war, yet light enough not to blight his future.

If Grace had the power to bend fate, she would sacrifice Charley's arm or Charley's leg or even one of his eyes to buy his life. Would her mother make the same exchange? Grace thought so, but it was, like so many other questions, something she could not ask.

She took the envelope, turned it in her hands. She would go to get a letter opener. No, she would go to get her father. He was either at the church or over at Port Union. The church was right across the road from the manse; he might be preparing Sunday's sermon. Perhaps if he was in the middle of opening the Word of God, he could call on divine power to change the words on the inside of the envelope.

"We should read it first. Then I'll go find Father."

Her mother made no move. Grace opened the envelope, read the words first silently, then aloud, as if they were lines in a play. As if they had no connection to her, to her mother, to her laughing older brother who had gone away just a year ago, looking oddly mature and serious in his uniform. She reached across the table but her mother pulled her hands away. "Excuse me, I—I need to be alone," she said. "Find the Reverend and tell him." Her voice broke on *Reverend* and she hurried out of the room. Why today, of all days, would she not say "your father" or even "Obadiah"? Why was it essential that she leave the room before Grace could see her cry? Shouldn't they be crying in each other's arms?

Grace searched her memory for a time when she was in her mother's arms, cuddled and petted, crying after a fall or a disappointment. She remembered words instead: "Don't make a big fuss over such a little thing." "You must be brave; don't complain." But this was not a little thing, not a skinned knee or an unkind taunt. Grace thought of following her mother upstairs. What would she say?

Instead, she left the telegram on the table, went out of the house. A mild April day with sun trying to break through the overcast sky. She practiced as she walked over the road to the church, tried to imagine what to say to her father. Could she say, with a steady voice and dry eyes, "Father, there's been a telegram. Charley has been killed in action"? Or would she say, "There's bad news—you'd better come home and read it for yourself"?

The church was empty. These days, if her father was not at home or in the church, he was often over at the Fisherman's Union site on the south side of the harbour, visiting Mr. Coaker. She left the church and climbed the path to the little graveyard, perched on the hill looking down towards the water. It was a sunny day, the clear blue sky making the air crisp and cold even for April: she shivered and wrapped her coat closer around her. There was a stone here in memory of one Catalina boy already: George Snelgrove died last year in the terrible July Drive. Charley was one of scores of boys from all

29

Trudy J. Morgan-Cole

around Trinity Bay who had enlisted after hearing about those losses: as if every time a boy was cut down in the bloody soil of France, another had to be uprooted from a Newfoundland bay and planted over there in his place.

She could see late-afternoon sunlight dancing on the water, and boats in the harbour— no fishing boats out yet, far too early in the year for that. She could see, distantly across the harbour, the skeletons of new buildings going up in Mr. Coaker's town. She couldn't hear the ringing hammers from here, but she knew from experience that if she took the path that led to the bridge over to the south side, within fifteen minutes of walking she'd be close enough to hear that sound.

A boy, a young man, ran down the road below her, towards her house, and for a moment Grace thought it was Charley. It was Jack Perry, Charley's best pal. Charley and Jack had talked about joining up together last summer, but Jack's mother had convinced him to go back to college in Canada instead. He was the youngest of four sons and the other Perry boys all worked in the family business: Jack was studying to be a doctor up in Montreal. He had just come home for his holidays.

"Jack!" Her voice steered him away from the manse; he bounded up the hill to the graveyard.

"Is everything all right? Mother saw the boy from the telegraph office going up your lane."

Grace shook her head. "I think...I think my father must be over visiting with Mr. Coaker. Can you go find him? Tell him to come home."

"Was it...?" Jack left the two words hanging: adding more would, Grace thought, make it more real. She shook her head again, then nodded, and tears came, finally. And there was, after all, someone who would take her in his arms and stroke her hair while she cried—not her mother but Jack Perry, her brother's friend, a boy she barely knew. She pressed her face into the rough cotton of his work shirt and felt his body rock a little from side to side.

When she drew away they both stumbled back a step. Jack handed her a big white handkerchief and she dabbed at her eyes and then blew her nose hard. He said, "I'm sorry," at the same moment she said, "Thank you," so the words got jumbled and it was impossible to tell for a moment who was sorry and who was grateful, and for what.

"I'll go find your father," he said. "You go on home, I'm sure your mother needs you."

Does she? Grace thought. If she did, Grace had no idea what kind of help to offer.

"Should I tell him?" Jack said. "Or just say there's been a telegram and he should go home?"

"No, tell him." *Then I won't have to say the words.* Maybe she would never have to say, "My brother is dead," and it would never be quite real. Especially if, like so many, he was buried over there in France somewhere. It would be as if he had simply gone away. Even after the war ended—if it ever did—it would be as if Charley had survived all the battles, married a Frenchwoman, and stayed there, and somehow forgot ever to write a letter home.

Jack went over the road toward the south side of the harbour, and Grace walked back to the manse. It was the maid's half-day off and the house was like a mausoleum. Somewhere upstairs, Lily Hunt Collins lay, or sat, behind a closed door, mourning her son. Her daughter walked half-way up the stairs, looked at Lily's bedroom door, then went back down to the kitchen and picked up the telegram on the table. She waited for her father to come home.

Trudy J. Morgan-Cole

Grace

CHAPTER TWO

"**Y**OU'VE WRITTEN THEM already? Given up your position?" Lily stood across the parlour from Grace; she wore a brown wool skirt and a beige linen blouse but in her mind's eye Grace saw a breastplate over her mother's bosom and imagined donning her own armour for this fight.

"I did. I told you I would."

"And I told you not to! Not without your father's permission, without mine. Now you've given up an excellent teaching position, and for what?"

Grace had taught school here in Catalina for two years now, ever since getting her second-class certificate from the Methodist College in St. John's. The best she could say about teaching was that she didn't hate it. In fact there were parts of it she liked very much: she liked the children themselves, especially the ones who had trouble in school, who came barefoot from the poorest homes and huddled close to the stove for warmth. She wanted to follow those children home, put shoes on their little cold feet and cook a good dinner for their sick, overworked mothers, instead of staying in the schoolroom and dragging the rest of the class through one Royal Reader after another.

"I've told you what I want to do," she said.

"And we've told you it's not possible." Lily was a formidable sight when laying down the law, which as far as Grace could see was all she ever did. She ordered the Sunday School teachers to stop letting the children run wild; she told the WPA their quota of socks for soldiers was unsatisfactory; she scolded the maid for burning the roast and explained how to cook it properly; she told Grace there was no possibility of her going overseas as an army nurse.

Two months had passed since the news of Charley's death. For the first fortnight Grace had thought her mother was broken. Lily spent hours, even whole days, barred in her room and Grace found the house empty and cold without that fierce energy she had spent her whole life battling against. Now, at the end of June, the WPA and the Sunday School still sailed on without Lily's firm hand on the tiller, but here in the house the iron had returned to her spine with the news that Grace intended to leave off teaching, go to St. John's, and train to be a VAD nurse.

"I want to do my part!" Grace said—shouted, really. Lily never raised her voice, which made Grace sound hysterical when she wanted to sound firm and brave. Jack Perry had gone off to St. John's to enlist: it was his turn, he said, to take Charley's place. Before Charley died, Lily used to rally the WPA women whenever there was word of a deadly battle in France or a ship lost at sea. *Send out the word: more men are needed to carry on the fight!* Grace would enlist if she were a boy, but girls were going overseas too. She pictured herself on a battlefield, wiping the feverish brow of a wounded boy with a clean white cloth. The soldier in her dream had Jack Perry's blue eyes.

"You will do your part here at home. That *is* a woman's part— to keep the home, to preserve the values the men are fighting for."

Trudy J. Morgan-Cole

Lily sat down and picked up her embroidery, as if to illustrate how to preserve those womanly values, though she used her needle to point at Grace for emphasis rather than to stab the cloth. "Nursing is no job for a lady. You have romantic ideas about it—in real life it's dirty and dangerous too, if you go overseas. It's not a profession for a well-brought-up girl. Nursing is not what you imagine. Nothing is. If you don't want to go on teaching you can help me here at home, but I don't want to hear anymore foolish talk about nursing."

Lily's needle pierced the thin cotton stretched over her embroidery hoop: the red thread of the roses she was embroidering looked like drops of blood on the white cloth. Her attention to her work was meant to signal the argument was done. Grace turned for the door, ignoring her own bag of work, which contained yet another pair of sturdy military socks.

"Where are you going?"

"Up to the church to see the Reverend."

"It'll do you no good. We've discussed this. He and I are in agreement. Don't think you can go behind my back and get a soft answer out of him."

Grace knew this was true. She had talked with her father last night but the Reverend was no good if Lily got to him first. He toed the party line and said that nursing was too difficult and dangerous. Anyway it was a lie. She wasn't going to the church. Outside, in the clear summer air, she felt better as soon as she started walking over the road to Catalina South.

A year ago, the south side of Catalina Harbour had been a quiet, grass-grown spot, empty of houses, stores, or stages. But then William Coaker, head of the Fisherman's Union, had bought up most of the land on that side of the harbour. Fishing and the war occupied the minds of most Newfoundlanders this summer of 1917, but here in Catalina there was another obsession and another source of paid work: Mr. Coaker was building a model town. He had built himself a new home and a headquarters for his Fisherman's Protective Union; now, a Union store, a fish plant, row houses for the workers were under construction. Every time Grace walked down by the harbour she could hear the ringing of hammer and axe.

Her father was a great admirer of Coaker's work and since the man himself had landed almost on their doorstep, Reverend Collins was found over at Coaker's premises nearly as often as he was in his own church. Port Union, as Mr. Coaker was trying to get people into the habit of calling it, would have electric lights and every modern convenience. It would be the finest town in Newfoundland because, as Reverend Collins explained to Grace, instead of being built like every other town in the world—for the rich to become richer—Port Union was being built from the ground up by the workers themselves, for fishermen and their families to have all the blessings a new century could bestow.

Even the war was supposed to be only a temporary interruption in the grand plan—young men like Charley were meant to go away, fight for King and country, then come home to build the new world that would rise from the ashes of the old. And even with Charley gone, buried somewhere in France, Grace felt a little of that old excitement pushing through her loss, like the buds that were just beginning to open on the trees. This was where she belonged— in a new world, a new century, of action and serious work. Even if her mother was determined to try to keep her in the last century, dutifully sitting at home knitting socks or embroidering pillowcases.

Jack Perry was going overseas: Grace had promised him she would write. But she was determined to be more than the girl at home writing letters to a soldier. Perhaps she could get Grandfather and Aunt Daisy to invite her on an extended visit to St. John's. Grace and Charley had both lived with their grandfather and his second

Trudy J. Morgan-Cole

wife while they were at school in St. John's; Grace liked her cheerful step-grandmother, who preferred to be called "Aunt Daisy" and who softened the edges of Grandfather's austere house. Perhaps, if Grace came to visit with her own hard-earned savings in her hand, Grandfather and Daisy would overrule her parents, let her train for the VAD after all. If she could get to St. John's anything was possible. Port Union was a stepping stone.

Her father was not at the FPU headquarters but Mr. Coaker was. Her father had introduced her to the great man months ago. Now she walked up to him boldly, like a brave girl who would defy her parents' wishes and make her own way in the world. *If I play the role well enough*, Grace thought, *someday it just might be truth.*

"So you're not going back to teaching, Miss Collins?" Mr. Coaker said when Grace had explained what she wanted.

"No, sir, I want to do something for the war effort. But I need to earn money this summer. I can take dictation, I have my second-class certificate, and my penmanship is excellent."

William Coaker sat behind his desk and looked out over the FPU office, at the busy hum of people coming and going with messages, articles being written for his newspaper, the *Fisherman's Advocate*, work orders going out for the new construction, shipping records for all the things coming in to Port Union, and the salt fish that would go out from there into the markets of the world. From the muffled ladylike stillness of her mother's parlour to this humming place, this masculine busy world—this was exactly the journey Grace wanted to make.

"I may have something for you here in the office," he said. "Just temporarily—during the fishing season. Let me see what I can do for you."

Grace

CHAPTER THREE

FROM HER GRANDFATHER'S house on Queen's Road to the Empire Hospital was a short stroll on a cool spring day. Grace enjoyed the walk through downtown St. John's: down over Prescott Street, across Duckworth, then on to Water Street. She liked being greeted by the giant advertisement for Minard's Liniment, King of Pain, on the side of O'Driscoll's. She loved the busy swarm of women going into stores and coming out with brown-paper parcels, men in their suits and hats entering office buildings, workmen in overalls going to the stonecutters' yard. The returned servicemen were recognizable by their military stride even when their regimental uniforms had been exchanged for civilian clothes. They looked strong and handsome and whole, these men who had come back unscathed.

At the corner of Hill o' Chips on the eastern end of Water Street stood the hospital, recently opened to deal with the growing numbers of wounded men returning from overseas. The building had once been a woodworking factory and a small section at the back was still used as a bakery, so the warm yeasty smell of bread and cakes mingled with the stench of antiseptics and illness. The men at the hospital were not the ones whose military stride identified them on the street. These men were not paraded out at dinner parties or honoured at Government House.

The armistice had been signed six months ago; soldiers and sailors returned on every ship that sailed from England these days. Grace had long since given up wishing her brother Charley had been wounded instead of killed two years ago at Monchy-le-Preux. Death was cleaner. She saw the broken men every day, brought them their soup and sometimes helped them drink it, looked into their bottomless eyes. The perfect wound she dreamed of for Charley—one that would get him out of the war alive but leave him whole and unblighted—did not exist. There were only two ways to end a war well. Either miraculously survive unharmed or die cleanly, leaving your family with a framed picture of a hero on the wall.

Grace went home at Christmas, to spend the holiday with her parents in the manse where Charley's picture hung in the parlour. Whatever celebration of the war's end that took place in Catalina happened in church and in the homes of her friends. No celebration in Reverend Collins's home, where the declaration of peace was a reminder of all they had lost.

It was a relief to return to St. John's, despite her love for home and the excitement that seemed to hum through the air of Port Union along with the new electric power lines. Her grandfather's house was less gloomy than her parents'. Grandfather Hunt, at sixty-eight, still went to work in his printshop every day. Aunt Daisy was a vigorous, chatty woman ten years younger than her husband. She was as much involved in the church women's guild and the WPA here in St. John's as Grace's mother was back in Catalina, but Daisy's involvement had a different quality than Lily's. Daisy was a follower rather than a leader, one who welcomed circles of women into her home to knit and sew because she enjoyed their company and liked feeding them home-baked treats, without needing to lay down the law to them.

Grace had lived with her grandfather and Daisy for a year and a half now, since the fall of 1917, when she finished work in the Fishermen's Protective Union office and moved to St. John's. Grandfather Hunt would not agree to her taking the VAD course without her parents' permission, but Aunt Daisy convinced him to allow Grace to stay with them in town as long as she was doing "something suitable," which Grace took to mean something other than a paying job that her family might see as beneath her. She volunteered three days a week at Empire Hospital and two days at the Poor Asylum, and taught a girls' Sunday School class at Cochrane Street Methodist church.

"Good day, Miss Collins," the matron, Miss Fitzpatrick, said as Grace came onto the ward, took off her coat and hung it up, and went to wash her hands. The hospital was understaffed and while Matron had little use for young lady volunteers who were too good to train as nurses yet wanted to be seen as do-gooders, she needed them. With the returning soldiers and the flu epidemic, volunteers who were actually willing to roll up their sleeves and work eventually earned her grudging respect. "Mr. Lloyd and Mr. Barry need their sheets changed and nobody's got time to do it. Then you might read to Mr. Barry. He's very unsettled."

Mr. Barry liked to hear selections from the *Book of Common Prayer* when the nightmares of shell shock kept him from sleep. He had a loving mother and sisters out in Humbermouth who could presumably be reading the Morning Service to him, but they had come on the train to visit him and could not bear to be in his presence for more than a few moments. He lost his nose, one eye, an ear, and a piece of his jaw on the Somme; his face was a cratered map of the Western Front and its horrors. He needed help to eat, though he could walk about fine on his own. Except for the ruin of his face

Trudy J. Morgan-Cole

and the rattle in his lungs he was otherwise hale. Even some of the nurses had trouble looking at him, but Grace found, to her surprise, that the sight of maimed faces did not revolt or horrify her. A face was still a face, after all. Mr. Barry's eyes were the colour of deep-woods ponds, brackish and still. She looked mostly into his eyes, but she did not shrink from the rest of his face, and she knew that he appreciated that more than her readings from the prayer book.

He told her once that he liked to hear the prayer book because he had planned to be a minister. At least, that was what she pieced together out of the tortured sounds he was able to get out. Speech was difficult for him, but Grace imagined that in another life Mr. Barry might have been a good minister. A better preacher, perhaps, than her father. Reverend Obadiah Collins was a great Bible student but he lacked the gift to convey what he had dug out of his Greek lexicon in a form that would excite the fishermen and their families in the pews. When she was young, Grace used to think her father was awkward in the pastoral role, as well, trying to comfort the afflicted, but that had changed since Charley's death. Parishioners seemed drawn to him now.

People were naturally suspicious, Grace thought—they didn't really believe that a preacher could understand their pain unless he had suffered pain himself. It was a shame Mr. Barry couldn't be a minister. Surely a man who had survived the trenches and come back with half a face, but with his faith somehow intact, would be able to talk to people about God's love. He could place a hand on top of theirs, and they would know he had suffered, like Jesus, in all points like as they had. Even Jesus, though crucified, got to keep His nose and His jaw intact.

By mid-afternoon when Grace left the hospital, a cold sleety rain had begun, making the walk home far less pleasant than the walk down in the morning. Aunt Daisy met her in the doorway. "I have a *surrrpriiise* for you!" she trilled. Grace used to think "trilling" was just something writers said in books and not something a person could actually do with her voice, but Daisy disproved this theory. The trill, the glow on her round face, the word "surprise," all effectively removed any possibility of Grace actually being surprised. She knew before she stepped into the parlour that she would see Jack Perry there, in uniform. Whatever made her gasp for breath at the sight of him, it could not possibly have been surprise.

She wanted to go to him, for him to fold her in his arms the way he did that day she told him about Charley. But two years had passed. She had shaken Jack's hand in farewell the day he left Catalina to go to St. John's to enlist. Jack was her brother's friend, nothing more. They had written often while he was away, the kind of friendly letters a girl wrote to her dead brother's best friend while he was overseas. The sorts of letters hundreds of girls all over Newfoundland wrote, were enjoined to write, to keep up the spirits of the men at the front.

In the past two years two young men had asked Grace to marry them; she did not think of Jack Perry as being in any way similar to those boys. He did not sign his letters with love or say that he was thinking only of her. He wrote about the things that happened around him, the men in his unit, funny incidents that punctuated otherwise boring days in the trenches. Daisy brought his letters to Grace saying, "Here's another from your young man!" and confidently expected that Jack's return would be a lover's reunion.

Jack put out his hand and she took it. "You're looking grand," she said. "It's good to have you home." They all sat down, Aunt Daisy perched on the edge of her chair like at any moment she might take flight and leave the lovers alone, if it weren't for the rules of propriety.

Jack was in uniform and he really did look grand. His slender form had filled out, shoulders broader, chest and arms more muscular. His face, though, was leaner, less boyish. Grace thought

Trudy J. Morgan-Cole

of Jack as having blond hair but it had darkened to a light brown. His eyes were light blue, very bright as he talked, smiled, laughed, turning from Grace to Daisy and back again. It was impossible not to compare him with Ivan Barry and the other men in the hospital.

"You haven't been home yet, then?" she said.

"No, our ship only docked here in town yesterday. I thought I'd take the train out tomorrow, see Mother and Father and all the family. I wondered if—that is, would you like to come out with me? Have you been home lately?"

"Oooh yes, Grace, you must, your mother would be so happy—" Aunt Daisy said, but was spared from explaining why exactly Lily would be happy by the arrival of the maid with a tray full of teacups and raisin buns, with rhubarb jam in a little silver pot. If she arrived back in Catalina with Jack Perry, would her parents jump to the same conclusion that Daisy seemed so happy to leap to? And would it please them?

Lily had said no to the idea of Grace training as a nurse; she had turned up her nose last year when one of Grace's old teachers at the Methodist College had suggested Grace could win a scholarship to go to college up in Canada. "A college education is no good to a young lady," Lily had said. The obvious assumption was that she wanted Grace to settle down, be a wife and a mother. But when Abram Russell had asked her father for Grace's hand in marriage— without so much as a preliminary discussion or even a hint to Grace herself—Lily had not been enthused about that prospect either. "They say he comes from a good family," Lily said, "and he's very ambitious, but there's something common about him."

Abe Russell was one of Mr. Coaker's protégées. He had come from Bonavista North to manage the newly built factory that would manufacture and bottle temperance beverages in Port Union. He had political ambitions too. People said he meant to run for a seat in the House one day. While Mr. Coaker hadn't moved Abe into his

A Sudden Sun

Bungalow the way he had with the Bailey boys—like the sons he never had—he was known to warmly approve of Abe Russell. Grace had spoken to him only a handful of times, and certainly had no interest in his marriage proposal: she was relieved that neither of her parents thought she ought to take it seriously.

She had not even told them of Harry Gullage's proposal, which he made directly to her on her visit home last summer. Harry was a nice-looking boy, good for a laugh; she had known him for years. He was a fisherman, son of a fisherman, and no matter how her father supported Mr. Coaker's desire to dignify the lot of the fishermen, Grace knew her parents would be shocked at the idea of her marrying one. She tried to be gentle in refusing Harry, and he was philosophical: it was as if he'd known he was aiming too high even by asking. He had married Lyddie Carter a few months after Grace turned him down.

Grandfather drove Grace to the Water Street train station to meet Jack two days later. Grace couldn't leave town right away; she told Jack she needed time to inform the hospital and the poorhouse that she would be away for a couple of days, and Jack had delayed his return home. Together they sat in an almost empty carriage. The only other passengers in their car sat at the far end so it was almost like having a private car.

The train began to roll—late getting out of the station, as usual. The route was familiar to Grace by now, but travelling with Jack, their knees almost touching as they sat across from each other, made it seem different, like a journey to someplace foreign. Grace imagined boarding a train at night in a foreign country, surrounded by people who spoke another language. The picture came accompanied by a stab of longing so intense it was almost like hunger.

"It's different from riding troop trains in France, I imagine," she said.

"It's a fair bit more comfortable."

Trudy J. Morgan-Cole

"I'd like to see it, though. France, that is. I always imagined I'd go there someday. That was before the war, of course. Is it all ruins now?"

"Not all. There are still beautiful places. Cathedrals, a few churches that didn't get shelled. The villages where the fighting was are in shambles. I spent a few weeks in Paris after the Armistice. It's still lovely." He was looking out the window at the Waterford River valley rolling by. "Maybe I'll take you there someday."

Grace looked out the window and hoped he wouldn't apologize for being presumptuous. For two years now she had been building a picture of Jack Perry, piecing together fragments from his letters to imagine what kind of man he was becoming. Laying those fragments on top of the boy she remembered, her brother's friend.

At Donovan's Station the train stopped to take on passengers, then again at Kelligrews. At Avondale there was a longer stop; Grace and Jack walked to the end of the platform and looked down the tracks, watching the line 'til it curved and disappeared in the woods.

"I don't suppose you'll be able to do a Grand Tour of Europe for a few years yet," Jack said, picking up the thread of the earlier conversation. "It'll be a long time before it's business as usual over there. Although already there's talks of them making the battlefields into parks, so people can go visit the soldiers' graves."

Grace thought about Charley's grave. "I never really wanted to go on a Grand Tour," she said. "I mean, I want to see the world, but…I can't imagine myself as a lady of leisure, just touring around for the pleasure of it."

"I know, it seems a bit…idle-rich, doesn't it?"

"Yes, exactly. I'm not rich, and even if I were I wouldn't want to be idle."

He laughed. "Very little danger of you ever being idle, I'd say."

"I suppose I'll take that as—a compliment?"

"That's how I meant it."

The train whistle blew. Jack took her hand as he helped her back onto the train. Grace took down the picnic basket Aunt Daisy had packed for them. Bread Daisy had baked herself—the maid was not allowed to turn her hand to bread—cold sliced ham and apples and a little jar of rhubarb jam. How simple and orderly it was, Daisy's way of caring for others. A woman's way, anyone would say.

At Shoal Harbour in mid-afternoon they waited on the platform for the branch line to Bonavista. On this last leg of the journey a stout older man settled into the seat across the aisle and nodded at them as he settled his bags and packages around him.

"Going to Bonavista, Captain? Miss?" the man said, taking off his hat.

"Catalina," Jack said.

"Of course, of course." The man took his seat, leaned forward a little and squinted at Jack. "Oh, you're Zeke Perry's young fellow?"

"Yes, sir."

"Thank you for your service, young man. The Empire owes everything to young men like yourself. And," he turned to Grace, lifted his bowler hat again, "to your brother. If I'm not mistaken you must be Reverend Collins's daughter."

"Thank you, sir." Grace searched her memory, trying to place the man. "Judge Hickey?"

"Very pleased to meet you young folks," the judge said. He turned back to Jack then and began quizzing him about whether Newfoundland could maintain the Regiment as a standing army in peacetime. Grace went back to staring out the window as miles of rock and barren rolled past.

When she glanced at Jack again he was deep in conversation with the judge. Jack Perry had always been handsome—all the Perry boys were good-looking—but with the added maturity and muscles earned overseas she thought he was fine-looking indeed. His

Trudy J. Morgan-Cole

ice-blue eyes, fixed on the older man, crinkled around the edges when he laughed: the few lines in his young face only made him more attractive. Just then he glanced over at her, and she looked away, feeling her cheeks flush.

As the train swayed and rolled along the track and the conversation plunged deeper into military matters, Grace dozed. A loud snore woke her, and she startled to see Jack laughing at her. "I must be a wonderful conversationalist," he said. "I've put the both of you to sleep, you and Judge Hickey."

"I was wide awake when it was just you and me."

"And now it's the two of us again." They were speaking in whispers, not wanting to disturb the older man who snored so loudly it seemed people in the second-class car must hear him.

She felt a nudge against her ankle, looked down to see the polished toe of Jack's boot. His smile suggested it hadn't been an accidental nudge, and he kept his toe there, gently brushing against her ankle. She lifted the hem of her skirt just a little, baring the top of her boot. Her skirts still covered her leg but still it felt as if she were being daring, even immodest, here under the closed eye of the distinguished magistrate.

Jack shifted in his seat, leaned a little forward as if to talk quietly, but he said nothing. Now his lower leg was pressing against hers, heat travelling through layers of fabric rather than contained by boot leather. It felt as if a trail of that heat shot up Grace's leg, coiling in her belly and spilling into her most intimate parts, then rose through her chest up to flush her cheeks.

When the silence seemed unbearable Grace said, "You said you can't see me as a lady of leisure, but what about you?"

"Well, I can't see myself as a lady of leisure either." He spoke lightly, but his leg still pressed against hers.

"You know what I mean! Isn't that what everyone asks when a soldier comes home? What are you going to do now?"

Jack looked out the window. "Did I ever tell you my mother had dedicated me to be a missionary? I was the son she was giving to God, either as a minister or a doctor, to serve the heathen overseas."

She nodded. Mrs. Perry had never been shy of talking about her ambitions for her children. Fred and Earl would take over the family business. Bill was to be a schooner captain. Jack, once it became clear how clever he was in school, would be either a minister or a missionary doctor. "When I was overseas," he went on, "working in the field hospital—well. I won't talk about it. Some days I thought if I got out alive I'd never want to see another wounded body again. Other days I thought if God spared me I'd do exactly as Mother wanted and go to the mission field. Now—well, I'll go back to McGill in the fall and finish my training. Then—who knows? None of it seems very real right now. Nothing but—" he dropped his eyes, smiled, and reached forward and took her gloved hand as an explosive snore ripped through the carriage. "Nothing in the world but you, me…and of course the magistrate."

CHAPTER FOUR

LILY KNEW THE story as soon as the two of them stepped off
the train. Any fool would know. Elizabeth Perry's son in uniform,
giving his hand to Grace to help her down onto the platform.
That was the picture everyone wanted to see this spring. The boys
coming home from war; the girls who had waited. There would be
half a dozen weddings all around the harbour this summer.

Lily hated him, of course, for being alive when Charley was
dead. When Charley was brave and signed up to go overseas Jack
had stayed behind, listened to his mother who was too much of a
coward to give a son to her country. Had Lily wanted to beg Charley
not to go, beg him to stay home? Of course she had. But she knew
his duty, and her own. It was what you raised a boy for: to go out into
the world, even to war if he was needed, to spend his life or lay it
down. If the world were arranged with any justice, the mothers who
allowed their sons to go to war would have them back safely, while
the cowards, women like Elizabeth Perry, would beg their sons to
stay home and eventually lose them in the mud of Flanders. But Lily
knew it was vain to hope for justice.

"Do you think young Perry wants to marry our Grace?" the Reverend asked Lily that night. They generally took a cup of tea together in the evening, before Lily went up to bed. The Reverend would stay up and read for another hour or so, then retire to his own bed in the room adjoining his study. Sometimes they drank their tea in silence; more often her husband made an attempt to initiate a conversation he thought she might be interested in. He usually misjudged.

"Didn't you see him—see the both of them?" Grace had come home from the station with her parents, dropped off her bag and announced that she was invited to tea at the Perry house and would be home later in the evening—by nine at the latest, she'd said. "They look like they're head-over-ears in love with each other," Lily added.

He glanced at her over the teacup, answering her tone rather than her words. "And you think that is a misfortune."

Lily shrugged. "What do you think? Have you ever known any good to come of anyone falling in love? Grace had enough sense not to throw herself away on young Abe Russell last year when he came sniffing around, but if she imagines she's in love it'll be a different story."

It was a story with many endings, Lily thought: the broken heart, the tarnished virtue, or perhaps the so-called happy ending, the wedding. Only the wedding was not the ending. The wedding led to the long years of housekeeping and one baby after another, and no matter which way it ends Grace would be ground down, damaged, broken. Everything Lily tried to spare her.

"You think it would be better, then, for her to make a sober choice? Should she marry some suitable young man from a good family, without any—er, any emotional attachment?"

The Reverend's tone and glance could not be construed as anything but a challenge. Lily clattered her cup in the saucer, some

Trudy J. Morgan-Cole

unfinished tea sloshing over the edge. "To be quite honest, I've not known that sort of marriage to have much success either," she said. "Good night."

Upstairs, she took down her hair, put on a nightdress, and got into bed, but she did not sleep. Sometimes, these last two years since Charley died, she slept far too much. Other times sleep eluded her. She would lie awake through the night, turning the pages of a magazine without retaining anything, watching the moon cross her window.

Those times, the sleepless times, could linger for days, up to a week, until finally, exhausted, she would sleep through a whole night and long into the next day. She thought of taking a few drops of laudanum but pushed the thought away. She had gone to see a doctor on her last trip to St. John's, when she could hardly sleep at all in those terrible months after the news had come about Charley. She didn't like or trust the Bonavista doctor, and didn't want anyone in Trinity Bay knowing she'd seen a physician. The doctor in town had said laudanum would settle her nerves and help her sleep. But Lily prided herself on a clear mind, on being beholden to nothing and no one. She would never be a ghost in her own house. She would never be Eleanor Hunt.

Doctors! She thought of that Perry boy, strutting around like a peacock, going to university to become a doctor, coming back from France without a scratch on him. How could Grace hang on such a boy, cling to his arm as if he were worthy of her? Grace, Lily's only remaining treasure, would go away with that boy if he so much as whistled for her. She would be hurt and used and shattered, and what could Lily do about it?

Lily didn't remember getting out of bed but she was pacing, pacing on the rag rug that protected her feet from the bare pine boards. She had made that rug in the first year of her marriage. She had torn the strips of fabric and hooked them through the brin when her eyes were a blur of tears. The rug was a promise, more of a vow than the words she'd said during the wedding ceremony. With every stitch she swore to God she would be a good minister's wife, that the mistakes of the past would be shredded and torn beyond recognition, worked into a pattern that would be, if not beautiful, at least useful. Lily had hooked a good dozen rugs since then but when she walked on this worn old rug she could still feel the bitterness seeping up through the soles of her feet.

Somewhere in the house, a door closed. The girl, Elsie, had finished her work and gone home two hours ago; she lived with her parents down in the harbour rather than up in the manse. The Reverend had gone up to his study. He might have gone downstairs for something—but the steps she heard were too light to be his. It must be Grace home from the Perrys' house. Lily glanced at the clock: quarter to ten.

Grace was home, going to the kitchen. It was an old habit of hers from when she lived at home. Whether she was at home or out in the evening, Grace would always make herself a cup of tea or cocoa in the kitchen before going up to bed. She was a night-owl and liked to sit up late, usually reading. Years ago, when Grace was young, Lily would go down to join her in the kitchen for a cup of tea. Those ought to have been easy times, warm and companionable. She heard other women talk of sharing confidences and secrets with their daughters and wished Grace would confide in her, but most of her memories of those late-night cups of tea and cocoa ended with harsh words, sometimes tears, Grace striding out of the room and up to bed offended. Lily's good advice, the guidance she tried to offer, never failed to upset Grace.

These last two years, since Charley died, Lily hadn't bothered anymore. When Grace was home she still went down to the kitchen for a mug-up at night but Lily left her to her own devices.

Now she was back home with a young man—maybe in love

with him. Surely it was for the first time. Lily could read her daughter, knew the language of her face and eyes and body. If Grace had ever been in love before, Lily would have known it. She had been alert for danger since the girl was fourteen.

Lily went downstairs to find Grace at the table, her hands cradled around the teacup. A little cup, with painted yellow roses, one of her favourites from childhood. The last of a service of eight, from Lily's wedding china. Despite the circumstances of the wedding the Reverend's mother, formidable old Mrs. Collins of Wesleyville, had ordered a full set of wedding china for her son and his bride. Over the years, various housemaids and Grace herself, as a young girl, had broken one cup after another, 'til only this lone survivor remained.

"Mother. Can I get you a cup? There's still some in the pot."

Now they sat at either end of the table, facing each other over teacups. Lily turned her cup—from a different set, bought later in their marriage—round and round in her hands, practicing sentences in her head.

"Has he asked you to marry him?"

"I—what?"

It seemed pointless to repeat the question. "Everyone thinks it's very romantic, war brides, boys in uniform. But there'll be many a girl sorry because she said yes hastily."

"He—Mother, Jack hasn't asked me anything. He's only been back from overseas a few days."

"Still and all there are plenty who'll jump into it without thinking. I don't want you to make that mistake. These boys who've been overseas—nobody knows what they've seen, what they've done."

Grace looked down at her teacup as if by dropping her eyes she could hide her answer, but it wasn't only in her eyes. It might as well have been inked on her skin. You'd have to have been in love like

A Sudden Sun

that yourself, once, to see how clear it was written.

"We're friends," Grace said. "I told you, he's only been back—well, since the day before yesterday." She looked surprised herself, glancing at the calendar, as if she thought it had been much longer.

Two days, Lily thought. And hours of that spent sitting on a train together. More than enough time. An hour was time enough; a moment, even.

"You always think you know best," Lily said. "But you know the saying: Marry in haste…"

"I'm doing nothing in haste." Grace set her teacup down in the saucer with a sharp clang.

"You never want to listen…."

"I never listen? Oh, that's brilliant, coming from you. When have *you* ever listened to me?"

"When have you ever tried to tell me anything?"

Grace had never been one to confide, even as a little girl. She talked to her father if she talked to anyone, but they talked about opinions and ideas and things in the newspaper, not the kind of secrets a girl was supposed to share with her mother.

"Well perhaps I would, if I ever thought you'd listen instead of telling me what to do, or barring yourself up in your bedroom to cry over Charley!"

Silence. A sip and another clang of the teacup. Grace swiped at tears with the back of her hand.

"I beg your pardon," Lily said. "I suppose there's something wrong with me because I couldn't just go on after Charley died, just forget about him like you and your father did."

"You know I never forgot, or Father either. But I'm still here. My life is going on, just like his would have, and I don't want to miss it all!"

"Big dreams, fine words, grand ambitions. I know what you want—but you can't have it. The world isn't like that, not for a girl

Trudy J. Morgan-Cole

anyway. Pride goeth before destruction and a haughty spirit before a fall."

"How would you know? If you'd ever *had* any dreams or ambitions perhaps you'd understand mine—but all you ever wanted was to have your only son back, your favourite child…"

Now Grace was crying full-on, her voice trembling, reduced to the language of childhood quarrels. *You love him more than you love me.* Until Grace bore a child herself she'd never understand, Lily thought—it wasn't about *more*; it was different. Loving a son was so much simpler than loving a daughter. It was a straightforward thing, like shooting an arrow and watching it fly. Loving a daughter was a tangle like embroidery, weaving one thing in and out of another, the whole thing wrong-side-up and looking like a mess until it was done and you saw the pattern.

Of course, Lily had never shot an arrow. She'd done plenty of embroidery, though.

She finished the last of her tea, watched her daughter cry. When had she last held Grace on her lap, put an arm around her? Five? Six? Not at seven, no. Grace already had her reserve then, her haughty spirit. Even younger than that, at three years old, she would squirm and pull away if Lily tried to hold her on her lap.

Lily stood up. "I'm going up to bed." She reached over the table and picked up the little yellow-rose teacup. "Look, you put a spall in the rim. That's no good now—and it's the last one of that set."

She went upstairs, closed her door, and listened for the sound of Grace's footsteps. When she heard them coming upstairs, she let out a breath she didn't know she had been holding. Grace was wilful and headstrong but she had always been, in the strictest sense, a good girl, and Lily could not really imagine her going out into the night, running away from the manse, seeking out Jack Perry in the dark spring night. Except that any girl might do the unexpected, if she imagined she were in love.

Lily Hunt Collins had been afraid as long as she could remember, of too many things to count. A particular kind of fear came with having children: she remembered the years of thinking of everything that could go wrong in the birthing bed and afterwards. Cot death, and diphtheria, and whooping cough; the myriad terrors of childhood. She had thought the fear might retreat when they grew up but if anything it became sharper. She imagined Grace in a boy's arms, embracing, yielding, then lost and abandoned and alone. Images of Grace in trouble turned easily to images of Charley dead on a French battlefield, lying in a cold grave far from home, and Lily sat on the edge of her bed and put her hands over her face. She was not such a fool as to think that because you had suffered one terrible loss, God would spare you a second. She learned long ago that was a lie.

Turning back the covers, she thought of the laudanum bottle. Perhaps just tonight, a little dreamless sleep.

Trudy J. Morgan-Cole

CHAPTER FIVE

"$\mathscr{I}$ SPOKE TO someone today who wants to meet you," Daisy told Grace. "Mrs. Parker—Abigail Hayward, she was. John Hayward's daughter. You know," she added, turning to her husband, "Hayward the lawyer? Abigail's lived in New York ever since she was married, but she's home visiting, now that her father's so ill."

"I remember John Hayward's girl," Grandfather said, ladling gravy over his roast chicken. "Flighty little thing. I never thought she was a good influence."

"Well, perhaps not—but she's over fifty now, I don't imagine she's flighty anymore." Daisy turned back to Grace. "She and your mother were great friends when they were girls. I told her all about you and she said you sounded like the spitting image of your mother. She'd like to see your mother again too, of course. I wonder could we convince Lily to come out here for a week or so?"

"It's hard to say," Grace said. Lily's visits to town were few, and Grace had the clear impression she did not enjoy staying in the house under Daisy's cheerful regime.

"Well, anyway I've invited Mrs. Parker and her sister—Violet Golding, you know her from church, of course—for dinner tomorrow night, so at least she'll meet you. And your young man as well, naturally."

Daisy adored Jack. Shortly after Jack came home, one of Grandfather's proofreaders had come down with pneumonia and Grandfather had hired Jack to replace him. As the proofreader was nearly as old as Grandfather himself, there was no telling how long the job might last, but of course Jack only wanted temporary work, to earn money towards his return to medical school in the fall. He boarded with his married brother, Earl, who ran the St. John's office of the Perry family business, but he spent many evenings at the Hunt home.

"He's not really *my* young man, Aunt Daisy," Grace said after her grandfather had excused himself from the table and the women lingered over their tea.

"You only mean he hasn't asked you to marry him yet—but he will. I hope your mother didn't scare him off too badly when you brought him home."

"My…my mother? Did she write to you?" Grace had, of course, said nothing to Daisy or anyone else about her conversation with Lily.

Daisy laughed. "Oh, Gracie, I know your mother. Sure I knew her back when her and Abby Hayward was girls, before your grandmother died. Your mother had some fine ideas of her own back then. Don't pay too much mind to anything she says about you and Jack. She's not a happy woman, is Lily, and you can't blame her too much."

"You mean…because of Charley?"

Daisy looked startled. "What, poor Charl? No, no, not that—I mean, that's a pity, of course, it's a tragedy. It'd be a setback for any woman. But poor Lily, no, that only knocked the last bit of life out

Trudy J. Morgan-Cole

of her. She had the good took out of her years before that, long before you was born, even before Charl was born, if you ask me." The more comfortably Daisy settled into a conversation, the more her Bonavista Bay accent came to the fore.

"What do you mean? When she married my father…?"

Daisy stared at her for a moment and then the expression on her face completely changed, like a child in school who has been daydreaming and has now been called to attention by the teacher. "Now, I've gone and said more than I should," she said. "It's running into Abby Hayward, that's what it is, is got me digging up old foolishness from the past. Don't you mind me." She stood up with her teacup, forestalling as she often did the maid's efforts to clear the table. Before marrying Grandfather, Daisy had lived in genteel poverty and had never gotten used to being waited on.

But she played the gracious hostess the next evening when everyone arrived for dinner. It was not difficult even before introductions were made, Grace thought, to guess which of the two visiting ladies had spent her married life in New York. Abigail Parker talked more loudly than her sister, her speech full of sharp American vowels. Grace knew little about fashions but even she could tell Mrs. Parker was more fashionably dressed than Mrs. Golding, her short beaded jacket neatly hugging her waist, her skirt reaching just to the ankle.

"My dear! Lily's daughter!" Mrs. Parker launched herself at Grace, grabbing both her hands and pressing them to her own beaded bosom. "I would have known you anywhere, no mistaking those eyes and cheekbones. And you carry yourself just like her— a beauty completely unaware. Turn around and step back, darling, so I can get a proper look."

Aunt Daisy introduced Jack as "Grace's friend, Captain Jack Perry. They grew up together in Catalina before the war. He was a great friend of poor Charley."

"Oh, poor Charley!" Mrs. Parker pressed her own hand, now, to her breast, and turned to her sister. "I told you, didn't I, Vi, about Lily's poor boy—lost in France—I'm so sorry for your loss, my dears," she finished, with a glance that swept from Grace to Grandfather, taking in Jack and Daisy along the way.

Once it had been commonplace for people to offer sympathy over Charley's loss: it happened every time Grace spoke to someone in the year after his death. Now it had been a long time and she realized with a start that she had, not exactly forgotten Charley, but had stopped feeling his loss every day. It was as if Charley had been moved to a different room, the room full of dead people, and she no longer expected to hear his voice or step among the living. That realization struck her like a second loss.

At dinner, Mrs. Parker carried all before her on a wave of conversation, and Aunt Daisy, who loved talkative guests, rose to the challenge. They talked about the flu epidemic and the difficulties of men returning home from the conflict, which drew Jack into conversation. Jack was the sort of man with whom older ladies were always charmed, Grace had noticed, and Mrs. Parker engaged him in a discussion of the differences between the American veterans and the Newfoundlanders. Then she asked Grace about her volunteer work at the hospital. Mrs. Parker herself, it appeared, volunteered in some capacity with the Red Cross in New York, "but not, of course, the sort of work you do. Mrs. Hunt has told me so much about how you are right in there working with those poor wounded men, and all the rest. You're like your mother in spirit, too—always going about doing good, as it says in the Good Book."

"Oh well—there's such a great need, you know," Grace said. "I do the little things—change sheets, and bring dinner trays, and sometimes read to the men to keep their spirits up." An image of Ivan Barry's ruined face appeared in her mind; she felt small, as if she were using his suffering to make herself look brave and generous.

Trudy J. Morgan-Cole

"The doctors and nurses do all the real work, of course."

"I'm surprised you didn't train for a nurse yourself."

"I thought of it, during the war, but …"

"But you'd have wanted to go overseas—so many girls did—and it would have been too hard on your parents—especially on your poor mother. Losing her boy overseas was bad enough. A mother is almost prepared to lose a son in war, but a daughter?"

Mrs. Parker steered the conversation in Grandfather's direction next, asking what he thought of President Wilson's idea of a League of Nations. She herself thought it was a grand plan, though she knew many people in New York who disagreed. Jack and Grace joined the discussion, leaving Daisy to talk with Mrs. Golding about mutual acquaintances, of which they fortunately had several.

In the parlour after supper Mrs. Parker positioned herself next to Grace on the small settee, and leaned in close. "You must come and see me while I'm here," she said. "I'm in town for another month at least—well, of course how long depends on what happens with poor Father. I've cabled your mother and she sent back a message that it's impossible to come this time of year. Is that true? There's a railway line all the way out there now, isn't there?"

"There is," Grace said. Honesty, and perhaps a desire to tarnish Mrs. Parker's warm memories of Lily, drove her to say, "It's not impossible. But Mother doesn't like to go anywhere much anymore."

"How sad." Mrs. Parker looked down at her own plump, pretty hands, playing with her fan. "I would go out to see her, but—dear Papa, you know. I must stay near him…. But I would so love to see your mother again. I feel she's had a hard time. There's no life without sorrow, is there? My own has been that I have no children alive—only two sweet angels in Heaven. Say you'll come to see me while I'm in town, darling, even if your mother won't."

Grace said she would, indeed, come.

"I work with some very interesting people in New York, you know," Mrs. Parker said. "Oh, I'm not the one to roll up my sleeves and get my hands dirty like you. I chair committees, sit on boards, raise funds, that sort of thing. Ladies devoted to good works—men dismiss us, but the fact is there's very little good works that would get done without ladies. So much suffering in the war, but so much here at home, too! Newfoundland seems a simpler, finer place, but I know—I remember—there's hardship here too. So, what do you think of Lloyd George?"

Grace felt like she was being given an oral examination in school by a very distracted and scatterbrained mistress who had forgotten to tell her what the subject of the test would be. Fortunately, Grace did have opinions on the subject of the British prime minister, and was able to gather them. The conversation broadened, then, like a stream widening out into a pond, taking in the whole group, and Grace had no more private conversation with Mrs. Parker until the guests were leaving. Her mother's old friend turned to her again at the door and said, "Expect an invitation from me within the week, unless poor Papa takes a sudden turn for the worse. Just you alone, so we can really have a proper talk."

Late that night, when the guests had gone and her grandfather and Daisy were in bed, Grace slipped out of her bedroom and climbed the staircase to the third floor. Grandfather and Daisy only used the first two floors of the three-storey house; they had given Grace what used to be the spare bedroom across from theirs. Annie, the maid, went upstairs once a week to dust but otherwise the top floor was unused, furniture shrouded with sheets so the rooms were like ghosts of rooms. Grace had not been up there since she was a child and had played hide-and-go-seek with Charley in the old house. Now she went slowly up the stairs, thinking of Abigail Parker telling her she was just like Lily in spirit, and of Daisy saying Lily had "fine ideas" once. What kind of ideas?

Trudy J. Morgan-Cole

She didn't know which of the old rooms was which. Even when her mother was young, would they have needed so many rooms? Lily had been the only surviving child, two others having died young of diphtheria. Had they had a cook or maids who slept in these upper rooms? One might have been a guest room, since the spare room on the second floor used to be Grandfather's study. And this room—this must have been Lily's bedroom, Grace thought, as she pushed the door open.

A broad bay window looked down on Queen's Road and the huddled shades of two wingback chairs flanked it. A mirror over the dressing table was unshrouded and thick with dust. Annie was not being particularly diligent, then, about dusting. And why should she? Grace stood in front of the mirror, seeing a greenish, distorted picture of herself—the old mirror, the dust, moonlight filtering in through the blind windows. Was she really the living image of Lily? People said so, but Grace had never been able to see it.

This could not, after all, have been her mother's room growing up, not this exact room, for Grace remembered her grandfather saying he had had to rebuild the whole house after the Great Fire, and Lily must then have been—Grace counted backwards—about nineteen, as old as Grace herself was now. So this room, if it was Lily's, must have been hers after the fire, in the new house.

She pressed the light switch and a dim bulb flickered to life. Grace folded back the sheet that covered a small dressing table. A silver comb and brush set sat on top of a lace doily. One drawer was empty except for sachets of potpourri. The one below that held ribbons and gloves. At the bottom of the drawer, a tiny key. But the dressing table had no locked drawers.

On the other side of the room, similarly shrouded, was a rolltop desk with one locked drawer. Not much of a system for hiding secrets, Grace thought—a locked drawer with the key just across in the dressing table. But perhaps there were no secrets in there, after all. Only things Lily had forgotten, things like the comb and brush that she had not deemed worth taking with her when she left home as a bride.

The key fitted the lock, the drawer slid open, and sure enough, it contained little except newspapers and clippings. Several copies of a paper called the *Water Lily*, with articles circled and words underlined. Clippings from the *Telegram*, the *Herald*, the *Gazette* — accounts of the Great Fire, accounts of attempts by the WCTU to pass a temperance law. Grace spread them all out on the bed, wondering if these were indeed her mother's youthful papers. Handbills from meetings promoting Votes For Women? Grace read through one: *In Newfoundland today a woman who manages her own business can have no vote, no voice in elections—yet the most incapable man in her employ may do so.* And every word still sadly true in the year of our Lord 1919, she thought.

Had Lily once been a suffragist? She certainly had no sympathy for that cause now. Grace remembered her mother glancing at a newspaper article last year when women in Canada got the franchise. "They say it's only for the wives and mothers of soldiers while the men are away at war, but of course they won't give up power once they've had the taste of it," Lily had said.

"It's only to bring in conscription, my dear," Reverend Collins had said. "The Union government knows they can count on the women who have men overseas to vote for it."

"Well, they'll reap the whirlwind," Lily said.

There were invitations here too, and calling cards, and a handful of postcards. Grace looked through these as well, feeling slightly guilty at reading her mother's private correspondence. But surely Lily would have destroyed or taken with her anything important, and most of the postcards were quite dull. She recognized the names on a few, her mother's cousins in Wesleyville or Harbour Grace. Only two were interesting: one in looping, girlish handwriting that read,

Trudy J. Morgan-Cole

"*It's a pickle and no mistake, but it needn't be a tragedy. Come to me,
darling, and we'll puzzle out what to do. Won't you?*" It was signed
only "*A.*"

A for Abigail, Grace wondered? If Grace were to visit with
Mrs. Parker, become friendly and confiding, could Mrs. Parker tell
her what sort of pickle Lily had been in, and whether they had ever
puzzled it out together?

Grace realized, looking through the scattered papers, how very
little she knew of her mother's life—who her girlhood friends
had been, what she had cared about, even what books she had read.
Lily talked a great deal, but seldom about her own past. The
other mysterious postcard showed a young man playing a guitar for
a willowy young lady, her hair in a Gibson Girl sweep and a bustle
accentuating her wasp waist. On the back was a scrawled and
male-looking hand, quite different from the careful feminine
writing that covered the other cards. Grace had to peer at it for a few
minutes to piece it out.

> *L Dearest —. Sorry for everything. It is never too late*
> *to change your mind. Or rather, soon it will be too*
> *late—for you, that is. I put no address on the envelope*
> *but you can find me at Mrs. Tulk's boarding house,*
> *642 President Street. Please come.*
> *— D.*

The letters resolved themselves into words. But the words made
no sense at all.

CHAPTER SIX

ABIGAIL HAYWARD PARKER. Well, well.

Lily held the telegram between thumb and finger, reading it over. It was the third one she'd received in the past fortnight. The first had announced Abigail's arrival in the capital city; the second asked if Lily might come to town so they could see one another again.

This one read:

> DINED WITH YOUR FATHER AND WIFE STOP IMAGINE DAISY GILL MISTRESS OF YOUR FATHERS HOUSE BUT SHE RISES TO THE OCCASION STOP MET YOUR DAUGHTER STOP SPLENDID GIRL AND A FINE YOUNG SUITOR STOP WILL TAKE HER UNDER WING STOP ARE YOU COMING TO TOWN STOP.

Stop, stop, stop, Lily thought. Stop dragging back people, names, images from the past. She did not like to think of Abigail Hayward, not the silly girl she once was nor the preachy Lady Bountiful she had become. Abigail frequently wrote about her various committees and hospitals and orphanages, thinking good works formed a bond between herself and Lily. She had no children of her own. It was almost inevitable that she should meet Grace and want to take her under a well-feathered wing.

Lily thought she ought to go to town and put a stop to this wing-sheltering business.

She avoided visits to town. She had no desire to walk the empty halls of the house she had once lived in, the beautiful house Papa had rebuilt after the fire. She had sweeter and more bitter memories of the two short years she'd lived in that rebuilt house than of any other part of her life, though very little had happened to her in the house itself. The house had been the place she returned: her tiny room on the top floor with its gable window looking out over Queen's Road was the place she waltzed back to as if there were air under her heels. There was the pillow she had hugged as if it were a living person in her dreams, the floor she had paced hour after midnight hour. There was the bed on which she had thrown herself crying 'til her throat ached, 'til she felt drained and empty of tears.

She had no desire to go back and see her father, who had steered her inexorably towards the only possible solution and never known what he was doing. She had no desire to go back and see Daisy reigning in her mother's stead. The happiness Papa had found with Daisy in his second marriage was an affront: not so much to her mother's memory—there was so little of Eleanor in the first place that her memory was almost completely insubstantial, like the shadow of a shadow—as an affront to Lily's own unhappiness.

The only person she wanted to see, of all that merry party in St. John's, was Grace. Lily wanted Grace home for one of the conversations they had only in her imagination, when they sat on the front porch in the sun. It was always warm and sunny in the land of Lily's imagination, and she and Grace sat in the sun doing some kind of fancy-work. Grace talked about the things that troubled or interested her, and Lily listened and gave sage advice, which Grace always accepted and thanked her for.

Lord, how her head ached. Keeping her hair up all day was such a burden. She was alone in the house now, except for the girl in the kitchen, and what did it matter? Lily pulled out one hairpin, just the one that was making her temple throb, and felt a split second of blessed relief as a rope of long, heavy hair snaked down over her shoulder.

Since Abigail's telegram had been delivered she had been restless. It would be a good day to polish the silver, a task no kitchen maid in Lily's experience had ever been able to do properly. She got as far as opening the box in the dining room that contained the silver, then sat down and stared at the beautiful pieces, starting to show signs of tarnish around the edges. Time was she would have been horrified to let the silver get into that condition. Lily had prided herself on her housekeeping, on managing the house and the maid and the menu and the silver as well as the Women's Missionary Society and the Sunday School. She had done everything expected of a minister's wife and more.

She had dropped all those responsibilities in the hard weeks after Charley's death, and then, knowing it was expected, she had taken them up again, one by one. She still did everything expected of her: this afternoon Elizabeth Perry and Rachel Snelgrove were coming over to plan the sale of work to benefit the wounded veterans, and Lily had promised to find a steady older woman to take the boys' Sunday School class since no reliable young man could be found to replace Bert Courage, who had gone off to Sydney to work in the mines. But as so often in this last year, Lily felt as if she were only going through the motions. Silver spoons with tarnished edges looked up at her like wide, unblinking eyes, accusing her.

There would be a rag in the kitchen, but if she went to the kitchen she would have to think of something nice to say to the girl.

Trudy J. Morgan-Cole

Nellie. Lily kept calling her Elsie, but that was the last maid, gone and married now. Nellie was fourteen years old and competent on her best days, but she liked to chatter.

Preparing to polish the silver became a litany of the house. The kitchen: to be avoided because of the girl. Parlour: her usual place to sit, sometimes for hours on end, sewing or doing embroidery. The window looked out on a long green meadow that ran down from the front of the parsonage to the path along by the harbour. Grace once kept up a bit of a flower garden there; Charley used to cut the grass in the field. They had moved to Catalina from Elliston the year war broke out, when Grace was fourteen and Charley seventeen. The children were away at school over the winter. They had both gone to town to live with Papa and Daisy at age twelve to attend the Methodist College. Charley moved on from there to study at Dalhousie up in Canada.

But in Catalina, just as they had done in Elliston, they came home for summer and Christmas, and Lily liked to remember that first year or so as a happy time. When she sat in the parlour now she remembered looking out on long summer evenings at clusters of young folk sitting on the porch, Grace and Charley and their friends talking and laughing and singing. Then Charley joined the Regiment and all that ended. Though Grace came home to teach school during the war and had had girlfriends over to the house in the evenings, still the house seemed in Lily's memory to have become silent after Charley left.

Ghosts paraded on the lawn; ghosts hung on the walls of the parlour. Not only the ghost of Charley, framed in uniform, but of the whole family when the children were very small and they had had a photograph done at Mr. Parsons's studio in St. John's. The ghost of an even younger Lily with the Reverend taken at the same studio a few days after their wedding, a stiff formal pose in which they both looked terrified. *With good reason*, Lily thought.

Neither silver polish nor a rag would be in the parlour. Lily shook herself out of reverie.

The cupboard under the stairs was a jumble. Nellie wasn't keeping it properly tidy, or perhaps didn't think it was part of her duties to take care of such things. After a little searching around on the narrow shelves, Lily found the silver polish poked behind a bottle of bleach. She pulled the string to turn off the light bulb. Oh, those light bulbs: the shining evidence of Mr. Coaker's dreamtown! Electric lighting all over Port Union and Catalina, not just here in the manse and in Coaker's Bungalow, but even in the simple homes of the fishermen. Electric lights, books and lectures, a clinic with a nurse brought over from England. How the Reverend and Mr. Coaker could go on about it, by the hour, when the great man visited their house. Still the lights were nothing more than a convenience when all was said and done: a good thing, but not exactly evidence of divine approval.

She was up the stairs, back up to her bedroom. The master bedroom, where the master had not slept these many years. Lily remembered their wedding night, a big bed in the Cochrane House hotel, in a room paid for by her parents. She remembered how cold the room was, and how she had clutched her nightgown about herself. She remembered lying awake beside him all that night, staring out the window.

She had no need to go into his study, that austere temple of the learned man. He could work late there on sermons and then go to bed in the adjoining room without disturbing her. That was the official reason for separate quarters. If anyone had asked, which of course no one ever did.

In Grace's room, she thought, there would be old clothing she could tear up for polishing rags. Grace had never cleared out the room because she had not really moved out. Not like a girl did when she got married. This gadding off to St. John's, volunteering at the

Trudy J. Morgan-Cole

hospital, trying to be a career girl—none of that ever lasted, did it? Fishermen's daughters went off into service and ministers' daughters taught school or did good works. No girl truly left home until she got married.

Lily had moved out of her old room in her parents' house when she married the Reverend, but even she had left things behind, old clothes, scraps of paper, and bits of writing and letters. Things she could not imagine taking with her into married life. Nothing that could reveal any secrets to a curious eye, should anyone ever search there—she had burned all the dangerous papers.

Grace's room had the untidy look of a place the owner intended to return to, which both irritated and comforted Lily. She never went into Charley's room. After word had come of his loss she had locked the door and never entered it. She wasn't keeping the room like a shrine, as some foolish women did. It was as if the room had ceased to exist at all, like a piece torn off the house.

In Grace's top drawer Lily found something she could tear up to make rags: an old blouse, far too small—something Grace had worn when she was eight or ten years old. Beneath it was a hand-made rag doll; a gift from Daisy when Grace was about six. They had been living—where, then? Before Elliston...oh, those were the years over on Cape Freels, the most godforsaken spot on earth. So Grace had dragged some of this stuff in her little trunk from Cape Freels to Elliston and then from Elliston to Catalina. They would have been packed up and gone to another place by now—the Methodist circuit liked to shuffle their ministers around—except that they were having a hard time finding a minister for Catalina so they were leaving Reverend Collins there for now. Another postwar shortage, Lily supposed.

She stood holding the cloth doll in her hands. It was a faded little thing, stuffed, she thought, with cotton batting, buttons sewn on for eyes. Grace used to streel it about with her everywhere and sleep with it at night. One arm hung half-off. Lily had a vivid memory of coming into Grace's room one day to find Grace cradling the doll and crooning to it, "My babby…My babby…My babby." It had startled Lily because that was what she had called both Charley and Grace when they were little, "My babby." But only for such a short time, when they were babies and it felt safe to be sentimental. She had stopped it, she was sure, by the time they were both weaned, if not before. She had always been careful to call them by their names and address them in proper English, no foolish baby-talk.

The year Grace was ten and Charley thirteen, Lily had accompanied the Reverend to some church meetings in Toronto—the one and only trip she and her husband had taken off the island together. In a store on Yonge Street, Lily had seen a doll: eighteen inches tall, dressed in a gown of real green velvet trimmed with lace, face and hands of exquisite china, real hair with a lovely auburn sheen, and emerald eyes that opened and closed. She bought it for Grace, had it packed in its own special box with layers of protective fabric and straw to preserve it for its long journey home on the train and steamer. She had bought a gift for Charley too of course— a toy fire-engine, she thought—but it was the doll for Grace that absorbed all her thoughts.

Grace's reaction had been gratifying. Her eyes had been wide and her mouth an O of delight. She had said it was the most beautiful doll in the world. She put it on its own shelf in her room and there it stayed; that doll, too, had moved from one parsonage to another, though by the time they got to Catalina, Grace had been too old for dolls. In the months after she first gave it to her, Grace's lack of attachment to the doll bothered Lily, though she couldn't quite put her finger on what she wished Grace would do differently. It wasn't that she ought to have played with the doll— it wasn't a doll made for hauling around from place to place, and

Trudy J. Morgan-Cole

indeed the few times Grace had attempted to take it down from its shelf Lily had told her to put it back and reminded her to be careful. After that she seemed content to let it sit there and glance at it from time to time. She took the doll for granted, while Daisy's tatty little ragdoll was her babby; even at ten she still dragged it about with her everywhere and seemed to love it more the more ragged and disreputable it became. It irritated Lily even now, when she walked into Grace's room and saw the Toronto doll inviolate on its shelf. It was behind her now, on a shelf by the bed. In the mirror its green glass eyes stared at her.

Lily laid the rag doll back in the drawer, covered it with the blouse. It was just possible that the blouse had been saved as the rag doll had, for some sentimental reason that only existed in Grace's mind. In another drawer she found a threadbare pair of bloomers and ripped them apart. Silver polish in one hand, rags in the other, she went back down to the dining room. Before the ladies came for their meeting, she would polish the silver.

Part Two

LILY 1893

CHAPTER SEVEN

"WHEN I STOOD there with our sisters in Boston, and heard the tales of women all over the world fighting for that same right that even the lowest and meanest of men may take for granted—sisters, it stirred me to the soul!" Mrs. Peters declared. She stood behind the podium in Temperance Hall, her face transfigured as if with a light from heaven, though Lily recognized that it was probably just a fine sheen of perspiration lit by the reflection of the lights. The building, only recently rebuilt after the fire, had been fitted with electric lights instead of the old gas lamps, and Lily found it hard to get accustomed to their harsher illumination. "How can we, the women of Newfoundland, do less than to stand with these other brave women around the world?" Mrs. Peters asked. "When we see all around us poverty, drunkenness, and degradation, when we see the women of Newfoundland suffering for the sins of men, how can we not hope to better those around us by standing up to make our voices heard?"

All around, women applauded, and some jumped to their feet. Lily stood up, drawn as if by a puppeteer's string, so powerful was the pull of Mrs. Peters's words. Over the winter, Mrs. Peters had attended a great WCTU rally in the United States at which a number of suffrage speakers as well as temperance speakers had taken the stage. "Imagine it!" she had said to the women gathered here in St. John's to hear her report. "All women speakers—not a man in sight! Women gathered to talk about issues of concern to women—first and foremost, Prohibition and the vote!"

After the lecture, women gathered in little groups for tea. Lily found herself pulled along with her old schoolmate Martha Withycombe in a circle that included Martha's mother Frances, Mrs. Ohman, and several other ladies. "The great pity is those who need to hear this message are not the women gathered in this room, but the men at the Colonial Building!" one said. "But when no woman can speak at a public lecture, who will hear our calls for justice?"

"If we can't speak, surely we can write?" Lily ventured. She brandished the new copy of the *Water Lily*, the first issue to roll off the press since July. Eight months had passed since the fire; most newspapers and periodicals had ceased publication since nearly all the printshops had been devastated in the blaze, as her father's shop had been. But now, as the burned city was beginning to rebuild, the presses, too, were rolling again. Mrs. Ohman's temperance paper was one of the latest to resume publishing.

"But it's only the same thing, my dear," Mrs. Williams said kindly. "Mrs. Ohman puts out a fine paper, of course, but it's written by women and read by women. Is any man going to pick up a copy of the *Water Lily* to see what the women of St. John's have to say about the issues of the day?"

Inspiring as women's meetings were, they always came down to this basic problem, Lily reflected as she circulated around the room at the end of the evening, picking up discarded papers and fans. Temperance women talked to each other, but women who were not concerned for the cause, or were actively opposed to it, remained uninformed. Meanwhile the great mass of men, who made all the decisions, thought of the temperance women as harmless do-gooders.

Lily had spent a long, dull winter shut up in her grandparents' house in Harbour Grace with little to do except read and write. By the time Papa had written to say the house was ready to move into, Lily longed to be back in town. A week after Uncle Wesley's schooner brought her and her mother back to St. John's, Lily had gone with a group of old school friends to the big Temperance Convention at St. Mary's Anglican church. She was thrilled to be part of such a big gathering, to hear the speakers who talked not only about the importance of passing a prohibition law but also about the important work the WCTU ladies were doing, how essential the women's voice was to the cause.

She had spoken to Mrs. Ohman there, who had told her she ought to come out to the regular WCTU meetings. When she learned that Lily liked to write, Mrs. Ohman asked to see something she had written, and chose a poem to be printed in the very first post-fire edition of the *Water Lily*. Seeing her own words in print— though not, of course, her name, since the piece had been published anonymously—had convinced Lily that she might, after all, have a little part to play in the great work that was now going forward.

The WCTU was circulating a petition to submit to the House of Assembly. It asked for a vote for women—not a general suffrage, but the right to vote in local elections on the prohibition issue. Lily had signed the petition at her first WCTU meeting and borrowed Mrs. Ohman's sheet for a few days to try to get more signatures.

She had tried at home: Mother wouldn't hear of it and told Lily to be quiet lest Papa should catch wind of what she was up to. Lily had also talked about it to her girlfriends, the young women with whom she had attended the Methodist College a few years earlier. Some of them were married or preparing to be married

Trudy J. Morgan-Cole

now. The brides and brides-to-be were least likely to want to hear about votes for women. The single girls were willing to hear her out, but Abby Hayward was the only one who actually signed. She had gone with Lily to the Temperance Convention—Abby was always ready to go any place there was likely to be a large crowd that included young men—but she refused Lily's invitations to come to WCTU meetings. "What, a bunch of old biddies clucking about closing down the rum-shops? A bit dull for me, I'm afraid." Abby had spent the winter after the fire in New York with her aunt, going to concerts and having new frocks made. "But as for the vote, of course I'll sign. The new century is going to be the century of women, haven't you heard? It's silly to let men hold us back."

Just yesterday, Lily had gone down to the kitchen to urge Sally to sign the petition. Sally had come back to work for them as soon as the house was completed, glad to have her comfortable little room up under the eaves again, since her family had been burned out of their home too. Lily and her mother had been unable to take Sally to Harbour Grace with them: there wasn't room in Grandmother's house for another servant girl. Sally had lived in a tent in the park with her own people for a fortnight and then moved into a crowded apartment with two other families. The Hunts' new house was still not fully furnished and there was finishing work to be done but Sally considered her little upstairs bedroom a great improvement over conditions her parents were living in.

When Lily explained about the petition, Sally had put up her hands as if warding off an angry goose. "Oh, no, Miss Lily, that's not for the likes of me."

"But it is, Sally! If we're going to stop the liquor trade we need the vote for all women, rich and poor. Why, Evans has the vote now. Why shouldn't you?" She knew that a few years ago the rules had been changed so that all men, not just property owners, had the vote. Educated ladies like Mrs. Peters and Mrs. Ohman and even

Lady Thorburn, whose husband used to be premier, thought it was most unfair that even a servant or a bum on the street could vote to put his man into government, while they could not.

"How would I know what to vote for? Sure, I can't even sign me name on that paper, all I knows how to do is make an X."

"It doesn't matter a bit. You know how hard it is on women when men go and get drunk on payday and then come home with no money for the market and beat the children? Don't you? Well, if you'd like to have the right to vote against that, for yourself and for other women, then you make your X and I'll print your name next to it." She put the pen in Sally's hand, but Sally dropped it on the countertop.

"No, Miss Lily, it's not right, is what. Do your mother know about this? Because she'll tell the Mister, and I don't want you to get in trouble. Your Pop don't have no time for folks who don't know their places, and I don't say he'd be happy with this vote business, neither."

The threat of Papa, who had never struck Lily as being so particularly strict or stern, hung over every conversation she had with anyone about the suffrage petition—except with Abby Hayward, who viewed it, like everything else, as a great joke. Lily brought her page of the petition back sadly to the next WCTU meeting with only her own signature and Abby's.

Now, as the meeting ended and ladies picked up their wraps and left the hall, Lily unfolded the paper from her handbag and gave it to Mrs. Ohman. "I'm sorry, it's not much. I only got one signature, besides my own."

Mrs. Ohman unfolded the paper, looked at the two written lines, then refolded it into her own bag. "Oh, Lily, you mustn't let it daunt you. Those of us who fight for the rights of women will face opposition on all sides, even within our own families! But it must never stop us. We must never be discouraged. Do you think

Trudy J. Morgan-Cole

you'll be allowed to come out to hear the debate, when our bill comes before the House?"

"Oh, I don't know if Papa will allow…"

"Well, you must see what you can do. We badly need you younger women."

Across the room, as if emblematic of the younger women, Mrs. Bulley's two daughters were going out the door, stepping into their father's waiting carriage. Not only was their mother a leader in the cause, their father posed no objection to his wife and daughters crusading for temperance and suffrage. It must be nice to live in an enlightened household, Lily thought.

At least she could show up to WCTU meetings. Mother and Papa would not oppose temperance work. A few days later Lily turned up the collar of her coat against a brisk cold wind with a swirl of flurries and walked to the office of the *Evening Herald*, where the WCTU did most of its printing business. Mrs. Ohman had asked her to pick up the latest batch of handbills. Lily was glad the WCTU did not do its printing with her father's shop; when the handbills were penned by Mrs. Ohman the language could get a touch strident.

The smell of a printshop was as familiar as the smell of bread baking in the kitchen to Lily. She stood in the outer office breathing the odour of paper and ink as she waited for the boy to come back with a parcel of handbills when a half-familiar voice said, "Hello, Miss Hunt."

She turned to see David Reid, the young newspaperman she had met on the day of the fire. They had had two chance meetings over half a year ago, yet it seemed he remembered her as easily as she remembered him.

"Mr.—Mr. Reid, was it? Of course, we met in Bannerman Park after the fire—didn't Mrs. Ohman introduce us?"

He smiled broadly. He had dimples: an odd sight on a grown man, but not an unattractive one. "She may have done or she may not have. I'd remember your face forever, even if we'd never been introduced."

"Mr. Reid!"

"Excuse me, I'm trying out my gallantry. I don't think it goes well, does it? Oh, nor does the hat," he added, removing his bowler. Flecks of snow dotted its brim. "Yes, Miss Hunt, I'm David Reid, sadly no relation to the railway Reid and thus no millionaire. Forgive me. The truth is I'm all out of sorts, seeing you unexpectedly like this. I've been planning out all kinds of clever speeches for when I saw you again, but they told me you'd left town for the winter."

"I've been back nearly a month now. You—you inquired after me?"

"I had some business with your father. Don't think he was best pleased at me making the inquiry, but you can't hang a man for asking, can you? Well, depending on what he's asking, I suppose."

There seemed no appropriate way to respond to any of this, so it was perhaps fortunate that just at that moment the boy came back from the shop with her parcel. Lily paid him and turned to go.

"What is it you're picking up here, then?" Mr. Reid asked, hurrying to get the door for her. "I'd have thought your father would take care of any printing you might want done. Not wedding invitations, I hope, is it?"

"Why, you are impertinent, aren't you, sir?" Lily knew she ought to stalk away with her head held high, but she couldn't suppress a giggle. She did walk away, but just a few steps, and then turned back to say, "As it happens, I am here to pick up handbills for the WCTU rally."

"Ah, the noble cause! What better reason could there be to carry a packet of handbills down Prescott Street? Are you going to Temperance Hall? Yes? I'll walk you there, will I? That couldn't possibly be improper, could it now?"

"I think it might be. Especially as I met you coming *into* the printshop, and now you've left without conducting your business."

"Oh no, I think this is my business. At least, it is now. Delivering an article to the press can always wait an hour, even when a man's two hours past his deadline. Walking alongside a lovely lady who left town the day after I met her—well, that's far more pressing. And to find out the lady has a social conscience and supports the women's franchise to boot—well, what more could a fellow ask?"

She hadn't mentioned the franchise, only the WCTU, but clearly Mr. Reid, like many people, considered the two causes closely linked. He was walking in step with her down Prescott Street regardless of her faint protests, and had managed to take possession of her parcel.

"You are mocking me, sir," Lily said.

"I couldn't possibly! How can you accuse me so cruelly?"

"You pretend to admire the suffrage cause."

"Why do you think it's a pretense?"

"Don't try to tell me you're a supporter of women's emancipation!"

He ran a step or two ahead of her and turned back, holding his hat over his chest. "I swear to you, I am a supporter of everyone's emancipation, women's no less than men's. Well, I write for the *Herald*, don't I?" The *Herald* was the anti-government, pro-reform paper. Its editor had published several articles supporting rights of women and carried a regular WCTU column.

"But the *Herald* is a temperance paper, and I don't think you're a temperance man, are you?" Lily said.

"Oh, you don't think so, eh! Do I have the look of a drunkard?" He glanced down at her and Lily looked away.

"Not that. But I know you're not a Methodist. If Mrs. Ohman hadn't introduced us, I might think you were a Papist."

"Ah, you see a bit of the Irish in me, don't you? Well, to be completely honest, my mother was Irish Catholic. But my father was Scots Presbyterian, and she promised him on his deathbed that she would raise his son Presbyterian, though she was free to do as she liked in the matter of daughters. She dropped me at the Kirk every Sunday," he explained, nodding in the general direction of where that church stood before the fire, "then walked on to the Basilica with my sisters, and then back to get me. Fortunately, Presbyterian preaching being what it is, she had plenty of time to spare. She never let me darken the door of a Roman church, and the truth is I don't darken the door of any church very often nowadays. And you are right in guessing I am not a temperance man. Though I don't say that around the editor of the *Herald*."

"Well then." Lily drew her hand away. They were near Temperance Hall now. "I thank you for escorting me, though it wasn't really necessary. After all, it was only the next street over."

"Of course. And an emancipated young woman should be able to walk a block in the city as well as any man."

"You are still laughing at me."

"I'm not, I swear it! I believe in the universal franchise as deeply and purely as you believe in God the Father, Son, and Holy Spirit."

"That's nearly blasphemy."

"So be it. In my grandfather's day, no one in Newfoundland could vote. We did as we were told by the governor from England. Men all over the world have fought for the franchise—first for the wealthy and then for the poor man too. Why not for the womenfolk as well? Whatever you think of me, Miss Hunt, I'm deadly sincere in supporting your cause." He handed over her parcel and bowed.

"Well, then—I commend your politics, if not your manners," Lily said. "You've been very impertinent, and I don't think it's proper that we should speak again."

Trudy J. Morgan-Cole

"That would be a shame and a sorrow indeed, Miss Hunt."

"Good day, Mr. Reid."

She meant to go straight into the hall but it was almost impossible not to watch his tall frame walking away down the sidewalk, hands thrust in his pockets, long strides swinging. He walked as if he were pleased with himself, as if he might be whistling. The nerve of the man!

Then, at the end of the street, he turned back and waved. As if he had known all along that she would be watching.

CHAPTER EIGHT

"*Y*OUR FATHER TELLS me you're active in the WCTU, Miss Hunt?"

Reverend Obadiah Collins leaned across the dinner table toward her. He showed early signs of both stoutness and baldness. Lily had been told that he was twenty-four years old but he looked as if he were apprenticing for middle age. Lily and her parents were dining at the home of Reverend Pratt, the Cochrane Street minister. Reverend Collins and Lily were the only younger people present, and Lily had no illusions about why her father had been so anxious to accept this dinner invitation, nor why he had talked with such warmth about the son of his old friend Jacob Collins. Young Reverend Collins shepherded the Methodist flock out in Greenspond. He was apparently learned, pious and, most important, unmarried. In need of a wife, that indispensable accessory for the hardworking clergyman.

"I am devoted to the cause of temperance, Mr. Collins," Lily said, keeping her eyes on her plate. She found it impossible to say "Mr. Collins" without thinking of the character from *Pride and*

Prejudice, and this young clergyman bore an unfortunate resemblance—in his manner, at least—to his literary namesake.

"I am so glad to hear that!" Reverend Collins had the air of a man interviewing a promising candidate for a position in his firm. A new partner in the business, as it were. "It's very well, of course, for those of us with the light of truth to accept the temperance message for ourselves, but there are folk all over this island—poor folk, uneducated—who will never see that light. Oh, Miss Hunt, if you could only see what I have seen—the poverty, the hardship, the ignorance. I have witnessed scenes I would not dare describe in a woman's hearing, all due to the evils of alcohol. And they will never put it aside unless it is taken out of their hands by force—the force of law." Mr. Collins's bay accent had been carefully schooled for sermonizing, but misplaced Hs slipped through the homiletic net: when he spoke of the Ardship and Hignorance, Lily had to hide her smile.

Now she looked up and met his eye. "You say you would not repeat what you have seen in a woman's hearing, and yet it's the women, and the children, who have to live with those scenes and bear the brunt of them."

"Of course, of course. It's the very reason why the WCTU ladies have been such a strong voice for us in the cause. I commend their desire to improve the lot of their suffering sisters." Dinner was a roast of beef, very tender: the Pratts had an excellent cook. Forks clinked against plates and conversation rose and fell.

"My daughter here is a great admirer of Mrs. Ohman," Papa said, "but I'm concerned about the way she links the prohibition cause to votes for women."

Reverend Collins bobbed his head towards Lily. "I would not tarnish the name of one you admire, Miss Hunt. But it is my firm conviction, as I'm sure it is of us all," he added, looking around the table for support, "that when woman steps outside of her proper sphere of home and family and seeks a role in public life, she is demeaned by it. Her natural purity and moral fibre are cheapened and coarsened. Do any of us really wish the ladies to be sullied by the grime of party politics?"

"No, of course, not," Papa boomed, and Reverend Pratt echoed him. Mama said nothing, but Mrs. Pratt put a hand to her throat as if she felt a sudden draft in the room. "I couldn't agree more, Reverend Collins. As a wife and mother I have always felt I'm fulfilling God's call. Why would I want to raise my voice in the public square when that is my husband's role? I might as likely expect to get up into the pulpit and preach on a Sunday morning!"

"Where we start listening to these votes-for-women agitators, we'll soon see women preachers as well as women politicians, and far worse," Reverend Pratt said. "But the sentiment is being taken up by so many people that it is hard to combat. I was most disappointed to hear that at the Temperance Rally a few weeks ago, some of the gentlemen who spoke—clergymen, even—were speaking in support of giving women the vote on this issue. I am glad to see we are all in agreement here."

Did Lily imagine her mother's eyes meeting hers over the table? Did she see a little headshake of warning?

Lily needed no warning. She said nothing at all as the conversation moved on from women's votes and Prohibition to the feud that was brewing at Gower Street Church over the reconstruction of their burned-out building. She nibbled at her roast beef, listened with a smile, but proffered no further comments.

Her silence bothered her. In bed that night she looked out at the slice of sky visible through her window and thought that she was like Peter on the night of Jesus's trial, warming himself by the fire, vowing he never knew the Man. She had not forsworn her beliefs, but she had not stood up for them either.

But the greatest test was still to come. On Tuesday evening the

Trudy J. Morgan-Cole

bill asking for the women's vote on the question of Prohibition would be presented in the House by Mr. Morison. Mrs. Ohman and Mrs. Peters were urging as many of the WCTU ladies as possible to attend. Some, like Mrs. Withycombe and her daughter Martha, had already declared they would not be there, claiming that even the gallery of the Assembly was an inappropriate place for a lady. Lily was sure her Papa would feel exactly the same about his only daughter sitting with a crowd of suffragists, watching men debate in the House of Assembly.

Yet how could she stay away? The only thing she could think of was to draw Abby Hayward into her confidence, gambling that Abby's love of secrets and conspiracy would outweigh her disinterest in politics.

It was a winning gamble. "If we're going to deceive our parents and sneak out at night, I can think of a dozen places more entertaining than the Colonial Building," Abby sniffed, "but I'll never be able to drag you anywhere interesting. If I invite you to spend the night here, and then we tell my parents that we're going to spend the evening at your house before coming back here to sleep, I'm sure neither of them will suspect a thing."

"Unless our mothers talk to each other."

"But they won't. Yours has the vapours again and mine is much too busy. The upstairs rooms are finally getting painted and papered again." Abby's house, unlike Lily's, had been undamaged in the fire but her mother claimed there was "soot everywhere" and had decided to redecorate anyway. "It's all she can think of. I'm sure I could smuggle myself out to a tavern on Water Street if I cared to. Shall we wear disguises, in case some friend of your father's recognizes you in the House?"

"Not disguises exactly, but I have a hat with a little veil, and if I keep a fan up in front of my face most of the time, I'm sure no one will recognize me." Lily's heart pounded at the thought of the subterfuge. She wanted so badly to sit with Mrs. Ohman and Mrs. Peters and the other ladies who were getting things done, who were really making a change in society. They had talked at the last WCTU meeting, tallying up the members of the House who would likely vote for them, who was soft on liquor and who was friendly to the women's cause. "We have a chance," Mrs. Ohman had declared. "Only a chance, but it's better than last year. At least my brother has come round." Her brother, Mr. Murray, had spoken against the bill the last time it had come before the House, and family feeling had not stopped Mrs. Ohman from roundly criticizing him in the pages of the *Water Lily*. Oh, to be so bold and daring: to be able to chastise even the men in one's own family!

On Tuesday, the fourth of May, the girls met after dinner at Lily's house and told Lily's mother they were going to Abby's. Instead, they walked to Temperance Hall, where about twenty of the WCTU ladies had gathered, with the intention of processing to the Colonial Building together.

"Lily! How wonderful to see you. And your friend—Miss Hayward, is it? Thank you for coming to add your support to the cause!" Mrs. Ohman looked around the room. "Not as many as I'd hoped. We had over fifty women marching, you know, a few years ago when we brought our first petition. Every time the bill gets brought forward and defeated, more women lose hope. But we must not abandon the ship! Last year we lost by only two votes, and I'm sure we are closer this time." She sailed off to greet another newcomer, and before long the little knot of women began making its way up Victoria Street towards Military Road and the imposing bulk of the Colonial Building. The government building was, along with the Roman Catholic Basilica, among the few landmarks that had not been touched by the fire.

"A song to raise our spirits!" Mrs. Peters suggested. She had a good, tuneful voice, and struck up a temperance tune that most of

Trudy J. Morgan-Cole

the women joined in with as their boots tramped the hard-packed dirt of the road. After "Would You Be Free from Your Bourbon and Gin" they began one that Mrs. Ohman had written specially for the Newfoundland cause:

Manhood suffrage for the fool
And clown, and knave and dandy,
But lets us keep our women down
And gulp our gin and brandy!

Faces appeared in windows as they passed, and people strolling down Military Road in the fine spring afternoon paused to stare. Lily pulled her hat a little down over her brow so the veil covered her eyes, but Abby tipped her own hat back and laughed. "Whoever would have thought I'd be out marching with a bunch of blue-stockings! If Norman Winsor were to see me now—well, wouldn't he get a shock? It'd serve him right, too!" Norman was the latest of Abby's many beaux.

Inside the Colonial Building, the women filed up the stairs to the Ladies' Gallery and crowded onto the benches. The session began at four o'clock. It was hot, and no subterfuge was required for Lily to take out her fan and keep it vibrating in front of her face. The veil on her hat had to be pushed back, though, for otherwise it was hard to see the rows of white-haired, mutton-chopped men on the benches below.

Still, now that she was inside surrounded by the cluster of ladies, she felt safe from discovery. Mother or Papa might still find out, of course, that she had not been at Abby's all evening: there might be a reckoning, but for now she was free and she was here. Here to see history being made.

The worst thing about making history was that much of it was awfully tedious. The old men below were fond of long speeches, and there were other items of business to discuss before the women's suffrage bill came up. Even when it came, the attitude of the speakers was disappointing. Mr. Morison presented the bill and spoke of the need for Prohibition. Mr. Morris replied with a stirring speech about how men had the right to vote for laws because they had a duty to go out on the battlefield and defend those laws. Mr. Morison had no good response to this.

In the row ahead of Lily, Mrs. Ohman leaned over the gallery rail, perching so far forward on her seat she looked as if she might tumble forward into the assembly of men below. If she did, Lily knew from the set of her shoulders and thetrembling of her hat that she would land with her mouth open, ready to defend the cause of women's suffrage even before she picked herself up off the floor.

But Mrs. Ohman kept her seat and kept silent even when the premier, Mr. Whiteway, rose to speak. There had been some speculation that he might come around to the cause, and indeed he started off by saying that he had originally been inclined to support giving women the vote in the local option elections.

"Oh, mercy," Mrs. Ohman said to Mrs. Peters. "If he says he was originally inclined to support it, that means he's decided not to."

The premier went on to say that after hearing several speakers who seemed to view this as a first step towards a general franchise for women, he had changed his view. "I am surprised," he said, his voice booming in the musty air of the chamber, "to see Christian gentlemen trying to upset the Biblical doctrine that the woman is subject to the man!"

Lily felt the hot waves of anger from the women around her, heard the murmur of comments. Premier Whiteway painted a vivid picture of the happy home ruled over by a contented wife and mother. "What would the condition be," he asked, "if the husband returned home to find his wife away on a political mission, and the comforts of home and children neglected?"

Trudy J. Morgan-Cole

Mrs. Ohman, unable to hold back any longer, shouted, "Disgraceful! Shame!" Her outcry was stifled by cheers and jeers from the gentlemen below, but Mrs. Peters jabbed Mrs. Ohman in the arm with her fan. "You'll do our cause no good if you get thrown out of the House," she reminded the other lady in a sharp whisper.

It was long past supper-time. Lily's stomach growled. Surely they would be missed at Abby's house. Surely her mother, however distracted she was by paint and paper, would send a messenger up to the Hunt house to see why the girls had not arrived. But when she whispered this to Abby, Abby smiled. "I thought of that ages ago," she whispered back. "When I went out for air I sent a boy round with a note saying we'd decided to stay at your house for the night instead."

It was nearly midnight when the vote was taken and, before anyone said Aye or Nay, Lily knew it would not go in their favour. The men below looked tired and cross: a fug of blue pipe-smoke and cigar-smoke hung in the air, and the men who were in favour of the women's vote would not hold out all night against those who so eloquently opposed it. They wanted to sweep the matter away, to be done with it so they could go home to their beds, beds no doubt occupied by docile wives who never questioned their place.

"We've lost, we've lost," Mrs. Ohman muttered under her breath as the men recorded their votes one by one. Mrs. Peters put her face in her hands when the tally was recorded: fourteen votes in favour of women's franchise, seventeen against. And then the session was over, and the members below filed out of the hall, and the ladies in the gallery did the same. They were quiet now, shoulders sagging, hats no longer jaunty. No thought of singing, now.

Outside, the night sky was black and the air cool and bracing. Only Abby seemed to have any spirit left. "Out 'til after midnight!"

she said, squeezing Lily's arm. "What a lark! Don't worry, we can slip in through the servants' door. I've promised Sadie a pair of silk stockings if she keeps quiet."

Lily watched as the women moved away in twos and threes, stepping into waiting carriages, disappearing into the night without calling goodbyes to each other, as though they had not even the spirit left to be civil. "What happens in the morning?" she said, falling into step beside Abby. "You've sent a message saying we're at my house. What will your mother think when we come down to breakfast in the morning in your house?"

"Silly Lily, always worrying," Abby said. "You read the Bible so much, don't you know 'Sufficient unto the day is the evil thereof'? Tomorrow will look after itself. I'll be sure to think of something."

Trudy J. Morgan-Cole

CHAPTER NINE

$\mathcal{T}$HE DAY AFTER the vote in the House of Assembly, Lily walked home from Abby's house where, as Abby had predicted, Mrs. Hayward was already out by the time they rose and did not question at which house the girls had spent the night. Back at her own home, Lily found her own mother lying down with a damp cloth over her eyes. She asked in a faint voice whether Lily had had a nice time at Abigail's. It seemed the deception had worked perfectly.

But to what end, Lily wondered. She had deceived her parents, gone somewhere Papa would never have approved, believing she was there to watch history unfold. Instead she had listened to learned and wealthy men talk about women and their place in the home. Mrs. Ohman, Mrs. Peters, and Lady Thorburn, who had all seemed so strong and confident when speaking at Temperance Hall, were reduced to chidden little girls. It scarcely even mattered that fourteen men had voted in favour of the motion: once the bill was defeated it felt as if every man in Newfoundland had told the ladies to stay in their place and keep silent.

In the early afternoon, Mrs. Ohman came to Lily's front door.

She gestured to her carriage, pulled up in front of the Hunts' door. Mrs. Peters, Mrs. Withycombe, and Martha Withycombe were inside. "Come for a drive with us," she said. "Disappointment shared is disappointment halved, I've always believed."

"Last night's vote will set back the cause of temperance ten years," said Mrs. Withycombe as the carriage rolled down King's Bridge Road.

"Not.to mention the cause of women's emancipation," said Mrs. Peters.

Mrs. Withycombe frowned. "Well, perhaps if the members of the Assembly hadn't got the idea that we were going to push for the full franchise next, they would have been more eager to give us the vote in the local option. That's what frightened them off, and now we're farther behind on our true cause."

"Perhaps we're not entirely in agreement on what our true cause is," said Mrs.Ohman.

"Now, now," said Mrs. Peters. "It does no good to quarrel among ourselves, does it, ladies?"

Both Mrs. Ohman and Mrs. Withycombe subsided into unhappy silence. The carriage rolled along the rutted roads. Mrs. Ohman unfolded her copy of yesterday's *Evening Telegram* and rattled its pages as she read. The *Telegram* was the government paper and was unsympathetic to the women's cause. A column in its pages had recently made reference to the "inane and hysterical criticism of those women's rights agitators in the columns of the strong-minded *Water Lily*." Needless to say, Mrs. Ohman preferred the *Evening Herald*, but she liked to keep a sharp eye on the opposing view as well.

All at once she gasped sharply. "Oh, monstrous! This is terrible!"

"What is it?" Mrs. Peters asked. The paper had come out yesterday evening while they were all in the House of Assembly; there would be no mention in it of last night's debate.

Trudy J. Morgan-Cole

"A letter—an infamous letter! Do any of you know anything about this?"

She read the letter aloud. It was from an anonymous member of the WCTU addressing the question "Should Women Sit in the House of Assembly?" The author's answer was a resounding no.

"'Besides the duties of a true and faithful wife'—that part is in bold type, by the way, 'there is a more sacred trust given to them, a trust which is every true woman's ambition to attain, that of a mother'," Mrs. Ohman read.

"But we never asked for women to sit in the House—much less said women shouldn't be wives and mothers!" Martha burst out.

"No, dear, but once the spectre of the women's vote, even on a single issue, is raised, every man in the Assembly believes women will run for office next," Mrs. Withycombe said. "Which is why we must be so careful not to give the wrong impression."

Mrs. Ohman continued reading the letter, which ended, "It must be obvious to all right-thinking people that the instant woman becomes independent of man for her support and protection, the collapse of the whole social system is at hand."

"All right-thinking people, indeed!" snorted Mrs. Peters, taking the paper from Mrs. Ohman. "This can't be genuine! The editors of the *Telegram* must have written this, to make it appear as if we are not united in our cause."

"But we are *not* united, are we?" Mrs. Ohman said, shooting a glance at Mrs. Withycombe. "I would not say that anyone *here* would be so disloyal as to send such a letter to the public press, but the sentiments are ones that we have all heard some of our members—including you, Mrs. Withycombe—express."

"I hope you are not accusing me of writing letters to the paper!"

Suddenly the carriage seemed very crowded. Lily's former pleasure at being included in this elite gathering of temperance women evaporated. The carriage was rolling past the Pleasantville cricket grounds; the shores of Quidi Vidi Lake lay broad and inviting on the other side.

Mrs. Peters followed her glance. "Oh, have your driver stop and let's get out and walk for a bit," she said to Mrs. Ohman. "It's a lovely day and I think we all need the exercise— at least, I know I do."

"Quite right," said Mrs. Ohman, leaning forward to get her driver's attention.

The day was sunny and mild. It was late enough in the afternoon that schoolchildren played on the banks of the pond, and a few rowboats dotted the surface of the water. Martha leaned against the bridge railing and watched the nearest boat, a far-off expression in her eyes. "It doesn't matter a fig to them, does it?" she said. "Everything we fight so hard for—votes and Prohibition and all that—that family out for a row on the pond doesn't care one bit, do they?"

"We don't know that for certain," Lily said, but Mrs. Ohman's voice, piercing as a piccolo, cut across hers.

"You may be right, Martha. They may know nothing about the battles we fight. But if that young father is sipping from a gin-flask and gets drunk and capsizes the boat, and all those pretty children are drowned, everyone will gather round the little caskets weeping. Then we'll see what a difference it might have made, had we succeeded in passing a prohibition law."

Lily had often admired Mrs. Ohman's ability to string together speeches that sounded as if she were standing on the platform in a lecture hall, just in ordinary conversation. But Mrs. Withycombe was less impressed.

"I didn't write that letter, but I do believe we'd have a prohibition law sooner if we hadn't distracted the Assembly and the press with the spectre of women voters. We ought to have kept our focus clearly on Prohibition from the beginning, and that family might be closer to being saved from a watery grave."

Trudy J. Morgan-Cole

In fact the young man pulling at the oars did not look in the least intoxicated, though Lily did see, as Mrs. Ohman apparently had, that he took a quick drink from a flask at his side. There was, in fact, something half-familiar in the set of the strong shoulders that propelled the boat along. When he took off his straw hat to wipe perspiration from his brow and she saw the shock of sandy hair, Lily realized with a start that the man was David Reid. Was he married and the father of a family?

She turned resolutely away from the pond, the man, the boat full of laughing children, and towards Mrs. Ohman and the other ladies. "What next, then? What do we do next?"

Mrs. Ohman sighed. For the first time she looked defeated. "I hardly know what to say, dear Lily. I am going to dedicate some time to thought and prayer before our next WCTU meeting."

It all seemed hopeless—after all their meetings and speeches, the petitions, the letters, the march and the handbills and signposts. It all came down to this: a group of women could do nothing if the men in power would not allow them to do it. And just a few yards away on the sparkling water of Quidi Vidi was David Reid, with three children and a flask of gin, and Lily's heart felt jagged in her chest, like broken glass.

He was rowing the boat to shore now, making the children laugh. The oldest boy, no more than nine, had his hands on the oars too, helping to bring the boat in, and on the shore a woman stood waiting for them. *His wife?* Lily looked at the woman's face, her red hair, the easy way Mr. Reid spoke to her as he lifted the children from the boat. The little girl shouted "Uncle David!" as he handed her to her mother—Mr. Reid's sister, surely. In spite of the quick, silver glint of the flask Lily's chest felt lighter. The heat of the day seemed joyful rather than oppressive.

The other women talked on and Lily gazed at David Reid, at his broad shoulders and the long line of his lean body as he pulled the boat into shore and tied it up. He wore no tie, waistcoat or jacket, only a blue shirt with the collar open and sleeves rolled up past the elbows. His trousers were rolled up too, above the ankles, and he was barefoot, splashing into and out of the water, then sitting on the grass to put on shoes and socks. The children clambered over him as he sat down: two little towheaded boys and, between them in size so presumably in age, a girl whose red hair was twisted into braids but escaped in small damp curls around her face. She had the same colouring as her mother and uncle: just at that moment Mr. Reid took off his hat again and laid it on the grass, and the gleam of sunlight made his hair shine like the polished bottom of a copper pot.

Then he looked up and saw Lily. He looked twice, as if making sure of who it was, waved, and came over, the little girl still clinging to his arm. He picked up his hat as he rose and put it back on his head just in time to lift it off again as he approached and said, "Miss Hunt. Mrs. Ohman. Ladies."

"Mr. Reid, good day," said Mrs. Ohman, a little stiffly. "You must have a holiday."

"Half-holiday. Promised my sister I'd take her and the little ones down to the pond as soon as we got a sunny day." He turned the full force of his charm on Mrs. Ohman as if he would burn through her chilly greeting like sunshine through morning fog. "I was in the House last night. I'm sorry. You must be greatly disappointed—I know I am. I'd dared to imagine it was the dawn of modern times in St. John's."

"I fear we will have to wait a long time for that, Mr. Reid," said Mrs. Ohman. "And at any rate you know that we wanted the vote so we could bring in Prohibition, so I hardly think you would be entirely pleased with the outcome."

"Ah well, I like to take the good along with the bad, as it were," he said. "Miss Hunt, will you come down and meet my sister and the little ones? This here is Annie. She won't leave go of me, but I know Catherine would like to meet you."

"Of course," Lily said. She excused herself from Mrs. Ohman and the other ladies, and found herself being introduced to Catherine Malone, Mr. Reid's widowed sister, and the two little boys, who were clamouring for a sweet now that the boat ride was over. Mr. Reid made a great show of searching his pockets and finding nothing, then pulling molasses kisses out of his ears and nose, which had the children falling on the ground in laughter.

"They can't get enough of him," Mrs. Malone said. "We don't see much of him, he's so busy with the paper, but he's as good as a circus when he comes by to entertain the children."

"Miss Hunt! We're leaving!" called Mrs. Peters from the bridge.

"Oh, stay with us awhile," Mr. Reid pleaded. "You can walk home with us, and who knows, perhaps we'll even get you out in the rowboat?"

"I'm not dressed for boating," Lily protested, but she ran over to the bridge anyway, to tell Mrs. Ohman that Mr. Reid would see her home.

Mrs. Ohman pressed her lips into a thin line. "Lily, have your parents met Mr. Reid? I hardly think they would approve of him coming to call on you. Mr. Reid is a member of the Kirk only so far as having his name on the books: he is neither a regular churchgoer nor a temperance man."

"It's a family outing, with his sister and her children. They'll see me safely home. It's not as if I'll be alone with Mr. Reid."

"Still, I know your father would not be pleased."

Lily's admiration for Mrs. Ohman was so great that it was difficult to stand her ground, but last night's escapade emboldened her. Perhaps the anti-suffragists were right: once a woman took it into her head to think for herself, who knew where the defiance might stop?

Mrs. Ohman shrugged. "Your parents trusted me to take you out for a ride and back. I suppose I will have to trust you, now, to get back by tea-time."

"I will, Mrs. Ohman."

The other ladies went back to the carriage as Lily returned to the lakeshore where the children were playing leapfrog with Mr. Reid. Lily sat on a bench with Mrs. Malone, who was easy to talk to and seemed surprisingly cheerful for the widowed mother of three small children. Her husband had gone down on a ship called the *Mary Rose* two years earlier; she was a seamstress who worked long hours into the night to earn enough to pay her rent and feed the children.

"David helps us a bit, when he can," she said, "though he makes little enough money himself. He loves writing for the newspapers even though it doesn't pay so well. He likes to believe newspapers can change the world."

It was, Lily knew, a bit dishonest to have told Mrs. Ohman that she would be with Mr. Reid, his sister, and the children. They all walked from the lakeshore to Water Street and took the streetcar to the west end, then got off and walked to Mrs. Malone's home on Cuddihy's Lane. It would have been far shorter and simpler to drop Lily off first at Queen's Road, which they had passed on the way to the streetcar stop, but she did not suggest that and neither did Mr. Reid. His sister asked if they would stay and have tea but Mr Reid said no, he would walk Lily home. Saying goodbye to the tangle of children and kissing his sister on the cheek, David Reid tucked Lily's hand firmly in the crook of his arm and set off on the walk back east along New Gower Street.

"They're a grand bunch of bairns, but they do get wearing after a few hours," he admitted.

"You're very good with them. I've hardly ever seen a man so much at ease with little children."

"Ah, it's only that I'm hardly grown up myself."

Trudy J. Morgan-Cole

They were walking so close she could feel the heat of his body. The triangle of skin at his bare throat was sunburned and so was the bridge of his nose: his fair skin coloured easily and it made him look even more boyish.

"I don't think your Mrs. Ohman likes me very well," he said after a minute.

"She thinks my father would disapprove of you walking me home, so she disapproves too."

"And me such a supporter of her cause."

"Only one cause. She told me to beware because you are not a temperance man." The silver flask, so briefly glimpsed earlier in the day, was an unspoken presence between them.

"I've already confessed to that."

"Why are you not, though?"

"There's worse things a man can do than have a glass of spirits to refresh him at the end of the day. I think the temperance crowd makes too great a fuss over a little thing."

"Are there worse things a man could do than beat his wife, neglect his family, drink away his pay packet at the tavern before he buys food for his family?"

He smiled, as if delighted she was debating him. "You're right of course, those are terrible things. But why not attack the problems themselves and the men who cause them, instead of punishing all the poor fellows who enjoy the odd glass?"

"Many a man says he only enjoys a sociable drink, but how many of those end up becoming drunkards?"

"Fewer than you'd think, Miss Hunt. And that sentence sounded like it came straight out of one of Mrs. Ohman's serial stories."

Lily couldn't deny that. How strong and determined Mrs. Ohman's heroine Alida had been, refusing to marry James, who was perfect in every other way, until he signed the temperance pledge!

A Sudden Sun

Lily could imagine herself as Alida, but Mr. Reid, unlike James, was hardly the perfect suitor even if he could be persuaded to take the pledge.

"Reverend Collins would like to come call on you the next time he's in town," her father had said, after that awkward dinner at Reverend Pratt's house.

Why should he? What would we ever have to say to each other? Aloud she had said, "Yes, if you wish, Papa."

Yes, Papa. Yes, Mother. Whatever you say. If you think that's best. The phrases that had been bred into her from birth came naturally to her lips. She was, had always been, a dutiful daughter.

"I don't understand how you can be so backward-thinking on this one issue and so forward-thinking on others," she said now to David Reid. There was something thrilling, as thrilling as deceiving her father, in arguing with Mr. Reid. She'd never spoken this way to a man before.

"It's because I see things differently than you do. I've listened to different lecturers, read different sorts of books. I've read Karl Marx; have you?"

"I don't know who that is."

"Well, when you do hear of Marx, some preacher or temperance lady will tell you he's a terrible infidel with dangerous ideas. But the truth is he's very right about some things, and there are a lot of people in the world who think so. The world is going to change a good deal in the next few years, Miss Hunt, and I intend to do more than just watch and write about it."

"That's what your sister says—that you think you can change the world."

"Why can't I? Why can't you? Would you be sitting up in the gallery of the Colonial Building with a crowd of lady suffragists if you didn't think it would change the world?"

"You saw me?"

Trudy J. Morgan-Cole

"I did, and admired you. In all possible senses."

"Much good it did us, sitting up there to watch them vote down our bill."

They passed the ruins of Gower Street Church and the Anglican Cathedral: both were busy sites now with men picking through the rubble for anything that could be salvaged and sold to finance the rebuilding efforts. Business owners worked more quickly than churches: while the congregations worshipped in temporary structures as the great churches started to slowly rebuild, most shopkeepers had already cleared the rubble of last summer's fire and some had erected new structures back in the fall. Now, with the good spring weather, new shops and houses were sprouting up everywhere. On Queen's Road, as they neared Lily's house, men were working on the new Congregational church that would replace the old Stone Chapel.

"Come, let's take a shortcut," said Mr. Reid. He took her by the hand and led her down behind the ruins of the old chapel. The lane was very dim and smelt strongly of horse manure.

"I don't think this is a shortcut. My house is just down the road there."

"I'm about to do something inappropriate, Miss Hunt." He turned to face her, put his arms around her, ran his large hands up and down her back as he drew her to him. Lily knew all the things she ought to say and do, knew it was a girl's duty to safeguard her virtue. But all she wanted was for him to go on touching her.

"Perhaps you should call me Lily," she said.

He laughed, a low laugh deep in his throat. "Well, that would be very improper indeed." He turned her face up toward his, leaned down, and kissed her.

She was unprepared in every way for his kiss, had never imagined how it might feel to have his mouth open a little and the warmth of his breath inside her own mouth. Her head was tilted

A Sudden Sun

so far back that her hat slipped off and she made no move to catch it.

David—impossible to think of him as Mr. Reid now—buried his hands in her hair, pulled loose a hairpin so that a long, thick rope of her hair fell down across her face and shoulder as she pushed closer to him. Every place he touched felt like it was on fire.

When he pulled out another hairpin she finally drew back, breathing hard. "I'll look dreadful!" she said, with a weak laugh. Everything in her felt broken, shattered, but what was shattered was a vessel that had held something delicious and warm, something that had now spilled out to flood her whole body.

"Here, I've rescued this anyway," David said, holding up her hat.

"That's no good on its own, I need my pins." He handed her one; it had landed on her blouse. She tried to put her hair back in place and shove the pin in but her hands were shaking. He took it from her, awkwardly skewered the pin through her hair.

She looked straight into his green eyes, as she might stare into the heart of the sun, to see how long she could without having to look away. She found she could hold his gaze, though it sobered her at once.

"Don't apologize," she said.

"I'd no intention of it."

CHAPTER TEN

OR THE NEXT week Lily went around in a cloud of mingled delight and confusion. She was upset about the defeat of the bill, and especially about the divisions it created among the WCTU ladies, most of whom seemed to feel it was time to abandon the franchise fight. Many of them felt, and said, that it had been a mistake ever to push the issue of the women's vote. At the Tuesday evening meeting a quarrel broke out between Mrs. Ohman and Mrs. Withycombe, and everyone left in a bad mood.

But outside the door was David Reid waiting to walk Lily home, though she had been promised a ride in Mrs. Ohman's carriage. "Tell her you're walking home," David urged.

"I can't –she'll see you there—you know she won't think it's proper that I'm walking with you."

"Better than walking alone, isn't it? It's coming on duckish. No time for a young lady to be on the streets alone."

"And no time for a young lady to be on the streets with a man who is not known to her family," said Mrs. Ohman, appearing beside Lily's elbow. "Come along, Lily." Her tone was sharp and clipped; she was still irritated with Mrs. Withycombe.

Despite the way she kept reliving David's kiss over and over in her memory, Lily could not imagine defying Mrs. Ohman yet again to go off with him. There was no convenient sister or niece or nephews around, nor could she pretend any longer that his intentions were entirely honourable.

"I'm sorry, I must go," she told David, and climbed into the carriage beside Mrs. Ohman. The older lady fumed the whole way home about the scolding she'd gotten from the Sons of Temperance, who had told her that the WCTU was tarnishing the good name of the temperance cause by agitating for women's votes. When the carriage pulled up in front of Lily's house, Mrs. Ohman told her driver to wait while she went in and called on Lily's parents. "Tell them I'd like to see them both, if your mother feels well enough. Just us older folks," Mrs. Ohman added with a nod that was hard to mistake.

Lily waited an agonizing hour in her room, wondering if she should concoct further lies or confess everything. Finally Sally tapped on the door. "The Mister would like to see you down in the study, Miss," she said.

Papa sat in his big wingback chair, papers and books all over his desk. Printing was a practical trade with him but also a passion. He loved books and reading, and collected first editions of books when his budget allowed. It made Lily sad to see the bare shelves in his rebuilt study; so many of his prized volumes had been destroyed in the fire, and he was just beginning to rebuild the collection. Papa's old study with its book-lined walls had been a favourite place when she was allowed in there as a child, but today Lily felt as nervous as she had when she was ten years old, the day she had accidentally torn a page in Papa's big Shakespeare book. She took a seat in a straight-backed wooden chair across from her father.

"Mrs. Ohman has told me that you have—not a suitor in the

Trudy J. Morgan-Cole

proper sense, but an impertinent young man who has made your acquaintance. Do you know who I mean?"

"I suppose she is talking about Mr. Reid, Father."

"Yes, that's the fellow. I've met him of course, in the way of business. He knows quite well I would never consider him worthy to call upon my daughter. He's a nobody, no family, a young upstart with radical ideas. He's neither a regular churchgoer nor a temperance man." He paused, drumming his fingers on the arm of his chair. "Of course, you may not have known all these things about him."

"Mrs. Ohman told me he was…not someone you could approve of." Lily kept her hands knotted in her lap. She looked down at them, studying the little knobs of her own knuckles and the tiny hollows between, glancing up at her father's eyes only once for each sentence she spoke. Against the dark green fabric of her skirt her hands looked very tiny and white. She remembered pressing them against Papa's big hand, not so very long ago—she might have been, what, eleven or twelve?—to see how big and strong he was compared to her. Then she remembered David's hand tangling in her hair, pulling her close to him.

"Lily?" Father said, and she knew she had missed the last question he asked her.

"I beg your pardon, Father? I didn't hear you."

"I asked if you have any feelings for this young man, or if he has just been bothering you with his presence. Either way, I will warn him to stay away from you, but if you have any fancies about him, it makes my task more painful."

"He hasn't bothered me. I only ever spoke to him because he was interested in the WCTU work; he wrote a piece for the paper about it, and I talked to him a little. I've been polite to him, but nothing more than that."

"Yes, but has *he* been polite to you? Are you sure he hasn't said or done anything improper?"

"No, not at all," she said, and then she did look him in the eye. She had never told Papa a direct lie before, though ever since becoming involved with the suffrage cause, not to mention since meeting David Reid, she had certainly misled him. It seemed important to look him right in the eye as she lied.

"You've always been a good girl, Lily. You know I've worried about your friendship with Mrs. Ohman. She's a good woman, but I don't approve of all her ideas and I was sorry to hear she had brought that petition before the House. Women have no place in politics. But Mrs. Ohman, regardless of her errors, is a good Christian woman and she was entirely right in coming to speak to me about this."

Lily was back to looking at her hands, at the little half-moons on the base of each nail. When she was little, she had used to bite her nails but Mama had painted them with iodine and broken her of the habit. "Mrs. Ohman has been very kind to me," she said.

"You know young Reverend Collins admires you. I hope you will come to like him too, as you get to know him better."

"He seems...very...*nice*." That was not as barefaced a lie as the other one but it was, at best, stretching the truth. And it seemed to content Papa, at least for now; he dismissed Lily and told her to go to bed.

Two days later, Abby Hayward came to call. "You have an admirer," she told Lily, her mouth drawn down as if trying to mask amusement with disapproval.

"I'm sure I don't know what you mean."

"Well if there's a young man who's brazen enough to walk up to a girl he doesn't know on the street and slip her a note with no more introduction than, 'I hear you're friends with Lily Hunt,' then I'd call him an admirer."

"What sort of young man?"

Trudy J. Morgan-Cole

"Threadbare. Barely respectable. I don't know him at all, and you know if I don't know him, then he's nobody. Red hair. Looks Irish. Might be a papist, for all I know. He's certainly not a Methodist, nor from any family worth talking about. Saucy manner. Why am I telling you this? It's perfectly clear you know who I mean!"

"You saw him once before, in the park, the day after the fire."

Abby shrugged and picked up her needlepoint. She had been working at this same sampler of roses and a pious motto ever since before she went to New York last winter: she was not much of a needlewoman. "I can't remember anything about the fire—that's all such a blur. Can you believe we camped all night in Bannerman Park? Anyway, it's clear you're not concerned about this fellow, so it's just as well I threw away his note."

"You what?"

"Ha, caught you out there!" Abby's smile broadened into a grin that made her look like a freckled schoolgirl again.

"I won't tell you a thing 'til you hand over that note."

"No, I won't hand over the note until you tell me a thing or two. And you know I'll win at this game, because you want the note more than I want the information." Abby pulled a small white envelope from a pocket of her blouse and held it up before her face. She pulled away, giggling, when Lily made a grab for it.

"There's nothing to tell. He's only someone I met."

"Indeed. A man without a name?"

Under pressure, and the desire to obtain the note, Lily finally admitted to David Reid's name and to their handful of previous meetings. She did not tell Abby about the kiss, nor about the conversation with her father.

To Abby's disappointment, Lily waited 'til she was alone to open the note. She took it up to her room and closed the door firmly. Papa was not even home but she somehow imagined that downtown, in the printshop, he could sense the presence of David's letter, tucked in its envelope, as if it radiated heat and light.

Her fingers trembled as she sliced open the note with her silver letter opener. The letter opener slipped and scratched the palm of her hand, and she dropped it on the bed beside her as she took the slip of paper from the envelope.

> *Lily of the Valley—I have been rude. I have taken*
> *liberties. Would like to take more if possible. Could*
> *you meet me in Bannerman Park at about four o'clock*
> *on Saturday? Some things in this world matter more*
> *than good manners.*
>
> > *– D (as in Daring).*

She read it again, twice, and noticed that her hand shook more rather than less with each reading. Was she really thinking of going, meeting with him secretly?

No, this was entirely wrong. He was handsome—moderately— and clever, and charming. And something else, something she could not put into words but that made her think of him all the time. But Papa had made it clear David Reid would never be allowed to call on her.

She tucked the letter inside her pillowcase, thinking she must find a safer place for it before Sally changed the beds again. Downstairs, a bell rang for dinner.

When the meal was over Papa pulled Lily aside. "You've thought about what we spoke of on Tuesday night?" he said. "After Mrs. Ohman's visit?"

"Of course, Papa. You know best."

"I'm glad to hear it. Do I have your promise that you will not see or speak to this young man again?"

He had not asked her to promise that before. That he asked

Trudy J. Morgan-Cole

now, in plain words, while the letter burned a hole through her pillowcase, must be a sign from God.

"I promise, Papa."

"My good girl," he said.

Up in her room, Lily lit a candle. She took David's note out and read it once more, then laid it in her washbasin. She touched the candle to the corner of the paper, saw the flames eagerly lick at the lines of his handwriting, swallowing up David Reid and any possibility of meeting him in Bannerman Park at four o'clock on Saturday.

When it was all gone she tipped the ashes into the grate and wiped out the wash basin. No one would suspect a thing.

$\mathscr{F}$OR THREE MONTHS she was obedient. For three months she remained the girl her mother had raised, the girl her father hoped would marry the Reverend Obadiah Collins. She went to church, went to meetings of the WCTU, the Women's Missionary Society, and the Ladies' Aid. She visited girlfriends for tea, she read books, she went for walks, and she did not see David Reid at all. Or rather, she did not speak to him. She saw him on Water Street one day as she and Abigail passed Clouston's storefront, a temporary booth the tinsmiths had set up to sell pots and pans while their shop was being rebuilt. As Lily paused to admire a china teapot, Abby poked her ribs with her parasol. "It's that man! Isn't that he?"

Lily shot a look at Abby that she hoped would freeze the blood to ice in her veins. She wasn't really good at giving that kind of look but she hoped that with practice she would get better, having seen Mrs. Ohman do it at meetings. She looked at the red-headed man walking towards them only long enough to know that it *was* David Reid, but she did not meet his eyes. She lifted her skirts and veered around a stack of barrels on the sidewalk to avoid him, though that

115

meant she had to step down into the street and barely missed a pile of horse dung.

"He tried to speak to you!" Abby protested, looking back over her shoulder. "You were very cold to him!"

"Why shouldn't I be cold? Father made me promise never to see him again."

Back in May, after she had failed to show up in Bannerman Park at the appointed time, Mr. Reid had sent two further notes. She burned them both. Sometimes she woke between midnight and dawn from a dream in which she was in an alley with David Reid again, his lips against hers, his fingers pulling the pins from her hair. She woke from those dreams breathing fast and found it hard to get back to sleep.

She said nothing of this, of course, to Abigail, who would have giggled and gasped with delight at such fantasies. That door was closed, Lily reminded herself. She prayed every night that God would cleanse her of evil desires.

In all that time, she had not seen him. But that was not strange. They did not move in the same circles. The only place she was likely to see him was walking along Water Street. Now it had happened and it had not been so painful after all. There had been just a moment when their eyes met and the urge to turn her head and look back had been like the force that must have pulled the gaze of Lot's wife toward Sodom. But Lily was made of tougher stuff: no pillar of salt for her.

The next note came the following day, slipped brazenly into her mailbox rather than hand-delivered by a messenger as the others had been. It was put in the box after the morning mail had been delivered but before Papa came home for his dinner, so its secrecy depended upon Lily checking the mail before Papa returned. Fortunately she did, and carried the small envelope up to her room, unseen by anyone. Her fingers trembled as she tore it open.

Tiger Lily—

Your heart is stone, and mine is like a poor stray tom-cat who has lost a dozen fights and is missing an ear and part of a tail but still goes out prowling. Which is to say, I thought I had given up hope 'til I saw you yesterday. And now I find I cannot put you out of my mind again. A note left at my place of work will always find me, if you choose to take pity, stone maiden.

— D (Discouraged, but not Defeated)

She read it over and over, and could not help smiling at the picture of the battered alley cat, still roving the streets, spoiling for another fight. In an endless battle he could not win, for the maiden with the heart of stone—Mr. Reid certainly did not mind mixing his metaphors—would never relent.

Still. She did not burn this note. She put it under her pillow and slept with it there that night. Woke in the morning from a dreamless sleep cursing herself for a sentimental fool. She was as bad as a girl in a novel, and not a sensible girl like Alida either. A silly girl like Alida's sister, Lottie, doomed to destruction for her selfishness. Sleeping with a note under her pillow! Lily threw it on the morning fire.

"A friend of yours is coming to town soon," Papa said that night at dinner. "He wrote and asked if he might call on you."

"You mean Reverend Collins."

"I hoped the news might please you."

"It does. It does—please me, Papa." Lily tried hard to put warmth and energy into her voice. "I know you think very highly of Reverend Collins."

"I hope that, in time, you'll come to think well of him too."

She tried to think, over the next few days, good thoughts about Reverend Collins. She had met him only that once, at Reverend

Trudy J. Morgan-Cole

Pratt's house. Her father had said that he was a very progressive young clergyman—though not so progressive, apparently, as to approve of votes for women. She struggled to recall his face. His thinning hair was—black? Dark brown? Some nondescript colour. Not red, certainly. And whatever colour his eyes were, they were not green.

Reverend Collins came a week later: came to sit in the parlour and make polite conversation with her father while Lily sat silent beside her mother. He was in town for the Methodist Conference and was full of talk about the wonderful sessions he had attended and the great speakers he had heard. He showed his excitement by a slight rise in the pitch of his voice, and by laying his teacup down in the saucer with a little clang. Every time he did it Mother started, either because the noise troubled her nerves or because she was worried about damage to the china.

Mr. Collins had invited Lily to attend a lecture in the evening, by a returned missionary who was also attending the conference, telling about his experiences in the Congo. It was held at the Tabernacle on Parade Street, the temporary home of George Street Church, and it was well-attended. Their seats were not as good as Lily would have liked. She was stuck behind a woman with a very large hat that blocked Lily's view of the speaker and his magic-lantern slides. The speaker's voice was dry and scratchy. He seemed to have had amazing experiences in the Congo but lacked the ability to describe them in a way that would keep his hearers awake.

What an unfortunate thing, Lily thought. It would be so much more convenient if the world was arranged so that interesting things only happened to people who were good public speakers or writers. Good experience was, after all, wasted on anyone who could not convey the sense of it. She thought of sharing the thought with Mr. Collins, but decided he would not appreciate the humour.

In the carriage afterwards he said, "You are very fortunate, living here in St. John's, to be able to hear good speakers and good music, to be in contact with the wider world. During the winter months in Greenspond, I think with longing of lectures such as the one we just heard, or some of the sermons that were given during the conference."

"Well, conference week is unusual. There isn't normally such a collection of great Methodist preachers in St. John's. But of course you are right, we have more diversions here than in the outports."

"There, a man must depend on reading to broaden his mind," sighed Mr. Collins. "You attended some of the ladies' sessions yourself at the conference, no doubt, Miss Hunt?"

"I did."

"And the Temperance Rally on Sunday night?"

"Yes, of course."

"Now that was inspiring! No doubt you were moved by it, as well."

Lily had gone with her father to the big Temperance Rally. The speeches had all been stirring, but not one of the speakers—all men, of course—had made any mention of the work of the WCTU. It was discouraging, after the heady excitement of the rally she had attended earlier in the spring when not only women's work but women's votes had been spoken of with such approval.

She tried to explain her disappointment to Mr. Collins. "Having been so involved with the women's temperance work, I felt it as a rebuke, to be quite honest." She had not intended to raise any topic that might be controversial, or even interesting, but he was the one who had brought up the rally and she was a little curious as to how he would respond if she shared even a sliver of her true opinions.

"Ah…yes, I suppose I can imagine how you might feel that way," Mr. Collins said. He seemed a bit taken aback that she had expressed anything other than admiration for the wonderful speakers at the rally. "But you know, there are other issues going on

Trudy J. Morgan-Cole

behind the scenes. I'm afraid many of the leaders of the movement are rather unhappy with the direction that the WCTU has been taking. Some of the ladies involved, and certainly Mrs. Ohman's paper, have been quite strident in stating that they want the women's vote. They talk not just about letting women vote on Prohibition, but of extending the franchise to women generally."

"Is that it?" Lily asked. "Is the WCTU being punished because the temperance men fear it's been taken over by suffragists?"

"Well, my dear, things are always more complicated than they seem. It's politics, you know, and perception. How things look from the outside. It's demeaning when women sully themselves with such things. You, my dear Miss Hunt, are a fine example of what I mean—a good and virtuous young girl, working in the temperance cause because of a sincere desire to end human suffering. But what if your name, your reputation, were to be tarnished by association with these striving and ambitious women?"

"I suppose that would be dreadful."

"Exactly," said Mr. Collins, who appeared deaf to sarcasm. "For women to concentrate on the ballot-box is a mistake. Indeed, many temperance men think we have little chance of seeing Prohibition passed in the next year or two, that we need to concentrate more on educating the public, and less on the legislature. No real change is likely to happen while Mr. Whiteway is our premier." He glanced over at her. "But I am boring you, of course. Nothing duller than people talking of things that are outside one's own experience."

The worst part was that he could say such a thing, so smug and condescending, without recognizing that he was giving her the equivalent of a slap across the face. But Lily said nothing. There was no value in arguing with Reverend Collins. She already knew she would strike no answering spark.

"I fancy you found Reverend Howlett a little dull as well, tonight," he went on, "and I promise the next time I come to town

I will try to find something more diverting to take you to. Nothing frivolous, of course, but perhaps a nice sacred concert?"

The thought that her obligation to him—to Papa, really—was not discharged, that she would have to go along with him to another event and sit stiffly by his side through a choral cantata or organ recital, felt as dispiriting as a downpour on a summer morning. "I'm sure that would be very nice," Lily said. It was as if she were an actress, reading someone else's lines. She could not help remembering that Abby had gone, this evening, to the dancing assembly at the Parade Rink with Frank Ayre. Much too frivolous an entertainment for a young clergyman, but Lily couldn't help thinking a little touch of frivolity might not hurt her. He might at least have offered to take her to watch the boat races down at Quidi Vidi.

The next day she went to the corner shop, bought a copy of the *Evening Herald* and read a scathing article about the way in which Premier Whiteway's government was bungling everything it touched. There was no by-line, but she needed none: she heard David Reid's sardonic voice in every line. She imagined him sitting in the gallery at the House of Assembly, his pen flying frantically across paper, copper head bent forward as he caught the currents of the debate. This was what he had been doing last night, no doubt, while she sat next to Reverend Collins watching lantern slides about the Congo. Being patronized by a man who thought she was bored by politics because she could not understand them.

The Herald. A letter sent to my place of work will always find me. She drew notepaper towards her, filled her pen.

> *Mr. Reid—You have been impertinent. Yet I am in-*
> *clined to forgiveness. You mentioned a place of meet-*
> *ing once. If you recall the place and can be there on*
> *Thursday at three in the afternoon, you may find me*
> *walking in the vicinity. Fortune favours the bold.*
> *– L (Lady Luck)*

Trudy J. Morgan-Cole

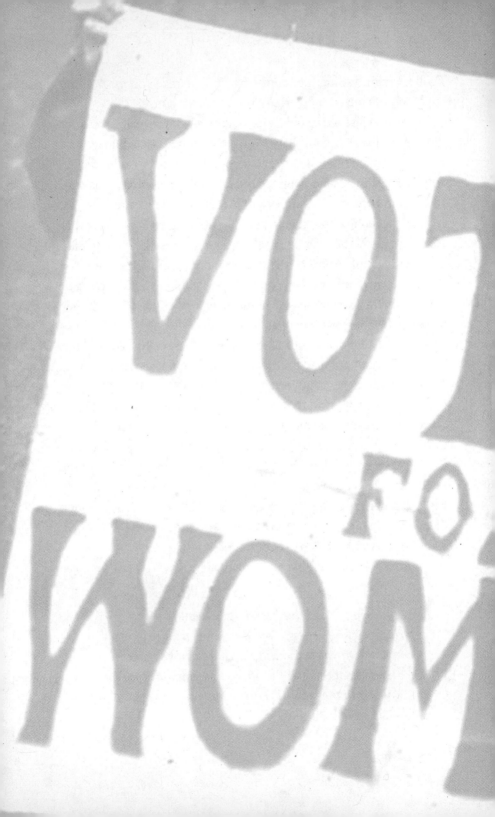

Part Three

1919–1920

CHAPTER TWELVE

"**D**ID YOUR MOTHER ever tell you about the time we sneaked out of the house to sit in the gallery of the Colonial Building, when they were debating votes for women?"

Grace shook her head. Language felt inadequate to convey the extent to which her mother had not told her about any adventure that involved "sneaking." Young Lily Hunt had been, by her own account, flawless in her obedience to her parents. "When—when was this?" she managed to ask.

Abigail Parker leaned back in her chair and took a sip of tea. "Well, we must have been—what, nineteen, twenty? Before either of us was married. You won't find it in the history books. None of the men thought it was important. In fact it was all a big joke to some of them. Oh, it was the year after the fire, I remember because Mama got new wallpaper with pink roses for my room. The House of Assembly wasn't my sort of affair at all, you know. I was an empty-headed little thing back then, couldn't have cared less about the vote or anything else. I mean, I did agree that votes for women were the thing, but I wasn't one for meetings or petitions like

Lily was. I arranged the whole escapade, though, because she was such a good girl, she wouldn't have known how to sneak out of the house or deceive her parents." So that much of Lily's self-portrait was true at least, Grace thought. "And your grandfather," Mrs. Parker went on, "well, he's mellowed a good deal in old age. That's Daisy's influence, I imagine. Back then, if we'd been caught, your mother would have been in plenty of trouble. But of course we were never caught. I was too good for that." She smiled as she passed a plate of sweet biscuits, English ones from a tin, to Grace, who laid one on the edge of her saucer.

Grace had reconciled herself to the idea that the version of her mother that lived in Abigail Parker's memory bore no resemblance at all to the mother Grace knew. Meetings and petitions, perhaps— Lily was a tireless organizer, not to say bossy—but suffragist rallies? Sneaking out of the house?

"She's changed, I can tell," Mrs. Parker said. "I know it from the tone of her letters—the few times she has written me. I wish I could see her, but I can't leave town. If it weren't for poor Father...."

"I'm sure Mother wishes she could come to town and see you," Grace said, though she was almost certain that was a lie.

"Ah, we could talk about old times, I suppose. How I laughed over that whole business. You know, I thought the suffragists were a bit ridiculous, silly old bluestockings who were more concerned about the vote than about fashion or catching a man. Goes to show how much I knew, doesn't it? I wanted the vote but I didn't want to be one of those women out marching for it! Expected others to do all the work. And as for catching a man, well, as your mother learned, it was quite possible to march for votes and still catch a man's eye. Though that turned out... Well, anyway, I've said too much."

She unfolded her fan, a pretty concoction of painted silk, and fluttered it in front of her face. Grace could see that Mrs. Parker took a good deal of pleasure in saying too much and then pulling back. Unlike Daisy, who had seemed genuinely shocked by her own indiscretion and anxious to cover it up, Mrs. Parker seemed to want Grace to coax more of the story out of her.

Grace thought of the postcard signed "D," of the scrawled intimacy of those hastily written words. *Was my mother ever in love with a man whose name began with D?* She thought of asking. But no, of course she would not do that.

That evening back in March when she and her mother sat in the kitchen at home and Lily had tried to warn her about heartbreak, to tell her that she should not marry Jack. Had she been speaking out of painful experience? *If so, it would have been a fine time to tell me what happened to you, Mother,* Grace thought. But she had not. What Lily had not chosen to share, Grace would not try to coax out of her old friend, even if that old friend looked most willing to be coaxed.

Instead, she turned the talk to other channels, and Mrs. Parker seemed eager to hear about Grace's work. "Do you still want to train as a nurse?" she asked. "I mean, if your parents were to give their blessing?"

Grace paused, thinking of the brisk, efficient Nurse Fitzpatrick at the Empire Hospital. Papist though Miss Fitzpatrick was, you couldn't deny she was doing God's work. "I wanted to very much, during the war," she said. "But I wonder if that wasn't as much about wanting to do something for the war effort as the nursing itself? I only know I want to do *something.* I taught for two years in Catalina," she added, "and Mother and Father approved of that. They wanted me to stay on there. I think it seems a bit more respectable to them than nursing."

"No one more respectable than your father," agreed Mrs. Parker with a smile that, again, invited Grace to ask about the story behind it. She gazed out the window as if lost in thought, then said,

127

Trudy J. Morgan-Cole

"I wish I'd been there when your mother got married. We'd always planned to be each other's bridesmaids, but she got married in St. John's and I in New York, and we didn't travel about in those days the way folks do now." Then, just as Grace thought they were about to head back down the road of reminiscence, Abigail Parker said, "There's a school of philanthropy quite near me in Manhattan, you know, where they train social workers. A dear friend of mine teaches there. Have you ever given any thought to social work?"

"I hardly know what it is," Grace said. "It's rather a new field, isn't it?"

"Very much so, but there's such a need—you know, working among the poor, going into the homes of the destitute, caring for orphans and for poor young girls who—well, unwed mothers and fallen women, you know. You ought to look into it."

"Are there entrance requirements? I only have my second-class certificate."

"Oh, I believe the official requirement is for people who already have a B.A., but they say 'equivalent experience,' and you know, the volunteer work you've been doing here—well, I know people on the board, I could make a few calls on your behalf. And if you did come—well, I would be so happy to have you stay with me, and to help you in any way I could."

Social work. College. Everyone was thinking of the future, with the war over and the returned servicemen trying to restart lives that had been interrupted. Why worry about anything that might have happened twenty-five years ago when everything seemed to be rushing Grace towards the future, towards decisions she hardly felt equipped to make?

The day after her visit with Abigail Parker, she sat in Ivan Barry's hospital room helping him eat his dinner. He told her that the girl he used to be engaged to had gotten married to his best friend. It was still hard to pick out his speech but Grace had become practiced at it. She leaned in close to hear him say that the girl was Myrtle—"Merr - uhh"—and that they had been engaged before he left Humbermouth in 1915.

"Best…for her," he said, when Grace said she was sorry to hear it. "But…one more…reen…harr to go…home."

Yes. One more reason it was hard to go home.

The government was putting money and effort into finding work for returned veterans, even retraining the men who had returned without legs or arms and would never be able to do manual labour again. The population of the hospital had thinned in the months Grace had been volunteering. Most of the men had recovered from the worst of their injuries, got used to using their prosthetic arms or legs, and gone home. Only a few remained, a few like Ivan Barry, for whom the world now seemed to hold no place.

Where could a man with only half a face go? He would never be able to work again, never go out in a fishing boat nor do the work he had hoped to do, that of serving as a minister. Yet when Grace tried, gently, to probe into the subject of his future and how he felt about it, Mr. Barry's one good eye still seemed to shine. "I sill…blee…Goh hah a play for me." *God has a place for me.*

Grace wished she had that much faith. She wanted passionately to serve God, and surely it should be easier for God to find a place for Grace Collins, well-educated daughter of a minister, than for poor shattered Mr. Barry. It seemed clear enough, on one level, that that place ought to be as a wife and mother, possibly even as the wife of Jack Perry. Faced with Mr. Barry, it seemed churlish to long for anything more than a normal life, marriage, and a home and family, the simple things that had been denied him.

When she left the hospital, Jack was waiting outside the door, as he often was. Instead of turning up towards her grandfather's house, they caught the streetcar at the Holloway Street stop and got off near Wood's Candy Store and Dining Room. Eating out at a

Trudy J. Morgan-Cole

restaurant was a rare treat they had indulged in three or four times over the spring, just for the pleasure of dining alone. Grandfather had said no the first time Jack had asked permission to take Grace out to eat: it wasn't proper, he said, without a chaperone. Daisy had waved that protest aside. "It's a different world now, Mr. Hunt. Different from when I was a girl, or even when your Lily was growing up. The war's changed everything. It's nothing for a respectable young lady to go to a restaurant with her beau, and it's not as if Jack is a stranger to us."

By now it was accepted that this was something they would do from time to time. Jack's favourite place was the Crosbie Hotel but Grace preferred Wood's. She liked walking upstairs past the bustle of the candy store and bakery to the quiet room above where deferential waitresses came and went, where the clink of glasses and silverware and the low tones of other diners created a sense that their table for two was a private world. At Grandfather's and Daisy's dinner table, Grace certainly would not have told Jack about Mrs. Parker and her indiscreet comments about Lily's past.

"I'm sure she's just the sort of person who likes to make everything out to be more scandalous than it is," Jack said, cutting into thin slices of pork roast. "She can't really mean anything improper about your mother, can she?"

"Apart from her being a suffragette? I can hardly believe that, but I did find all those old broadsheets and press clippings in her old room."

"But that's not shocking. If anything, it's admirable."

"Yes, but it's out of character." Grace looked down at her plate, watching the flaky crust of her mutton pie—Wood's specialty, and her favourite—crumble as she attacked it with her fork. "It makes me wonder what else I don't know about my mother. Was she in love with someone—someone before my father, I mean? If she ever *was* in love with my father."

"You think she wasn't?"

"I can't ever remember them being...affectionate. But then, I don't suppose parents are, in front of their children, are they?"

Jack smiled. "I don't know. My father, now, he's the most proper man you'll ever meet—you know what he's like in public—but at the end of a busy day at work he'd come home and put his feet up, and my mother would sit on the humpty and unlace his shoes and rub his feet, and he'd say, 'Oh my Bess, you're a wonderful girl,' and she'd say, 'I know old man, that's why you married me.'" His face warmed at the memory.

"Really? They would do that?"

"Oh, all the time. Now they weren't what you'd call romantic, I don't recall them hugging and kissing in front of us—I'm sure Mother would have died of shame—but he'd come into the kitchen in the morning when she was cooking breakfast and tell her she was a grand girl for looking after us all, things like that. And if she was dressed up for church or going out he'd always tell her she was lovely. Didn't your parents do things like that?"

"No, never." By comparison with those fleeting sketches of life in the Perry household, Grace felt her own childhood homes, those outport parsonages, as bleak places, empty of marital affection. She tried to remember an unguarded moment between her parents, a kiss or an embrace or a word of affection, but none came to mind. Even the mildly flirtatious teasing that Aunt Daisy directed at her much older husband, whom she always called "Mr. Hunt," was a bit shocking to Grace; she realized now it was because she was unused to seeing a married couple show affection for each other.

"You're lost in thought," Jack said.

"I'm sorry—no, I'm thinking of my parents. Maybe my mother really was in love with someone else. I suppose I'll never know. Anyway, Mrs. Parker said some more interesting things—not about the past, but about the future."

Trudy J. Morgan-Cole

"She wants you to go to New York, doesn't she? What would you do there?"

"There's a college—a school of philanthropy. I don't know very much about it, but from the little I know I think it's what I would like doing. I know that I want to be of some use in the world." Grace wondered if Jack would say that he couldn't bear for her to go so far away.

Jack looked down at his plate, pushing boiled potato and cabbage around with his fork, then took a bite before looking up at her. "I'm going away in September—back to McGill to finish my degree."

"So you wouldn't be here anyway."

"Grace, I—you know I want to marry you, don't you?"

Now it was her turn to look down at her plate. It was hard to know how to respond to such a question; it was far more complicated than "Will you marry me?" To say "yes" would sound vain and presumptuous; to say "no" might be an offense.

She settled on the answer that was closest to the truth. "I…I had hoped you felt that way."

"I do—so much. But I want you to be free to go to New York, to learn and to work and find out what you want to do. It doesn't seem fair that I should be the only one of us to do that."

"You're an unusual man, Jack Perry."

"Am I, I wonder?" He looked out the window, at the dark street punctuated by the yellow glow of streetlamps. "I don't think I always was. I think I was pretty ordinary, before I went overseas. Something of what I saw there, what we did there, gave my ideas of ordinary life a kick in the teeth. I don't know yet if that's good or bad. But I can't be the only one, so there must be a change coming, Grace."

"So—you'll go to Montreal, and I'll go to New York?"

"I have two years more of medical school, and then an internship. At best it would be a long engagement."

"I'm not opposed to long engagements," she said, and he laughed.

"To tell the truth I hadn't planned on this tonight—I have no ring—and I haven't spoken to your parents."

"Let's not be in any hurry to do that," Grace said. "It doesn't need to be official yet. I don't have to wear your ring to know that we...that we have..."

"An understanding?" Jack raised his glass.

"An understanding," she agreed.

Trudy J. Morgan-Cole

CHAPTER THIRTEEN

"YOU ARE NOT going to New York. It's simply impossible."

Lily stood at the parlour window, her back to Grace. She could not even bear to look at the girl as she talked about going so far away, starting a new life tucked under Abigail Hayward's wing. Abigail was the sort of mother Grace wanted, urging her forward. Lily wondered would Abigail be so eager to encourage adventure if she had a daughter of her own.

"Last time I came home you thought Jack was going to ask to marry me, and you told me I'd regret rushing into a hasty marriage. Now I come home to say I'm not getting married, I want to go back to school, and you're forbidding that. Mother, if you don't want me to marry, you don't want me to go to college, and you don't want me to work, what do you want me to do? What kind of life can you possibly imagine for me?"

A life here, with me, Lily thought, but that was impossible. When Grace was born, Lily already knew about sons, about loving and losing them. She knew that no boy, whether he lived a few hours or twenty years or seventy years, would stay by his mother's side. On the morning the midwife laid Grace in her arms, Lily had thought, *This is my daughter, my reward. This is the child who will love me, the child I can hold.*

But Grace had only seemed to be that girl for those few quiet minutes while she nursed at Lily's breast. Then she had wriggled, and squirmed, and opened her mouth in an ungodly howl, and ever since that moment she had been fighting to get away. *Why can't you be content here?* Lily wanted to say. Not that Lily herself had ever been content in Catalina or in Elliston or any of these other barren outports the church had stranded her in. But if she had a daughter by her side, if she and Grace could be together all the time, she would feel that all those hard and lonely years had been worth it. She would finally have her reward.

Now Grace wanted to go off to New York, of all places. *Can any good thing come out of New York?* Lily thought. No city on earth—not London or Paris or even Berlin—could have laid a colder chill on Lily's heart. She would no more give her girl up to that city of wickedness than she would sell her into slavery.

Aloud she said, "New York is a hard place. It makes people harder."

God knew the last thing Grace needed was to be made harder. The girl had had a shell on her since she could walk and talk, like a beautiful piece of furniture lacquered over and over 'til you couldn't put a chip or a spall into it. Grace at three, struggling out of her mother's arms to go play. Grace at six, her knee skinned and bloody: Lily had dabbed at it with Mercurochrome and told her to be more careful, but Grace had bit down on her lip to keep from crying out at the sting and said, "It doesn't hurt." Grace at seventeen, running off to St. John's as soon as she could after Charley's death, talking about joining the VAD and going overseas, as if she thought Lily could bear another loss.

"Is that what you think? That going to New York will turn me

Trudy J. Morgan-Cole

into some kind of hard, modern woman? Do you think I'll come back with a Castle bob and short skirts, smoking a cigarette? I want to go to a school of philanthropy, for goodness sakes!"

"Watch your tongue!" Lily said. "A girl who'll talk back to her own mother like that, who knows what you'd be like after a year in New York. What is social work, anyway, when it's at home? Do you even know, or is Abby Hayward filling your head with fool ideas you don't know a thing about?"

Grace started pacing the room—at least, she walked to the door, then hesitated and walked halfway back, and then turned again, so the effect was much the same as pacing, like a cat in a cage. "Nothing I do will ever please you, will it? I can't be a nurse, I can't go to college, I can't get married. You had dreams of your own once. Can't you remember? Or is that the reason? You won't let me have any work or life of my own, just because you never did!"

Abby Hayward. Foolish old Abby with her unguarded tongue, dragging up old stories to tempt and amuse poor Grace, who was hungry for romance and excitement. Who knew what other things Abby might have told Grace? That was the worst of Abigail Hayward: the past would never be dead while she was alive.

"Don't talk about things you know nothing about."

"Then you don't deny it?"

"Deny what? That I did foolish things when I was a girl? Did you ever stop to think that's the reason I don't want you making foolish mistakes—because I know where it gets you?" Lily had a memory, vivid as a stab wound, of herself lying across the bed in her parents' house, crying so hard her throat ached.

If she could spare her daughter even one night of crying like that, it would be worth all Grace's resentment. Lily would lash Grace to the front porch if it would guarantee she would never have to cry like that. "All young girls want today is to go away from home, have careers, excitement, adventure. Do you know what happened to Eve when she wandered from Adam's side?"

"You are impossible! I'm going to talk to the Reverend!"

"Don't you go bothering your father now! He's working on his sermon—"

But Grace had already gotten up, walked out of the house without even saying goodbye. The sound of the door closing was so firm and so familiar—Lily thought she could probably remember, if she tried, the very first time Grace had run away after a quarrel, run out of the house and slammed the door. She was punished for the door-slamming, of course, but though her touch had gotten gentler with the years, her method of escape hadn't changed. It was just the same when she went off to Port Union and got herself a job, or when she went to St. John's to live with her grandfather against Lily's express wishes. Out the door, always. What fate might befall a girl who chose the outside world as her refuge?

Grace would go to her father. The Reverend had not been a supporter of emancipation for women back when Lily secretly marched with the suffragists. But his views had changed in his middle years. He thought now that it was appropriate for a young woman to get some education and work in a suitable profession until her marriage, or instead of marriage if God had ordained her for a spinster. Social work, working among the poor—yes, he would approve that. He would have been in favour of Grace training for a nurse if it had not been for the possibility of her going overseas.

There was only one way Lily might sway him. She never brought up the past—neither of them did. But if she were to allude to it, to tell him that Abigail had not only been privy to her own darkest secret but had aided and abetted her at the time, well, the Reverend might agree that Abby was no fit woman to be in charge of the morals of a young girl. It would be worth dredging up that painful subject, if the Reverend would agree that Grace should not be allowed to go to New York. Lily might still prevail.

Trudy J. Morgan-Cole

Grace

CHAPTER FOURTEEN

PEOPLE FLOWED DOWN Fifth Avenue like a living river. Grace thought that if she were to lift her feet she would still be borne, wedged between the shoulders of the people on either side, down the broad Manhattan street towards Macy's. She had been in New York for a week now and was amazed at how there were more people on any given street than in all of St. John's. Until she had come downtown to go shopping alone she had not really realized how vast and swift-moving the crowd was, how small a droplet she was in this mighty torrent of humanity.

Mrs. Parker had wanted to go shopping with Grace, driven in their car by Mr. Parker's driver. "He brings Mr. Parker to work every morning as it is; he can tuck us in alongside, drop us at Macy's and come back after we've shopped a bit and had our lunch. Don't look shocked, Gracie dear; that's how we do things here. Buying you a few new frocks is the least I can do, for your poor mother's sake."

Your poor mother. Mrs. Parker liked that phrase, which rang oddly in Grace's ear. It was usually used of the dead, and Lily was very much alive and still heartily disapproving of Grace being in

New York. "Your poor mother wrote me a letter—" Mrs. Parker had said the day she arrived. Then she shook her head. "She worries about you. I wrote her and promised I would take care of you as if you were my own, Gracie."

The week of what Mrs. Parker called "settling in" to her fifth-floor apartment on the Upper West Side was full of unfamiliar experiences, of which being called "Gracie" was only the most obvious. Mrs. Parker kept trying to buy things for her. The Reverend was paying Grace's college tuition but there was no extra money for living expenses; Grace had suggested she find work tutoring young girls so she could give Mrs. Parker something towards her room and board.

"I won't hear of it, I won't!" Mrs. Parker had insisted. "Not that there's anything disreputable about teaching—it's not as if you were working a shop. But I want you to be like a daughter to me, and no daughter of mine would work her way through school. You should be able to devote yourself entirely to your studies, not scurrying around to jobs at all hours. No, if you go looking for pupils I shall be completely heartbroken." Tears formed at the edges of her eyes and Grace, unused to this particular form of manipulation, was forced to concede.

It was hard to believe that Abigail Hayward had ever been Lily Hunt's best friend. Certainly their methods of dealing with an unwanted situation could not have been more different. Mother had harangued, harassed, and peppered Grace with arguments about why she should not go to New York. Grace appealed to her father, who at first had been wholly in favour.

"I know of this school. It has a good reputation. We had a little money set aside for poor Charley to finish college. I'm sure he would have approved of it going to your education instead."

Then Mother got her hooks into the Reverend. At least that was what Grace assumed, for a day or so later her father had expressed

Trudy J. Morgan-Cole

doubts about whether Mrs. Parker was a fit guardian for a young girl far from home. That made Grace wonder: if Mrs. Parker knew secrets about Mother's past, did Mother also know secrets about Mrs. Parker, things that would make Reverend Collins suddenly doubt her generous offer?

Grace confronted her father in his study at the church, far from her mother's field of influence. She had thought it all out carefully first, trying to decide what ammunition she had that might hold some weight with him, enough to outbalance her mother's refusal. As calmly as she could she told him that she wanted to go to New York more than she had ever wanted anything. "I'll go anyway," she said, "no matter what you say."

"Grace, I've never thought of you as a rebellious girl. I know your mother wasn't happy with you moving back into St. John's, but then at least you were still living with the family. You understand that she worries about you—it's not like you to be so defiant."

"No, it's not, but this matters to me, Father. I have my passport and enough money for steamer fare at Grandfather's house in town; I can go on my own, without your permission. I'll throw myself on Mrs. Parker's mercy, and you know she'll take me in and pay my tuition. Then I'll be even more beholden to her. Is that what you want?"

Her father had relented, over Lily's objections, and here Grace was. Catalina train station, where she had said goodbye to her parents and Jack a few weeks earlier, seemed as far away as the moon. Today she had taken the subway and then a streetcar: nothing less like the streetcars in St. John's could have been imagined. She stood shoulder to shoulder with people of every imaginable size, shape, and even colour, for there were Negroes on the streetcar too, and old men speaking a language she couldn't even guess at, and one impossibly fat woman whose parcels almost equalled her own bulk—how could she be carrying so many packages downtown just at the time the stores were opening? How much more would she have once she had actually done her shopping? But perhaps she was not going shopping. *Perhaps she was*—and here Grace's imagination failed her, for riding the subway and streetcar, and walking down Fifth Avenue, reminded her of how little she knew about people in New York.

If she walked on the street in St. John's she knew everyone. Not literally, of course; she knew only a few people by face and name, but the rest she knew by type. She could identify at once the office worker, the factory girl, the housemaid coming from her mistress's home, the schoolmaster off to teach his classes. People at home were as clear and simple as illustrations in a child's primer, while here in New York some half-mad artist seemed to be at work, illustrating the grimy streets with every variety of human, clothing and decorating them in ways that gave her no clue who they were and what they were about.

The positive side to that, Grace realized as she stood before a long mirror in Macy's, holding skirts up before her, was that she might be as opaque to New Yorkers as they were to her. Nobody knew or cared where she came from, who her father or mother was, what business brought her to the city.

She picked out sensible clothes: three wool skirts that would seem heavy now but nice and warm in winter. One black, one brown, one grey; they could be mixed and matched with the four cotton blouses she bought, two white, one pale blue and one a very soft rose. Everything was good quality and would stand up to plenty of washing and wearing. Grace was pleased with her purchases.

She was ready to leave that floor and go look for good walking shoes when she saw the red dress hanging on a mannequin. It was perhaps only her imagination that made Grace think the mannequin looked a little like herself: the same shade of dark brown hair, though the mannequin's hair was bobbed and Grace's braided and pinned in a neat coil. Something about the tilt of her chin, maybe, made Grace imagine herself in the dress. But where? It wasn't a dress she could wear to church, or to school, or walking on the street. She had no idea why she searched for it on the rack in her size, why she slipped it off the hanger, why she took it into the fitting room.

When she slipped it over her head and looked at herself in the mirror she caught her breath. The coiled braid of hair looked out of place now: she needed bobbed hair to match this dress, and silk stockings instead of heavy lisle ones. The dress made her silhouette boyish-straight, no nipped-in waist but a clean downwards line, only a beaded belt around the hips giving a token nod to the idea of a waist. The red satin was edged with black piping, and the skirt ended half-way between knee and ankle, showing more leg than Grace had ever displayed even in a bathing costume. She looked up to meet her own eyes in the mirror and saw that her cheeks were red.

She stepped outside the change room to catch a glimpse of herself in the three-way mirror. As she turned to look at the back of the dress over her shoulder she saw a man pause and shoot her a bold look and a smile. Quickly, she ducked back into the dressing room and peeled off the gown. It was silly—and so impractical. And even at a sale price, far outside her modest budget. She could buy another two good skirts and a hat for what that dress cost, and where would she ever wear it?

Back at the Parkers' apartment, Ida, the maid, answered the door and took Grace's packages. "Just put them up in my room, Ida, that'll be fine."

"Yes, Miss. Got yourself some lovely new things, have you? So much nicer here than the shops in St. John's, ain't it? More choice, like," said Ida. Ida came from Fortune and was some kind of poor cousin of Mrs. Parker's family. "I always hire girls from home," Mrs. Parker told Grace. "I like to help them out, and they make far better servants than anyone else in the city. We Newfoundland girls know how to work, don't we?"

Grace very much doubted that Mrs. Parker had ever "worked" on anything like the scale of Ida or her cohort Liza Jane: they scrubbed and dusted and polished and cooked and served at the table, and lived together in a tiny room off the kitchen. But they had not mastered the art of appearing silent and invisible like servants in the better New York homes. They were Newfoundlanders not easily put down or kept silent, and the fact that their mistress was a fellow-countrywoman and a shirttail relation gave them leave, in their eyes, to be familiar.

"A letter from your beau," Mrs. Parker said, sailing into Grace's room to inspect her purchases and hand over the mail. Grace imagined Mrs. Parker's reaction if she had brought home the red dress. She would approve, probably offer to pay for another in yellow. "Nothing from your parents?" Mrs. Parker added.

"I cabled them to say I'd arrived safely. I don't expect a letter yet. And of course mail takes longer from Newfoundland than from Montreal." Grace wondered why she felt the need to excuse her mother's silence. She had never known her father to be a letter-writer. His pen was employed only in sermons. When Charley had been alive, away at college or overseas, it was Mother and Grace who wrote to him. When Grace herself had been at school in St. John's, a weekly letter had come in her mother's hand. Lily's letters had been lengthy and full of local news, woven in and around reminders of duty, responsibility, the importance of behaving properly and doing well in her classes. Grace had often been annoyed by her mother's constant stream of written advice. She tried to imagine now what it might be like if those letters no longer arrived.

Grace wanted to put up her aching feet and read Jack's letter before supper. But Mrs. Parker leaned against the doorjamb and Grace felt obliged to invite her to come in and sit down.

"I'd always imagined having your mother here, you know, in this very bedroom, after I married Mr. Parker and we moved into this apartment. But of course she was married herself then, and, well, I think she wanted to put the past behind her."

Grace laid aside Jack's letter and sat upright. "Mrs. Parker, you keep dropping hints about my mother's past. Is there something you want to tell me?"

The direct approach surprised Mrs. Parker, who looked like she had been planning to continue the game of cat and mouse for several more months. "Well now, dear, I didn't mean—well, yes, I suppose I have been a bit indiscreet. I see you, Grace, looking so very like her, like she was at that age when we were such friends, I find myself going back over it all. I keep wondering—oh, dear, Grace, all I want to know is—do you think your parents are content together? Do they have a happy marriage?"

How strange, Grace thought, *that this is what she wants to know*. She would not have imagined Abigail Parker lying awake nights worrying about the state of Reverend and Mrs. Collins's marriage. "There was someone else, wasn't there? Some other man my mother was in love with?"

Mrs. Parker said nothing, which was so unusual for her that it was an answer in itself. "She asked me not to talk to you about the past," she said finally, between pinched lips.

Grace thought of telling her about the silent parsonages she had grown up in, the master bedroom that was Lily's alone, her father's austere bed next to the study. "Perhaps my mother is right," she said instead. "It's best not to dredge up the past. After all, if my mother had never married my father, I wouldn't be here today, would I? So from my point of view, it's all worked out for the best."

CHAPTER FIFTEEN

Come for Christmas. I know a couple you can stay with,
Newfoundlanders—she is anyway—says she knows
your mother and will write with a proper invitation. Please
say you'll come. Montreal is impossible without you.

"IMPOSSIBLE"? GRACE WONDERED what she would write in reply to Jack's postcard. New York without him was not impossible, but it was lonely. She was getting to know the other students in the Social Work program, but had made no real friends yet. Women greatly outnumbered men in the program, but most of the lady students were several years older than Grace, had college degrees as well as several years' experience working in the field. Despite Grace's "equivalent experience"—and, more relevant, Mrs. Parker's calls to her friends on the board—that had earned her entrance, a few of the ladies seemed to look down on Grace for not having a degree. Or perhaps it was because she came from a backward outpost of the British Empire that none of them had ever heard of. She had made a couple of friends—Miss DeWitt, a soft-spoken girl from the South, and Miss Clark of Chicago, both girls about her own age with whom she often studied and chatted between classes. But both were doing what Grace would have been doing without Mrs. Parker's generosity—working to earn extra money in their hours outside of class. There was little time for strolls in the park and lunches at the Automat. Grace missed home; she missed Jack.

But Montreal was not so far by train. A Christmas visit was certainly possible. Grace wondered who was this woman in Montreal who knew her mother. Another relic of Lily's past, like Abigail Parker?

"This is our stop," announced Miss Everett in her crisp, no-nonsense voice. Everything about Miss Everett, from her tone to her boots, proclaimed that here was a woman who had serious work to do and would brook no foolishness from man, woman nor child—especially man. She was in her forties, a church deaconess and founder of a home for unwed mothers in Utica, New York, and was a great believer in the idea that work for the poor must be conducted on modern, scientific principles.

For the first month, all their studies had been theoretical and confined to the classroom, but observation and fieldwork formed an important part of the first-year students' programs. In the second year each student would select a specialty and a work placement in the community; the first year was intended as a general introduction to the field of social work. On this chilly December morning their destination was a settlement house on the Lower East Side where social workers lived alongside immigrant families and the poor.

It was an ideal Grace had read about and heard her professors lecture on and she found it exciting that rather than handing down charity from on high, those who wanted to help the poor would go and live among them. She had read about Toynbee Hall in Britain and Hull House in Chicago and she was excited to visit an actual settlement house, though when the students left the subway station at Delancey Street she was shocked by what she saw. She thought she had gotten used to New York crowds, but these crowds were composed almost entirely of dirty, shabbily clad people speaking in foreign tongues. The tenement buildings all around looked as if they were falling to pieces. Many had windows broken out and all looked as if far more people swarmed in and out than even these tall buildings could hold. Miss Everett led her charges down the sidewalk and the mass of people parted like the Red Sea before Moses. Grace looked at the faces around her and wondered, *Am I still in America?*

The settlement house on Eldredge Street, when the students arrived, seemed to be everything Grace had read and heard about. In the large first-floor rooms she saw a group of young women trimming hats, a roomful of men taking English lessons, and in the yard out back, a group of schoolchildren playing. The settlement worker who served as their tour guide, a young woman about Grace's own age, described the dozens of different clubs and organizations that operated out of the house. "Just today the doctor is in for a medical clinic, seeing people from the neighbourhood who couldn't possibly afford to pay for medical care," she explained, gesturing at the closed door of the examination room.

The whole place seemed to hum with busy energy. Grace watched a line of men going down the stairs to the lower floor. "The public baths are down there," their guide explained. "Most of the tenements don't have running water, so a great many people from the neighbourhood come here to bathe, often before they go to work or when they return home in evening."

In the yard outside they stopped to watch a slightly older woman leading the children in a vigorous series of calisthenics before she sent them inside to do their homework. "There'll be

Trudy J. Morgan-Cole

tutors in there who can help them with their work," the guide explained. "Many of them come from families where there's no English spoken at home, so schoolwork is quite challenging."

"I imagine so," Grace murmured to Sharon DeWitt. "I'd love to work in a place like this, though."

"I would too," her classmate whispered back. "I've heard tell how back when our college started, all the social work students had to come live here at the settlement house for a few months. I wonder why they stopped that?"

Grace shrugged as Miss Everett shot a chilly glance in their direction. Clearly she did not approve of students talking amongst themselves during a tour. But she unwittingly answered Miss DeWitt's question herself a little later. The social work students watched as a dark-haired woman approached the group of children, wailing and sobbing. She pulled a girl of about ten or eleven away from the group, drawing her away into a corner of the yard for private conversation. "Excuse me a moment," said the settlement worker who was leading their tour. "I must just go talk to her." She left the group of students and hurried past the playing children to speak to the crying woman and the child.

"Come along, we'll pay a visit to the library and the kitchens, then catch our subway train back," Miss Everett said. "I imagine this conversation will take a while; best not to wait." Her look of disapproval was even clearer than it had been while Grace and Miss DeWitt had been whispering.

"Do you know what is going on there?" Grace dared to ask, nodding towards the conclave in the corner of the yard.

"Not this particular situation, but I've witnessed enough similar ones to guess," said the lecturer. "One of the weaknesses of the settlement house model is that workers are often sympathetic with those who require firmness. Some mothers, for example, ought not be left in charge of their own children. Mothers who drink, who cannot be trusted to run a household, want to keep their children with them when the children would be much better off in a well-run orphanage. Many of the workers here are of the view that they can keep families together by providing support within the settlement community, but I'm afraid that all too often that is sentimentality and wishful thinking. The settlement ideal," she continued as she led them through the halls, apparently not concerned who heard her, "sounds fine on paper—that the workers come in and treat the poor as equals—but it fails to take into account the limitations of the people with whom they are working."

"But surely," Grace ventured, "there's something to be said for a mother's love for her children."

Miss Everett paused in her walk to fix Grace with an icy glare. "Perhaps you will be able to speak more cogently about the value of a mother's love, Miss Collins, when you have had, as I have, the duty of removing the body of a deceased fourteen-year-old and her unborn child from the care of a mother who sold her daughter into prostitution to pay for her own gin habit. High-flown sentiments about family love and the inherent nobility of the poor sound a little hollow at such times. You look shocked, Miss Collins." Her gaze swept from Grace to the rest of the group. "You will all need to see a little more of life in neighbourhoods such as this one before you are equipped to judge whether the settlement house model or the scientific approach works best. Perhaps then you will also be able to judge whether you are cut out for work such as this. And this is the library," she announced, opening a pair of broad double doors to reveal a book-lined room where three or four people sat at tables reading or writing.

Her words still rang in Grace's ears when she took the train at Grand Central Station to Montreal on the twenty-second of December, immediately after writing an examination on racial characteristics in the population. She was well aware by now of the

Trudy J. Morgan-Cole

divisions within the social work school over the best ways to help the poor, and understood that "scientific" educators such as Miss Everett had the upper hand over those who had once knitted the school closely to the settlement houses. Grace might disagree with some of Miss Everett's theories, but she worried the instructor's opinion of her own capacity might be accurate. *Am I really able to do this work?* Grace wondered. *Or do I simply like the idea of helping the poor. Or even more*, she thought with a stab of sudden honesty, *do I just like the idea of working in neighbourhoods and with people that would shock my mother?*

She tried to imagine Lily's face if she had seen the squalid tenements clustered around the settlement house. Her horror was so easy to visualize that Grace felt a kind of distant fondness for her mother's intense propriety. Lily had not, as Grace feared, cut off contact altogether when Grace went to New York. Her weekly letters still arrived, neat, closely written pages on which she documented which ladies had crocheted what for the fall sale of work and how impossible Mrs. Hapgood, the Anglican minister's wife, was being about the plan to unite their charitable forces to benefit the families of veterans. Seeded among the parish news were the usual admonitions for Grace to study hard, behave herself, and not get carried away with any foolishness no matter what she might see or hear in the city. Lily had read an article in a church magazine about how jazz music was destroying the morals of the young. She clipped it out and enclosed it with passages underlined, and urged Grace to avoid any place where jazz might be played.

Grace had written weeks ago to tell her parents of the invitation to Montreal for Christmas. Lily had replied:

> *The lady that has befriended Captain Perry wrote to me already to confirm her invitation. I knew her long ago in St. John's and do not approve of all the causes she supports but she is entirely respectable.*

*Remember that you are a guest in her house and
if your young man comes to visit there I trust you will
conduct yourselves appropriately. It will seem dull
here at Christmas without you.*

The journey home was of course far too long and expensive to make for Christmas break but for a moment Grace wished she could be there. The manse would be dull even with her there, she thought, but it would be familiar, and there were far too many unfamiliar things in Grace's life these days.

But she forgot the thought of going home when she saw Jack waiting at the station in Montreal. He held out his arms and Grace went straight to them, as shameless as she'd been on that day they'd gotten news of Charley's death. Here, far away from families and everyone who knew them, she allowed him to pull her into a tight embrace and lifted her face for a kiss.

"I've got a cab waiting to take us to Mr. and Mrs. Ohman's house," he said, picking up Grace's bags and taking her by the hand to lead her through the crowded station.

"I knew I'd heard the name before. Jessie Ohman, isn't it?" Grace said. "She used to edit a ladies' paper back in St. John's." The name Ohman had tickled at the edge of memory when Jack had told her of the invitation, and on the strength of his statement that Mrs. Ohman had known her mother Grace went back through the packet of papers she had taken from her mother's old room in St. John's. She wasn't entirely sure why she had taken those papers all the way to New York with her—some idea, perhaps, of showing them to Mrs. Parker, asking about them? She never did; it seemed disloyal. But when Grace went back to that packet of papers she saw Mrs. Ohman's name all over—as editor of the *Water Lily*, as an outspoken proponent of the prohibition laws and votes for women.

"That's the one. She's quite a firebrand still, though she must be well up into her seventies by now. Her husband's the quiet one. He's in the jewellery business, not a Newfoundlander by birth. She is, and she's always saying how she misses home, like any Newfoundlander, I suppose." Jack handed Grace's case to the cab driver and helped her into the motorcar.

The Ohmans' home was a fair-sized house. For some reason Grace had been thinking of an apartment like the Parkers', imagining Montreal would be just like a slightly smaller New York. Inside, a grey-haired, slightly stout woman in dark green velvet trimmed with what looked like hand-crocheted lace, welcomed them into her sitting room.

"My dear Miss Collins, how very good to meet you," she said, drawing Grace into an embrace. "Young Captain Perry—Doctor Perry as we shall be calling him soon—has told me so much about you. Oh, dear—how much like your mother you look!"

They took tea in the sitting room, Mr. Ohman nowhere in evidence, and Grace gave Mrs. Ohman a brief summary of her studies in New York.

"Such an excellent field for young women to enter. There is a great need, in every city. Not just in large places like New York and Montreal, but in St. John's too. There is terrible poverty there. At least, there was in my day, and I don't imagine it has gotten any better. I tell Captain Perry here that I fully expect him to dedicate his talents and his medical degree to working among the poor once he has finished his studies."

"My mother always wanted me to go into foreign missions."

"Oh, there was a day when every good Christian thought their calling was to go to the mission field, but many of us have come to see over the years that the mission field here at home is just as great. Wouldn't you agree, Miss Collins?"

"I think she's a little bit in love with you," Grace whispered to Jack later that night, after Mr. Ohman had come home and he and

Mrs. Ohman had gone upstairs. In the next room a maid clattered dishes loudly enough to assure them they were not left entirely unchaperoned.

"She's doomed to disappointment then, as she's not the kind of girl I admire."

"Oh, and what kind is that? A modern young woman, I suppose, with her hair bobbed and her skirts short?"

"There's only one girl who's the sort I admire, and the length of her hair and skirts doesn't matter at all." Jack drew his face close enough to hers to kiss, almost, then pulled back. "But I've hardly got any time to spend with her. I'm on shift at the hospital 'til noon on Christmas Eve and then I'm back again on Boxing Day, a twelve-hour stretch. I hope you don't have a dull time."

"Of course not! We'll be together when you're not working, and when you are, I'll visit with Mrs. Ohman and see something of Montreal."

Jack ran both hands through his hair. "You're a good sport, Grace, and I know you'll make the best of whatever happens. It's only that—oh, I shouldn't get started talking about it. Just don't expect me to be the best company, even when I do get away from the hospital."

"I suppose you must be very tired, after twelve-hour shifts."

"Tired doesn't begin to touch it. There's a kind of exhaustion. It goes right down to the bone. I can't explain it unless you've felt it. I felt it in the trenches, but you expected it over there, everyone was going through the same thing. Now I come off a night shift and walk out into the daylight and it feels like I'm staring into a black hole, like I'll never—" He looked around as if only now realizing he was speaking out loud. "I'm sorry. Oh, Grace, I'm so sorry—I shouldn't have said anything."

"No, it's all right. We ought to be able to tell each other how we really feel, even more in person than we do in letters." She had told

Trudy J. Morgan-Cole

him in her last letter about Miss Everett's cutting words after their visit to the settlement house, and her own doubts. Now she said, "I went off to New York all fired up with the desire to do good, but I wonder if Miss Everett is right—if it's too hard for me."

"I don't think she means that at all," Jack said. "I know I'm saying that without even seeing the woman, but I don't see how anyone could look at you and not know how strong, how good, how dedicated you are. I think she wants to test you. But I don't think she really doubts you. And even if you doubt yourself, I never do—not for a minute."

"Thank you for saying that." Again, she heard the clink of dishes in the adjoining room—that maid really was taking an incredibly long time to clear the table. "Surely it's the same for you. Haven't you told me before that the long hours, all the hard work in medical school, are just meant to test you, to prove that you're strong enough to do the work? And you've proven that already, overseas, a hundred times over."

Jack looked away, out a darkened square of window through which nothing was visible. "You'd think so, wouldn't you?"

"But...you don't believe it?"

He sighed, looked down at his fingers twined around hers: they were sitting hand in hand. "Most days I don't. I try to put the best face on it in front of everyone, even in my letters to you, but—I'm not sure I can do it, Grace."

"I'm sure you can. I don't know what to say. If I could take that feeling away from you, I would."

"I know you would. But I don't think anyone or anything can. I pray...It feels like I spend hours on my knees, begging God to get me through the next day, to give me just a little bit of hope and strength to go on."

"And He answers. You do go on."

"I do. But I never feel strong."

A door opened somewhere else in the house and Mrs. Ohman's voice called, "Grace dear, are you ready to come up to bed? I'd like to show you where the clean towels are."

"In other words, it's time for me to be going," Jack whispered, brushing his lips across Grace's. "I'm sorry I said all that."

"No, don't be sorry. But look—that's true courage, isn't it? Going on when you don't feel you can. I want to help, I just don't know what to say. But I love you. If that's any help at all."

"It is. It's all there is."

Trudy J. Morgan-Cole

CHAPTER SIXTEEN

At the words "Come in!" Grace pushed open the heavy oak door to Miss Everett's office and stepped inside. "Here's my paper," she said, and watched the woman's eyes dart to the clock on the wall, making sure it was in on time. Grace had an hour to spare before the paper was due.

Miss Everett glanced at the title before laying it with the stack of student papers on her desk. "'Causes of Delinquency in Immigrant Boys,'" she said. "I look forward to reading your conclusions, Miss Collins."

"Thank you, Miss Everett." Grace turned to go.

"Miss Collins?"

"Yes, Ma'am?"

"I suppose you have selected your area of specialization for next year?"

"Yes, Miss Everett. Family work in the community."

"Ah, of course." Miss Everett nodded. She would already have known that Grace had not chosen Miss Everett's own speciality, child development; she must have had her list of the second-year students she would be supervising some weeks ago. "And I suppose you will hope to do your placement at one of the settlement houses."

"I hope to, yes."

Miss Everett only nodded; you couldn't read either approval or disapproval in her nod, but something compelled Grace to add, "I still believe very strongly in the settlement model, but I have learned a great deal from you about the scientific approach. I hope it needn't always be…exclusive. One or the other, I mean."

"I know what you mean, Miss Collins. I hope your tendency to idealism will not overwhelm your very fine scholarly mind. Good day, Miss Collins. Enjoy your summer holiday."

Grace walked back from college rather than taking the subway. It was a warm afternoon and she let the sun drench her back and shoulders through the cambric of her blouse. The hem of her new spring skirt was two inches above the ankle: she fit in, fashion-wise, with the younger women in her class, though by comparison with many of the ladies she passed on the street, she still looked dowdy. She liked the feeling of the spring air circulating around her stocking-clad ankles. She thought about the red dress she'd tried on in Macy's, wondering would she ever be daring enough to wear such a costume.

Soon college would end for the year and with it, the social work program. Next week Jack would write his final exams at McGill; he was coming down to visit her in New York for a week before they both returned to Newfoundland for the summer. After that—well, who could tell?

She wondered if he might propose—here, under the trees in Central Park. Jack had another year of medical school and one of residency after that, but that was fine by Grace, who was anxious to work for a while and use her new qualifications.

I want too many different things, she thought. She wanted to be walking through Central Park in New York and also to be back home, to be a working woman and also to be Jack's wife. She wanted to be independent, here in New York, connected to no-one, and yet she also wanted Jack by her side. She wanted to be free of her family and yet she yearned to go home and have Lily welcome her with open arms, approve of the life Grace was building. She wanted everything, all at once. That was her problem.

What she did not want was what she found when she got to Mrs. Parker's apartment: Jack's suitcase in the hallway. Her heart leapt, at first. He was here early! But by the time she got to the parlour door, even before she saw him siting with elbows on his knees, face between his palms, she knew it was wrong. This was the first day of his examinations. Jack should not be here.

He stood slowly, crossed the room to her but did not take her in his arms. After a moment he reached out and took her hands instead.

"No one was home. The maid let me in," he said. Not the explanation she was looking for.

"What—when did you arrive?" Not the question she wanted to ask.

"This morning. I took the night train down from Montreal. It took me awhile to find the place."

He looked as if he hadn't slept. "I'm sure Ida's getting the guest room ready," Grace said. "Do you want to lie down?"

"No, no, I want—" He looked around the room as if caged by its gentility, its expensive furniture and excellent taste. Words failed him. He could not tell her what he wanted.

"Do you want to go for a walk?"

He must have walked all the way up from Grand Central Station, yet he said quickly. "Yes—please. I—we need to talk."

She led him out of the building and back across to the park, the wide sunny paths she had walked just half an hour ago. She tried to imagine what kind of news he might be bringing that would have

A Sudden Sun

him here when he should still be at McGill. He said nothing at all until they were in the park, and then he asked whether her classes had finished yet for the year, whether she had written any examinations.

"You had one to write today, didn't you?" Grace said. "Whatever you have to say must be important, if you've missed an exam for it. You'd better go ahead and tell me."

"I didn't miss an exam to come down and tell you anything," Jack said. He walked looking straight ahead, his stride still long and military, his arms swinging, as though he were forever marching to some battlefield in Flanders. "It's the other way around. I came down to tell you I'm not writing my exams. I can't do it, Grace."

She looked at him, but he would not return her gaze, so she had to search the lines of his face and body rather than his eyes for clues. She remembered how he had talked at Christmas about fear, about feeling overwhelmed. Then he had seemed like a man struggling to swim in deep waters. Now there was a calm without peace. It was the calm of a man who has been sucked under the waves and ceased to struggle.

"What happened?" she asked finally.

"I couldn't do it. That's all. I did try, even though I couldn't study and I knew going in it was no go. Sat down in the examination hall and took the pen in my hand. Couldn't write a word—just doodled on the page until it was time to leave. Today's exam would have been a practical. I was supposed to stand there in front of a live patient—a human being!—and tell a supervising doctor what was wrong with him. God, how could anyone even think—" He held up his hands, out in front so she could see how they trembled. "I can't do it, Grace. I've failed."

"Failed—this year, this term of your program, that's all." She laid a hand on his arm.

Trudy J. Morgan-Cole

He broke stride then, stumbled to a halt. "I'm not going back, Grace. Can't finish medical school, can't be a doctor. What kind of doctor breaks down in tears, has to rush from the room when he sees a wound? What kind of *man*, even—?"

She led him to a nearby bench. He sat in the same posture as when she had found him in the parlour, elbows on knees and head in hands. He ran his fingers through his hair, over and over 'til it stuck out in all directions, and started several different sentences but finished none of them.

"I'm sorry," he said at last. "I thought we had a future because I thought I had one. But now I see that won't wash."

"It doesn't matter to me if you're not a doctor," Grace said.

Then, on those words, he finally looked up at her. "It doesn't. At all?"

"Of course not. You know I was never—I mean, being the doctor's wife didn't matter to me like it would to some women. I'm not like my mother, or even yours."

"My mother. Oh, she'll—I can't even imagine telling her, Grace. Or Dad, even worse. They were so proud, Grace. I thought I could make them—so proud…"

His voice broke the second time he said "proud." Grace put a hand on his shoulder and as if that touch had made him collapse like a house of cards he leaned towards her. She gathered him into her arms, against her shoulder, and she felt him shake with sobs. She sat on a park bench in open sunlight, holding a man against her breast and letting him weep. She thought of Charley. She thought of Ivan Barry with his blind eye and the gaping mouth that was supposed to preach sermons one day. She thought of every dream shattered and broken, and after a while she cried too.

CHAPTER SEVENTEEN

EVERY TIME LILY looked at Jack Perry, she wished he were dead.

It was, admittedly, a harsh reaction to have to a pleasant young man: handsome, devout, the son of a respectable merchant. But Lily could not clap eyes on him without picturing his body in the mud of a French battlefield, torn and broken, his lifeless eyes staring up at her.

It was wrong that Jack was alive and Charley dead. She thought it before Jack left for the Front and she thought it, too, when he came home, strapping and healthy. If Jack had been brave, he would have signed up with Charley, and been at Monchy-le-Preux, and taken Charley's death.

But now he and Grace were keeping company, and Lily had another reason to wish him dead. It would have been fine—ideal, in fact—if he and Grace had been sweethearts before the war. He could have gone off to war, and Grace could have written him letters, and then when he died, Grace's heart would have been broken.

In Lily's imagined life, she and Grace sat together for hours in the parlour or on the front porch of the house on warm days, content to knit and embroider in each other's company. In that life, a dead soldier lover would fit perfectly. She did not wish Grace to live entirely without love; a little girlhood romance added colour to life, if only it ended with the girl's innocence intact and a bittersweet memory to cherish.

It was a pretty picture, Grace safe and contented at her mother's side, dreaming about her brave lover who gave his life for his country. Lily could not shake her resentment of Jack for surviving to shatter that image, though she felt wicked knowing that she was wishing poor Elizabeth Perry the same anguish she herself had known. But then, Mrs. Perry had three more sons.

The Catalina station was busy this June morning. Even Mr. Coaker himself was there, to greet his daughter Camilla, he told the Reverend as they waited for the train. *Now there's a good girl!* Lily thought. Coaker and his wife had been separated for years and the girl lived with Mrs. Coaker: she was about Grace's age and entirely devoted to her mother, though she came for a few weeks each summer to visit her father in Port Union. It was shameful, of course, that the Coakers lived separately—a bad example to the people, and one reason Lily refused to join in her husband's admiration of Coaker. People whispered that the great reformer was so cruel to his wife that she could not live under his roof. But the girl was a model daughter, and when Lily had seen Camilla with Mrs. Coaker in St. John's she felt a pang of envy. Imagine having a daughter whose only ambition was to stay by her mother's side!

Now the train was here, and there was Miss Coaker, and Abe Russell with his new wife, and a knot of other people, and then Grace and Jack. As soon as Jack stepped off the train and reached back to give his hand to Grace, Lily saw that something was wrong with him. Nothing as wrong as what was wrong with Charley. Nothing as irreparable as death. But the boy who had carried a sort of golden sheen on him ever since returning from the war looked tarnished now.

When Jack and Grace were home last summer, there had been an ease to their laughter, a confidence. As if, despite the fact that one of them had been through a war and another had lost her brother in that war, they still walked through the world with the belief that all would be well, that oceans would part at their feet. Such confidence in Grace had frightened Lily: no girl should go out into the world with her head held so high. A girl should go out guarded, watchful for a thousand dangers or, better yet, not go out into the world at all, but stay safe at her mother's side. And clearly Grace had caught a hint of those dangers, for both she and Jack seemed guarded, the sunny light of their faces shadowed as they came down from the train.

There was a moment, before the two families parted ways at the station, when Grace and Jack stood very close gripping each other's hands. She said something to him in a low voice, her forehead crinkled as it had done when she was very serious ever since she was a tiny girl. Jack shook his head, and then Grace pulled away to go with Lily and the Reverend back to the manse, and Jack went off with his parents.

Lily had no words to ask Grace what had happened. Nor would she ask about Abigail Hayward, even after Grace settled her bags around her feet in the carriage and said, "Mrs. Parker sends her love, Mother, and still wishes you would come for a visit."

"Abigail Parker knows very well New York is the last place on earth I'd want to go for a visit. If I had any interest in gadding about."

After supper the Reverend excused himself to visit an ailing parishioner. Lily was about to go into the parlour when Grace said, "It's a lovely evening, I'm going to sit out on the verandah."

"Very well."

Trudy J. Morgan-Cole

At the door she turned back. "Come out and sit with me, Mother?" She sounded hesitant as a schoolboy asking a girl to his first dance.

"The flies will have you eaten alive," Lily said.

"I don't mind. I've missed the fresh air and the view."

"Suit yourself." Then, as the door closed behind Grace, Lily went into the parlour to pick up her work bag. She took the set of table napkins she was embroidering—a wedding gift for a friend's daughter—out on the verandah and pulled up the straight-backed chair across from the rocker where Grace was lounging. The evening air was pleasant, still holding a trace of the day's warmth.

"See? It's lovely out," Grace said, swatting at a fly that buzzed near her nose.

"The insects will get worse as it gets dark."

"If they start bothering me, I'll go inside."

They sat silently for a while as Lily picked away at her embroidery and Grace stared out at the harbour. "Don't you have any sewing or knitting?" Lily asked.

"Nothing unpacked yet. Can't I have a few minutes just to sit and enjoy a lovely evening? I don't have to be doing something all the time, do I?"

There now, Grace had her back up already, and the subject of Jack Perry had not even been broached. Truly, there was nothing Lily could say to the girl, nothing at all. It had always been like this— Grace took offense so easily. But Lily knew she must not stop trying. Considering and discarding several possibilities, she finally put together a sentence that might get near the information she wanted without angering Grace too much. She practiced it several times in her head before she spoke.

"Will Jack be coming to speak to your father while he's in town?"

Grace said nothing for a moment, then, without meeting her

mother's eyes, she said, "I don't know. I wouldn't imagine so."

Lily had hit somewhere close to the mark. Something must have gone wrong between the lovebirds.

"Oh. I suppose since you both still have another year of school…"

She let the sentence trail off, but this suggestion of delay in their engagement seemed to trouble Grace even more. She hopped out of the rocker and went and leaned out over the railing. "Careful," Lily said—not that there was any real danger of Grace overbalancing and tumbling into the rhododendron bush, but it was a habit as accustomed as breathing, to warn her of possible danger. In another habit just as ancient, Grace responded by leaning out further, 'til only the tips of her shoes grazed the porch.

"Exactly," she said finally. "I've got another year of college; plenty of time to talk about the future when that's done." Grace had already secured a job at the FPU offices for the summer.

"So you're still determined to go back in September, are you?"

"I suppose so." Grace shrugged.

"And what will you do after that? Does it really make sense to spend two years and hundreds of dollars getting a diploma if you're going to get married as soon as you finish?"

"Oh, I don't know, Mother! Stop badgering me, will you?"

Lily swatted her embroidery at a whining buzz in the air near her head. She gathered her work back into her bag. "I knew those flies would have me tormented," she said. "And it's getting chilly. Put on a sweater if you're staying out here." She stood up and went inside.

In church the next morning Jack sat with his parents and Grace sat next to Lily as the Reverend expounded upon the good and faithful servant who would enter into the joy of his Lord. Jack walked Grace home from church, but Lily got no hint as to the reason for the strain in the air until Monday night when the Ladies'

Trudy J. Morgan-Cole

Aid met at Mrs. Perry's home.

Grace said she wasn't going. "Don't be ridiculous," Lily said. "Everyone round the harbour knows you're keeping company with her son. It will look bad if you don't go."

"I don't care how it looks."

"That's all very well for you, but I'll be plagued with questions. People will think that you and Jack have had a falling-out. Worse yet, they'll think you're on bad terms with his mother."

"I don't mind what they think! Can't you just tell them I've gone to bed with a headache? I'll go to bed, then it'll be half true."

"I'm not in the habit of telling lies, or half-truths," said Lily.

"Oh, aren't you?" Grace said. A queer smile lifted the corners of her lips and she went to get her sweater. "I suppose I'd better come, after all."

As Lily had suspected, Grace was the centre of an eager group, not just of the girls her own age but their mothers too, all eager to know about her time in New York, even if most of them were more interested in New York fashions than in social work. Midway through the evening, Lily overheard Mrs. Snelgrove ask Mrs. Perry, "So, will young Jack be working for his father this summer, until he goes back to college?"

"Oh, I don't know," Mrs. Perry said, and laid down the cup of tea she was holding. "Truly, Clara, I don't know what to make of that boy. He tells me now he may not—" she looked around and lowered her voice, but not so much that Lily, positioned a little behind her, could not hear "—he may not even go back to school. Imagine! He's always been so good, so hard working, and now, well—I don't know what to make of him. His father's very upset, and—oh, I shouldn't have said anything. I shouldn't."

Once again, Mrs. Perry glanced around as if to make sure no one overheard, but this time she looked behind her. Lily dropped her eyes to her needlework, but not before she met Mrs. Perry's eyes

A Sudden Sun

for one unguarded second.

Later, with the younger women out talking in groups on the lawn in the twilight, Mrs. Perry glided up to Lily in the parlour. Most of the women were gone now. Mrs. Perry's maid came and went with teacups and trays.

"You overheard me talking to Mrs. Snelgrove about poor Jack," Mrs. Perry said. "I'm sorry, I know it's wrong to talk outside the house—I never do it—but I can talk to you, can't I, Lily dear? We're almost family, aren't we? Poor Grace must be distracted. Did she tell you the whole story?"

Lily's tongue was stilled by the easy assumption of confidences between mother and daughter. Elizabeth Perry had three daughters in addition to her fine handsome sons: did they all confide in their mother all the secrets and sorrows of their little love affairs, their private lives? Two of the girls were married now, of course, yet they were in and out of their mother's house all the time with an easy intimacy Lily could not help but envy.

"Grace doesn't say too much," she admitted finally.

"Oh, she's very discreet, I should be more like her myself. But the truth is it's broken my heart, and to hear Zeke losing his temper over all the money we've spent on his education, and poor Jack just sits there and takes it, like a dog that's been beaten— that's not my boy, not at all. I don't recognize him." She pulled a handkerchief from the sleeve of her blouse and dabbed her eyes. "When he came home from overseas I was so glad, I thought God had spared us, and I thought I'd never ask for anything again. But now, to see him come back all—all defeated like, as if his spirit's broken. Even the war didn't do that to him!"

Or perhaps it did. For half a moment Lily allowed herself to feel sympathy.

But she could harden her heart as easily as Pharaoh. She almost felt it hardening, like putting on armour inside her rib cage. "At least

Trudy J. Morgan-Cole

he came back," she said. "Whatever happens to him, he is alive. You should be grateful."

"Of course, of course," sniffled Mrs. Perry, "and we are, but…" She broke off, her head lifting to the sound of a male tread on the stairs. Her husband and son had been banished during the women's meeting; Lily had thought they were gone out but Jack, at least, must have been upstairs. Now he came and stood in the doorway and took in his crying mother and the woman who might be, might have been, his mother-in-law. He looked haggard. That was the only word for it.

"Mother…Mrs. Collins," he said. "I'm sorry, I thought all the ladies were gone."

Elizabeth crossed the room to him, took hold of his arms and laid her head against his chest. Jack looked over her head at Lily, embarrassment covering over the terrible weariness in his face. "Is Grace still here?"

"I believe she's out in the garden."

Jack looked through the window but made no move to go. He let his mother cry against his shirt-front as Lily excused herself and made her way out of the Perrys' house.

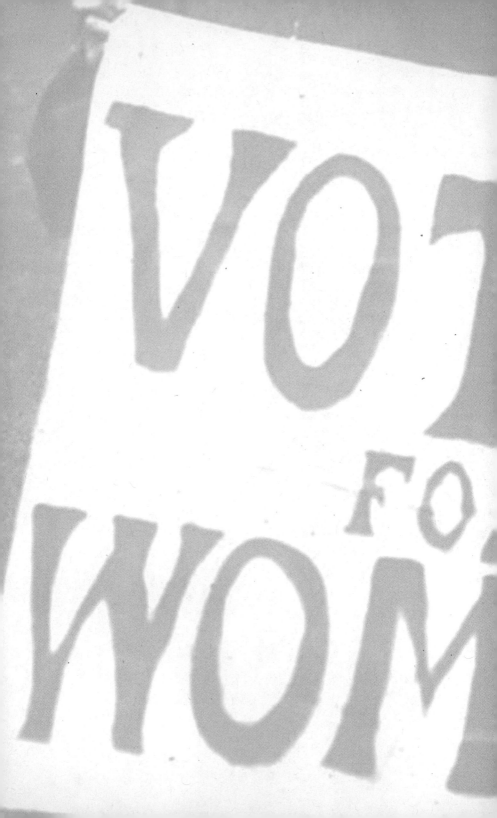

Part Four

LILY
1893–1894

CHAPTER EIGHTEEN

$\mathcal{L}$ILY STEPPED OUT of the flustered heat of Temperance Hall into the cool of a September night. Behind her, Abby exited arm in arm with Martha Withycombe. Martha's mother, newly elected secretary of the WCTU, had given a stirring talk about the Rescue Home for girls in trouble that the Salvation Army had just opened with support from the WCTU. There was to be a fundraising drive for the home, and the ladies had been sent forth to embroider pillowcases for the inevitable sale of work.

"I've been working on the dearest little set of needlepoint cushions," Martha said, "intended for my hope chest, of course, but after Mother's speech tonight I'm moved to donate them. It can't be right, can it, that I have so much and others so little? And I do have so much—two dozen pillowcases and a dozen sheet sets, four tablecloths and five complete sets of linen napkins...."

"Not monogrammed yet, of course," said Abby.

"Well, of course not."

"Perhaps you might pick some nice initial, embroider it, and then look for the man to match the letter?" Abby suggested.

A moment's silence from Martha, then she laughed. "Oh Abigail, you're shocking. Isn't she just dreadful, Lily?"

Lily laughed, letting her laughter mingle with that of the other two girls. Martha had been keeping company for two years with Edward Miller—a fine catch, any girl would have to admit, heir to a button-factory fortune. But Edward had gone off to England for a year and before he'd been away three months, word came back that he was engaged to an English girl. Martha's hope chest continued to grow, though hope was wearing thin.

Now Abby unhooked her arm from Martha's arm and took Lily's instead. "Come along, your poor mother will be distracted if you're not home," she said, barely hiding her giggles. She swept Lily off to the waiting carriage. Lily hoped neither Martha nor any of the ladies coming out of the hall noticed a tall, lanky figure detach itself from the shadow of the building and walk a few paces behind the girls.

By the side of her family's brougham Abby squeezed Lily's hands. "Don't do anything I wouldn't do, now, will you? My good reputation rests in your hands."

"I'll be back at your house by ten, I promise."

"Make it eleven. My good name isn't *that* precious," said Abby. And under cover of darkness, she climbed into the carriage as Lily slipped her arm through David Reid's arm.

A little rush of danger flooded Lily's veins, as it always did when she went off alone with David. She knew she was safe with him, if she was willing to stretch her definition of safety a little farther than she had been accustomed to do.

By now they had something of a routine to their courtship—if courtship it could be called. Their brief encounters in public—if Lily, for example, attended an event that David was covering for the newspaper—were always distant and proper. If they spoke at all they called each other "Mr. Reid" and "Miss Hunt." No one would be able to report to Lily's father that they had seen David Reid being familiar with her. As far as Papa was concerned, Lily was being courted by Reverend Obadiah Collins, whose letters arrived from Greenspond with dull regularity.

David tucked his hand over hers as they set off along Duckworth Street, heading west, away from Abby's house where Lily was spending the night. The Upper Path, as many older people still called it, looked less like a path and more like a proper street in the last year; it had been widened and straightened after the fire. They turned down Prescott to Water Street, past the ruins of the Market House. Merchants' premises stood with their fronts facing the street and their backs to the harbour, where every merchant had a wharf for ships to load and unload goods. The familiar street looked different after dark. The life-sized horse in the window of Ring's Saddlery and the Indian in Cash's Tobacco Shop, taken inside for the night, stood silent sentinels over the dark street. Once the shops were closed, respectable young girls like Lily weren't seen downtown. The saloons drew rough men and loose women from every corner of the town and harbour. The same people from the same streets where Lily sometimes went with other WCTU ladies, bringing food and clothing to the destitute. At night the poor inspired fear rather than godly pity.

She had never really seen places like these, rum-shops whose doors spilled smoky yellow light and fragments of songs and curses, before she and David had begun taking their night-time walks. Lily had been terrified the first time she walked past a string of Water Street saloons after dark. "What do you think, that people will take you for a woman of easy virtue?" he had laughed. "I promise you, nobody who knows you will see you and think, 'What is Lily Hunt doing in such a place?'"

"If anyone did see me, they'd be quiet about it," Lily pointed out. "All Papa's friends are temperance men. If they were down here themselves, they'd never want anyone to know it."

Trudy J. Morgan-Cole

"They won't be down here," David assured her. "If a good temperance man sneaks a drink he does it in secret, from a bottle in his well-locked cupboard. These places are for fishermen and dockworkers and factory men, not for the likes of your father and his cronies."

By now Lily had learned that the anonymity of these dirty streets was a better cover than a shady, tree-lined lane by Rennie's River—though she and David had walked there, too, on summer evenings. She truly was no one here, only David's shadow. She had seen men brawling in the street outside a saloon; she had seen ladies of the night too, though those poor women were far less glamorous than such names implied. *Fallen women*, she thought. That was a better word for it, fallen from the pedestal of pure womanhood down onto these filthy streets.

And where am I? Lily wondered, as David pulled her into the alleyway between two shops for another kiss. *I am a falling woman.* Not fallen—but not on that pedestal either.

"Does it trouble you?" he said. Had she spoken her thoughts aloud?

"Does what trouble me?"

"Lying, sneaking around. You don't seem the kind to relish it."

"Not like Abby, you mean," Lily said, and they both laughed.

Next to having a clandestine love affair of her own, the best thing that could possibly have happened to Abigail Hayward was for a friend of hers to have one. Lily had agonized for a week after her first secret meeting with David, wondering whether to confide in Abby. It was one thing to bear the burden of guilt, of dishonesty, herself, quite another to foist it upon her friend. But Abby had been delighted. She entered into the conspiracy with even more enthusiasm than Lily herself. True, she didn't have the thrill of receiving stolen kisses, but then Abby had no burden of guilt to carry either. Abby wouldn't know guilt if Jesus Himself appeared in her room and told her she was disobeying His holy law. Whereas Lily, even in the midst of her happiness, carried guilt with her constantly. But she noticed that over these last weeks that guilt, though never disappearing, had shrunk a little. She had carried it at first like a heavy sack on her back, then like a bundle in her arms. By now it was more like an unusually large locket around her neck: something she was aware of but able to ignore.

"What story is Abigail telling for you tonight?" David asked.

"A true story—that I am spending the night at her house. Only she's told her parents that I went home to pack a bag before coming over, and that Evans will drive me over. Whereas I told Mama I would go to Abby's house directly after the WCTU meeting."

"Clever indeed. As long as your mother doesn't compare notes with Abby's mother, I suppose."

"She won't." Lily's descent into falling womanhood had been greatly aided by the call for a general election in November. The demand for printed material—handbills and such for political candidates—had kept her father's shop unusually busy. He worked most evenings since the election call, and it was usually her mother who received the news that Lily was going to stay at Abby's house, or go to a meeting with Abby, or go out with Abby to dinner at a friend's house. Abby's role was to tell blithe lies while Lily went for long evening rambles with David Reid.

"It's a bit foolish, though, isn't it?" David said.

"What is?"

"This. You and me. Sneaking about like children playing hooky from school."

"Well, but we have to, or Papa would—I don't know what he'd do. Send me away, perhaps. Off to Harbour Grace with Mother's family."

"Yes, of course, but what I mean is—d'you ever ask why?"

"Why what?"

"Why it should be your father's say, and not yours, who you keep company with?"

"Well, because—because. He's my father. I'm his daughter."

"And that's the way it's been since time immemorial? You're his property, to care for and dispose of as he sees fit." David's fingers tightened a little around Lily's hand; he sounded as if he were angry.

"Not property, no! Papa wouldn't understand about—well, about us—but he has my best interests at heart. I mean, it's not as if he would force me to marry someone I didn't want to, or anything like that."

"But he might stop you from marrying someone you did want to?"

"I don't—I don't know." The mention of marriage seemed to make the whole discussion weightier and more dangerous. Lily looked away, not wanting to meet David's eyes. "Anyway, I'm not marrying anyone. Not now—"

"Not even the good Reverend Collins?"

"Of course not!"

"He'd like that, though. Your father, I mean."

"Probably, yes. Of course he would."

"But why should he have a say in it at all? Why should he control who you talk to, where you go, who—who kisses you?" David leaned forward and illustrated the word "kisses" appropriately, though they were right out on the street.

The kiss ended; they turned up Williams Lane. It would soon be time to head back towards Abby's house. Lily was still thinking about David's question. "All the same, a father is responsible for his daughter, isn't he?"

"Responsible for treating her like a child? You're twenty years old, Lily. Why aren't you responsible for yourself?"

Lily was spared the necessity of answering what seemed an unanswerable question by the loud entry of two drunkards into the narrow lane, which boasted a saloon on each corner.

"Come on now, what do we got here?" one of them bellowed. "Oh, sweet'earts, sorry sweet'earts!"

The sweetheart drunkard seemed friendly enough, inclined to do nothing more than call out a greeting, but his companion called "Das a mighty sweet piece you got dere, buddy. Wanna give us a bit?"

She moved instinctively closer to David's embrace but he was turning already toward the intruder. The muscles in his arms tensed: his whole body was becoming a different machine.

"Now b'y, you just go on your way and leave us be," David called. "I don't want no trouble and neither do you."

"Don' want no trouble? Don' wannit?" slurred the man, swaying down the lane towards them. He was not so very close yet, maybe thirty or forty feet away, but David had moved to place himself between Lily and the drunkards. "I'll tell ya what she wants!" the man bawled. "She wants a real man, and I'll show ya, I'll show ya, buddy…"

"Come on, Jim b'y, get outa here, let's get outa here," his companion urged as David took a step toward them. Lily looked over her shoulder. She could run for the other end of the alleyway and get out of there before the men got close. But what would she be running into? Who knew how many other drunkards might be up on Duckworth Street at this hour of the night?

David took another step towards the men.

"There's two of us and only one of you! Lemme at her now and I won' give you no more trouble. Das what you wants, right, no trouble? And I knows what she wants…"

"Clear off!" shouted David, in a voice she'd never heard from him before. Surely he must have fought, growing up—boys did, especially boys of the lower sort, but probably all boys to some extent. He seemed taller and broader as he walked slowly toward the men, and though she was still trembling she felt sure he could defend

Trudy J. Morgan-Cole

her honour—if there were only one drunken opponent. But against two?

Only it wasn't two, because the other man was already in retreat, shouting, "Come on, Jim, come on home out of it! You don't want a fight with the likes of him, he'll have you up before a magistrate! Leave him alone with the girl—come on Jim, come on!"

Whether it was David's steady, unhurried approach or the mention of the magistrate, something slowed Jim's steps. "Ah, go on, b'y, yer makin' much out of nudding!" he shouted at David, backing up a step or two. "I was only foolin'—you knows dat, right, only foolin' around wit' ya!"

David said nothing, only stood his ground, his hands still fists. The drunkard backed up further, further, and finally turned around. "Devil take ya, I never meant nudding by it!" he shouted. "You can go to hell, you and yer little whore too!"

He was out of the alley before he flung the insult, and David lurched forward as if to follow him, though until he heard that filthy word he'd seemed content to stand his ground and watch the man walk away. Lily grabbed for his arm, felt the hard cords of muscle tensed there. "Leave it, David. He's gone now."

He turned. "But he said—"

"I know what he said but it's only words, isn't it? A man like that doesn't know anything else to say about a girl."

A girl standing in a dark lane with a man's arms around her, Lily added silently. Maybe Jim the drunkard was no fool after all. Maybe he called it as he saw it, and what he saw was a woman falling.

As they turned their steps east on Duckworth Street towards Abby's house they heard the clamour of church bells—a thinner sound than it used to be, in this city after the fire, with so many church steeples still crumbled and empty. The surviving bells struck eleven. "I'm late," Lily said.

"I'm sorry."

"It doesn't matter. I'll be there by quarter past."

"Not just for being late. For—all that."

"It's not your fault what a few drunks say or do."

"It is if I bring you to places like that."

I don't mind, Lily wanted to say, but he would have known it wasn't true.

"Next time we'll walk along Rennie's River," David said. Her heart leaped with relief. Another man might have said there would be no next time, that it wasn't worth the risks they took to be together.

They walked home quietly, making no effort to pick up the threads of their interrupted conversation. But the questions David had asked played over like a gramophone record in Lily's head. She'd struggled to find the courage to defy her father and see David. But she had known always that her father was right and she was the one in the wrong. It had never occurred to her to question, as David did, a father's fundamental right to make such rules for his daughter. And yet if she truly believed all the fine words she'd heard about women being the equals of men, why should it be? If she had the right to vote, and to go out to work and earn her living, just like a young man might do, would her father still have a say in who she courted, who she married?

There was a reason to it, she knew. Preachers might say it had to do with Genesis and God making man head of the woman. But Lily thought it might have more to do with what had just happened in Williams Lane. For what would have happened to her if she had been in that place alone tonight? How could any woman walk through the world without a man to protect her?

She wanted to try to explain this to David, but she was very tired, and they were nearing Cochrane Street and Abby's house. A conversation for another time, perhaps.

Trudy J. Morgan-Cole

CHAPTER NINETEEN

$\mathscr{A}$BBY'S MOTHER SWEPT in to her parlour. Mrs. Hayward moved like a schooner running with a strong headwind. She had a list of things she wanted Abby to do, and as she was on her way back out of the room, almost as an afterthought, she turned back and said, "Oh, Lily, did your father's man find you, the other day?"

"What day was that, Ma'am?"

"Oh, two or three days ago—Tuesday, was it? Evans came to the kitchen with a message for you. He seemed to think you were here, but Abby was out visiting the Ayre girls that afternoon. I told Cook to tell him he must have been mistaken."

"Oh—of course," Lily said. On Tuesday she had met David in the park for half an hour as he was leaving the office. She had told her mother she was going to Abby's. Walking back from the Park alone she had run into Evans, who gave her a note from her mother asking if she could pick up soap and some Minard's Liniment at the druggist's. It wasn't on her way at all, but she did the message and congratulated herself that once again she had gotten away with meeting David in secret.

Abby didn't hesitate long enough to take a breath. "Oh, Mama, I decided at the last minute to take Lily along with me to the Ayres's."

"That was a dangerous story to tell," Lily chided Abby after Mrs. Hayward had gone. "What if your mother talks to Mrs. Ayre and finds out I was never at her house?"

"Mrs. Ayre wasn't even there, it was just the two girls and me and the old grandmother who's deaf as a post. Besides, to tell the sad truth, Mama's not interested enough in your comings and goings to play Sherlock Holmes. Why, she's not even interested enough in my comings and goings, as long as she's assured I'm someplace respectable. She'll have forgotten this whole conversation before she's up the stairs—more important things on her mind, you know."

"So all in all, it's a pity you're not the one sneaking around to see a secret lover."

"Isn't it! Believe you me, I think that every day."

"Would you, though?"

"What, me? In a heartbeat."

"No, but really. If it were real, a real-life young man your parents wouldn't approve of, would you see him secret?"

Lily's tone was serious enough to sober even Abby. "I'd love to do something so naughty," she said after a moment. "But I'd have to ask—*why* would my parents not approve of him?".

"Because he's not a churchgoer. Because he drinks—a bit, anyway. Because he's half-Irish and his mother was a Catholic and his family are—nobody really. Any of those reasons."

"In this scene you're painting, is he rich?"

"No."

Abby took a deep breath. "The problem with the whole scenario, when you lay it out like that, is—why am I doing it? Do I hope to run away with him, to marry him, in the end? Because it seems to me— well, I know I'm very silly and I talk a lot of rot about being wicked and all that, but the truth is, anyone Papa wouldn't want me to

Trudy J. Morgan-Cole

marry is probably not anyone I'd want to marry, either. I mean, you do want someone…compatible, someone who can socialize with your friends, someone who can provide for you. Papa's very concerned that I marry a good provider, and I'm even more ambitious. I want a rich man!" Abby laughed, her serious mood dispelled already. "And if he's rich, and respectable, and all the rest, then there's no need to sneak around. He'd just come calling."

"Yes. I suppose so."

Abby leaned forward, took Lily's hand. "Oh, sweetheart, I don't want to make you feel sad. You are in a bind, aren't you? But do you really think Mr. Reid would ask you to elope with him? And if he did, would you risk it? The shame, and all that? And you'd be so poor!"

"Well, he hasn't asked. But what if it—I mean, what if it were you, and he weren't planning to marry you? If it were just—" Lily's voice trailed off. She couldn't think of a word for what she was imagining.

But Abby could think of several. She squeezed Lily's hands. "You mean to be his lover—his mistress? Oh Lily, you haven't— have you?"

"No! Of course not! I'd never be so wicked—or foolish."

"Foolish is the important part, not wicked. It's dreadfully wicked for a married woman to take a lover, but it's safe enough if you're discreet. No, I'm not saying I'd ever do it, but people do and they're not struck by lightning from heaven. But an unmarried girl—darling, we can't be too careful. Once a man has his way, he'll toss you aside, and no one else will marry you. I know it's harsh but it's only the truth."

"I know—of course I know all that. Let's talk about something else. Or, no, let's do something else. I'm tired of sitting inside and I'm tired of turning this whole thing over and over in my head. Let's go walking."

"A drive instead of a walk, please," Abby said, leaping up. "I want broader horizons than I can see on shoe-leather. Let me ask Mama if Wilson is free to drive us. Or no, wait, I'll ask if she'll let us take the gig. I do love to drive, but she hates to let me."

Predictably, Abby's mother said no to the gig, particularly as both the horses would be engaged in taking her on an afternoon call. She suggested the girls join her.

"I'd rather be hung, drawn, and quartered," Abby said, returning to the parlour with this news. "Two hours sitting with Mrs. Monroe in her parlour discussing china patterns and middle-aged gossip? And now Mother's got it into her head that we should go with her and I'll never be able to cry off for anything as frivolous as a walk. Unless I can come up with something improving and good-works-ish to do instead, I'm afraid I'm doomed—and you along with me."

"Martha did ask if we could come help deliver baby blankets to the Rescue Home this afternoon," Lily said. "I put her off, but they were meeting at her house at two, so we've still time to get there."

"Perfect!" Abby jumped up to tell her mother the revised plan, then lifted her hands in despair. "See what my life has come to? So desperate for entertainment that I jump at the chance to bring blankets to—ugh, a poorhouse?"

"You still have a concert with Frank Ayre to look forward to tonight, haven't you?"

"No, tonight is Norman Winsor. Now I'll be able to be all aglow with virtue when I go. Very well, I'll ask Mother if we can ride along with her as far as the Withycombes' house. It's not a perfect plan, but for lack of time to invent a better, it will have to serve."

To make some of their lies plausible it had become necessary for Abby to accompany Lily to a number of WCTU events. Abby turned out to dislike the efforts of the "earnest bluestockings," as she called them, far less than she pretended to. Lily herself was becoming a bit disillusioned with the WCTU. In the wake of their latest defeat in the

Trudy J. Morgan-Cole

House of Assembly, the women who opposed pushing for the vote had won the upper hand in the temperance organization. Frances Withycombe had been elected secretary, replacing Jessie Ohman, who now seemed sidelined. Not silenced—she was impossible to silence—but the latest issue of her *Water Lily* had had to be postponed twice due to lack of funds and nobody seemed to know when it would be printed. Lily had written a little piece for this issue and was beginning to despair that she would ever see it in print.

So Lily had not committed herself when Martha asked about the blankets, worthy though the work was. Martha insisted, as her mother did, that this was their real work, to alleviate the suffering caused by drink and other social evils. Getting the vote would have been only a means to that end, and if it stood in the way of achieving their real goal it was best to abandon it.

"But I can't help feeling," Lily said, trying these ideas out aloud on Abby as they walked up the long path to the Withycombe house, "that we're being pushed off into a corner, told to go and do woman's work. Not that the work isn't good, but it's not enough."

"Well, if Martha's parroting her mother, you're parroting Mrs. Ohman," Abigail said. "I've heard her say almost the very same words."

"I don't—oh, perhaps I am. What do *you* think?"

"I think the afternoon would be more pleasantly passed if you and I were both dining at Cochrane House—if it were still standing, of course—then going on from there to assignations with our secret lovers. But one can't get what one wants all the time, so it's good to learn how to make do with next best."

Lily said no more, for they were at the Withycombes' door and this was not a house in which one spoke lightly of secret lovers. But she supposed Abby's words might be applicable to her own question after all. If women couldn't have the vote, perhaps they would have to make do with bringing blankets to the poorhouse.

Inside, Mrs. Withycombe, Martha, and three other women were folding the blankets they had sewn, knitted, and crocheted over the past weeks. Most were white, some pale pastels. Lily herself had knitted a pale blue one and trimmed it with white crochet lace, and was particularly proud of her work.

"Oh, Miss Hunt, Miss Hayward, how good to see you both. Martha said she'd asked you but we thought you must have decided not to join us. I've hired a carriage—why don't we ladies go in that? Martha, you girls can follow us in our buggy. I'll get the boy to hitch it up."

Lily had not yet visited the new Rescue Home, for all she had heard about it. She imagined an orderly house, clean-scrubbed but shabby, with poor girls who all looked a bit like her maid Sally. Babies would nestle in their mothers' arms whimpering softly because of the lack of blankets, and both mothers and babies would smile with appreciation when the blankets arrived.

A middle-aged woman in a Salvation Army uniform met the WCTU ladies in the front hallway. Lily didn't know a great deal about the Salvationists except that they had only come to town in the last few years, they had noisy musical meetings, and they weren't considered entirely respectable despite being such devout Christians. She also knew they dressed up in uniforms as if they were in the military, and when Mrs. Withycombe addressed the matron as "Captain Jost," Lily realized it must be possible, in this army, for women to hold positions of rank as well as men.

Lily saw no fallen women, though she could hear a baby crying somewhere. The lady captain took the blankets from Mrs. Withycombe. "Thank you, I can take these and distribute them."

"No, no, we'd much rather do it ourselves, meet the mothers and babies," Mrs. Withycombe said.

Lily saw a flicker of irritation cross the other woman's face. No doubt it would be easier to drop off the blankets and have the staff

Trudy J. Morgan-Cole

distribute them—it wasn't that the girls and their babies needed to see the WCTU ladies, but rather that the ladies wanted to look at them. But then, if WCTU funds were going to support this place, perhaps it made sense to drop in for occasional visits.

"No need to make ready, we shall greet them just as they are," Mrs. Withycombe said, moving towards the staircase.

"First let me show you our workroom." The captain steered the ladies away from the steps and opened the door of what must have been a large parlour and a dining room when this was a private home. The wall between had been opened up to make a single, large, sunny room where four young women sat at sewing machines with large baskets of work beside them. "Here we train our girls for useful work." The ladies all stood there for a minute looking; the girls kept their eyes on their machines. It was a clean, bright room and the clickety-hum of the treadles and needles made a pleasant sound.

Upstairs, when the captain led them up, was the room where the four babies slept in cots. Two had been born there in the home to girls who were with child when they came there, Captain Jost explained; two had come in with their mothers. Just now two of them were in their cots, one scooting about in the cot and making small grizzling noises, the other asleep. A young girl sat on a stool nursing a baby while another girl was down on the floor on all fours, face to face with a child who was old enough to crawl.

"Nancy, get up off that floor!" said the woman, who really did sound like a captain now.

The girl scooped up her child and cradled it on her hip as she turned a sulky, pouting face to Captain Jost. "I ain't doin' nothin' wrong, Ma'am," she said.

"Getting down on the floor with her encourages bad habits—in both of you," the captain said. "Baby should play quietly in her cot until you come up for a feeding; she must learn to be on her own and not expect to be picked up every time she cries. These ladies have

A Sudden Sun

come to bring us some blankets."

Nancy's baby reached out a hand for the pink blanket that Lily carried over her arm, but Captain Jost pushed the little hand away. "Perhaps a blue one for her, Nancy. That lovely rose colour would be nice for Aggie's little boy." She turned to the girl who was nursing the squirming baby.

Lily handed the blanket to the girl. She pulled the baby away from her breast; the front of her dress still hung loose.

"How old is your baby?" Lily asked as the girl wrapped him in the blanket.

The girl called Aggie dropped her eyes: there was no boldness in her stare as there had been in Nancy's, and Lily found that this girl made her less nervous. "Thank you, Miss," she said. "He's two months. Just startin' to sleep through the night. 'Tis some hard to hear them crying when we're not allowed in to feed them."

"Hard, but necessary," said Captain Jost. She reached out to pry the baby from his mother's arms. "Too much fussing spoils a child, Agnes. Go on now that he's fed, there's dishes to be done in the kitchen." Aggie scurried away as Captain Jost whisked the baby, now wrapped in Lily's pink blanket, to a nearby cot. The girl glanced back once before she went to the door, not at Lily or at the captain but at the cot. Her eyes looked like the eyes of a starving dog.

She's younger than I am, Lily thought, *Fifteen? Sixteen? What happened to her? Did she fall in love with a man who abandoned her? Or did some man take her by force?*

A year ago she would not even have thought of the latter possibility. Abby had been the one to tell her, when they were sixteen, that babies resulted from a man and a woman "having relations," though she did not explain what those mysterious relations might be. She said it was a bit like dogs or horses mating, only not as nasty. Lily had always assumed the act to be inevitably a part of marriage, or at least of romance. Mrs. Ohman had had to explain to her that girls of

189

Trudy J. Morgan-Cole

the poorer class were often forced into "relations" against their will. *More like dogs and horses after all*, Lily had thought.

"I have some hopes for Agnes," Captain Jost was saying to Mrs. Peters. "She's a good, biddable girl, and we should be able to place her in service if the baby dies. If he lives, we may be able to find a good home for him. It's a sin the orphanage won't take illegitimate children. They're the ones who need care the most." She led the ladies back out of the room and downstairs. "That one Nancy, now, she and her baby were living on the street—actually on the street—and she was selling herself for gin. They've been here six weeks but Nancy's still hard as nails, and she won't be parted from the child. I don't see much of a future for either one."

The squalls of babies followed them down the stairs, and even when the Rescue Home doors had shut behind her Lily still heard those cries in her head. The WCTU ladies swept into the carriages back to the Withycombe house for refreshments: Abby and Lily were to be collected there when Abby's mother had finished her calls.

Lily sat next to an open window—it was a mild day for October—and drank tea while she listened with half an ear to a conversation that Mrs. Withycombe was having with Mrs. Ritchie out on the verandah. Only when she heard the words "*Water Lily*" did she rouse from her reverie to listen to the older women.

"My dear, she's relentless," Mrs. Withycombe said. "She's come back to me twice this month looking for money to pay the printer. Of course I've put her off as gently as I can."

"But will we pay?"

"Well, you are the treasurer, suppose you tell me!" Mrs. Withycombe laughed. "Of course, she's not entirely reliant on us for money. Her husband puts some of his own cash into it, but it's not enough to keep it going. Mr. Macpherson was funding her for a while, because he's such a strong temperance man, but I've heard tell that he doesn't want the good name of the Royal Stores associated with votes for women, so that money has dried up. If she can't get anything from us, I don't think she'll be able to put out another issue."

"It's simply too damaging to the cause…in these times…all this suffrage rhetoric. Nobody wants to hear it."

"I'd rather not come out and say it, of course—so much better if one can avoid unpleasant scenes."

"I don't believe Jessie Ohman thinks so. I think she fairly relishes unpleasant scenes."

The women's laughter tinkled like little brooks running over stones. Smooth stones, like beach rocks that would never cut your foot or show a jagged edge but were as unyielding as the cliffs rising above.

"Well, if it comes to unpleasantness, you know you have my support," Mrs. Ritchie said. "And the support of most of the ladies, I think." The voices lowered to an indistinct murmur as the two women moved along the gallery to the door at the far end of the house, and as they did, Abby appeared in front of Lily with the news that her mother's carriage had arrived and it was time to go.

Lily said nothing on the ride home. She would have had little opportunity anyway, for Mrs. Hayward interviewed Abby about the visit to the Rescue Home with all the tenacity of a news reporter cornering a member of the House. "Those poor girls," she said when Abby described the young mothers with their babies. "Be grateful, both of you, that you've been raised in good homes with good morals and every advantage. The horrors that await poor girls with no one to protect them out in the world, well, let me just say that the plight of those girls you have seen today is by far—by *far*—the best possible outcome. How much worse it might be, well, I could not describe for innocent ears like yours, but many a young girl has been brought to ruin in this city, and…"

Lily stared out at the streets rolling by, at the construction sites where hammers were still swinging and brick being laid, men

191

working as late into the fall as they could on houses and shops being rebuilt from the rubble of the fire. Mrs. Hayward's monologue became as much a part of the background as the carriage wheels and the horses' hooves. Lily had, in fact, been deeply shaken by the sight of those poor girls. Could their fates change? Or once a girl fell, was she fallen forever?

But with a different part of her brain Lily couldn't stop hearing Mrs. Withycombe's laughter as she plotted to keep Mrs. Ohman from getting funds to print the *Water Lily*. Had they schemed like that to get Mrs. Withycombe elected secretary instead of Mrs. Ohman? All the speeches and pamphlets about women's franchise said that politics would be better, nobler, cleaner, if women were involved: women were too pure and fine for the dirty old game that men had been playing for centuries. But what if that weren't true? What if women, given a chance, were just as nasty and back-stabbing as men?

"You're lost in thought," Abby said, and Lily realized that Mrs. Hayward had fallen silent—they all had.

"It was the Rescue Home," Lily said. "Those poor girls, the babies…what will become of them?"

"Nothing good," Mrs. Hayward said crisply. "One can't drown babies like puppies or kittens, of course, but when I see children like that I can only think how much more merciful the Lord would be if He had taken them to Himself as soon as they were born."

"Mama! That's terrible!" Abby said. She sounded, for once, genuinely shocked.

"I know it sounds harsh, darling, but think practically. Think of their lives, their suffering. If there were a way to sterilise the poor it would be a great advancement for society. Ah, Lily, here we are. Give my regards to your poor mother, won't you?"

A Sudden Sun

CHAPTER TWENTY

"*I* WON'T GIVE give up, regardless of what anyone says," Mrs. Ohman insisted. Her voice was pitched to carry over a large roomful of listeners, though only Lily, Abby, and two other women sat in her dining room folding leaflets. "If the WCTU is no longer willing to support the cause of votes for women, then we need to speak directly to those who care about the real issue."

"So it is the real issue, isn't it, Mrs. Ohman?" Lily asked. This was, of course, the very charge that Mrs. Withycombe levelled against Mrs. Ohman as if it were a slander: that she cared as much about getting the vote as she did about ending the liquor trade.

"It's at the heart of all the other issues. I'm coming to believe that more and more since our defeat in the House," Mrs. Ohman said. "We can pick away at the liquor trade, homes for unwed mothers, better conditions for factory girls and whatnot. But the key to all these issues is to get women's voices heard."

She was even standing in speech-making posture, feet slightly apart and chest thrust out a little, a leaflet held in her outstretched hand.

"Well, it'll never happen if we don't get anyone out to meetings," said Mrs. Bulley, taking a new pile of leaflets from the tall stack. Mrs. Ohman had paid for these to be printed out of her personal funds. Lacking a paper to publish her views, and lacking a voice at WCTU meetings, her latest idea was to start a local branch of the Woman Suffrage League. With a general election just a few weeks away, Mrs. Ohman declared it was the ideal time for women to throw their support behind candidates who supported the suffrage cause.

So far, she had garnered little support, and her first attempt at a meeting had drawn only six women, including herself and Lily. Abby had begged off that one, but Lily had insisted on bringing her today to help distribute five hundred leaflets. The leaflets advertised an organizational meeting to be held in Gower Street church's temporary tabernacle. They had had to be printed up a second time because Mrs. Ohman had originally planned to use the parish hall of the Presbyterian Kirk until some members had complained and the minister had told her she couldn't hold her meeting there.

"Now we'll each take a few of these home to give out to ladies in our churches this Sunday," Mrs. Ohman said as their little procession reached the main shopping section of Water Street, "but apart from that, try to get them all handed out today. Lily, Abby and I will be here in front of Ayre's. The rest of you go on to cover the Royal Stores and Bowring's."

"I'm going into Ayre's," Abby said in Lily's ear. "I'll take a handful of leaflets to keep her quiet, but I've no intention of handing them out. I'm looking for a new hat. Come with me."

"No, I'm going to stay here by the door," Lily said. Unlike Abby she felt no embarrassment at being associated with the cause, though she did worry about being seen by someone who might report her to Papa. Still, as women came out of the shop, singly, in pairs, or with husbands, she joined Mrs. Ohman in thrusting leaflets into their hands. "Women deserve a voice in the most important issues of our day!" Lily said, over and over, while on the other side of the Ayre's entranceway Mrs. Ohman said, "Find out why Premier Whiteway is determined to silence women!"

Some women took the leaflets without looking too closely. Several waved their hands in protest or said, "No, thank you!" Lily saw several crumpled and tossed in the gutter just a few feet down the road, as though the ladies had thrown them away as soon as they realized what they were. A few ladies paused to read. Some stayed to argue. "Really, Jessie," said one who obviously knew her well enough to be on a first-name basis, "what would poor Nils say if he knew you were down here, a few feet away from his shop, hawking political pamphlets?" The giant watch and chain marking Mr. Ohman's watchmaking shop was visible just down the street from Ayre's.

"My husband supports my endeavours fully!" Mrs. Ohman said.

"But does he know you're passing out leaflets in the street?"

"Of course he does. Just because some people are married to men who want to keep them slaves to the household, doesn't mean we all are!"

"This is hardly the appropriate place for a Christian lady, a merchant's wife," said another lady.

"Isn't it? We who are fortunate enough to be well off are the very ones who need to speak out!" Mrs. Ohman said. "The Christian's job is not just to comfort the afflicted, but to afflict the comfortable!" Lily had heard that quote from her before: Mrs. Ohman said she had read it in an American newspaper and would embroider it in a pillowcase if she ever had the time to do fancywork.

A few more ladies stopped to join the discussion, including

Trudy J. Morgan-Cole

Mrs. Ritchie, Mrs. Withycombe's supporter. News of Mrs. Ohman's latest antics would be all through the WCTU by teatime, Lily knew.

"Is it going to break out into a street brawl? Because I'll want to write that up for the *Herald*," came a familiar voice close to her ear.

Lily looked around to see David just behind her. She thrust a leaflet in his direction. "We've been giving them to ladies, but I think members of the press should be informed too," she said. Her spirits, which had sunk as low as her boots when she saw Mrs. Ohman quarrelling with her opponents, were buoyant again. "Are you working this afternoon?"

"Just got away from covering a speech by Mr. Fox—going home to write up the article before press time tonight. Can you sneak away with me for a little while?"

"I promised Mrs. Ohman..."

"Very well, I'm going into Ayre's to look for, er, a pair of new shoes. If you happened to come in and pass out a few leaflets inside the shop you wouldn't be abandoning your post, would you?"

"Abby's in there, I suppose I ought to go find her."

"Of course you ought. You'll find *me* in gentlemen's shoes," David said, and slipped through the doors of Ayre's before Mrs. Ohman had a chance to see him—or so Lily hoped.

"Mrs. Ohman, I have to go into the shop and find Abby. Could you take the rest of these?" Lily said a few minutes later, pushing the rest of her leaflets into the lady's hands. Mrs. Ohman was explaining to a plump grey-haired lady that when God made the husband head of the wife, He never intended to make every man on earth the head of every woman. She barely registered Lily's defection.

Inside, Lily moved past shelves of pots and pans, through racks of ready-made clothes, to bolts of fabric and sewing patterns. Men's shoes and women's millinery were both near the back of the shop, and it was a peal of Abby's laughter that led her to the right aisle. To her surprise she found not just Abby but David there. David leaned, arms crossed, against a shelf while Abby posed with a feathered hat.

For just a moment, before either of them saw her, Lily froze. She knew that Abby would never consider keeping company with a man like David Reid; for all her talk of naughtiness, Abby had told the truth when she said she would marry the sort of man her parents would select for her. Yet the easy, open way she smiled at David caught at Lily's heart. If Abby wanted to ensnare him, she surely could. Why, out of all the inappropriate girls he could have fallen in love with, had David chosen quiet, straitlaced Lily instead of laughing, flirtatious Abby?

"Well, here you are finally," Abby said. "Come save me—I've been chatting to a strange man. If anyone saw me, my reputation would be ruined."

"Not too strange, I hope," David said. He was holding his hat by his side with two fingers and now laid it across his chest and bowed slightly. "Miss Hunt can introduce us properly."

It was true; Abby had once carried a message from David to her, and had conspired in a dozen intrigues to allow them time to be together, but they had never been introduced. Lily hesitated. Was it that stab of foolish jealousy that gave her pause, or was it the knowledge that when she introduced David to anyone else she knew, she chipped away at a barrier that separated their private world from her everyday life?

"Miss Abigail Hayward, this is Mr. David Reid. He writes for the *Evening Herald*."

"Pleased to meet you at last, Mr. Reid," Abby said, extending her hand. "And now I am going to be very busy looking at hats for a quarter of an hour. I find that the area over there behind the men's flat caps is quite secluded at this time of day, if you're interested."

David laughed as he led the way and Lily followed him to the secluded spot behind the caps. "You're right. She's every bit as shameless as you described her."

"Shameless? Did I say that?"

"Oh, she's not really. She just likes to appear it," he said, leaning against the wall with his hands in his pockets. "I know her sort—all men do. Pretty girl, good family, likes to flirt. Pretends to be bold and daring. But in the end she'll do exactly as expected—marry a nice boy, have a family, become her mother. They all do."

"Will I?" Lily looked into his green eyes as if she really could read her own future there.

"You're a different type entirely. No coquetry, no foolishness. But still waters run deep. If ever a girl were going to do the unexpected—to run off with the wrong sort of man, say—well, it wouldn't be your friend Abby there."

His words laid a cold chill over her, so real Lily shivered. "I don't know," she managed to say finally.

"Neither do I, I'm only speculating. Wishful thinking, you might say."

"Talk about something else. What was Mr. Fox's speech like?"

"Deathly dull. He wouldn't stand a chance except he's running against a man even duller than himself. I'm much more interested in what your friend Mrs. Ohman is doing out there."

"Trying to drum up support for her Woman Suffrage League."

"I thought you told me that was a bust?"

"She's calling another meeting."

"This is strong stuff." David unfolded the leaflet, still in his hand, and read aloud. " 'In Newfoundland today a woman who manages her own business can have no vote, no voice in elections, yet the most incapable man in her employ may do so. Women of

Newfoundland, demand your rights!' Marvellous. I'd like to print something about this, but it'll only get her in more trouble."

"I think she's past caring about trouble. She's tried the whole plan of catching flies with honey and it's gotten her nowhere so she's opening the vinegar bottle, and…devil take the consequences." Lily dropped her voice to a whisper, hoping no one else was nearby to hear her bad language.

But Abby was there, of course, her beribboned head poking around a towering display of men's bowlers. "I'm buying this hat," she declared, "then I'm going out to tell Mrs. Ohman that you were called home all of a sudden," she told Lily. "Then I'll make the supreme sacrifice of handing out leaflets in your place."

"No, you don't need to—"

"You're not expected back 'til dinnertime so it gives you an hour or so of freedom. Use it wisely."

"I'll walk you home," David offered, giving Lily his arm. "We'll take the back streets so Mrs. Ohman and her comrades are unlikely to see you."

It was a risk, going out in the public street in broad daylight, but they took the side entrance out of Ayre's and cut up over McBride's Hill and Church Hill, past the building sites of the churches, to avoid the busier traffic of Water and Duckworth Streets on a weekday afternoon. "We'll saunter through Bannerman Park," David offered, "and perhaps steal a kiss behind a tree. That is, unless you'd like to go in the other direction, come by my sister's place. Her and the young ones have gone out to her husband's family in Upper Gullies for the fortnight to look after the place while her mother-in-law's sick. I've been looking in on their place every day. We could go there for a few minutes' privacy—if you wanted."

Lily said nothing. "I'm sorry," David said after they had walked along for a silent moment. "I shouldn't have asked that. I didn't mean to imply you were the kind of girl who'd…well, who'd do

Trudy J. Morgan-Cole

anything she didn't think was right and proper."

But you already said I was, Lily thought, remembering their conversation. He had as good as said that while Abby would play the coquette's game, Lily was the one who would actually sin. Lily was the falling woman.

"I couldn't do that," she said. "Go there with you—to an empty house, alone."

"Of course not. I know that," he said. He sounded a little distracted now. After a moment he added, "and I wouldn't ask it of you. Only I'd like to believe, if you said no, that it was because you thought it was wrong. You, yourself, not because of what your parents or the church or everyone around you said."

She turned his words over in her mind before she replied. "How does anyone know what's right or wrong, without parents or church or God? You can't just make up right and wrong for yourself."

"What if we did, though? Just sort of puzzled it out for ourselves? You know, thought through the consequences of whatever we did, and answered to our own consciences?"

"Is that what you do?"

"I suppose I try to."

"I think it's different for a man," said Lily.

CHAPTER TWENTY-ONE

"LILY, PLEASE COME to my study after dinner." The words she had been dreading for months.

October was nearly over. Since July she had been meeting David in secret, relying on Abby's lies and subterfuge and, increasingly, on lies of her own as well. *It has to end sometime,* Lily thought, not for the first time. *Perhaps it ends today.*

Ends how? she wondered as she spooned the last bite of trifle into her mouth. Papa had left the table as soon as the main course was finished: he never stayed for dessert, though Sally made something every night—a trifle, a few slices off a fruitcake, jelly or blancmange. Tonight it was trifle, innocent, like everything in their household, of the rum that laced most people's trifles and cakes. Neither Mother nor Papa would allow alcohol in the house for any reason at all, not even medicine or cooking. They were stricter than even most of the Methodist teetotallers Lily knew. Abby's family were temperance people too, but Lily vividly remembered her first taste, as a girl of ten or eleven, of rum-soaked trifle in the Hayward house. It tasted wrong, like sin but not in a delightful, naughty way. Like something spoiled and sinister.

Her mother sat across the table, taking tiny bits of cream on the tip of her spoon, licking it off and putting it back, without ever plunging into the fruit and cake below. "Do you know why Papa wants to talk to me, Mother?" Lily tried.

Eleanor's eyes rested on hers just a moment, then slid away. "Somebody told him something about you that upset him."

"What? Do you know who, or what they told him?"

Eleanor laid down the spoon, put her hand to her forehead and rested it there, as if her head were too heavy to hold up any longer. For as long as Lily could remember her mother's headaches had been like an additional member of the family, far more vivid and strong and demanding more attention than Eleanor herself. Now Eleanor pushed back from the table, blinking two or three times. "Excuse me, I must go up and lie down," she said. In the doorway she turned back for a moment. "He's a very fair man," she said, looking at a vase on the mantelpiece rather than at Lily.

Her father, in the leather wingback chair behind his massive oak desk, looked like a fair man. "Lily, I heard something today that troubled me. I wanted to lay it before you, to give you a chance to explain yourself. The person who spoke to me might, after all, have been mistaken."

"Yes, Papa." She was going to ask, *What was it you heard?* But why should she ask? Let him chart the course.

He leaned back in the chair, frowned, made a church steeple of his fingers. Lily thought it looked as if he had been hoping for a teary-eyed confession or a protestation of innocence. "Mr. Withycombe called by my office on a matter of business this morning," he said. "His wife thinks very highly of you, you know, admires your dedication to the temperance cause. So he thought it was his duty to let me know his wife and daughter had reported seeing you the day before in a very…how will I put it?…a regrettable situation."

"Regrettable," Lily echoed. She could not regret, could never regret loving David. But she regretted the lying, the sneaking around, all the subterfuge necessary for her to enjoy those rare moments of happiness. She had not Abby's temperament. Oh, what would Abby do if she were called into her father's study at such a moment? Blithely deny it all, or burst into convincing tears and beg forgiveness?

The silence stretched out. Lily clenched her teeth, fought back the urge to add something helpful, to ease this difficult conversation.

"Regrettable. Yes, indeed." Papa bowed his head a little. The point of his steeple touched his chin now. "You remember, of course, when we had a similar conversation like this in the spring. I asked you to promise me that you would not see a certain young man, or have anything to do with him again?"

"Yes, Papa." Not one word more. She imagined turning a key in her chest, as if she could lock her secrets into her heart. She knew his next question would be: *Have you kept that promise?* And then she must decide how deeply to damn herself.

"It was Mrs. Ohman who spoke to me about your behaviour in that instance. And I told you then that while I disagreed with her on certain issues, I believed her to be a good Christian woman and I knew she had done right to speak to me."

"Yes, Papa."

"Some events in the months since then have led me to, well, to question my judgement of her. Mrs. Ohman, no matter how noble her intentions may have been at first, is no mere temperance crusader but a blatant agitator for women's rights. She misled the WCTU into seeking votes for women, and though Mr. Withycombe assures me that his wife and most of the other ladies involved now see their error, Mrs. Ohman has not. She continues to agitate for that cause, as I believe you well know, for Mrs. Withycombe informed her husband that yesterday afternoon you were standing on the pavement in front of Ayre and Sons with

Trudy J. Morgan-Cole

Mrs. Ohman, handing out copies of this—this piece of trash."

As her father passed the familiar broadsheet across the desk, Lily clenched her jaw again, this time to bite back laughter. She had been braced, in every muscle, for the news that Mrs. Withycombe had seen her walking arm-in-arm with David Reid along Duckworth Street, or seen her leaving the side door of Ayre's with him, or even—heaven forbid—seen David kissing her behind a tree in Bannerman Park. To be confronted instead with the crime of handing out suffrage pamphlets came as a heady relief.

"Is this true?" her father pressed as she read over again the words she had scanned so many times.

Lily looked up from the paper. With the greater danger removed for the time being, it was easy to confess to the lesser crime. "I'm sorry, Papa, but it is true. I did help Mrs. Ohman give out these leaflets."

"Surely you must have known I would not approve."

"I thought only about the fact that I believe the cause to be just."

"You mean that Mrs. Ohman has convinced you of it!" Papa shouted. Quicker than she could see, his hand-church collapsed into two fists, one of which he slammed on the desktop to punctuate his words. "That woman has led you astray! You have believed the cant with which she's filled your mind, and listened to her counsel over that of other, wiser women, like Mrs. Peters or Mrs. Withycombe."

"I think Mrs. Ohman is right. The battles will never be won 'til they are fought on the right ground. If we women don't have our voice in society and in government, then—"

"Stop parroting her!"

"I'm not a parrot! These are my own thoughts!"

"Silence! A girl of your age and experience has no thoughts of her own, save what she hears or reads, which is why it is so important to guard the influences to which you are exposed." Papa sighed and buried his face in his hands for a moment, his fingers twining through his thick grey beard. "I blame myself, in truth. I have been negligent, knowing that your poor mother is not well. I have trusted too much in women like Mrs. Ohman."

Now that he had taken some of the blame on himself, the advantage was tilting slowly back towards Lily. *If Abby were in this chair*, Lily thought again, *she'd know what to do.* Abby would know that now, with her father blaming his own poor guidance, it was the moment to humbly bow her head, promise to hand out no more leaflets in the street and to always be ruled by his good judgement.

But Lily was discovering in herself something more rebellious than Abby, in her most daring moments, could have dreamed up— a defiance that flared even when it was clearly against her own best interests. "Are you so certain, Papa, that Mrs. Ohman is in error? For I don't think so."

"That you can even raise such a question shows how far you have been led astray, Lily."

"Does it, Papa? I have searched the Scriptures, and I am convinced that God created woman with the same gifts and responsibilities as man, and—" her voice wavered a little under her father's incredulous glare "—and if I hand out leaflets or go to a meeting to urge that women have the vote, I believe I'm doing God's will."

"God's will! You see, Lily, this is what comes of the line of thought Mrs. Ohman has been feeding you. Determining God's will is not your task. Your job is to obey those in authority over you!"

It had taken all the courage she possessed to defy him. Now all she could do was to sit silently. Silent, without apologies or promises, without showing the contrition she knew he wanted to see. And it was easy to do that, because she felt no contrition.

His face grew harder and angrier, and then in a moment it seemed to melt, and he looked sad. "Oh, Lily, you are so innocent.

Trudy J. Morgan-Cole

When a young girl begins to think that she can defy her father's authority—when she begins listening to strong-minded women talk about women's rights and the like—it's the first step on a slippery slope. Every man knows what can happen to girls in such a situation. Be glad you have a father to protect you from that fate."

Lily thought of the young girls at the Rescue Home, who surely had had no god-fearing fathers to protect them. But whatever had led them astray, she doubted it was speeches about the rights of women.

More silence, while Papa waited for the words Lily would not say. The carriage clock on the mantle clicked like a disapproving tongue.

"You are not to see, or speak to, Mrs. Ohman again under any circumstances," Papa said at last. "You are not to attend any meetings to do with suffrage business, nor to read any literature about women's rights. Is that clear?"

"Yes, Papa."

"Nor are you to attend any more meetings except the Ladies' Aid, and then only if Mother is well enough to attend with you."

"I understand."

"And you have no more to say?"

"No, Papa."

"You may go to your room now."

Lily went to her room. Disbelief had burned off to anger before she set her foot on the first step. She climbed the stairs to her room, sat at her desk and pulled out writing paper and pen. She scribbled furiously for a few moments, tore up the paper and threw the scraps in the fire, and started again. A shorter message this time, only a few words. A place and a time.

She went down the back stairs, not passing Papa's study but going straight to the kitchen where Sally was scrubbing out the pots from dinner. "Hello, Miss," Sally said.

"Hello, Sally." Lily passed on through the kitchen door into the yard, wondering if her father had thought of setting Sally to spy on her. But then, he was all unaware of the possibility of secret assignations or messages sent to lovers. He thought only of keeping her away from political gatherings and strong-minded women.

She was out of the yard and onto Queen's Road, then up around the corner onto Garrison Hill before she found the right sort of grubby nine-year-old boy, the kind who would always carry messages for a penny. She gave him the address of David's boarding house and a penny, and he ran off as if his heels were on fire. Lily went back down the street, into the yard and back through the kitchen. Sally only nodded this time, and Lily went quietly up the back stairs to her own room.

Trudy J. Morgan-Cole

CHAPTER TWENTY-TWO

*T*HE HALLWAY WAS as narrow as the passage between the kitchen and pantry in Lily's house. It struck Lily that this was the poorest house she had ever set foot inside, and David's sister and her children were humble but by no means destitute. *I tell myself I want to help the poor*, she thought, remembering that day at the Rescue Home, *but I know nothing about them*. And she was here today, not as a bringer of charity but as an intruder, coming when Catherine would surely not approve of her being here.

She thought of leaving. No one had seen her arrive: David's note had told her to come at three, let herself in and wait 'til he arrived at three-thirty. She went into the small parlour, crowded with furniture, and eased herself onto the pink velveteen settee as if afraid to make any impression on any part of the room. Spidery ferns in brass pots draped the bookshelves: watering the plants was part of David's duties while Catherine and the children were away.

What if they came back early? They were due back on Sunday, but what if something had gone wrong in Upper Gullies and they came home sooner than expected? She imagined Catherine Malone, carrying bags and bundles and surrounded by her three young children, opening her front door, saying, "Miss Hunt! What are you doing here?"

When the door did open, she jumped. "It's only me! Are you here, Lily?"

She stood up as he came into the parlour. He stopped two feet away, took his hat off but made no move to hang it up or to step closer to her. It was the first time they had ever been alone with each other in a building, with a roof over their heads and a door shut between them and the world. Goosebumps rose on Lily's arms, but perhaps it was just that the room was cold.

"I was afraid you wouldn't be here." His voice sounded gritty, as if he had a sore throat.

"I almost didn't come." Lacking the excuse of WCTU activities or church women's meetings, she had found it difficult to get out of the house alone for a few hours. When she proposed a visit to Abby, Eleanor had offered to go with her and visit Abby's mother. A swift exchange of notes with Abby changed it to a walk in Bannerman Park—a subterfuge they soon would not be able to resort to, as the days were growing chillier. Eleanor decided her head was not strong enough for a walk and had contented herself with warning Lily to go to the park, meet Abby, and be back by suppertime.

Abby, of course, had to know the real plan. "You're actually going to his sister's house alone with him? Aren't you frightened?"

Yes, of course. Lily was frightened of almost everything now—frightened her father would catch her out in lies and discover the truth was so much worse than passing out women's suffrage tracts. Frightened that David would interpret her frantic note, her scribbled desire to meet him, as permission to take liberties. But frightened, most of all, that her life was closing in, narrow as the hallway of Catherine's house. Reverend Collins's letters arrived every fortnight and Lily knew that when winter passed and ships came to town again, he would come with a proposal of marriage. Then she would be a minister's wife out in Greenspond, and everything she loved would be barred to her forever.

So here she was in Catherine Malone's parlour on Cuddihy's Lane, alone with David Reid.

David bent down to light the parlour fire. When he had it going he put his arms around Lily, as if lighting the fire had dispelled more than just the chill of the room. She hadn't imagined the luxury of a kiss in an empty house, with no one nearby to see and judge. He pulled her closer 'til her body was pressed tight against his and she could feel every line, every muscle. *One flesh*, she thought. *Is this what it means?*

Then his lips left her lips and began to trace a path down her jaw, onto her neck. Shivers that had nothing to do with cold or fear of discovery travelled over her body. His mouth was at the collar of her blouse now, then his fingers were there too, unbuttoning, kissing the hollow of her throat, caressing bare skin that had never been touched since, she supposed, she was a baby in her mother's arms.

She wanted to touch, to feel his skin too, wondered what his bare chest and arms would look like with his shirt off. His shirt was untucked already. She slipped her hands beneath it, found his skin warm and a little sweaty to the touch.

"Lily. Ah, Lily." He pulled away from kissing her throat, closed his eyes and then straightened up and opened them again. "Lily. Wait."

She left her hands where they were, touching his bare skin, but he pulled them away and held them in his tightly.

"I'm sorry, I don't want to—to take advantage. I know you've got your—well, what you believe about right and wrong and all that. I didn't bring you here to—" His usually quick tongue groped for the words, words she didn't know herself. She knew there were coarse words for the things a man and a woman did but she had only heard them muttered in the street. What would she call it, if she talked about it? "The joys and troubles of the marriage bed," she had heard a lady of her acquaintance say once, but this was no marriage and there was no bed.

"It's all right." She didn't know if that was the truth or the boldest lie of her life. She couldn't think of the right words either. *Show me the pleasures of the marriage bed* would hardly do it. All she wanted was to keep touching him, for him to keep touching her. Surely they could do that and she could still keep at least some of her virtue intact.

"Are you sure?"

She shook her head. She wasn't sure at all. In fact she had come here thinking that she would have to be very strong, very firm with him if he tried to push her. Thinking of her virtue as that castle she had always been told it was, surrounded by a moat, the drawbridge securely pulled up and the walls guarded. But she thought instead of words like *yield, surrender.*

He unbuttoned her blouse and touched the curving line of the tops of her breasts, covered in the light fabric of her shift. Then his hands moved down to her waist, enclosed in the stiff bones of her corset. "Pardon my language, but this thing looks bloody uncomfortable," he said.

She giggled, feeling as she were gasping for air. "It is. You could...I wouldn't mind taking it off, but I'd need some help. Sally usually laces it up for me in the morning and unlaces it at night."

"You'll have to show me what to do."

She turned her back to him so he could untie the laces of the corset. It took some time; David kept interrupting the process to kiss the back of her neck. But every loosening of the laces was a release.

"Is that it? It just comes off then?"

Trudy J. Morgan-Cole

"No, there's a hook down there…I thought you'd be a man of experience." Now her voice was the one that sounded hoarse, her mouth dry.

He laughed a little. "Only a man of very little experience, and not with the sort of ladies that wear corsets. Ah, there it is, then."

And then she was free, free of the corset, and it was easy to slip off her shift so he could touch her bare skin. Her petticoat was on the floor at her feet. "Are you quite sure?" he said again, coming up from kissing her like a man breaking the surface of water, gulping for air. She was not at all sure and at the same time completely sure. Sure only that whatever right and wrong meant, whatever virtue was, whatever God might say, she could not stop touching David and feeling his touch, could not stop this lovely sensation that flooded through her whole body when he touched her bared breasts.

"Oh, God. My God, my God," he said. A man's hands on her breasts, and instead of shame she too, was *thinking My God, my God*. A hymn of praise. The only hymn that mattered, because commandments and rules were a thousand miles away, and all Lily wanted was David, here and now, skin against skin.

"It will hurt," he warned her later. They hadn't talked in what seemed a long time, absorbed by kisses and touch and the intricacies of her undergarments. Her clothes were a bed below her now, covering Catherine's parlour rug. "It's not like in some romance."

She knew nothing of the kind of romances that enumerated these details. Jane Eyre said only, "Reader, I married him," and left the rest to imagination. Cathy and Heathcliff, for all their talk of dark passions, had never even gotten in a bed together. Lily had no idea what to expect. But she was, now, absolutely certain, all doubt washed away under the touch of lips and hands. The drawbridge was down. There was nothing in the castle worth guarding. Everything good had been waiting outside all along.

CHAPTER TWENTY-THREE

*T*HAT NIGHT, LILY could not sleep.

She had arrived back home just in time for dinner, dazed and wary, sure that as soon as Papa looked at her he would know what she had done. But Papa was working late and Mother had gone to bed. Lily sat down in the dining room alone to the slices of roast pork, turnip, and cabbage. "The Mister says you're not to wait, he'll have his when he gets home later—about eight," Sally said.

So Lily was left with her own thoughts, and at first she felt nothing so much as drowsy, warm and tired. She thought she would go up to her room and curl up and sleep at once.

But when she had picked at a little of the pork she went upstairs, barred her door, and undressed. David had done a poor job of lacing up her corset again and she had rolled her hair up in a quick untidy bundle. Now she took it all off. First her blouse and skirt then, with some wriggling and squirming, the loosely laced corset, then her shift, petticoat, even her drawers—let her hair down, and stood looking at herself naked in the watery green mirror over her dressing table.

She had never done this before—stared at her own naked body rather than covering it as soon as her bath was over. She did want a bath, but if she rang for hot water Sal would wonder why she wanted a bath on Sunday evening instead of the usual Saturday night.

It had been a shocking mess. She hadn't known about that. Who would have told her? Mothers only told their daughters such things before wedding nights. A girl was prepared for a bridal bed, not for a pile of clothes on top of someone else's parlour rug. David had worried about the blood on her petticoats but she would pass it off as an unfortunate accident during her time of the month. The woman who took in their washing would hardly have cause to comment.

Now that she was here in the bedroom she was no longer sleepy. She washed up with the cold water in the basin and got out her nightdress and clean bloomers but kept drifting back to the mirror, looking at herself undressed, though the room was chilly. All the places he had touched her. It felt like there were warm red handprints all over her body, despite the chill in the air. And inside—somewhere deeper than her soul, she thought, a part of herself she'd never known before—was rubbed, raw and sore. Yet the pain felt triumphant in a way, like she imagined a man's muscles might feel after a hard day's work.

She had had, since childhood, a trick of turning one eye lazily inwards, a sight that used to amuse and horrify her playfellows, and when she did it her vision doubled. She did it now and there were two separate mirrors, two naked Lilies, each a little blurred. One was marked with shame and blood: she should have Hester Prynne's scarlet A on her skin. No, not A but F: Fornicator.

The other Lily was free of shame. She had been kissed, caressed, loved. The other woman bore the loss of her virginity like a badge of pride: a man had valued her so much, had awoken so much pleasure and delight from her body. She was no longer a child. This was the real marriage, after all: she belonged to David forever, and he to her.

Finally it was too chilly to stand there buck-naked staring at herself. Lily pulled her voluminous flannel nightdress over her head, put on fresh drawers and wrapped herself in a robe. She rang for Sally to build up the fire. "You're going to bed early tonight, Miss," Sally said, and Lily realized it was not even eight o'clock.

"I had a long walk this afternoon. I'm tired," Lily said.

"And you don't need any help getting ready?" Sally's quick glance took in the fact that Lily was already in her nightdress. She moved to gather up the discarded clothes from the chair.

"No, I managed on my own tonight. That'll be all, Sally."

She curled up on the bed, still in her robe, pulling the quilt over her. The dark outside her window grew deeper, the fire burned down to ashes, the lamp burned out. Queen's Road was quiet at this hour of night and with the window closed against the biting fall night she could hear no sounds from farther afield, though she knew that just as on summer nights there were dogs barking and people still awake, people laughing and swearing and fighting somewhere in the city.

When David kissed her good-bye in Catherine's hallway he'd said, "I love you fiercely. I always will. Never doubt it."

But she was, already, doubting it. She might not have read romances that described these intimate scenes in detail, but she had read plenty that described what happened to a girl once she had given up her virtue. Whether she was a scullery maid or an heiress, the end was always the same. The man who had stolen her virtue scorned her once he had had his way with her. Lily had surrendered her citadel and got nothing in return, not even a name or protection.

That was the bare truth of it. She had wanted it, begged for it even, but in the end he'd taken her virginity and now she was just

Trudy J. Morgan-Cole

an unmarried girl who was no longer pure. If David Reid didn't marry her—and how could he? Her father would never consider him for a moment—what good would she be to Obadiah Collins or anyone else? And the act they'd done today could get her with child. But how would she know? Was there some way to tell if she had fallen pregnant?

Who would know these things? A married girl asked her mother, but who did a fallen woman ask? She was sure Abby, for all her worldly posturing, knew nothing of such intimate matters. Abby was a little girl playing at being a woman. The time when Abby could be her confidante was over.

What she needed was to talk to some old, wise, anonymous midwife, or to look it up in a book. *What sort of book might have such information?*

"Oh God, please, please, if there's a way to stop it from happening, please let me not be with child. I'm sorry. I promise, I promise it won't happen again, please forgive me, I know I've sinned, but don't make me bear a child, I couldn't—I couldn't." She pictured herself on her knees at the Rescue Home, scrubbing like Nancy or Agnes, her baby wailing in a cot nearby. Would Mother and Papa really throw her out into the streets?

"Oh God, please," she begged again, and then was silenced by her own terrible hypocrisy. She was praying to be spared the consequences of a sin she had committed knowingly, eyes wide open, knowing it was a sin and fully intending to do it anyway. And she hadn't even been truly repentant, not until she thought about the chance of having a baby. Now she was crawling back to God, a shameful hypocrite.

Only with that thought did real repentance come, as if the two Lilies in the mirror had finally merged into one. With her sight clear again Lily saw what she had done, the deceitful, hypocritical creature that love had turned her into. She loved David, truly, but what was that love against the love of Jesus, the love of One who had died for her? She had believed she was called—had insisted to Papa, even, that she had a work to do for God in this world. And rather than doing that work she had allowed herself to be led astray, into paths of sin.

It took Lily a week to find the right book, after painstaking hours searching the shelves in her own family's library and then the bookshelves at Abby's house. She finally found a dusty old volume—*The Doctor's Home Companion*—at Abby's house, and spirited it away to her own house where she could read it without fearing someone would come into the room behind her. It told her that when a human female was impregnated, her monthly courses would cease for nine months. Lily knew her visitor was expected again in a few days, so if it came on time, she was safe. Until then, she lived in terror.

"There's something wrong with you," Abby insisted on the day she finally coaxed Lily over for a visit, though Lily's real reason was to return the book she had silently stolen. "You haven't tried to plan any secret trysts for nearly a fortnight. Have you quarrelled with him?"

"Of course not," Lily said.

"Because it wouldn't be entirely bad if you had, would it? I mean, a little romance is a good thing, but in the end, where can it lead? Better to break it off now than let it go any farther, isn't it?"

"Of course. I'll marry Reverend Collins, will I? Is that better?"

"Oh, don't be so cross," Abby said. "I'm only trying to make you feel better. The problem is that I'm not very good at it. I'm terrible, in fact. I'm so selfish. You're here, obviously broken-hearted, and all I can think of are my own silly affairs and whether I should say Yes or No to Frank Ayre."

The eminently eligible young Mr. Ayre had finally proposed, and Abby was taking time to think it over. He seemed to have every

Trudy J. Morgan-Cole

desirable quality—rich, hardworking, generous with his money, extremely respectable and kind to Abby. He wasn't even half-bad-looking, both girls had agreed in happier times when Lily was in the mood to join in making such judgements. "If only I were even a little bit in love with him!" Abby sighed tragically. "I don't believe in marrying for love, exactly, but I'm not sure I believe in marrying without it. Oh, there I go again, talking about my own troubles."

"They're every bit as real as mine are, and you've every right to talk about them," Lily said. She felt weary of the whole conversation, of Abby's company, of constantly turning over and over in her mind her fear, her sin, her guilt, and her raging desire to go back to Catherine's house with David and do it all over again.

She circled November 15th on her calendar—the day her visitor was due to arrive—but it did not come. Lily was usually fairly regular, keeping track of her days so she could plan in advance not to wear a white dress in summer, for example. A day late wasn't unusual and most months she wouldn't even have noticed, but that day felt endless. She was going to be cast out, branded as a scarlet woman. Papa would turn her out of the house. Where would she go? She could think of no one, nowhere. Except David, of course. And she hadn't replied to his notes for nearly two weeks, so surely he would give up soon and forget her.

The next day, she felt the familiar cramping in her lower abdomen, the dull backache. After she went to the lavatory, relief flooded her. She had her reprieve. It was tangible evidence that God had forgiven her. *Washed in the blood*, she thought, and laughed out loud.

The same day, Abby came for an unannounced visit. "I've gotten tired of waiting for you to come see me again. I think you're determined to become a recluse, and I won't allow it."

"I've told you, Papa's banned me from everything but church. He's afraid I'm going to turn into a crazed suffragist and start marching up and down Water Street with a signpost."

"Well, please don't do that, or I won't admit to knowing you," Abby said. "I must say, you're sounding a bit more like yourself today. Made up your quarrel?"

"There never was any quarrel."

"Ah, that must be why he gave me this." Abby pulled a small envelope out of her reticule. "I passed your Mr. Reid outside the rink on Parade Street last evening, and he pressed this into my hand."

Lily took it slowly. There had been two other notes delivered by boys on the street. The notes were short, scrawled, and pleading. She had replied to none of them. How could she explain, on paper, that she knew she had sinned and must never be alone with him again? She felt like a rag soaked in kerosene. She wouldn't even need to touch the flame, only get close, and it would all be over in a second.

"Are you going to open it?"

She did, but not until after Abby was gone. Lily had insisted there be no more discussion of David or the letter. They talked instead about Abby's decision, almost definite now, to refuse Frank Ayre.

She read it alone in her room.

> *Lily-white—I'd beg forgiveness if it made any sense—*
> *but how can I ask forgiveness for a thing I'll never*
> *regret? But your silence is rebuke and I've driven you*
> *away. God yes I'm sorry for that, will be sorry 'til I die.*
> *Can you send a note at least to say "Let me alone"*
> *and I promise I'll try? Put me out of this misery of not*
> *knowing, anyway.*
> *   – D (as in, Driven Mad)*

That was more than he'd ever committed to paper before— more dangerous, harder to explain if the note fell into the wrong hands. Papa's hands, of course. And she could end all this, all her

Trudy J. Morgan-Cole

guilt and torment, she could be Papa's good girl again if only she sent that note.

Three words: *Let me alone*. She could even send back his own note with those words circled; no need to add anything more of her own.

She burned the note. And she thought all night about writing a reply, but finally fell into an uneasy sleep: nothing written, nothing decided.

Sunday morning. The sermon was long and tedious. Lily looked at Reverend Mrs. Pratt, wondering what it would be like to be the minister's wife, having to sit and look pious and interested through one's husband's sermons week after week.

The final hymn over, the parishioners of Cochrane Street filed out through the doors slowly, stopping to shake hands with the minister. Papa, as always, had to stop and talk with half a dozen other men—often, Lily suspected, about business, even though he would have said he didn't discuss business on Sunday, much less in the narthex of the church.

She felt someone tug at her sleeve and turned around to see the last person she ever expected to see in church—David Reid.

"I'm sorry," he said, bending close to the brim of her hat. "I had to try. I know you didn't answer the notes, but…"

"Hush!" Lily looked around. Papa was nowhere in sight, but a few church ladies glanced over with interest. There was that nosy Daisy Gill, a spinster lady who used to teach Lily and Abby's Sunday School class when they were younger, peering over her fan at Lily and David while she chatted to Papa's cousin Sadie. "It's not—it wasn't because I was angry."

"So all is not lost?"

She couldn't hold back a smile. "Not all."

"I'm off work today like any good Christian. If I went to Bannerman Park about three, is there any chance I might see you?"

"I—I'll try. I will. I must go."

She walked to the park with Abby, who obligingly gave them half an hour alone. There were hardly any people in the park today, only children of the rougher sort playing. None of the well-dressed crowd who strolled here on a summer Sunday would come out under chilly grey skies to walk through leafless trees past dead flower beds.

"I don't dare to be alone with you," Lily said. "It was lovely but—it was wrong. You know it can't happen again."

David said nothing. She had her hand drawn through his arm, her fingers pressing so hard into the crook of it that she thought she must be hurting him.

Finally he said, "I know that you believe it's wrong. I know most people would think that."

"But you don't. You have your own commandments, I suppose."

David shrugged. "You might say that. Anyway the Ten Commandments don't have anything to say about what we did. It's not adultery, so the seventh doesn't apply."

"Hush!" Lily said, though no one was nearby.

"I'll promise you never again, if that's what it takes to stop you crying. But can I still see you, and talk to you? Or should we end it all now, since we know that it can't end well?"

She knew that was the simple truth, had known it for ages: it couldn't end well. Though seeing him in her church this morning had given her a ray of hope. He had come only to find her there, she knew, but perhaps if he came again—

He was a good man, she knew that. A good man to his core, no matter what radical things he said, no matter what they'd done together. He didn't call himself a Christian but he was not beyond saving, surely. If David could change, if he were a believer, nothing else would matter. That he was poor, that he had no family

Trudy J. Morgan-Cole

background, that he was only a newspaperman: no matter what Papa objected to, Lily would pay no attention. If only she could win him round—as the love of a good woman always did, in storybooks—to a life of faith and virtue, all would be well.

She said nothing of this aloud, of course. She knew David well enough to know that if she told him she was embarking on a crusade to save his soul he would either laugh or get angry, or both.

But it was her secret vow, and she made it before God on her knees that night. She would not have intimate relations with David again, she would pray every night for him, and every time they were together she would do all she could to influence him along the right path. The Holy Spirit would have to do the rest.

CHAPTER TWENTY-FOUR

"IS THERE ANY sight more degrading, any greater disgrace than that of the drunken man who squanders his pay packet in the tavern and weaves his way home to beat his wife and children? Why, the only thing more shameful is the female drunkard! You gasp in shock, ladies, but I assure you that such women exist—poor, depraved creatures, who neglect their own babies and deny their God-given natures for the gin-bottle. How could a woman further degrade her pure and noble nature than to embrace the demon drink and give herself over to its evil ways?"

Mrs. Withycombe's voice was clear and carrying. In the seat beside Lily, Mrs. Ohman stirred. Behind her fan she said in Lily's ear, "If poor women were given fair wages for their work and protected from husbands who beat them, they would never turn to drink."

Mrs. Withycombe heard the interruption, and glanced in their direction, but then turned her steely gaze back out at the WCTU ladies gathered before her who listened without arguing. She continued with her speech about the shocking spectacle of the drunken woman. Lily had noticed that few of the ladies argued directly with Mrs. Ohman these days. It was more common for her to raise a protest and everyone else to continue the discussion as if she had never spoken.

"Until the problems that cause drunkenness are addressed, railing at women for getting drunk does no good!" Mrs. Ohman piped, half-rising from her seat.

"Thank you, Mrs. Ohman, your views are well known," said Mrs. Withycombe. "Most of us are realists enough to know that we cannot reform society from the ground up. We can only address those areas to which we are called to relieve suffering."

"If we had the vote we'd be able to reform society from the ground up!" This time it was a bit louder than a whisper but not as loud as an interruption. She could easily be heard by women for the next two rows around her, but Mrs. Withycombe could ignore her if she chose to.

"Imagine the plight of this wretched creature, who knows in her heart that her duty is to her family, who day after day resolves that she will care for them, but who is lured away by temptation, time after time. Night-time finds her insensible in the gutter while her little ones cry at home, their bellies empty. Such is the curse of the demon drink, and women as well as men can fall into its chains! And it is our duty—nay, our calling, our vocation—to rescue such creatures where rescue is possible, to care for the abandoned children, and to end the ravages of the liquor trade once and for all!"

Hearty applause from most of the women. Lily's attention was caught by the tragic image of the woman who struggled to live up to her duty but was waylaid time and again by temptation, for Lily felt that she was that woman. Only she was tempted not by gin or rum, but by a man's caresses. She, too, made resolutions to reform, told herself over and over that she would never let it happen again. And, over and over, she tossed aside all her resolutions and ran to her lover's embrace.

"I have simply had enough," said Mrs. Ohman, standing up. Mrs. Withycombe, still in the full flower of her speech, hesitated, glanced at Mrs. Ohman, but went on speaking. So did Mrs. Ohman, not quite at the pitch to carry to the whole hall but certainly clearly enough that anyone who wanted to listen could hear. "A full year since our bill was defeated in the House and we are farther than ever from achieving our goals, farther than ever from making a real change. How long are we going to muddle about being—*ladylike*?"

"Mrs. Ohman!" Mrs. Withycombe broke off her speech. "If you have something to say, please save it for the discussion afterwards. You are out of order!"

"Order! The things we submit to, in the blessed name of order!" Mrs. Ohman said, and shuffled past the seated ladies to the end of the row. "I've tried to preserve order all my life and where has it gotten me? Nowhere! Perhaps the time has come, after all, for a little disorder!"

The hall was far more silent than it had been for Mrs. Withycombe's speech. Every eye was on Mrs. Ohman, waiting to see what kind of disorder might be about to break forth. But all that lady did was turn with a swish of her skirts and stride out the back entrance.

Silence hung in the air for a moment after the heavy doors banged shut behind her. Lily wondered whether she ought to leave in solidarity with Mrs. Ohman. But that would attract attention. She had finally wrangled from her father permission to begin attending WCTU meetings again after months of apparent good behaviour. Everyone in town would know by morning that Mrs. Ohman had made a scene and stormed out of the meeting. If Lily got up and left with her, Papa would find out.

Mrs. Withycombe cleared her throat. "Ladies, just because some among us choose to forget their womanly natures and attempt to create the kind of scandal and uproar we associate with men at

Trudy J. Morgan-Cole

political gatherings, does not mean the rest of us should follow suit."

"Hear, hear!" shouted Mrs. Peters, then subsided, perhaps realizing that she was behaving a little like a man at a political meeting herself.

"We are women, and not politicians, nor agitators. We are here to do the simple and humble work to which God has called us, lifting up the downtrodden, feeding the hungry, clothing the naked, and comforting the afflicted."

Her choice of words was perhaps unfortunate, since Lily vividly remembered Mrs. Ohman's favourite saying about afflicting the comfortable and thought other ladies might recall it too. Mrs. Withycombe was doing all she could to make clear that the WCTU was not in the business of afflicting the comfortable.

Lily had no time to stop and chat with anyone during the chaotic tea-time after the meeting, for Papa's condition upon letting her attend the meeting was that Evans drive her to the front door of the Temperance Hall and collect her there exactly two hours later. Papa was still keeping a very close eye on what kind of meetings Lily attended, never suspecting that under the cover of Sunday afternoon visits with Abby she had managed four times to slip away and spend an hour alone with David at his rooming house.

It had to be Sunday: her sin was compounded by committing it on the Lord's Day. Only on Sunday was David likely to be free all afternoon. Papa, of course, was also off work on Sunday, and in the cold winter months she could not plausibly claim to be going for a walk in the park. But she had established a habit of going visiting to Abby's house, and often from there paying calls on others. If the odd time she managed to slip away and go to a rooming house on New Gower Street, she had not yet aroused her father's suspicion.

All this subterfuge was made more difficult by the fact that Lily kept promising herself she would never be alone in a private place with David again. And since public places carried the greatest risk of discovery, this meant in practice that she rarely met him at all— once or twice a month, at most, ever since that fateful day back in October when she had yielded up her virtue to him.

If only they could have courted openly, as Abby courted her many beaux, going to concerts and lectures together. But that kind of courtship was reserved entirely for Obadiah Collins's spring visit. If only the hours spent with Reverend Collins could have been with David instead, Lily thought. Hearing the Methodist College orchestra saw its way through a Mozart symphony, listening to a debate on "Has the Human Condition Deteriorated Since the Days of Our Ancestors?" or even sitting on the velveteen settee in her family's parlour, would have been bliss with David. They could have talked, then, long and freely, of all the subjects they wrangled over in their stolen moments together. In the privacy of the parlour with David she could have properly taken all his objections to organized religion, even his questions about the very existence of God, and answered them, one by one, in a rational fashion.

And in her parents' parlour, she would not have been tempted to illicit embraces. There, he could have seen her for the pure and virtuous girl she had once been. Her godly example, coupled with the power of her arguments, would have won him over to sign the temperance pledge and take his place beside her in the church pew. Lily often went back and read over Mrs. Ohman's lovely story of Alida in those old issues of the *Water Lily*, and knew that she could have been an influence for good over David just as Alida had been over James. If only they had been able to meet freely and respectably, to talk, not forced to set up secret trysts and hide in corners. If only.

It was a lovely image, that idea of herself keeping company with David openly, gradually winning him to the light. So different from

227

the stilted conversations she had had with Reverend Collins when he visited, when most of her effort had been directed towards steering the conversation away from personal matters so he would not propose to her. So different, too, from her real relations with David, to which, when she thought about them, she could only attach the adjective "sordid." It had been all very well in summer when they could walk about the streets or lanes, but in winter they could only be outside for a quarter hour at most before David would suggest his rooming house. "We can talk there. I can bring you up a cup of tea." Lady callers were, of course, not permitted, but the landlady was famous for turning a blind eye.

They had been there again just this Sunday past, and Lily had insisted, even as they passed through the door of the room, even as she sat down on a hard-backed chair and tried to ignore the bed that took up most of the room, that they were only there to talk. He was not forceful. Yet somehow they were never in that room more than a quarter of an hour before they were in each other's arms, arguments and debate forgotten, all Lily's resolutions heaped around her in as crumpled a pile as her petticoats on the floor.

She never told David how ashamed she was, how bitterly she prayed for forgiveness. The sin and repentance was all between her and God, nothing to do with him: in David's eyes what they did was not even a sin.

Five times. Five times, now, from October 'til May, she had had relations with him. Jesus had said to forgive the sinner seventy times seven and presumably He would do the same, but what if all the sinner's promises to mend her ways were a hollow sham?

The carriage pulled up in front of the house and Evans helped Lily down. It was May now, but unlike the blooming warmth of last May when she'd gone with Mrs. Ohman and the others to the House to hear their bill being defeated, this was a raw, chilly May— there hadn't yet been a warm day that felt like spring. Leaves on the trees were still clenched into buds, weeks away from opening. Though it didn't get dark now 'til nearly seven in the evening, the sky above remained a uniform white, the clouds rarely pierced by sunshine. Last year's May had been a hopeful one, full of possibility: this one was grim, locked tight as a fist. Lily wondered if people in other places were always confident that summer would come, year after year. She herself always hid a tiny seed of doubt: perhaps this would be the year summer would bypass Newfoundland entirely, and they would slide straight from one winter to another without even a few short weeks of relief.

The house echoed with emptiness, as it always did. If she stood in the hall and listened for a minute she could hear sounds behind the emptiness: the ticking of the grandfather clock, the muffled thuds and clangs as Sally prepared the dining room for dinner, the creak of a chair in the study above that proclaimed Papa was home from work. She listened for a sound that indicated her mother, but there was none. Silence was Eleanor's signature note.

A note from David came after supper, delivered by one of their trusted street-urchins as Lily went out in the garden. There was no great pleasure in walking in the garden with the weather they were having now, no flower beds to check on although the daffodils had bloomed and gone in a sudden burst of optimism a week earlier. The boy's name was Johnny. He looked about ten years old and had ears that stuck out under a cap two sizes too big. He ran down the lane behind their garden and passed an envelope, much creased and folded as if he'd been carrying it for days, through the fence palings. Once he had left it for her stuck into a crack in the palings. The next time she saw him after that, Lily had rapped him on the head with her knuckles and refused him a penny. It was too dangerous, she told him, to leave letters lying about.

"When did the gentleman give you this?" she asked now.

The boy shrugged. "Dunno. Yesterday, day before."

Trudy J. Morgan-Cole

"You'll have to do better than that to earn your penny."

"He already give me two."

"Yes, but you expect another one from me, don't you?"

Johnny shoved his hands deep in his pockets. His cap slipped down over his eyes as he screwed up his forehead with concentration.

"Today's Thursday, ennit? So it was Tuesday he give it me. I seen 'em outside the Colonial Building after all the bigwigs come out, and then I come by two, three times last night but you wasn't out here. So, Tuesday. Day 'fore yesterday. I don't mess around, Miss. He gives me a note, I comes and gives it to you first chance I gets."

"I know, I know," Lily said, handing over the penny. She wasn't sure why she felt the need to grill the boy, only that when she held the note in her hands and read David's words she wanted to imagine him writing it, to know what day it was and what he was thinking when he'd penned them.

> *Lilith—Been thinking of you since Sunday afternoon, wishing it were still Sunday afternoon. O that all of life could be one endless Sabbath day, as the hymn-writer says of heaven, though no doubt he was planning different activities. Forgive me again—do I ever speak to you, or write a letter, without running up an endless bill of impertinence, of idle words for which I will be held account at the judgement? But you know the only judgement I fear is yours—and I count on clemency, I gamble on grace. When, oh when will I see you again?*
>
> *Write when you can. The faithful Johnny is more than eager to earn his pennies. He is as trustworthy as God, for I have told himself myself that if he betrays us, I will hang a millstone about his neck and throw him into the harbour. I told him it was in Scripture and he believed me, for he'd heard something to that effect in*

Sunday School once when forced to go. Do you see
what foolish prattle you've reduced me to? To which
you have reduced me. Forgive the preposition—it's
out of place, as I am when from you I am apart.
With foolish yearning…
– D (as in Desire).

She read it over and over. She loved his letters, even the hastily scrawled notes. She wished she could lock them in a secret drawer and read them over and over. Her actual time with him was so short and his notes were like being with him for the few moments they took to read. But while she had kept a few—the most non-committal ones she could find, in which no eyes but her own would ever see anything compromising—she burned almost everything he sent. What if Papa were to find this—or, more likely, Sally, who could not read, found it and felt duty-bound to turn it over to Papa on the strength of the fact that it looked like a man's writing? The signature alone would damn her. D as in Desire! Lily knew *desire* was a word she should not even think, nor should anyone think it in connection with her. "Your desire shall be for your husband, and he shall rule over you," God had told Eve in the garden. No husband, no desire. Unruled and unruly desire was a dangerous thing, and it flamed through her like the tongues of fire that licked and consumed David's note as she burned it in the grate before bedtime.

Trudy J. Morgan-Cole

CHAPTER TWENTY-FIVE

"*I*F I SIT on the lid of the trunk, do you think it will close?" Abby wondered. "No. I'm too delicate, aren't I? Maybe I'll call Wilson up and have him sit on the lid. That would work. He's quite hefty."

"Or you could just pack fewer things," Lily suggested.

"Oh, you *are* adorable. Although, now that you mention it, I suppose it's a bit silly to pack gowns from St. John's to wear in New York. I'll probably toss them all on the fire my first week in the city."

Abby was off to New York in the height of summer. "Hot and dirty, but better than cold and dirty, which it will be if I stay here," she pointed out. She was staying until at least Christmas, "If not forever," she told Lily. "I fully intend to find a millionaire and marry him. Aunt Sarah has half a dozen picked out for me to sample." Two years of flirting and coquetry among the well-off young Methodists of St. John's had earned her proposals from Frank Ayre, Norman Winsor, and two others so inconsequential Lily couldn't even remember their names. But Abby had rejected them all.

"What will I do here alone? Without you?"

"Poor thing. You'll pal around with Martha Withycombe 'til you expire of boredom, I suppose. But soon I'll be married and in an apartment of my own, and you could come to stay. You will come, won't you? When I'm married? If you're not married yourself by then?"

"I can't see how I will be," Lily said.

Abby stopped flitting around the room, sat down on the still-unclosed trunk lid, and took Lily's hand. "Darling, you know I never speak seriously because I believe serious talk is a kind of death. Don't contradict me: it is. But I will, just this once, because I'm going away tomorrow and I don't know when I'll see you again. You must give this up—this thing with David Reid. You know it can't go anywhere, and as long as it goes on you won't even look at any other perfectly suitable man. And there are other men, not just the Reverend. Remember, wherever there's a Mr. Collins, there's a Mr. Darcy lurking somewhere near by."

"And you mean to tell me David Reid is no Darcy."

"Darling, I'm afraid he's more of a Wickham, and meanwhile there are perfectly nice boys from good families who would love to court you. We're twenty years old, Lily. The future is upon us."

"It all sounds very easy and practical when you put it like that."

"It is easy and practical. Everything is. You just have to put aside your feelings, or pretend you don't have any."

Papa still suspected nothing. All his parental wrath was focused upon Mrs. Ohman and the spectre of women's rights agitators. As Lily had expected, he heard about Mrs. Ohman's stalking out of the WCTU and chastised Lily for going even though he had given her permission. Mrs. Ohman's attempts to start a Suffrage League had failed over and over. Bookings for halls were refused, ladies failed to show up when a hall was booked, and no new copies of the *Water Lily* had been printed since November of last year. Meanwhile, Lily had managed two more secret meetings with David—once to the boarding house where, again, she proved unable to resist temptation, and once just to walk about by Rennie's River on a chilly grey day. That had been the previous Sunday, and she was sure everything would be better if they stayed clear away from the possibility of transgression. But instead they'd had a terrible argument—she had actually shouted at him—and though they both apologized, she had been in tears when they parted.

"I won't even have to end it," she told Abby now. "It will end of its own accord, for without you to cover for me, how will I ever see him again?"

"It's all for the best," Abby said. "Please say you'll come see me in New York."

"I will," Lily said, but it seemed as unreal as saying that some-day she would die and go to heaven and pluck the strings of a golden harp. It could happen. It might happen. It was impossible to feel that it really would happen, at least anytime soon. Everything felt remote and distant. From the first time she had succumbed to David's embraces she felt her life had been held in abeyance, unable to move forward or back.

Or perhaps that feeling had begun even before the affair with David; perhaps she had become suspended, like a fly in a spider's web, the night she sat in the gallery of the House of Assembly and heard the learned men strike down the bill for women's votes. Until then Lily had believed she was working for something, that she was part of a movement that would eventually prevail, that would change the world. Now here was the world unchanged, and Lily unable to fit into it. She had girded herself to ride into battle in a war that had not been declared, after all: her army had withdrawn from the field and she was left with armour and a useless sword.

Pretty metaphors, of very little use. She stood up. "I'd better get home. Mother said four o'clock."

"Kiss me. And don't forget to write," said Abby.

Three days after Abby's departure on the steamer for New York, Lily was shopping with her mother, who for once felt well enough to go out, in the Royal Stores. She saw Mrs. Ohman looking at bolts of cloth and went up to her, since Mother was absorbed in trying on boots.

"Did you go to last week's WCTU meeting?" Mrs. Ohman wanted to know.

"No, Papa's forbidden it again, after you made your grand exit the last time."

"Well you know, you're not missing anything. I didn't go myself, but I'm sure it was more of the same. Mrs. Withycombe and her crusade to make the WCTU so respectable that no one dare disapprove. Whoever changed society by trying to be respectable? Name me one person."

Lily could not.

"Anyway I don't think the politics of my hometown will concern me much longer," Mrs. Ohman said. "Mr. Ohman is in Montreal, looking at a business opportunity there. I'm sick of this town and everyone in it—except for you, Lily darling, and a few others."

"I'll be sorry to see you go, even though I'm not supposed to be talking with you at all. Papa doesn't like your influence."

"Your Papa and others like him will wake up someday," Mrs. Ohman said. "I only fear it will be too late. But what about you, dear Lily? You mustn't languish. If we can't work for the vote we must find other work to do. And you have prospects, haven't you? What about that nice young minister friend of yours—is he coming to town again? You know, a minister's wife can have a great influence within the community."

Abby was gone. Mrs. Ohman was thinking of going. David was kept busy reporting political stories: the fall election had given Premier Whiteway a majority but results were overturned in more than a dozen districts, so by-elections were being held almost every week. The end result was that there would likely be a new premier and government, and anyone who made his living reporting on politics was busy attending meetings and writing about them at all hours. He still sent notes by way of Johnny every few days, most of which Lily dutifully burned after reading.

Summer came, finally. Grey skies with cool sunshine filtered through rain. It wasn't much of a summer, but it was July now and the days were as fine as they were going to get.

"Things happen in threes," her mother said one day, opening the mail. Eleanor often spoke in clichés. Lily wondered was it because it took less energy than inventing original things to say. The news that things happened in threes—bad things of course; there was no need to modify the noun—was often coupled with the observation that this life was a vale of tears. The letter announced the death of an ancient great-aunt—ninety-five if she was a day— in Harbour Grace.

"Well, poor Aunt Hepsie gone—things do happen in threes, they say."

Lily rarely challenged her mother, but she was so restless that even an argument with someone so completely yielding seemed possible. "Why, Mother, what were the other two?"

"The other two?"

"You said things happen in threes. If Aunt Hepsie was the third thing, what were the first two?"

"Uncle Tom Gill, in the spring, and then your grandfather's storehouse catching fire."

The storehouse, like Uncle Tom and Aunt Hepsie, was in Harbour Grace, so it hardly seemed an immediate crisis, especially as no one had been hurt. But Eleanor said she had a dread of fire, even hearing about it, since the terrible one here in town two years ago. Two years! Had it really been so long?

"Ah well, this life is a sad vale of tears," she said, folding the letter.

"Then you must be glad Aunt Hepsie is free of it," Lily said.

"Glad? No, I can't quite be glad, but she's better off, poor soul." Eleanor stood, tucking the letter into her skirt pocket, and went upstairs. Papa was in the study; Lily was alone again in the parlour. She was reading Emerson's essays, which she found pretty slow going. Emerson had come up in an argument she'd had with David a few weeks ago—the last time she saw him in fact—and she wanted to understand his writing for herself rather than just hearing about it second hand from him. Most of the books he mentioned she wouldn't have dared bring in the house. Imagine if Papa caught her reading Darwin or Karl Marx! But Mr. Emerson seemed safe enough, and David had loaned the book to her, so it was like holding a little piece of him.

She had taken to writing longer letters in response to his notes. After all, he had no need to burn her letters—she could be as indiscreet as she liked, as long as she kept the letter safe from discovery between the time of writing and the time of sending.

Thinking of David, and letters, and Johnny the messenger boy, drove her out into the garden to read, though it was a bit chilly and she had to go back for a shawl. It really was not a very promising July. She thought almost with longing of the July day of the fire, how hot and dry it had been. Certainly a fire starting today would have a harder time devouring the town, with everything so damp and soggy.

Sure enough, after she'd been out there about an hour grappling with *The Over-Soul*, she heard, "Hsst! Miss—I got sumpin'."

"Hush," she said, going down to the back fence where Johnny waited in the lane. "I've told you to be quiet."

"I am bein' quiet. You got a letter for me? I got one fer you."

Lily had written three pages to David the other day and sent it

Trudy J. Morgan-Cole

off with the boy: she never allowed herself to write until she'd heard back from him. She didn't want to seem like some pathetic lovelorn girl, badgering him because she had nothing better to do than sit around writing love letters.

The boy passed an envelope through the slats of the fence to her. As always she shivered a little, taking it from him. Her father had never wandered out into the garden or glanced out a window during one of these exchanges but she was always aware that he might do so. If he were to appear, demand she hand over the letter, the game would be up.

> *Waterlily—*
> *I know it's not been easy for you to get away since*
> *the butterfly has flown. But I must talk with you.*
> *Something has arisen—an opportunity golden for me,*
> *one I can't pass by. I don't know what it will mean for*
> *you—for us. Have I said too much? The family is*
> *away again. Can you come to that house—you know*
> *the one I mean—on Saturday afternoon? I must see*
> *you alone and tell you what's happened.*
> *– D, as in Desperation*

D as in Desperation? She had told him before of the need to be discreet in letters and he had taken that as an excuse to make up silly codes—"butterfly" for Abby was suitable enough, she supposed—while leaving the most damning sentence of all—"I must see you alone"—blazing on the paper. She twisted the note into a knot in her hands while she walked back and forth in grass still damp from the morning's rain, the hem of her dress getting soaked. What kind of golden opportunity did he mean?

He wanted to meet at Catherine's house. She had never been in that house since the first time they met there, months ago. All that time she had been living a life of sin, telling herself it would be all be redeemed when he was redeemed. Now he spoke of desperation,

and of an opportunity he could not pass up.

The message came on Thursday. Where could she claim to be going on Saturday afternoon, when no one would lie for her? Lily still had no plan when she came down to dinner on Friday evening to find her father chatting to Reverend Obadiah Collins.

"Ah, here's Lily," said Papa in a tone that indicated she had been the subject of their conversation. "Lily, Reverend Collins came to town on today's steamer. He's staying 'til the middle of next week. I've invited him to have dinner with us, and given him permission to take you and your mother for a drive tomorrow afternoon. Mother thinks she'll feel well enough to pay a call on cousin Sadie, so you and Reverend Collins can drive out there with her. She has a lovely garden and you young folks can have a pleasant stroll while Mother and Sadie visit."

Saturday was the nicest day they'd had yet this summer. Two years to the day, Lily thought, since that scorching July day of the fire, the day she had met David. Today was warm, not hot, a model day for a drive out to the far western reaches of the city, where Cousin Sadie lived in a large house at Riverhead. She did have a lovely garden; the roses were budding and the rhododendrons and laburnum in full bloom. Mother looked pale and drawn but she and Sadie sat on the back verandah wrapped in shawls, discussing the shocking story in last week's newspaper about a young woman who, against parental warnings, had been seen riding a new-fangled bicycle about the streets in company with a young man. "They'll be wearing bloomers in public next, you mark my words," Cousin Sadie said. She shot a sharp look at Lily as if to ensure she was not about to strip down to her drawers and hop onto a bicycle.

"Excuse us while we take a little stroll," the Reverend said to the ladies, and led Lily to a bench at the bottom of the garden. Why, Lily wondered, was it acceptable to go for a walk with a young man but not for a bicycle ride?

Trudy J. Morgan-Cole

"What a pleasant spot," Mr. Collins said. "So civilized."

"Unlike Greenspond, you mean?"

"Well now, I truly believe God has called me to work on our remote little isle, for the time being, anyway. From Greenland's icy mountains to Greenspond, Bonavista Bay, eh Lily? All the way my Saviour leads me."

Lily wondered if he would be able to string together an entire conversation using only hymn titles. "Anywhere with Jesus you can safely go, I suppose," she said.

He chuckled, a dry sound like the wind passing through a heap of autumn leaves. "But I will admit," he said, "that it is a pleasure to get into town, to drink from the well of civilization, as it were. There's such need, Lily my dear, you would not believe, among the fishermen and their families—well, you know a little of it, for I've described it in my letters."

She had not read his letters with much attention. She knew that she ought to care about the plight of the poor fishing families in the outports as much as she did about those in the slums of St. John's, but when the concern came attached to the unctuous person of Reverend Collins it was difficult to take it to heart.

"But for that very reason there's little out there in the way of intelligent conversation or, well, the gentler influence. My parsonage, like my life, wants the woman's touch, if you get my meaning."

Belatedly, horribly, Lily did get his meaning. If her thoughts had not been so consumed with David's letter, their planned meeting at Catherine's house and the trouble of how to arrange it, she surely would have seen that this meeting, too, was carefully arranged. When had her mother had the energy to pay a call? Why were she and Reverend Collins needed to drive Mother to Sadie's house? Because Mother was the perfect chaperone who would understand the need to leave them alone in the lovely garden.

He was taking her hand in his. "I hope you don't mind—I know I'm taking liberties, but our correspondence these long winter months has given me reason to hope—"

Yes, she had written dutiful letters in reply to his. Papa expected it, and it had seemed harmless enough. Surely, she had thought, he would not propose by letter. And sure enough, he had made a trip into town just to do it.

"...so I've dared to hope that you might, perhaps, consent to share my life and my ministry. I've prayed about this, Lily, and of course I've spoken to your father first, set your mind to rest about that. He and your mother would be sad to see you leave town, but they both believe you would be a wonderful partner in ministry. Will you make me a very happy man and agree to be Mrs. Obadiah Collins?"

She had never found the name Obadiah particularly funny before but suddenly, intoned so solemnly by its owner while he spoke of being "a very 'appy man," it stood out as the funniest thing in what was, in some ways, a rather funny speech. Funny, that is, if it were being said on stage, by the pompous clergyman character in a farce. Less funny if it was your real life, and the man was actually sitting beside you on a bench—thank goodness he hadn't knelt!— holding your hand in his large sweaty one.

She looked up at the verandah. Mother and Cousin Sadie were both bundled in shawls, fanning themselves vigorously. They glanced down into the garden just as Lily looked up. They knew. Mother must have told Sadie the plan. The plan everyone had known but Lily.

In the distance, a church clock struck three. Was David waiting for her at Catherine's house?

"Reverend Collins, this is—it's such a shock. I can't—I mean, I haven't thought at all...forgive me."

"No, no, forgive me. I ought to have given a bit more warning,

Trudy J. Morgan-Cole

but—it's so rare that I get into town, and I didn't wish to leave such an important question to a letter. Of course you may have time to think—I assure you I didn't assume we would announce our engagement this very day." It was clear from his face and tone that he had assumed exactly that. He still had not let go of her hand.

Lily's stomach clenched; she thought she might throw up. "I want to go home—I'm sorry—this has all been such a surprise," she said. She hoped that he would continue to attribute her reaction to maidenly modesty rather than aversion. But he would have to know the truth sometime. Why not now? It was too final, to tell him a definite no and then face Papa's disapproval.

"Of course, of course, my dear. Only tell me that you'll hold the question in your heart and won't leave me without hope. Can I ask that of you?"

"Oh, I don't know—I'm terribly confused. Please don't—I really don't want to think about marriage at all. I don't feel ready. I don't—can you please drive me home?"

Mother was more than ready to leave; the visit, short as it was, had already tired her out. She hesitated, though, searching first Lily's face and then the Reverend's, as if waiting for a happy announcement that did not come.

As they drove past the post office on Water Street a clock somewhere struck four. An hour. All that had happened in only an hour.

"Mother?"

Eleanor opened her eyes to look at Lily.

"I'm going to ask Mr. Collins to let me off, to walk home. I'm very—I have a great deal to think about. I need some time to clear my head, and a walk would do me good."

"My dear, I couldn't possibly." It was the Reverend who answered, turning back to look at her. "This far from your house— unattended..."

"Mother, please? I need an hour to myself, and it's such a fine day, I'd like to walk."

"Mrs. Hunt, I insist—surely it's not safe for Lily to walk so far on her own?"

"She's a strong girl, and it's broad daylight," Eleanor said. "Just stay to Water Street, Lily, don't go off on any side streets."

When the carriage was out of sight Lily immediately began climbing the steep side-streets towards Cuddihy's Lane. She wondered how long David would wait for her. It wasn't a long walk: she arrived at quarter past four.

"I didn't think you were coming," he said. "Did you walk? Is anyone expecting you?"

Lily shook her head and sank down on the settee. David sat beside her.

"He asked me to marry him," she said.

"The minister? The one your father wants you to marry?"

"I told him I wasn't ready, that I needed time to think. Why would I need time to think?"

"But—you didn't say yes. You're not coming here to tell me you're engaged to be married."

"No! Anyway, it was you who had something to tell me," she reminded him.

So he told her. He tried to look sad and solemn as he talked about going away from her, but he couldn't hide the light in his eyes or the grin that occasionally broke through as he told her about it.

"New York, Lily—think about it! All the things I'm interested in, the things I want to learn about and write about—it's all possible there! Ideas you'd be blacklisted for even mentioning in St. John's. Why, in New York there'd be a whole newspaper just for that one thing. Socialism, communism, anarchy even. Votes for women, equality for the races, real change for the poor. If those things are going to start anywhere, it'll be there. And I can be there, in the

Trudy J. Morgan-Cole

middle of it, learning about it all, writing about it."

He looked like someone had struck a match and set him on fire, as excited about going to New York as Abby had been, although the worlds into which they were about to plunge couldn't have been more different. He talked about writing for a socialist paper and sleeping on a couch in his friend's brother's apartment, and all she could think was, *He is leaving me. Everyone is leaving me. The only person who wants to stay by my side is Obadiah Collins.*

"You want me to be happy for you," she said.

"Oh, Lily darling. I want more than for you to be happy for me. I want you with me. Could that happen? Would you leave all this—your home, your life here?"

"For—what? Sleeping on your friend's brother's daybed?"

"Well, if you were with me I'd find something a bit better than a daybed, of course." A little line creased the middle of his forehead. She saw that as soon as he broadened his dream to include her it became muddled, less clear and beautiful to him. He wanted her, yes, but he also wanted to be a young man alone, the brave journalist going off to adventure in the big city. He had not pictured a wife, an apartment of his own, bills to pay.

And…a wife? Did he even mean marriage? Reverend Collins had proposed to her, but David had not. Was he suggesting she come to New York and live in sin with him?

"You haven't given it much thought, have you?" she said gently. "Me coming with you, I mean. You never really thought I'd say yes."

He raised his hands, a gesture of surrender. "It's true. I didn't dare to hope. But would you do it? Run away with me, get married down there somewhere? You'd be far away from your family, and I know they'd never approve."

"They wouldn't approve even if I stayed in St. John's and married you in Cochrane Street Church," Lily said. "If we ran away together, they'd cut me off forever."

"Is it too high a price to pay?"

"I don't know. Are you asking me?"

He was silent then too. "I love you, Lily," he said, "but I don't know how to make sense out of you and me. I can't ever be the kind of man you want to marry. I can't live that life. And I can't ask you to live the life I want."

She was crying without transition, without sobs or tightness in her throat, just tears running down her face all at once. He took her in his arms, pressed her cheeks against the rough cloth of his suit jacket. "Ah, there girl, come on now. I wish it could be different. I swear to God I do."

"Do you?"

"I do. But you know what you want—a good churchgoer, a man who's taken the pledge, a good provider."

"And why couldn't—couldn't that be you?"

He heaved a great sigh, like all the burdens of the world were on his shoulders. He was pulling the pins out of her hair, running his fingers through it, kissing her hair. All that instead of answering. Such a simple question.

"Would it be so hard—so awful, to live that life?" She ought to have a better way to put her case than this. When Alida refused to marry James until he took the temperance pledge she had made stirring speeches to convince him. All Lily could do was beg. Beg him to be a different man from the one he was.

"Lily. I don't believe any of it, you know I don't. I don't believe in God at all, certainly not the one who made the world in six days and expects me to show up on Sunday and listen to a sermon. I don't believe having the odd drop to drink is any great sin. I want what you want—a better world—but I don't think we're agreed on the way to go about it. And maybe that shouldn't matter when you're in love, but it does."

Trudy J. Morgan-Cole

"When are you going?"

"I've booked passage for the fourteenth."

"Of this month? The fourteenth of July." Barely a week away. She looked at the clock on the mantel, an ornate little thing in a gold filigree frame. By now Reverend Collins had dropped her mother off and was no doubt driving back along Water Street looking for her. She had burned the bridge behind her this time: whatever time she got back there would be tears, lies, threats, and punishment.

"Do you have to go?" he asked, seeing her look at the clock.

"No. I have to stay."

He moved in to kiss her again but she stood up, reaching for his hand. "Can we go in the back? Would it be all right to be in—in Catherine's bedroom?" She tried to sound calm and certain but her voice trembled on the word "bedroom."

"Are you sure?"

"We might not see each other again," she said. "I'm sure." David was right; he would never be the man she could marry—didn't even want to be that man. And as for Lily herself, what would, what could happen to her? She couldn't leave home and family, go live in a boarding house in New York, walk the alien streets while David learned and wrote and argued about socialism. She was twenty years old and had never had a marriage proposal and now she had turned down two in one day.

Afterwards, they did something they had never done: rested in each other's arms, lying so quiet they might almost have slept. "Come away with me, Lily. Run away with me to New York," he said in a voice as soft as a sigh, as she lay curled under the crook of his arm.

She wondered what he'd do if she said yes. It would change his dream, certainly. Shatter it, perhaps. But he was a man of honour. Not a man who went on and on about his honour, making sure you knew it, like Obadiah Collins would do. But having asked, if she said yes he would take her with him, marry her in front of a justice of the peace. She couldn't even think about that life, but then, she couldn't think of this life, either, without him in it.

Lily didn't even think this time of counting off the days. She thought only of the days until he went away; she didn't remember that her monthly visitor was due in a fortnight. She didn't know that she would be counting the days again, waiting and waiting, as his steamer sailed off to New York. She didn't know that in Catherine's clean sheets they had conceived their child. If she had stopped to think about it, she might have guessed. But she didn't think.

Trudy J. Morgan-Cole

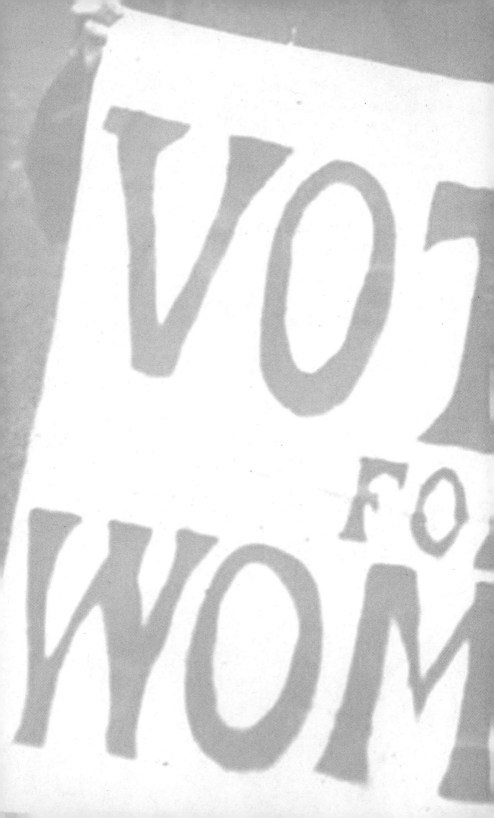

Part Five

1922–1923

Grace

CHAPTER TWENTY-SIX

"THANK YOU, MISS." The little girl's lips were so badly chapped they looked like thin slices of raw meat in her narrow face. "Yer some good to us, Miss."

Grace started to reply, then lifted her shoulders in a shrug and let them fall helpless. Being "some good" today consisted of bringing a barrel of cast-off clothes to the two-room flat where Effie Butler lived with six younger siblings. Grace had sorted through the mounds of castoffs donated by church ladies, thinking of each of the children in those squalid rooms and what would fit them before making her visit on Sunday afternoon—the only day Effie would be off work and home to receive the bounty.

Effie and her siblings should properly have been in the Methodist orphanage: their mother had died of pneumonia last winter and their father was away for months at a time fishing on Grand Banks schooners or, this time of year, gone to the ice. When he was home he spent little time in the rooms where his children lived. He preferred the company of a woman the children called Aunt Loll who lived on the bottom floor of the house, entertained a lot of gentleman callers, and was supposedly "looking after" them. But the father insisted no children of his were going to no orphanage.

Effie was about fourteen. She told Grace she used to work in the Ropewalk factory before it closed down, so she must have been working since she was at least twelve. After the Ropewalk closed she had found a job in another factory; her brother Frank, a year younger, worked on the docks. Between them they sometimes earned enough to feed the five younger ones, though not enough to keep them clothed or heat the rooms on a regular basis. Grace had encountered the little Butlers when they tumbled into her Sunday School class months ago. Now they were part of the ever-growing network of families to which she, as the deaconess of Gower Street Church, attempted to extend enough charity to keep them alive.

Grace had graduated with her diploma in social work last June. She could have had a job in New York, but Jack was back in Newfoundland and so was all her family, and she still found New York a lonely place much of the time. So she moved back into her grandfather's house and began volunteering everywhere she could, hoping to find paid work. Finally the deaconess at Gower Street Church was forced to resign due to ill health and another trained deaconess could not be found. The church offered Grace a position. Because she lacked formal deaconess training her title was "lady assistant" but her duties were the same as those the old deaconess had done, primarily serving the poor of the parish. And it was a saving for the church: they paid her the deaconess's stipend of a dollar and fifty cents a day, but they did not have to provide her with room and board as they would normally do.

Grace knew that her stipend, much like Effie's earnings at the factory, was not nearly enough to address her actual needs. If she had wanted to live anywhere other than her grandfather's house, or to wear fashionable clothes, or purchase anything more for herself than books or the occasional train ticket home, she would have had

A Sudden Sun

to ask her parents for money. Every time she left a house like Effie's, Grace was keenly aware of the luxury of her own position. She could afford to do work she enjoyed for little pay because her family was well-off enough to allow her such an indulgence. She could, she supposed, have lived in a boarding-house room, taken on extra work—tutoring in the evenings, perhaps—but it would have been a much more difficult life.

The Butlers were her last family to visit this afternoon. Sunday was the day of rest, but it was often Grace's busiest day of the week; she taught a girls' Sunday School class and made calls to families who would not be home any other time of the week, as well as going to morning service at Cochrane Street with Grandfather and Daisy, and evening service at Gower Street, usually with Jack. She wasn't sure of Jack this evening, though.

As she climbed back up into Grandfather's buggy, which she often borrowed to carry around the boxes and barrels of clothing she had to deliver, Grace made a note of calls she had to pay and letters to write tomorrow. Apart from the direct acts of charity, much of Grace's workload consisted of speaking up on behalf of her charity cases to employers, landlords, and merchants. Effie's brother Frank had been unable to work for a fortnight because his shoulder had been injured when a crate he was unloading fell on him. While Frank was off work the rent went unpaid and if Grace had not spoken to the landlord, all seven Butlers would have been homeless.

It was hard, as she hefted the empty clothing barrels onto the cart, not to think of the settlement house on Eldredge Street where she had spent her second-year placement. How wonderful to be part of a team of people, all working together to improve the lot of the poor, sharing the same goals and ideas. She was, of course, part of a team on the ministerial staff of Gower Street Church but their concerns were not necessarily hers, and she often felt very much alone, going about from house to house trying to be all things to all people. Nobody in

Trudy J. Morgan-Cole

St. John's had the kind of vision that the settlement workers in New York did, of everything that could possibly be done for, and even by, the poor in the cities if all worked together. Indeed, as she had learned in her classes, even many social workers didn't share the vision of the settlement house ideal, condemning it as sentimental and unscientific.

Thoughts about work occupied Grace's mind during the drive home, but underneath that was a niggling worry about whether Jack would come to walk her to evening service tonight. If he was not coming, he would send a note round to the house; Jack was far too much a gentleman, even at the worst times, to leave her waiting without sending word. But she was beginning to fear this was one of the worst times.

Nearly two years, now, had gone by since Jack had left McGill in the middle of exams. He had moved into St. John's and found work in the office of Mr. Coaker's *Advocate* newspaper, drawing on his experience in Grandfather Hunt's printshop and his father's Port Union connections. Jack admired Mr. Coaker's work and was glad to have a small part in it, but "God never meant me for a printer," he told Grace. "I'd appreciate it if He'd give me some inkling of what He did mean me for." The comment was tinged, as were many of Jack's comments now, with faint bitterness.

All through the year that Grace had been finishing her course in New York and Jack working here in St. John's, they had kept writing to each other, though there was a constraint in their letters that had not been there before, when Jack was in Montreal. Grace had hoped that when she, too, came home, their situation would be clearer. But she had been back eight months now and though they were still, in some sense, keeping company, Jack said nothing about marriage or about the future. He took her to church on Sunday evenings and sometimes, if there was a lecture or a debate she might enjoy, he took her out on a Saturday night as well. Aunt Daisy badgered Grace to invite Jack to dinner, but he accepted less than one invitation a month. He was like a man holding himself at a careful distance, not wanting to sever the connection but not wanting to commit himself either.

One Sunday night in October, Jack had sent a note saying he could not escort her to church that evening. Grace had thought little of it, but the next evening she dropped by his brother's house, where he was boarding, to see if he was feeling under the weather. Jack's sister-in-law, Evelyn, met her at the door and looked relieved. "Oh, Grace—I was hoping you'd come. He's having another bad spell, and I never know what to do. Can you talk to him?"

Grace could not, because Jack would not see her. And she had no idea what a "bad spell" meant, though according to Evelyn this had happened three or four times during the last year. Two days later he sent a brief note of apology; the following Sunday night he came to take her to evening service as usual.

"Were you sick?" Grace asked.

He took his time answering. "The manager at the *Advocate* seemed to find it easy to believe I was sick. Maybe that's the best way of putting it."

"I don't understand."

"There's not much I can tell you, Grace. I just couldn't—face things. Anything. It happens sometimes, is all."

"But you're all right now?"

He was all right—until the next time. Bad spells came every couple of months, never for more than two or three days at a time. When they came, Jack refused to see or talk to anyone, sent a note to work saying he was sick, would not come out of his room or even eat. The last one had been in the middle of February, over a month ago, but there was no pattern, no rhyme or reason to it that Grace could see. Every Sunday afternoon, before Jack was scheduled to come and get her for church, Grace felt a sick knot of fear in the pit of her stomach. Was this going to be another of his bad Sundays?

Trudy J. Morgan-Cole

But he was there on the doorstep at six, smiling when Daisy said that next week he must come earlier and have supper with them. Smiling, but making no promises. As they walked down Gower Street, Grace told Jack about her afternoon visits. "What did you do this afternoon?" she asked finally, feeling that her words were falling into a well of silence.

"Went to sleep for a few hours. Blessed Sabbath, day of rest, you know."

The speaker at Gower Street this evening was not the regular minister, not a preacher at all in fact. It was a young English doctor who had spent the last year working in Dr. Grenfell's mission hospital in Labrador. Despite the fact that his training was medical rather than homiletic, he was a good speaker: he lacked any rhetorical flourish but spoke earnestly, with a furrowed brow that hinted at how strongly he felt about his subject, though his voice was pitched low and there was no shouting.

"Do you remember," Jack said as they left the service to walk home, "my mother wanted me to be a missionary overseas? I still think about that."

"I remember."

Grace remembered, as if it were something from another lifetime, how easily she and Jack used to be able to talk in those months before he went to Montreal. She missed his ready laughter and the way his eyes lit when they made plans for the future. Now the time they spent together was nearly always at public events that allowed little time for conversation, and when they did talk—as on the walk to and from church on a Sunday evening—Jack kept the conversation light, steering her away if she tried to probe too close to his thoughts and feelings.

But tonight he was pensive. "I always thought the mission field meant, you know, Africa or India. Like everyone thinks, I suppose. What that fellow said tonight—it opened my eyes. I mean, think of the things we saw, growing up around the bay, how hard the fishermen have it. Then you imagine, on the northern coast or down on the Labrador, how it must be—so far from any civilization, the fishermen and trappers and the natives. That's a mission field, right there—a place where there's real need."

"You're thinking of going up there?"

Jack shrugged. "Better than spending my life doing something I don't care about, I suppose."

"I know you're not happy working with the *Advocate*."

"It's a job, and I'm lucky to have one with times as hard as they are now." The brief postwar boom in Newfoundland business had ended. Last winter several factories had closed and businesses had gone bankrupt. Hundreds of people in St. John's were out of work. "But when I try to look ahead it's like looking down a dark tunnel. Mr. Coaker wants to move the *Advocate* out to Port Union and he'd like me to go with it. Your grandfather thinks I should come back to his shop. I believe he wants me in place of Charley, to pass the business on to. My own dad wants me to go into the family business, and Mother still hopes I'll finish medical school someday. And I don't—I just can't make any plans. Just when I think I'm going to be all right, and I can start thinking about the future, it's as if—oh, I don't know." Looking at him as he spoke, Grace thought, was like watching a fire struggle to catch. One bright spark began to glow, then flickered out, turning dark and cold again.

Grace wanted so much to see that flame, to see the old Jack instead of this defeated man. It would be worth losing him to the Labrador if he came back someday, whole and himself again. If whatever he'd lost during those long months in Montreal—or earlier in France—could be won back.

"I think you should talk to Dr. Shelby," Grace said. "He'll be in town for a week, and I can find out his address from the church tomorrow. Go see him, if you think you might be interested in working for Dr. Grenfell's mission."

Trudy J. Morgan-Cole

"No, don't you go finding out his address for me," Jack said. "I'll take care of it, if I decide I want to talk to him. I've got to turn it over in my mind a bit."

"Well, don't turn it over too long. He is just here for a week, and—"

"For heaven's sake, Grace, let me do this myself, will you?" There was a bite in his tone she'd never heard before.

"I'm sorry. I only thought—"

"I know what you thought."

They walked along in silence. Distant and untalkative as he had been these last months, Grace had never seen him angry.

"You make it sound like I'm always pushing you to do this or do that, like I should just leave you be," she said, knowing silence was better but driven to speak nonetheless. "That's not fair. When have I ever pushed you to do anything?"

She had, she thought, been a model of patience. Accepted his leaving medical school, accepted his coolness and his strange behaviour, accepted that the subject of their marriage was suspended. She had gone about her own work, kept company with him when he asked her to, not pushed and prodded him with questions or advice.

"I'm sorry, Grace. But you don't know—you can't know what it's been like for me, all these months."

"Of course I can't know! You never tell me. You act as if nothing's wrong, and then you disappear for days at a time with no explanation except that you're sick, only you're not really sick. Do you ever think about what it's like for me?"

She never raised her voice in public like this; the thought that she and Jack might be a couple shouting at each other on a street corner would have shamed her half an hour ago. He looked like he might shout back, but then he took a long breath and said, "I do think about it. All the time."

"That day in New York—on the bench in the park? I'd give anything to go back to that day, awful as it was. At least then you were truthful with me."

He walked ahead, quick steps slapping the road, hands shoved deep into his pockets—Jack, who would no more forget to offer her his arm than he would leave the house without putting on his hat. He strode four or five paces ahead, and she did not quicken her pace to meet him but kept on, sure that no matter how angry or upset he was he would not walk far enough ahead to leave her unprotected on the street.

She was right about that. When he got to the bottom of Garrison Hill he stopped, hands still in pockets, and looked not back at her but out the harbour and the Narrows. "I want to get away, is all," he said when Grace stopped beside him.

"Away from what? From me?"

"Good Lord, no. From this city, from people with their polite questions about whether I'm going to finish medical school. From myself." He kicked a loose stone savagely with his toe. "And yes, I suppose from you too. Look, I love you—you know that, don't you? But I'm not myself. I haven't been for a long time. What do I have to offer you?"

"You still think I care? About being the doctor's wife? I wouldn't care if you were splitting fish down on the flake in Catalina! It wouldn't change a thing about how I felt about you!"

He smiled. "I doubt you really mean that. Haven't you passed up a chance to marry a fisherman before?"

"Yes, but that was Harry Gullage, not you! Don't you see the difference? I wasn't in love with Harry Gullage!"

"And love is all that matters, right? I used to believe that too. Now I wake up in the night screaming from dreams I can't remember, and when dawn finally comes I hate the fact that it's another day I have to live through. Is that the life you want, Grace?"

Trudy J. Morgan-Cole

She had asked him to be honest; now she didn't know what to say. He sat down heavily on the stone wall in front of the Benevolent Irish Society, ran both hands through his hair.

"I wish I knew what to say."

"There's nothing you can say."

She did not see him or hear from him again the rest of that week. She started several times to write him a note, but tore it up each time. He was right. There was nothing she could say.

Jack was waiting for her outside the church the next Sunday afternoon when her Sunday School class was over. He stood straight with hands in his pockets, a half-smile on his face; there was something different about the way he carried himself and she knew at once that he had made a decision.

"I'm going," he said. "To Labrador. I mean, at least, I'm going to apply to go, and hope they take me. I met with Dr. Shelby a few times. He thinks I'd fit in well up there."

"I'm sure you would. And—it's what you want, is it?"

"I think so." He offered her his arm. It was a cold March day but the sun was shining and the wind was not strong. "Do you want to go straight home, or walk about a bit, or do you have calls to make?"

"No calls today. Let's walk down Water Street and see what ships are in."

The cobblestoned expanse of Water Street was hushed with Sunday silence. Shops and offices were closed, and there was no clamour of ships being unloaded at the docks. The whitewashed words in the window of W.J. Allison announced parsnips were five cents a pound and potatoes were fifteen cents a gallon, but none could be bought 'til Monday morning. "I'll miss you," Grace said, as they crossed the cobbled street.

He sighed. "And I'll miss you. You've never had frostbite, have you?"

"What? No, have you?"

A Sudden Sun

"Only the once, when I was about thirteen. Pop took me and Earl back to a tilt in the woods cutting wood one January, and we got stranded out in a blizzard—couldn't find our way back to the tilt for hours. Got frostbite in two toes. It's the strangest thing. It hurts and hurts 'til you'd think it can't hurt anymore and then—it doesn't. It doesn't hurt, but you know in spite of the relief it's not a good thing. Am I making any sense at all?"

"I suppose you are." When he came to her in New York and told her he had left college, he had been in such pain; most of the time this year in St. John's he had seemed numb. A sort of frostbite of the soul, perhaps, though not having experienced either kind of frostbite Grace wasn't sure she really understood.

"I don't know if you ever get back all the feeling once you've lost it—in toes or anywhere else. But at least if I go to Labrador I can get rid of this damned—sorry—this blasted feeling that I'm wasting my life. I don't want to hold you to a lot of promises—that wouldn't be fair."

"I don't mind. We've made promises before."

"We've been apart so much," Jack said. It was true: he had been overseas, then he had come and gone to Montreal while she had gone to New York, and when he returned from Montreal, thinking himself a failure, she had gone back to college. Now they were both in St. John's, but it was no good; she knew it as well as he did. "I can't make plans, can't think about what's next," he went on. "What if I go to Labrador and find I want to stay? Or worse yet, what if I'm no good there either? What if all I find out is that I'm no good anywhere?"

Grace untucked her hand from the crook of his arm and held his hand. They walked along the cold quiet street, hand in hand.

Trudy J. Morgan-Cole

CHAPTER TWENTY-SEVEN

*J*ACK LEFT TOWN six weeks later. He had applied for work with the Grenfell Mission in Labrador and been accepted, and sailed down to Labrador on the *Kyle*. Grace was not sure what kind of good-bye to say. "God go with you," she said finally, as he kissed her cheek and turned towards the gangplank.

"I was going to suggest He should stay here and look after you," Jack said with a grin, so that her last picture was of him smiling and making a joke.

She walked back to her grandfather's house from the steamer dock; it was a warm day for this early in the spring. In her room she looked at her reflection in the mirror and thought: *A spinster. A maiden lady*. She had not thought of herself in those terms before. During the war she had been a young girl with a special friend overseas. Now Jack was gone and he had said they should not make or keep promises. Grace was twenty-two years old, with a diploma in Social Work, a post as lady assistant with the Methodist church, and, she supposed, a more or less broken engagement.

She thought of the room upstairs that had once been Lily's, of her mother looking at her own reflection in that mirror up there. Lily had been married at twenty-one. Grace didn't know if her parents' engagement had been short or long: she knew so little about her mother's life before marriage. Had Lily ever looked at herself in the mirror and thought of herself as a maiden lady, a spinster?

Over dinner that evening, while spreading butter on a thick slice of her own home-made bread, Daisy said to Grace, "Do you ever think of going back to teaching? I mean, not in some little outport school, but with your college education I'm sure you could get a decent position at a nice school here in town—maybe even teach at the Methodist College. Wouldn't you like that?"

Grace laughed. "No, I don't think I'm cut out for teaching," she said. "I only ever did it for those two years when I was young, and I don't have the patience for it. Or the interest, really."

"That's a pity," Daisy said. She didn't need to explain that if poor Grace was going to be jilted and condemned to a spinster's life, she ought to get herself back into the one profession deemed wholly respectable for a single woman. It was clear she thought that any potential Jack had as a suitor was erased by his decision to take off for the Labrador, but to her credit, Daisy didn't harp on things.

"Going off to another meeting tonight, dear?" she asked as Grace left the table. "Must be the suffrage ladies, is it?" If it were Ladies' Aid or the Women's Missionary Society, Daisy would have kept her company, but she drew the line at the Women's Franchise League. Not that she disapproved of the cause. "It's time women had the vote, but it's for young girls like yourself—educated girls, not a simple housewife like myself," was the sort of thing Daisy would say. "I think it's grand for you—go, get involved in all these things, Grace."

Grace darted a look at her grandfather, who sat at the head of the table paying more attention to his roast than to the conversation of his wife and granddaughter. He had snorted under his breath a few times when she'd mentioned going to meetings of the Franchise

Trudy J. Morgan-Cole

League, and she wasn't entirely sure how he felt about the suffrage cause. But he made no fuss about it.

Grace herself had only recently started attending the meetings when one of the ladies at church had invited her to come. At the franchise meetings she felt, more than at the Ladies' Aid or the Missionary Society, that she was in the midst of a group of like-minded women. Women like Mrs. Gosling, Mrs. McNeil, and Miss Kennedy all believed in improving society by reforming the liquor laws, educating the poor, and cleaning up the slums. Above all, they believed that for real change to occur women had to have a vote and a voice in how the country was run. Sitting in their meetings, Grace felt a strange sense of kinship with her mother's younger self, even though she had never heard Lily speak of women's votes with anything other than disdain.

"Oh yes, I remember Lily Hunt from back in the WCTU," Fannie McNeil told Grace. "I was a few years younger so I didn't go to the meetings, but I was always interested in the cause. I think your mother wrote for their paper too—it had some good pieces in it, all written by women. That was Mrs. Ohman's project, of course."

"I met Mrs. Ohman in Montreal." Grace had kept in touch by letter with the older lady since her visit two years before. She didn't know if Mrs. Ohman and Lily had ever corresponded, other than the time Mrs. Ohman wrote to Lily inviting Grace to stay with her in Montreal.

"You don't remember Grace's mother, do you, Miss Kennedy?" Mrs. McNeil turned to May Kennedy.

"No, but if she was in the WCTU that's hardly surprising—there was no place for Catholic girls in that. Nearly all Methodists and Presbyterians. It's the one thing we've done right so far here in the Franchise League—cut across the denominational lines and got women from all walks of society."

"Though only the well-off," Grace pointed out. "I mean, we

don't see any poor women here, fishermen's wives or factory girls, do we? They stand to benefit from the vote, but we don't include them."

"Ah, you need to talk to Mrs. Earle—pardon me, Mrs. *Salter* Earle," May Kennedy said, with an arched eyebrow.

"Salter is her husband's name?"

"No, Salter is her maiden name. She didn't want to lose it entirely when she got married so she uses both. Now, the urge to hang onto one's own name is something a spinster lady like myself can well appreciate, but only Julia Earle would be headstrong enough to think she could have it both ways—keep her name *and* get a husband." Miss Kennedy laughed. "But you must have met her, she's one of your Wesleyan crowd."

"I think I have seen her at Cochrane Street Church," Grace said; her grandfather and Daisy attended there and she had a vague memory of being introduced to a formidable woman who was secretary of the Women's Missionary Society there.

"You would have, surely. She's a big wheel among the Methodists, and she's hung onto another thing a lady usually loses when she marries. No, don't look shocked, I mean her job! She's a secretary in the House of Assembly, and goes to business every day along with looking after her home and raising her children. Though truth to be told, the word on the street is that looking after the house is fairly low on her agenda—she's not much of a homemaker. I suppose she must have a maid, at least."

"She sounds formidable," Grace agreed, trying to remember what she'd heard about the woman, "but why do you recommend her to me?"

"Why, she started up the ladies' branch of the NIWA—you know, the factory girls' union. She shows up here once in every blue moon to lecture us all on how women's rights mean nothing if we don't include the rights of the working woman. She's quite the character."

Trudy J. Morgan-Cole

By chance Grace heard a second mention of Mrs. Salter Earle and the NIWA that same week, from Effie Butler who announced that she was having Aunt Loll look in on the children on Thursday evening so she could attend the union ladies' meeting. "Oh, we have a lovely time," Effie said, "they always gives us tea and biscuits, and after the business part there's recitations and sometimes music, and Mrs. Earle always haves something to say—you should come sometime, Miss Collins, you'd love it."

With recommendations from two such different sources, Grace thought she ought to go, so on Thursday evening she left Aunt Daisy to attend the Ladies' Aid on her own while Grace went off to the old Temperance Hall to attend the NIWA meeting. She didn't see Effie Butler there, but she did see Julia Salter Earle, who crossed the floor to greet her before the meeting started.

"Ah Miss Collins," she said, gripping Grace's hand in a handshake as firm as any man's, "I've been wanting to invite you here for a while. You're doing good work there at Gower Street I hear. Or at least as good as one can do under the present circumstances. I always feel charity work is a bit like putting bandages on people who are bleeding to death, yet we can't seem to get by without it, can we? Sit here with Miss Foster, we're about to begin."

Julia Salter Earle, it seemed, knew all about Grace Collins. In fact, she seemed to know all about everyone. Grace sat and listened as Mrs. Salter Earle chaired the meeting, tabling resolutions about regular lunch breaks and restroom breaks for factory employees. "We've made good progress these last three years," she reminded the assembled women, "but with businesses facing hard times and factories closing, the owners think they can take back the rights we've fought for. I've had men who call themselves Christian businessmen tell me to my face that if the girls on a factory floor— I won't say which one, but I'm sure some of you can guess—if the

A Sudden Sun

girls go on strike, they can fire the lot of them, replace them the next day with unemployed girls, and never have to give an inch. You know it's true. If we don't stand together, they'll pick away at your rights, one by one, 'til you're worse off than you were before the war! Solidarity forever!"

"Hear, hear!" shouted the women around Grace. Mrs. Salter Earle referred to them as "girls" and they were, on average, several years younger than Grace herself, since so many girls worked for a few years and then gave up outside employment when they got married. Girls of sixteen and seventeen, some, like Effie, even younger, in threadbare blouses and home-sewn skirts, sat ramrod-straight hanging onto every word their leader uttered, and joined together to sing the union anthem "Solidarity Forever." Grace had heard it sung at meetings in New York, but never here in St. John's.

Grace was stirred by the sight: she wasn't sure what to make of Mrs. Salter Earle's strident, abrasive manner, but the young women she had collected around her were inspiring. And her vision was like that of the settlement workers—not just handing out charity, as Grace was doing, but working among the poor themselves, enlisting their own efforts to raise them out of poverty. It was strange to sing "Solidarity Forever" and applaud the suggestion of a strike, when at home that evening Grace had listened to Grandfather fuming about how the printers' strike, which had dragged on for months, made it impossible to run his business. Yet she couldn't help agreeing with much of what she heard. She already knew that girls were exploited in factories, and united effort was necessary to improve their lot.

After the business part of the meeting there was, as Effie had said, tea and biscuits, and some of the girls got up to do songs and recitations. Mrs. Salter Earle settled herself and her teacup into the seat next to Grace as a slim girl of about seventeen stepped up

Trudy J. Morgan-Cole

to the front of the room and cleared her throat. "I read this poem in a magazine," the girl said, "and the paper said a crew of women out in the States carried it on their signs when they went on strike, and I think it's the best thing I ever heard." She cleared her throat, clasped her hands before in school-recitation posture, and raised her voice.

As we come marching, marching in the beauty of the day,
A million darkened kitchens, a thousand mill lofts grey,
Are touched with all the radiance that a sudden sun discloses,
For the people hear us singing: "Bread and roses! Bread and roses!"

As the recitation continued, tears sprang to Grace's eyes. Mrs. Earle listened dry eyed, nodding slightly at the end of each stanza, but Grace was lost in the poignant beauty of the words, and of hearing them recited by a working girl who must surely have known from experience what they meant.

As we come marching, marching, we bring the greater days.
The rising of the women means the rising of the race.
No more the drudge and idler—ten that toil where one reposes,
But a sharing of life's glories: Bread and roses! Bread and roses!

As the room full of women burst into applause, Mrs. Earle leaned over to say in Grace's ear, "Seamstress at the Royal Stores. Mother was a seamstress too, 'til the arthritis crippled up her hands so she couldn't work. Father's a drunkard, good for nothing. Young Theresa there did well at the convent school—family's Catholic, of course—up 'til she was ten and had to leave to go to work. Fine reciting voice, fine mind. Shame she couldn't stay in school."

When the recitations and songs were done and the women sat around chatting, Grace turned to Sylvia Pearcey, another of the young women she knew from her church work. Sylvia worked in the same factory as Effie Butler and Grace asked her, "Do you know where Effie is? It was she who invited me to come this evening; I

A Sudden Sun

thought she'd be here."

"Oh, didn't you hear what happened today at the factory?" said Sylvia. "There was an accident with one of the machines and Effie got her hand caught in the works. She's in awful bad shape."

"Is she at home? Did anyone take her to a doctor?"

The girl shrugged. "Don't know. We had to shut down an hour early today because they couldn't get that machine running again, that's the only reason I had time to get me tea and get here for this meeting."

"Oh dear—I ought to go look in on her and the children, see if she's all right," Grace said.

Mrs. Earle, who was engaged in lively conversation nearby, turned and said, "Is that the young girl who was in the accident at the boot factory? I heard she's been taken to hospital."

"Yes—Effie Butler," Grace said. "I was just going to go by the house."

"I'll come with you," Julia Salter Earle announced. She clearly knew who Effie Butler was and where she lived. Remembering her thumbnail life sketch of Theresa McGrath, Grace wondered if she knew every factory girl in St. John's by name and address.

At the crowded flat they found four of the five younger Butler children. Frank was away fishing on the Labrador, and Jennie, who was ten, was the next oldest. It was Jennie who answered the door.

"No, Miss, Effie's gone, they took her to hospital. I tried to find Aunt Loll to tell her but she's been gone this two days. And I don't know where Jimmy went to neither, he took off with them Morris boys and Effie always says they're a hard crowd and he shouldn't go around with them. And all the little ones are bein' bad and I don't know what to do!"

"Did you have anything to give them for their tea?" Mrs. Earle asked, wading into what seemed like a sea of small children.

"There was only half a loaf of bread, and no butter, Ma'am, and

Trudy J. Morgan-Cole

they're still squallin' at me like they wants more."

"I'm going to the shop," Mrs. Earle said to Grace, "to get something for these children to eat. You try to find out what hospital they've put poor Effie in and how badly off she is."

Grace remembered May Kennedy's comment that Julia Salter Earle was an indifferent housekeeper. She had an untidy look to her—her clothes were serviceable but unstylish and her greying hair was pinned up any which way, with no impression that she had taken time over it. But she was able to perform housewifely duties when the situation required. By the time Grace had spoken to the neighbours and determined that Effie was at the General Hospital, Mrs. Earle had bread with butter and jam, and slices of bologna and hard cheese ready for the Butler children along with a fresh pot of tea—a better meal than those children had had in months, Grace guessed.

It was the next morning before Grace was able to visit Effie. She found the girl feverish, her hand swathed in bandages, in a bed with the word "**PAUPER**" hung on a sign over it. Effie drifted in and out of consciousness. She told Grace the story of her injury and insisted she was well enough to go home, but didn't seem to know who Grace was. "Infection," a nurse told Grace. "We can't put her out on the street in that condition."

Grace went back to the house to shepherd the younger Butlers off to school. The baby, Rachel, was only three and not yet going to school, and Jennie wanted to stay home to look after her, but Grace insisted everyone go to school. She took Rachel downstairs to Aunt Loll, who had reappeared but seemed to have little interest in the Butler children's plight. Grace left the child with her anyway, not knowing what else she could do.

When she stopped back by the hospital in the evening to see Effie again, she found a very different scene from the morning. Effie was asleep and the "**PAUPER**" sign had been removed. A bouquet of flowers sat on the table beside her bed, and Julia Salter Earle, looking pleased with herself, sat in a chair nearby. Where another woman would have occupied her idle hands with knitting, Mrs. Salter Earle was scribbling notes on a large pad of lined paper.

"Did you bring the flowers?" Grace asked as she pulled up a chair.

"No, they were sent by Murrays—the factory owners," Mrs. Salter Earle said. "I stopped by and had a little chat, and pointed out a few provisions in their policy book that bound them to pay the medical expenses of an employee injured on the job. After putting up a little protest they agreed to abide by the policy, and I suggested it might be a nice touch to send flowers as well. We've won all these concessions in the past, you see. It's all down in writing. But as soon as times get tough and workers are desperate for jobs, the owners think they can go back on what they've agreed to. Someone has to hold their feet to the flame."

"And that's your job."

"It is one of my jobs."

In the dimmed light of the hospital ward, Grace looked at the older woman. She was a bit scared of Mrs. Salter Earle, though she felt as if they had something in common now, having gone together to the Butler home last night. "May Kennedy told me I ought to meet you," she dared to say now. "Though she said you only drop by the Franchise League meetings once every blue moon."

Mrs. Earle snorted. "That's about right."

A nurse moved through the ward, checking on patients. She paused beside Effie's bed and felt her forehead. "She's sleeping a bit more peaceful now. I think the fever has broken," she said to Mrs. Earle. "You ladies will have to go soon, it's nearly the end of visiting hours."

Trudy J. Morgan-Cole

"I was just hoping she'd wake so I could tell her that the children are being looked after," Grace said. "I'm sure when she does wake up she'll be worried." Effie stirred and shifted a little in the bed but did not open her eyes.

"The Franchise League ladies are well-meaning," Mrs. Earle said to Grace when the nurse had moved on, "but they're wealthy women with all the advantages of their class. They're glad to have poor women mark their names—or their Xs—on a petition, but they don't really see those women as equals, as sisters."

"Do you? Really? I mean, do you really believe—" Grace gestured towards Effie, who murmured a little in her sleep, "she is your equal?"

"In education, in opportunities, in breeding, of course not. But those are external things. Raise a girl like that in a different family, give her a good education at the Methodist College, put the right clothes on her and she'd be indistinguishable from me or you. That's what equality means—recognizing we're all the same underneath, and working to strip away those external differences."

Effie's eyes fluttered open. She looked around the hospital ward and then at Grace and Mrs. Earle, who had been sitting there nearly an hour, waiting to give her the good news that her bills were paid and her brothers and sisters fed.

"Glory be, is that the two of ye there chattering?" she said, meeting Grace's eyes with her own fever-bright gaze. "I kept havin' a dream there was seagulls perched all around the bed. Can ye quiet down or go home so I can have a few minutes' peace?"

CHAPTER TWENTY-EIGHT

"YES MAID, AND 'tis about time too." Sarah Gullage wiped her hands on her apron and took the paper from Grace. "I know they says 'tis only the young ones wants it and the old folks are standing in the way of change, but you mark my words, we're not all old-fashioned just because we're on the wrong side of fifty. I say 'tis high time, when you looks around and sees what the men has done, that we gives the women a chance. I hope I lives to see a woman prime minister—be better than that one Squires, I 'low." She took the paper to her kitchen table, where two mixing bowls full of dough sat ready—she was just about to put bread in the warmer to rise. Grace handed over the pen as well, and Sarah took it, frowning in concentration as she carefully etched out the letters of her name.

"You wouldn't believe it, I had a lovely hand when I was a girl—went to school up to the third Royal Reader, I did, and I could write all kinds o' things. But for nearly forty year now I never had to write nothing except births and deaths in the family Bible, and my hand is getting shaky these days." Sarah was nearer sixty than fifty: she had borne twelve children and raised ten—the nine of her own that survived plus one that was either a nephew or cousin. One of her nine was Harry, who had long ago asked Grace to marry him; Grace didn't know if Mrs. Gullage ever knew about that.

They were all grown up and married now, and old Bill Gullage was still fishing with his sons Harry and Bert. Now at the end of October, with the cod landed and made and sold, Mr. Gullage and his boys were repairing and repainting the dory and mending their nets before winter closed in. Sarah, freed like the other fishermen's wives from labour on the flake, was still busy around the house but glad for a few moments to stop and chat as she signed Grace's petition. "You got a nice few names there," she said, handing the paper back to Grace. "Do you find most of the women round here are sensible enough to want the vote?"

"Oh, I'd say it's about half and half so far," Grace said. She had knocked on doors of houses like this one where she and her petition had been welcomed warmly, and she had gone to others where the door had been slammed in her face. At Heber Bursey's place she had never even gotten to talk to the woman of the house; the mister told her to get out. "Minister's daughter or no minister's daughter, I'll kick you off the gallery if you comes waving that piece of trash in my missus's face again." After a reception like that it was nice to sit in Mrs. Gullage's warm kitchen and hear how it was high time for women to have the vote.

Heber Bursey's missus, Betty, cornered Grace outside the church on Sunday. "Have you got that petition of yours? I means to put my name to it while himself got his back turned." Heber was not a churchgoer so Betty did not have to look out for him as she made a careful X and Grace wrote "Elizabeth Violet Bursey" next to it. "I hope 'tis not a sin to sign it on a Sunday. I suppose it is a sin to go against my lord and master but what he don't know will never hurt him, so I 'lows he'll live forever since he don't know nothin'."

Grace took the petition back from Betty and saw her own mother beckoning. "Hurry up, dinner will be stone-cold," Lily said. The Reverend had finished his after-church handshakes and conversations with parishioners and only a few people were left in the churchyard.

On the road that sloped down from the church to the parsonage, Lily said to Grace, "I suppose I can't stop you from passing around that petition altogether, but could you at least refrain from doing it on Sunday right after service? It's unsuitable."

"I wasn't passing it around—Mrs. Bursey came looking for me," Grace said. "Anyway, I happen to think it *is* suitable. I believe women's suffrage is God's will."

"And you're qualified, all of a sudden, to tell the rest of us what God's will is? That's presumption, is what that is."

"Oh, Mother. How is anyone qualified to say it's not God's will? And don't quote me a proof-text about women keeping silent in church or being submissive to their husbands. In Bible times nobody had the vote, men or women, so it's not relevant."

"Now you're just being saucy," Lily said, and hurried a few steps ahead to walk next to her husband, though as usual, she did not take his arm.

"What do you think about women's franchise, Papa?" Grace asked over dinner.

Lily sighed heavily. "Haven't you already said enough about it, Grace? Let the subject drop."

"But I think it's right to get Papa's view on the question, both as my father and as my pastor," Grace said. "Shouldn't we be guided by him?"

Lily made a sniff that was almost a snort and rolled her eyes but said nothing. The Reverend, apparently unaware that he was being used as a playing piece in a game his wife and daughter were playing, waved his fork in the air like a conductor's baton as he

Trudy J. Morgan-Cole

spoke. "It's a most interesting question. I know that when I was younger I was quite convinced, as were most of the clergymen I knew, that women had no place in political life. Why, your mother and I had some quite lively discussions about it when we were courting—she was well acquainted with some of the women in the suffrage movement."

"So I've heard," Grace said, and caught a sharp glance from Lily.

"I don't remember that they were particularly lively discussions, myself," Lily said to her husband. "I knew your views on the subject, and in time I came to agree with you."

"But my own views have changed over time, as society has changed."

"Truth doesn't change. If a view is correct it should be held to regardless of what the world is doing," said Lily.

This was the liveliest conversation Grace could remember at the family dinner table since Charley had died. Besides genuinely wanting to know her father's views on the question of women's votes, she wanted to keep it going. "Mr. Coaker has told the Franchise League he supports the cause," she said.

"Yes, he's one of the people with whom I've discussed it," her father said, returning his fork to its usual task of conducting roast beef to his mouth. "He thinks, as I do, that making a truly fair and equal society means extending voting rights to women as to men. As I study my Bible I've come to believe that God made man head of the home, but he didn't intend to keep women from having a voice altogether. It's all a question of balance," he went on, warming to his subject so that he sounded as if he were in the pulpit again. "Of course there are extremes; of course there are people who want to break down the barriers between the sexes entirely and see women in the House of Assembly, women on the magistrate's bench, women out of the home circle entirely. Now, I couldn't countenance that. But the vote? There's no harm in that, and plenty of good."

"I agree, Papa—although I'd go farther, and say that the House or the magistrate's bench might not be bad places for women. Someday."

"And there's the danger, you see?" Lily turned not to Grace but to her husband. "The downhill slope. You let down the standards in one area, and people think they can upset the apple cart entirely."

"Now, I don't think that's completely true—"

"Haven't you just heard your own daughter?" said Lily, who never interrupted her husband in conversation. "You said you supported the vote, with reservations, and she charged ahead and said the reservations don't matter. You mark my words, the men who support women's franchise will live to regret it one day." She turned to Grace. "And women will come to regret it too. Girls your age will long for the day when their fathers and husbands protected them!"

"Perhaps we don't need protecting," Grace said. "Perhaps the apple cart *should* be upset."

Lily laid down her fork: somehow that one statement from Grace seemed to have drained all the animation from her face and voice. "Until you become a mother yourself, you have no idea." She sat for a moment longer, staring at her plate as Grace and her father continued to talk about the franchise vote and whether Mr. Coaker would give it the support of the Fishermen's Party when it came up in the legislature. Suddenly Lily said, "Excuse me, I'm not hungry, and I have a meeting with the Sunday School teachers to prepare for." She pushed back her chair with a scrape and stood up, her roast barely touched.

"You should try not to upset your mother," the Reverend said mildly, when they heard the door to her room close upstairs.

"I didn't *try* to upset her," Grace said. "She was the one who

Trudy J. Morgan-Cole

brought it up."

"I think perhaps it troubles her that you're soliciting signatures. Quite apart from her view of the cause, which I'll admit is old-fashioned, she may think it's not appropriate for you to be knocking on doors for a political cause."

"Do you think it's not appropriate, Papa?"

He looked down at his plate. "I think it's better for a girl's mother to judge what is and isn't appropriate behaviour for a young lady," he said. "Talk about women's rights and the franchise upsets your mother. It brings back memories she would rather forget."

Why, was she bitten by a suffragette in her cradle? Grace wanted to ask, but knew her father, tolerant as he sometimes was of her brand of humour, would not appreciate levity on the subject of her mother. He treated Lily the way a man who was no gardener might treat an exotic orchid someone had given him—with a kind of wary, nervous pride.

"Why should it stir up bad memories?" Grace said. Her father seemed like the least likely person on earth to give her any insight into Lily's past, and yet, presumably, he had been there for it.

"Oh, she had many friends who were involved in that cause when she was young. She had some experiences that were— hurtful. She had to put certain people, certain associations behind her. It's no wonder if those ideas are painful to her now."

"I won't bring it up again around her," Grace promised, not at all sure whether or not she would keep that promise. But she was anxious to end the conversation on a conciliatory note, before her father actually ordered her to stop bringing around the petition.

At the end of a week she had gotten sixty signatures in Catalina and was starting on the ladies of Port Union. This time of year, late fall, was the best time to catch women at home, with the fish in and the gardens harvested. She got a few signatures as well from the tiny class of well-off ladies in Catalina: her own mother did not, of

course, sign, but the Anglican minister's wife did and so did Mrs. Perry, who was still teary-eyed after Jack's departure in September.

"What good work you're doing, I admire it so much," she said, signing the petition in her lovely script. "You out campaigning for women's rights, and Jack off to the Labrador to look after Esquimos and trappers—what a pair you are. I don't mind saying, Grace darling, I thought the two of you would have been married long before this, but I tell myself all the time that God moves in mysterious ways."

Grace could think of nothing to say to this. After all, hadn't she, too, thought she and Jack would be married by now? The Lord's ways were mysterious indeed and she did not think she wanted to discuss them with the woman who was supposed to have been her mother-in-law. Instead she asked, "Have you heard from Jack since he left?"

"One letter on the last boat. He sounds like he likes it up there, doesn't he?"

Grace had had two letters and Jack did indeed sound happier. She wasn't sure how much to trust letters. The year he was in Montreal, his letters to her in New York hadn't hinted at his growing panic and despair. Even in person, he had become good at hiding his true feelings. She thought of all those times last year that Jack would retreat into his room for days and then reappear as if nothing had gone wrong.

Mrs. Perry, too, was thinking of those times. "Earl and Evelyn were so worried about him, you know, last year? I'm sure you were too—I mean he had a good job with the *Advocate* but they told me how he used to send word he was sick sometimes when he didn't seem to be. They were afraid he had taken up *drinking*?" She lowered her voice on the last word. "But I said I couldn't see that, not Jack...."

Grace couldn't see it either. She thought Earl and Evelyn had latched onto that explanation because the idea of a stalwart young

279

Trudy J. Morgan-Cole

Methodist secretly taking to drink was more believable than the idea that a brave war veteran would lie on his bed staring at the wall for hours on end, unable to face another day. And she couldn't say that, exactly, to Jack's mother. Instead she said, "I'm praying Labrador will do him good."

"I am too, my darling. You'll understand when you have children of your own, how you just have to leave them in the Lord's hands. Anyway I think it's wonderful work you're doing, with the petition and all—you just keep it up."

Grace intended to keep it up. She walked over the bridge from Catalina to Port Union one morning when the ground was hard with the season's first frost. The sound of hammers and saws still filled the air: not until snow covered the town would the men of Port Union stop erecting new buildings. Here there were more ladies of leisure to contact than in Catalina. Coaker's new industries all required managers, and managers had wives. Grace went door to door knocking at each of the row houses—just like a miniature St. John's street—first the little ones up on the hill where the labourers lived, then the nicer ones down by the harbour where most of the managers' wives were happy to sign the petition.

Then she thought of the shopgirls in the Union Store, and continued down the road by the harbour to the tall white building with its lofty towers. Inside, the shop sold the same things available in most outport merchants' shops, but in greater quantity and variety, and in a much more impressive setting. It boasted two storeys connected by an elevator—probably the only elevator outside St. John's, Grace thought—and nearly a dozen employees, all young and female. When she stopped by the fabric counter to show the petition to the girl there, several others gathered around, curious.

"I'll put me name to it," said Sandra Courage, and two or three others did the same.

"Don't be so hasty," warned another girl Grace didn't recognize—

an Anglican, she thought, whose father fished with Skipper Bob Howley. "I don't know if Father would be all right with me signing this, and your Pop might not either, Sandra."

"Ain't that the whole point of it, though?" Sandra said. "Why should a girl have to ask her father's say-so to sign a piece of paper? Or her husband's either, for that matter."

"Now, you goes talking like that, you won't have to worry about getting your husband's say-so on anything because you won't get a husband!" said Elva Hallett.

"Go way with you, maid! Just cause you can't hook a man don't mean I can't—signing this paper or having the vote got nothing to do with it one way or the other."

It was hard to steer the conversation back to the franchise but in the end Grace got eight signatures and was just ready to leave the store when the front door pinged and an older man walked in and lifted his hat to the girls gathered around the fabric counter. They scurried to their different stations like insects scurrying after a log had been turned over.

Only then did Grace recognize William Coaker. She had met the man only a handful of times in the years since she had defied her mother's wishes and gone to ask him for a job. He was not always home when she came to visit her parents; he travelled not just back and forth to St. John's but also to America and Europe on union business. She remembered her father saying that Mr. Coaker had just returned from a trip.

If she had taken a moment to recognize him, he had no such difficulty knowing who she was and what she was doing. "Ahh, Miss Collins. I hear you've been bringing the Women's Franchise League petition around town. Is that what you're doing here today?"

"Yes...Sir?" Grace didn't mean to turn it into a question. Mr. Coaker, or at least his union, owned most of the town, but it

Trudy J. Morgan-Cole

wasn't as if she needed his permission to get the signatures of the town's women.

"May I see?" he asked, and she handed him the paper, somewhat reluctant to let it slip from her fingers.

He nodded as he looked up and down the list of names, and some Xs, for the women who couldn't write their own names. "Very good, very good, Miss Collins. I'm impressed with the work you're doing."

"Mrs. McNeil tells us you've promised your support in the House, Mr. Coaker."

"Of course, of course. The women's vote is an issue whose time has come. I've always stood up—the Fisherman's Party, that is, and the Union, have always stood up for the rights of the oppressed and that includes our women as well. The time has come," he said again.

"Then no doubt you'd be willing to be the one to introduce the motion into the House? It would stand a far better chance of success if it's brought in by a member who's so widely respected."

"Well, he got out of there so fast I thought he was going to start walking backwards," one of the girls said after Mr. Coaker had left the store. "I never saw a man go back on what he said so fast since Uncle Wilf Gullage asked Phoebe Chaulk did she like his new house and she said yes and she'd love to marry him."

All the girls laughed. It was certainly true that Mr. Coaker had checked himself very quickly once Grace asked if he intended to bring the bill in himself. "Still I don't know why," she said. "If he supports the bill, why wouldn't he introduce it in the House?"

"Miss Collins," Sandra said, "I know you got a lot of book-smarts and you knows all about what goes on in the House of Assembly, and I don't know none of that, but I knows this much: 'tis one thing for a man to say he agrees with an idea, and another thing altogether to put his own name to it. Especially if the idea comes from a woman, right?"

The girls nodded. "Anyway, Mr. Coaker can't go taking no chances these days," said Elva.

"What do you mean?"

"My pa says Mr. Coaker's taking hits from all sides—not just the merchants and the bigwigs, but even some of the union men don't support him anymore."

"Don't be talkin'—they don't know what's good for them," said the girl whose name Grace couldn't remember. "Fishermen would be nowhere without Mr. Coaker."

"Sure, he does lots of good for us, but he does all right for himself too," Sandra said, nodding in the direction of the Bungalow, Coaker's spacious house that crested the hill like a little castle.

"And lots of people never forgave him for voting for conscription," Elva added. "My pa says that's the real trouble."

"The war's been over for four years," Grace pointed out. "And we never had conscription anyway." She didn't add that the conscription law had been, in her view, necessary, and would have had to be put in place if the war had lasted. She knew that people who had lost a family member in the war, like herself and Mr. Coaker, believed conscription was needed. Those who hadn't lost anyone thought the very idea of military conscription was terrible, and there was no getting past that divide.

"It don't matter," Elva said. "Once they lost faith in him, he'll never win it back. People remember. They hold grudges."

Grace left the store with a bolt of gingham cloth, a packet of needles and eight signatures—and more insight than she had expected from a group of shopgirls. *When*, she wondered, *will I learn to stop underestimating people?* She found the same thing in her work in town. She was always leaping ahead, thinking she knew better than others just because she had a college education and they were poor.

Trudy J. Morgan-Cole

Effie Butler had taught her a valuable lesson. Back in the summer Grace and Mrs. Earle had worked hard to get Effie compensated for her accident so she could provide for her younger brothers and sisters. Effie had been grateful, but as soon as she was back on her feet she had marched the four youngest ones up to the Methodist orphanage and signed them in.

"I thought you wanted to keep the family together!" Grace had protested.

"Now Miss Collins, you been awful good to us and yes, I woulda liked to keep us all together if I could. But having food on the table means more than all being under one roof. I learned something from all this, and that's that I can't provide for the youngsters on just what Frank and I makes. They could have starved. Them little ones will be better fed and better off in the orphanage. Anyway it was our da who never wanted them in there, and what do I care what he thinks?"

I thought I knew what was best for Effie's family, Grace thought now. *And I thought a bunch of shop girls would know nothing and care less about politics.* But the girls in the shop, all fishermen's daughters, knew more than she did about how Mr. Coaker was viewed by the union members. While the minister's daughter might believe that the great reformer was a hero, the fishermen's daughters heard what their fathers and brothers said about him around the dinner table, and that was a more complicated picture.

The next day was Grace's last at home before returning to St. John's. Her train was to leave at noon and she packed her bag after breakfast. The suffrage petition was on the downstairs hall table, ready to go in her handbag—except that when she looked for it, it wasn't there. Grace asked the maid if she'd seen it, but the girl had no idea.

The Reverend was out visiting; he would be home later to drive Grace to the station. Lily was in the parlour. Grace tapped lightly on

A Sudden Sun

the door and opened it a crack to Lily's faint "Hello?"

"Mother, have you seen my petition? I left it on the hall table." Grace hated to bring it up again—her father had asked her, after all, not to upset Lily—but she couldn't leave without it.

For a moment Lily didn't say anything. She sat in a chair by the window, her knitting needles clicking furiously at what looked like a mitten. She looked neither at the knitting nor at Grace but out at the rain slapping the glass.

"Mother? Did you hear me?"

"I told you I didn't want you at that petition business. Nothing good will come of getting yourself mixed up with those kind of women, Grace."

"I just need to know if you saw the petition."

Lily shrugged. All her attention was on her knitting as she finished off a row of stitches. "There was a jumble of papers on that hall table. I assumed if no one had put them away they must be all garbage."

Grace felt ice-cold. "What did you do with them?"

"I put them in the fire." Lily rolled up the ball of blue wool with neat, efficient movements and began working with the red wool.

"You did what? Was my suffrage petition in there? Did you look at them at all?"

"I don't know. If your papers are so important to you, you should take better care of them."

"That's a lie!" Grace burst out. "You wouldn't have burned them without looking! You knew what it was! You burned my petition on purpose, because you don't approve! How could you do that?"

Still Lily didn't take her eyes from her knitting, though Grace knew from years of watching she was well able to knit without looking down at the work. "If that petition did get thrown on the fire it's all for the best."

Trudy J. Morgan-Cole

"You—you—" Grace shook with anger, tears springing to her eyes.

"*You* stop and think before you say words you'll regret. Anything I've ever done was for your own good."

"How can I go back to those ladies, to Mrs. McNeil and Mrs. Gosling and the rest, and tell them I don't have my signatures because my mother burned the papers? Those women *remember* you— some of them anyway. They remember you marching with the WCTU and fighting for the franchise. How can I tell them you did this?"

"I don't give a tinker's damn what you tell them," said Lily who, to Grace's knowledge, had never uttered a curse word in her life. "And I certainly don't care what they think of me. Do you think I'm *proud* of those days, of what I did?" Now she did look up, her needles still moving, and Grace saw tears in her mother's eyes, tears that matched her own. Though Lily's hands were steady her voice shook a little as she said, "Grace, my dear, if throwing one handful of paper on the fire could save you from making mistakes you'll regret all your life, I'd do it again. I'd do it right in front of you."

"You selfish, opinionated old *hag*, you always say you're only thinking of me when all that matters is *your* opinion, *your* views. Nobody can be right but you!" Hot tears spilled down Grace's cheeks. "I'll never forgive you for this, never!"

She slammed the door behind her, ran out into the hall and through the front door. She was halfway up the road to the church before she remembered her father was not there, but visiting with a parishioner.

She would tell him. She would. He understood; he thought her cause was just. But what could he do? He couldn't unburn paper.

In the end, Grace said nothing. She sat on the front porch of the house in the drizzle with her bag 'til the Reverend came with the horse and buggy to drive her to the station. Lily did not come out to say goodbye and Grace did not go back in the house. She took the train back to town, and told Mrs. McNeil at the next Franchise League meeting that her petition papers had got mixed up with some others and accidentally been put in the fire, and she was so very sorry for the terrible mistake. She told no one what had happened, did not even put it in her letter to Jack.

She could have gone back to Catalina at Christmastime, told the same story and tried to get the women to sign all over again. Getting those signatures again would have been the best thing for the cause. But Grace wrote to her parents and said Christmas was a busy season in church work, as the Reverend knew so well, and she could not spare the time to come home.

Trudy J. Morgan-Cole

CHAPTER TWENTY-NINE

"*N*OW, WHAT ABOUT the Port Union area? Oh, I'm sorry, those were yours, weren't they, Miss Collins?" said Mrs. McNeil, sorting through stacks of petitions. "Of course, such an unfortunate mistake. But these things happen." Over the fall and winter the Franchise League leaders had heard more than one story of petitions that had mysteriously gone missing or been destroyed outright. Despite returning empty-handed Grace had been invited to join a committee that would draft a covering letter to accompany all these petitions when they were presented to the prime minister. She sat around a table with the most powerful women in the League— Fannie McNeil, Edna Bulley, May Kennedy, Armine Gosling, none of whom knew what had actually happened to the hundred signatures she had collected back in October.

"I've tried to see if there's someone else in the area who can circulate a petition for us, but we've had no luck so far," said Mrs. Gosling. "And Mr. Coaker told me just what he told you—he and the other Fishermen's Party members will vote for the bill when it comes up in the House but that he won't be the one to introduce it."

"That might be just as well," said Mrs. Bulley. "I'm not sure Mr. Coaker's support is the support we want, with the *Telegram* and the *Daily News* both calling him a Bolshevik." Grace thought of the shopgirls in Port Union. Mr. Coaker seemed to be in trouble with the fishermen for supporting the established parties too much, and in trouble in St. John's for being too radical.

"Sir Richard says he will bring it in as a government bill," Mrs. Gosling said, "and that will be much better than having Mr. Coaker sponsor it. If it's a government measure it's sure to pass." Armine Gosling certainly knew the value of having the ear of the man in power: her husband had been mayor of St. John's, and while he was in power, council had made it legal for women to vote in city elections—as long as they were property-owners. It was a step toward the franchise, but only a small one. The government of Newfoundland still needed to be roused to the suffrage cause.

"I don't know what to make of Sir Richard," sighed Edna Bulley. "He claims to support the cause when we talk to him in private, but then you read things like this article in the *Gazette*—and we all know that paper has Squires's money behind it."

The women around the table rolled their eyes—they had all read the article—but May Kennedy put her hand over her heart and recited a line from it all the same: "'It would be interesting to know whether any of these true-hearted, honest Newfoundland women from Fortune Bay or Bonavista support the franchise cause.'"

"It just makes my blood boil, how the papers—the *Gazette*, anyway—try to make us out to be nothing but a bunch of rich townie socialites instead of 'honest Newfoundland women,'" Mrs. McNeil said.

"Well, anyway, these petitions should answer that accusation," Grace said—it was the first time she'd spoken up without being asked a direct question. As the other ladies passed her the petitions she had been copying down a list of the communities they came

Trudy J. Morgan-Cole

from. She began reading off the list of communities—"Bonavista, Baie de Verde, Cormack, English Harbour, Heart's Content.... How can anyone say now that the outport women aren't in favour of the vote?"

The next day, after making a call to the Methodist orphanage, Grace was off to another meeting—this time to the Ladies' Branch of the NIWA. At tea-time afterward the imposing Mrs. Salter Earle pulled her aside. "What went on at yesterday's Franchise League meeting, Miss Collins? I do rely on you to keep me up to date on their gatherings." She snorted at the news that Sir Richard was going to bring in the franchise bill.

"Government measure, my foot! When are those fools going to stop believing everything that sleveen Squires tells them?" Unlike Mrs. Bulley, Mrs. Earle had no difficulty deciding what to make of Sir Richard. Since she worked at the House of Assembly she knew the ins and outs of what went on there. "Squires makes promises to put people off, then makes excuses about why he can't keep his promises. That's just the way the man works. The way his government works. I don't know why anyone trusts him further than they can throw him."

"I suppose he's the man in power, people have to work with him if they want to get anything done."

"Nothing *will* get done as long as he's the prime minister. Including women getting the franchise—you mark my words. Those women are barking up the wrong tree if they think anything is going to change as long as Squires and his crowd are in power."

Grace admired Mrs. Earle but found her exhausting. She was a tireless worker but also a tireless agitator: you couldn't fault her for saying the world, or Newfoundland, was an unjust place because she certainly was doing all she could to make it better, but her energy was fuelled by a kind of anger that Grace found hard to take. It was an anger harsh and powerful as lye soap, useful for getting things done. Still, Grace wanted to believe the world was essentially a good place and could be made still better with prayer, dedication, and a little kindness.

But Julia Salter Earle was rarely wrong. Weeks slipped by and the franchise bill had still not been introduced. "I'm afraid the session will go by and nothing will get done 'til the fall—if then," May Kennedy said one evening in February, as their small committee sat down around the table to talk after the next Franchise League meeting was done. "I had so hoped that when I went to the congress I could report that the women of Newfoundland have finally joined the rest of the English-speaking world. Now that even the Americans have the vote, any country that hasn't given women the franchise looks more and more backward."

After working with these women throughout the fall and winter, Grace was becoming a little bolder about speaking up. "You'll have to tell them instead that our government is dragging its heels," she said now. "Maybe you can get the ladies in other countries to write letters to the government of Newfoundland, shame them publicly in the papers for being so slow to give us the vote."

"That is exactly what we ought to do!" Mrs. McNeil said. "Do you know, we asked the government, and the international alliance petitioned them too, to send a delegation of Newfoundland women to the Rome congress. But Sir Richard said there wouldn't be a penny to send suffragists off to Europe for any such thing."

"Thank goodness I've the means to go at my own expense," May Kennedy said. She was a well-off spinster who lived with her aging mother; their needs were provided for by a generous inheritance that allowed for plenty of household help and left May free to devote herself to good works. "Are we done here for tonight? Mother will be in bed by now, but my cats will think I've abandoned them. Miss Collins, do you have a ride home? It's far too cold to walk."

Trudy J. Morgan-Cole

Grace rode to her grandfather's house in the comfort of Miss Kennedy's side-sleigh; it was every bit as cold as walking in the knife-sharp winter air, but the journey was much faster. Miss Kennedy leaned her fur-hatted head close to Grace's ear and said, "There are a few months to go 'til the congress. It may be possible to collect enough donations from our wealthier members so that we can send a second delegate to Rome. If we can do that, I think it ought to be you."

"Me? By rights it should be Mrs. McNeil or Mrs. Gosling, or someone else with more experience."

"Not all the older ladies enjoy travel as I do. And we all agree we need a younger woman, someone who can represent the voice of the next generation. You're articulate, Miss Collins, and it's quite stirring to think that your mother marched with our first woman suffragists way back in '93. You can talk about that, and say that here we are, her daughter's generation, and we still don't have the vote."

They were turning onto Queen's Road, almost at Grandfather's house. The bells on the horse's bridle jingled merrily. Grace was used to the fact that Lily's suffragist past was an open secret to a certain generation of women in St. John's. But what a lie it would be, to go all the way to Rome carrying the banner of a second-generation suffragist.

After leaving the house that day back in October, Grace had written no letters home until she wrote her father to say she was not coming for Christmas. She got a Christmas card from both her parents with a five-dollar banknote inside and, in her mother's handwriting, the note, "May the Lord bless you in 1923. Your loving mother and father."

Grace had wondered for a while if her mother would write again—and if she even wanted to hear from Lily. Perhaps the business of the burned petitions had severed things between them forever. She felt oddly relieved, now, to see a letter in her mother's handwriting on the hall table. It was full of the usual: Catalina news, church doings, and advice for Grace. She made no mention of the petition nor of the months of silence between them.

That night, Grace sat down to compose a short but newsy response. She rewrote it several times before she was able to match her mother's neutral tone, devoid of the anger and regret she felt. She could not forgive what Lily had done, but she could not leave the letter unanswered. Cutting off all ties to home was unthinkable.

After that, Lily's letters once again arrived weekly, as they had always done, and Grace replied to each one. But among all the letters she received that winter, from her mother and other relatives and her college friends, she missed Jack's familiar handwriting. His last letter had come before Christmas, when ships were still leaving Battle Harbour. They had agreed to keep writing to each other in instalments over the winter, keeping their letters in a journal they would send each other in spring. It was April before the Labrador steamer arrived and the next day Grace found a parcel on the hall table with a black leather-bound notebook inside.

"Oh, a package from your friend, you must be so pleased," said Daisy. But the usual bubbly trill was missing from Daisy's voice, along with the phrase "your young man" that she used to use as if it were Jack's name. His months-long absence had clearly demoted him in Daisy's eyes. She had hoped Grace would begin courting someone else; several times she asked if Grace would be willing to meet the nephew or grandson of some friend of hers. Grace declined all such offers. Once during the winter an earnest gentleman who attended Gower Street Church and was articling at a law firm had invited Grace to a concert with him. The evening had been pleasant enough but she had felt no more desire to spend more time with the young lawyer than she would with any other casual acquaintance of any age or gender. She busied herself with work, with reading, and with the activities of the Women's Franchise

Trudy J. Morgan-Cole

League, and thought it possible that her interests, taken together, did not add up to a whole that made young men particularly anxious to court her.

Grace waited 'til she was alone in her room in front of a small fire with a cup of hot cocoa, before she opened the notebook to read what Jack had written through the long months of winter. Even when she was settled in her chair, she found herself strangely reluctant to open the cover. She hadn't heard from Jack since the last steamer sailed in the fall. Busy as she had been, she had never stopped wondering how he was faring.

Just his tidy, close-written script on the first page—"My dear Grace"—made her heart race. So many months had passed since his last letter and she had spent more nights than she would ever admit to anyone lying awake, trying to imagine what Jack's life was like in Labrador. She had imagined terrible things—that the work, the loneliness, those long cold winter nights had driven him to despair. That he really had taken to drink, or worse. She knew of men who had been overseas who were so tormented in their minds that they had been driven to take their own lives. What if work on the Labrador coast, which Jack had hoped would be his salvation, had been his undoing instead?

She had tried to comfort herself with the thought that if anything truly terrible had happened, some news would have come back—a cable to his family, perhaps. And then in the winter silence she imagined other things—that he was well, and happy in his work, and had forgotten about her. Perhaps he was contented because he had fallen in love with some fresh-faced English nurse or even an Esquimo woman. The jealous thoughts were petty and Grace tried not to dwell on them, but stranger things had happened, and he had said, after all, that no promises should bind them. One promise he had kept—the promise to write. He had written a great deal. She supposed he had little else to do except for work. As she read the first page she found, as always with Jack's letters, that it was as if he were in the room with her, his voice filling the empty spaces both outside and within.

> *November 23*
> *My dear Grace—I was right to come here. I know that already, and if in later months I write you to say that I'm discouraged, that the work is hard, that it all feels hopeless—for those who've worked here longer have warned me I will feel all those things, and that the winter months are particularly hard here—still believe me, that I have done the right thing by coming here. Only I fear the winter, not just for the cold and dark but because no mail boat will come with letters from you. Only in this journal, writing words that you won't read 'til spring, can I confess how much I depend on those letters.*

Grace read the first entry in the journal over twice before she turned the page. Just to see on paper Jack's admission that he relied on her letters made her feel like a key had turned in her heart, unlocking something she hadn't known was locked. He had still felt that way in November. Would he have sent the journal, after all, if he hadn't still felt that way when spring came?

> *December 15*
> *I don't know why it should be that the very thing that froze and terrified me when it occurred at medical school—the sight of an injured person—should have such a different effect here. In this case it was a trapper who had half-severed his foot while chopping wood— and of course it took far too long for him to come to the clinic, the wound was deeply infected and the foot far past saving. It was every bit as gruesome as things I saw in the trenches.*
> *But I felt exactly as it did back on the battlefields of*

Trudy J. Morgan-Cole

France and entirely unlike the clean and antiseptic
hospital in Montreal. I thought only of the suffering man,
and the injured limb, and what might be done to save
him. In the end it meant amputating the foot—a hard
blow, but he's a brave fellow and was already learning to
get around well on a crutch when I saw him last.
I suppose I am much in the same situation—not having
lost a foot, I mean, but having lost a piece of myself. Since
coming here I have begun to see two things: that what I
have lost will never be wholly regained, and that I may
be able to go on without it.

In mid-January he wrote about the early dark and late dawn of
the northern winter.

It's dark by four in the evening and not light again 'til
nine in the morning. I know it's worse farther north, the
land of the midnight sun in summer and the long dark
winter. But it's more than dark enough here… I go to the
clinic in the morning darkness and return home, if I
don't work late, in afternoon darkness. And sit in my
room looking out at the dark night, which seems endless.
I was never afraid of the dark as a child but I'm
beginning to fear it now—how foolish is that? The worst
things, the deepest fears and doubts, seem to surface at
night, and at this time of year up here it seems to be
nearly always night.

I write to you that I'm happy here, happier than I was in
St. John's, and then I lie awake these nights and can
think only dark thoughts. But it's better, I've come to
believe, to feel the horrible things than to feel nothing at
all. You can't imagine—I know you can't, because you
are so much alive, always glowing like a flame just lit—
you cannot imagine feeling so dead that it would be a
relief, almost, to be back in the trenches in France, braced
for the whine of shells, if only to feel something again.

A Sudden Sun

Grace did not want to picture Jack like that, sitting alone by a dark window, thinking what he described as "dark thoughts" and glad to be feeling anything at all, even if it was something terrible. She read on: it was not the only entry like that. His dark thoughts were all there on paper for her to see. All the things he had kept hidden during that year in St. John's when she had wished he would talk to her were committed to writing now, as if he had to be hundreds of miles away before he could tell her the truth.

Yet through it all, as he wrote about the hardship and the loneliness, his terrifying dreams and the chasm of self-doubt that yawned before him on the darkest nights, he wrote, too, about loving his work and realizing he could still do it, and the joy that gave him. Grace's eyes burned—sometimes with tears, sometimes just with the strain of reading so late at night when she ought to be asleep. But the same words that chronicled Jack's despair also carried more hope than she'd heard from him in years.

> *March 12*
> *I am leaving Battle Harbour for now; I've been sent down the coast to the clinic at Forteau, where there's no doctor at the moment and a greater need for the services of an almost-doctor. The clinic, and the community there, is even smaller than at Battle Harbour, so, I imagine, even lonelier.*
>
> *I wish you were here. And yet that's not right because you seem so very much in your place in town that I can't imagine transplanting you to Labrador. I think the only people who make it up here are the ones who do feel called to it—and I think, for now at least, that I am one such.*

When Grace closed the black notebook her eyes ached with the effort of reading forty pages of handwriting by lamplight. She blinked at the clock: it was two in the morning. She had read

Trudy J. Morgan-Cole

Jack's stories of gruesome injuries, long hours, endless nights, an epidemic of flu that wiped out two entire families in a tiny village. He had written about his work, what he was learning, about his own pain and anguish and the glimmers of hope he saw. He had spoken to her more freely in his winter journal than in all the long months before he went away. He had written of missing her, and wishing she were there. But he had not written that he loved her, or said anything about marriage or the future.

She closed the book with the feeling that Jack had just been in the room, that she could still hear the echo of his voice. He was so close and yet he was far away, much further than the distance between St. John's and the Labrador coast. As to when, or whether, she would see him again, Grace had no idea.

CHAPTER THIRTY

"IT HAS BEEN thirty years since my mother joined a group of women who marched to our Colonial Building and presented a bill asking for the right to vote," Grace said, her voice shaking a little. She paused for translators to repeat her statement in French, in Spanish, in Italian. "And still the women of Newfoundland do not have the right to vote!"

"Shame! Shame!" cried some voices from the crowd. It was a crowd indeed, the largest Grace had ever spoken in front of— women from England and America and Europe as well as other parts of the world, brown and black faces mingled with the white ones at this ninth Congress of the International Woman Suffrage Alliance. The women of Newfoundland properly belonged among the brown and black faces, Grace thought, for the fact that they still didn't have the vote put them among the backward countries of the world, like that poor woman from Egypt who had spoken with such passion the day before. Italy, the host country, had still not given women the vote, though the country's new leader had promised it would come soon. Among the British Dominions, only the women of South Africa stood along with Newfoundland on the side of those who had not yet been given the franchise.

Speaking to such a group was both exhilarating and frightening. Grace's speech was a brief coda at the end of Miss Kennedy's presentation, and she felt disloyal to Lily as the words came out of her mouth. The very thing Lily had worked hard to conceal from her, the past that she was so ashamed of, Grace was telling this large group of strangers. Speaking as if suffrage was a cause she had learned about at her mother's knee.

When she finished with a plea for the ladies to petition the Newfoundland government for women's franchise, a burst of applause met her speech—something Grace's previous experience speaking in Sunday School and to church women's groups had not prepared her for.

It was not making speeches, though, but listening to them that was the most exciting part of the week—hearing the great Carrie Chapman Catt speak as she laid aside the mantle of leadership she had borne for nearly twenty years and the new president, Mrs. Ashby of England, was elected. Later, Grace was introduced to Mrs. Catt and shook her hand. Then there was the fact that, incredible as it seemed, she was in Rome. Grace spent as many hours as she could spare walking the streets, looking at the ruins. There was the Coliseum, and there the Roman Forum, just as they had been when Caesar was murdered on the Senate floor, when St. Paul and St. Peter preached here.

On Sunday, their last day in Rome, Miss Kennedy asked if the Italian lady who was acting as their tour guide, Signora Rignotti, could take her to St. Peter's. "I would so love to catch a glimpse of the Holy Father, and perhaps get some holy medals to bring home to dear Mother—it would mean so much to her," she said. Grace sometimes forgot that Miss Kennedy was a devout Roman Catholic; she was the only papist Grace had known well since the days when she worked under Nurse Fitzpatrick at the old Empire Hospital. Both women had done a great deal to erode Grace's wariness of Catholics, but her staunch Methodist soul shrivelled at the idea of going to St. Peter's Square to see the Pope and get holy medals blessed. "I believe I'll stay at the hotel," she said.

"I will bring you to a group of ladies who are making a—a pilgrimage, you would say?—to St. Peter's," Signora Rignotti said to May Kennedy. "Then I take Grace to the Coliseum. I am not so very good a Catholic; the Pope can say mass without me there." She laughed and hooked her arm through Grace's.

Italy was a country rebuilding itself after the ravages of the war that had ended five years earlier. Everywhere in Rome new roads were being built and new monuments erected. Grace exclaimed as she stepped over a metal drainage cover emblazoned with the eagle of the ancient Roman legions and the "SPQR" legend that she knew represented the Senate and People of the Roman Republic. "Goodness! Surely the drainage covers haven't been around since the time of the Caesars, have they?"

Signora Rignotti laughed. "No, no, not at all. Italy is an old country and a very new one, too. Much of our past was buried and forgotten. All this, bringing back the eagle and the old Roman symbols—that is all Mussolini and the Fascists. They want us to think the Roman Empire is great again. A bit foolish perhaps, but they are also putting in the new drains, so who am I to complain?"

The name and image of the new leader, Mussolini, was everywhere. He had sat on the dais and greeted the suffrage delegates on the first night of the conference, a blunt, plain-looking man who spoke what sounded to Grace like blunt and plain Italian. Nothing was poetic or eloquent about him, but when he spoke, people listened. Since coming here she had heard Italian ladies speak almost with reverence of their new leader—they called him *Il Duce*, "The Boss"—while others rolled their eyes and shook their

Trudy J. Morgan-Cole

heads when the great man's name was mentioned. One way or another, this man was the centre of everything in this city.

In a strange way Rome reminded Grace of Port Union—on a far grander scale of course, but the ancient city had the same endless string of new building projects that the little outport did, the same air of energy and optimism, and the same sense that behind it all was one man's vision, one towering personality. Over dinner that evening with Signora Rignotti, May Kennedy, and some ladies from the Canadian delegation, Grace tried to explain to Signora Rignotti. The Italian woman nodded, then shook her head. "Yes and no," she said. "I see what you mean about these great men—they build cities as their monuments—but if your Mister Coaker is a union man I do not think he and Mussolini would get along well, for Il Duce is set against the unions. His Blackshirts break up the strikes and promise they will save us from the socialists. Me, I'm not so sure we need the saving, but he says he will give our women the vote."

"I suppose time will tell," Miss Kennedy said, and when Signora Rignotti shot her a questioning glance, she added, "Your Mussolini—whether he is a good leader or not. And whether you, and we, get our rights."

"Ah yes, time. Time does not heal all wounds, as you English say, but it makes many things clear."

Signora Rignotti walked them back to their hotel that evening. At the door she turned to Grace. "It move me very much, what you say about your mother. I pray you in the New Found Land soon have the vote, and we here in Italy too. I am sure your mother will be proud of you." She put her arms around Grace, who was still struggling to adjust to the frequent kisses and embraces of southern Europe.

Then the Roman interlude was over, and Grace and Miss Kennedy were on a steamer headed back across the Atlantic. Their ship was bound for New York, from where they would catch the *Nerissa* to St. John's a few days later. Grace had arranged to spend those days staying with Mrs. Parker, who was eager to hear about everything: Grace's family, her work in St. John's, Jack, the conference in Rome. Abigail Parker was a most gratifying audience: she was never bored.

"What a wonderful opportunity, not just to attend a conference like that, but to speak. I tell you, Grace, I'm ashamed sometimes to think I come from Newfoundland when I see how backward our country is, but now I really think we might be seeing change in the air. And you're going to be a part of making it happen! Your mother would be proud, really she would."

Abigail Parker—who had known Lily so well, so long ago—unconsciously echoed the Italian woman who had never met her: *I am sure your mother will be proud of you.* And they were both wrong.

Grace took a long breath. "Do you really think she would, Mrs. Parker? She's told me over and over that she doesn't want me involved in the suffrage movement. Why would she think that, if she fought for women's votes herself once?"

For the first time since Grace had met her, Abigail didn't start talking immediately, treading on the heels of Grace's question. She took the time for a long sip of tea and laid cup and saucer down with great care. She picked up a scone, looked at it, laid it down again.

"Your mother was very badly hurt once, Grace. Perhaps she made some—poor choices. And perhaps she blames the suffrage women for some of that. She thinks that—well, that one thing led to another."

"She was in love with someone else before she married my father, wasn't she?"

Another sigh, like a soft puff of wind in summer. "Yes. Yes, she was. Madly in love, I'd have said."

"I can't picture that."

Trudy J. Morgan-Cole

"No, and that's the tragedy—not that she fell in love, but that it turned her into a woman you can't imagine ever being in love. It's as I told you. She was very badly hurt."

"Who was he?"

"No one. I mean, no one you'd know of. No one any of us knew of, really. He didn't move in our circles. He was a nobody — a journalist, very ambitious, very radical ideas."

"This was in St. John's?"

"Yes, hard to believe there was anyone radical in St. John's in those days, isn't it? He left eventually, of course. Came here, to New York."

"He left my mother?"

"He, ah—yes, he went away."

"And that was the end of things between them?"

"I can't tell you the whole story, Grace. Your mother begged me never to tell you...."

"But there is a whole story. And you know it."

"I helped your mother—I mean, I thought at the time I was helping. I helped her see this man, spend time with him. I thought it was all fun, a great lark—you know, secret admirers and all that. I didn't know how badly she would be hurt when—oh dear. I've said too much already."

"I'd pieced together a lot of it anyway. Things my mother and father said, and some old postcards I found in her room at Grandfather's house." The two postcards that had mystified her for years, the one signed A and the one signed D, were in Grace's purse, worn soft on the edges from carrying around. She had brought them knowing she would see Mrs. Parker in New York, though it wasn't until Signora Rignotti said *I think your mother will be proud* that Grace had decided to show them to Abigail.

Now she passed her the one signed A, the one that said, "*It's a pickle and no mistake.*" "You wrote this, didn't you?"

Mrs. Parker looked at the card, her lips forming the words as she read. "Yes," she said, almost a whisper.

"And this other one. He wrote it—the man my mother loved."

Mrs. Parker nodded, reading the card. "I suppose so. Yes, of course he did. I saw his hand writing often enough. I used to pass notes for them, sometimes. I should have known better."

"Can you tell me his name?"

"I can't. I shouldn't."

Grace wasn't sure why she persisted. For so many years she'd known there were secrets in her mother's past but had been willing to let them lie. It wasn't as if she had any right to them, if Lily didn't choose to tell her. But she had gone to Rome, and told women from around the world that her mother had once been a suffragist— her mother, who burned the suffrage petition. Last fall, when Grace had written to tell her parents that the Franchise League had raised money to send her to Rome, the Reverend had written back to give her his blessing. He had made it clear that he was going against Lily's wishes, something he rarely did where Grace was concerned. He also wrote, "We would like to see you at home again," but Grace had not been back since Lily burned the petition. She pleaded the need to stay in town and work, to save money for the Rome congress. The last letter she had from Lily before leaving Newfoundland was full of news about what everyone in Catalina had contributed to the Ladies' Aid sale of work, but had made no mention of Grace's trip to Rome.

Abigail Parker, who hated keeping secrets, needed little persuasion to tell Grace about a man called David Reid, a New-foundlander who, like herself, had lived in New York all these years. They didn't see each other socially, of course—not the same circles at all—but David Reid looked her up from time to time. Asked about people from home. Asked about Lily. He was a journalist. He lived in Brooklyn. And he had never married.

Trudy J. Morgan-Cole

"You have an address for him, then. Or at least you know where to find him," Grace said.

"Oh Grace, that wouldn't be a good idea. That wouldn't be a good idea at all."

Two days later, the day before her ship sailed for St. John's, Grace walked down the Brooklyn street where David Reid lived. The streets grew narrower and more crowded as she moved further into the heart of Flatbush. May in New York was as hot as May in Rome had been; she missed the cool of a St. John's fog. This Brooklyn street was a different world from Mrs. Parker's neighbourhood in Manhattan. She heard a babble of voices in different languages, saw dark faces, saw old Jewish men in black hats with long fringes of hair by their ears, woman in long dark dresses with veiled heads.

Mrs. Parker had given her the address after some protest. It really hadn't been a fair fight, Grace thought, pitting her own will against Abigail Parker's. Abigail still had that romantic, foolish side. The same part of her nature that had once helped Lily arrange meetings with a secret beau also wanted to know what would happen if Grace were to meet her mother's old lover. Grace had considered coming here and knocking on the man's door, or walking into his newspaper office, but she had sent a note instead explaining who she was and asking if they could meet. She had hesitated before adding the postscript. *My mother does not know I am contacting you.*

He had replied by return post, suggesting a restaurant in his neighbourhood at four o'clock this afternoon. She stood looking at the house a moment longer—it was four now, so if he were punctual at all he had left—and then went down the street, checking the address on the now crumpled piece of paper in her hand.

The restaurant was small and almost empty, since it was neither lunchtime nor dinnertime. A few people passing on the street gave her sidelong glances as she opened its door: presumably a well-dressed young lady going alone into a restaurant in the late afternoon was enough to attract attention.

The small, olive-skinned man who bustled towards the door when she opened it apparently thought the same. He gave her a nod deep enough it might have been called a bow and said, in heavily accented English, "Good day, Miss. Are you—you are not alone, are you awaiting someone?"

"She is awaiting me, Hassan," said a man's voice from the back of the room. Still blinking from the contrast between the brilliant sunshine outside and the darkness of the restaurant Grace could not at first see the man attached to the voice, but she followed Hassan to a table by the wall.

The man—tall, thin, grey-haired—stood up, thanked the waiter, and offered his hand to Grace while Hassan pulled out her chair. "David Reid," he said. "I'm very glad to meet you, Miss Collins."

"I'm—I'm not sure *glad* is the word in my case," Grace said, taking her seat. "I didn't even know of your existence—not by name, anyway—'til quite recently."

"And now you know that I am—what? An old friend of your mother's? I don't know what Abby told you."

"An old—what's the phrase? An old flame, I suppose. Someone my mother kept company with before she married my father."

He raised his glass and turned to the waiter. "Another of the same for me, Hassan, and the lady will have—what? A cup of tea? You won't like the coffee here, even if you like coffee."

"I've just come back from Rome. I drank Italian coffee there."

"Really! So you were at the women's suffrage conference? Did you hear Mrs. Catt speak? Still, Turkish coffee is another thing altogether." He glanced back at the waiter, and Grace said, "I will have a cup of Turkish coffee, thank you very much."

Trudy J. Morgan-Cole

David Reid burst out laughing. "Oh, you are so like Lily! You ordered that coffee exactly as she would have—full of spite and determined to have her own way even if she choked on it." His laughter died as quickly as it had come. "Or perhaps I'm not really remembering her. Perhaps I'm imagining her as she would have been if she'd lived in a time and place that had let her sit in a restaurant with a man and order her own coffee."

"I'm not even sure it's proper for me to be here," Grace admitted. "But having just come back from the conference in Rome I feel less inclined to worry about what's proper." She was impressed that he knew about the suffrage congress.

He looked old, older than her father, she thought, the way thin men often looked older than fatter ones because the wrinkles of age stood out more. Her father was fifty-five and her mother not yet fifty. David Reid could easily have been sixty. His face was lined, his hair iron-grey. He wore a light summer suit and fidgeted with his necktie, loosening it around a long, thin neck as he spoke.

"So, how did you convince Abby Hayward to tell you about my existence? Or did she just blurt it out? She's quite the blurter."

"She is, but she's a loyal friend too. My mother had asked her not to tell me anything about the past. Mrs. Parker told me a few things, but only after I guessed a good deal myself. I gather your…friendship with my mother didn't end very happily."

"Not very happily, no. I'm not surprised Lily never told you about me."

"It turns out there are a lot of things about my mother I didn't know. I only found out by accident that she was a suffragist when she was young. She never spoke of it."

"Quite the opposite, I'd guess—she disapproves of modern young women being independent and having careers, all that?"

"Yes." He seemed to know Lily's way of thinking quite well for someone who hadn't seen her in thirty years.

Hassan returned with a miniscule cup of coffee, which he laid before Grace, and another glass of whatever Mr. Reid was drinking—something alcoholic, Grace supposed, though she was hardly an expert in that area. Half a small glass tumbler full of amber liquid.

"So she's become quite conventional. It doesn't surprise me. People react in many different ways to—well, to things that upset them. Has she told you that pursuing women's rights will lead to free love and the end of morality?"

"Something like that, yes." Grace sipped the coffee, which was at least as strong as three cups of what she had drunk in Italy, distilled into a single tiny vessel. She wondered what Mr. Reid would say if she told him about the petition Lily had burned.

David Reid nodded. He cradled his glass in two long, bony hands. Then he looked up. "Tell me about Italy," he said. "Was it your first time abroad?"

So instead of talking about Lily, they talked about Italy. Mr. Reid had been there before and during the war but not since. He wanted to know about the conference but also what she had thought of Rome. "This Mussolini will be bad news, you mark my words," David Reid said to her, when she said how clean and well-run the ancient city had seemed to her. "People are looking around for saviours just now, in Europe, after all the chaos of the war, but here in America too. Perhaps even in Newfoundland."

"I don't think there's any hope of a saviour arising in the east—only Sir Richard Squires, in office again, forever and ever amen."

He laughed again. He had a wonderful laugh that filled the whole room and lighted his thin tired face. "Ah, dear old Newfoundland. I've travelled so much but I've never gone back home. I went to Russia, you know, in '19—just after the revolution. I wanted to see if the Bolsheviks had really got it right after all."

Trudy J. Morgan-Cole

"And had they?"

"Well, they're trying. It's a noble dream, you know, the best in the world. Better than Christianity even. I'm sorry, you're a minister's daughter—am I shocking you? But whether it's Christianity or communism, the problem is always the same—human nature. The serpent in Eden. Russia is a communist Eden, but it has its share of snakes."

They talked about politics in Newfoundland, in America and abroad, about Bolsheviks in Russia and Blackshirts in Italy and a world trying to remake itself after a war that had seemed like the end of the world. About the franchise for women and about Prohibition, which was in force in the U.S. as in Newfoundland but widely ignored in both places. "It's what women like your mother fought for," Mr. Reid said, "At first they only wanted the vote so they could outlaw the liquor trade. But do you really think it's done any good?"

Grace shook her head. "Not at home, because it's not properly enforced." Many of those who had once supported Prohibition in Newfoundland, even Mr. Coaker and the FPU, had turned against it in practice, seeing it as just one more way for the rich to oppress the poor. Those who had money could still get liquor if they wanted it; those who hadn't brewed their own.

"It's the same story here." David Reid lifted his glass. "I couldn't walk into any restaurant in New York and order a glass of whisky, but Hassan, who is a devout Mohammedan and doesn't touch a drop of the stuff himself, has a quiet understanding with his regular customers. People who want it can still get it, and those who abuse it always will."

Grace nodded. "If a man is a worthless drunkard who beats his wife and children, making liquor illegal doesn't change him—only forces him to buy it or make it illegally. If he had no way of getting liquor at all he might still beat his wife and children. The problem is deeper than the tavern or the wine-shop."

"Exactly. And the corollary is that if a man isn't that sort—if he's a decent kind of fellow who treats his wife like a queen and just wants a stiff drink to relax at the end of a hard day's work—then it's not fair to deny him that small pleasure, on the grounds of keeping it out of the other fellow's hands. You see? That's a thing your mother and I could never agree on, and I can see your forehead wrinkling up too—oh, you do look like her. You're not convinced."

"Not entirely, no."

"You know, if I could have given up that one drink at the end of the day, if I would have signed the temperance pledge and gone to church, Lily might have married me. Imagine. I suppose we're both thinking that then I could have been your father."

Grace nodded and forced herself to take another sip of the coffee. "Only, not really. Because I wouldn't have been me. I'm Papa's daughter too as well as Mother's."

"Yes, and with my blood in the mix instead of the good Reverend's who knows how you might have turned out. I don't know him, you know—your father. Never met the man, only heard your mother talk about him. He was courting her at the same time I was. But he was the one her father approved of."

"You couldn't have been so much in love, if you wouldn't take the pledge for her."

"Either that or I was a slave to the bottle, eh?" He laughed, a quieter laugh this time, one that didn't fill the room but barely left the table. "I wasn't, you know. There've been a few times in the years since when I drank too much—after Lily left me that last time, and once during the war when—anyway, sure. But it's never been my vice. Drink didn't ruin me, you know, the way she thought it would. I'm not sure I even *am* ruined, except by old age. That gets us all in the end, whether we take the pledge or not."

He was silent a minute, staring down into his glass. They had

Trudy J. Morgan-Cole

talked for two hours about the whole world and it had finally circled back to Lily. "She wanted me to be someone I wasn't, and I guess I wanted the same from her. I mean, I pictured us running away here to New York, living some kind of bohemian life together, but she wouldn't have been happy. And so in the end, I wouldn't either. That's the problem with love. It's a damned shame, Grace, but loving someone doesn't matter that much in the end if you don't want the same things. She didn't love your father, but I always thought she was much better cut out for his kind of life than mine. Tell me, did she manage to find a bit of happiness out of it all?"

It was almost the same question Abigail Parker had asked four years ago. Both of these people, her mother's old lover and her mother's old friend, had been tangled up in a sad situation that had left them both desperate to learn whether Lily had been happy after all.

"Not really. I don't think so. She's kept busy; I think she liked church and parish work, being the minister's wife and all that, at least until my brother died during the war. But even before that— I can't say I ever thought of her as particularly happy." Even as she said the words, Grace wondered if they were true. How often did she, did anyone, take a step back and look at a parent as a fellow human being, happy or unhappy? She had always seen Lily only in relation to herself: as kind or stern, over-protective or distant, depending on the mood between them at any given moment. But happy? Grace thought not, but how could she ever know for certain?

"Ah. That's too bad," David Reid said. "Too bad for her, and too bad because it makes a mess out of my theory. I've been—well, I haven't been unhappy. It's been a decent life and I've done most of the things I wanted to do. I hoped she could say the same. I've come to think living the kind of life you want is more important than being with the person you love. But maybe Lily hasn't even had the life she wanted."

Grace took the second postcard out of her purse. "You wrote this, didn't you?" She passed it across the table and watched his face as he read it.

He laid it on the table in front of him when he'd read through it, at least twice she thought, from the time it took. "I was in a boarding house in South Brooklyn," he said, "sitting up on the bed with a book on my lap, because I didn't even have a desk, writing this and trying to imagine bringing her here, into this life. I couldn't do it, but I couldn't abandon her either. The easy thing would have been to go home and pretend to be the man she wanted. Maybe that's what I should have done after all." He looked up at Grace. "I'd been down here for months when she wrote me. She wouldn't come with me, you see, when I left St. John's, so I thought it was all over between us. I was down here, working all hours and still broke, going to political meetings and, yes, that was probably one of the times I was drinking a bit too much. And then Lily wrote to tell me."

"That she was coming to New York?"

"What? No. Lord, no. She wrote to tell me she was going to have a baby."

Trudy J. Morgan-Cole

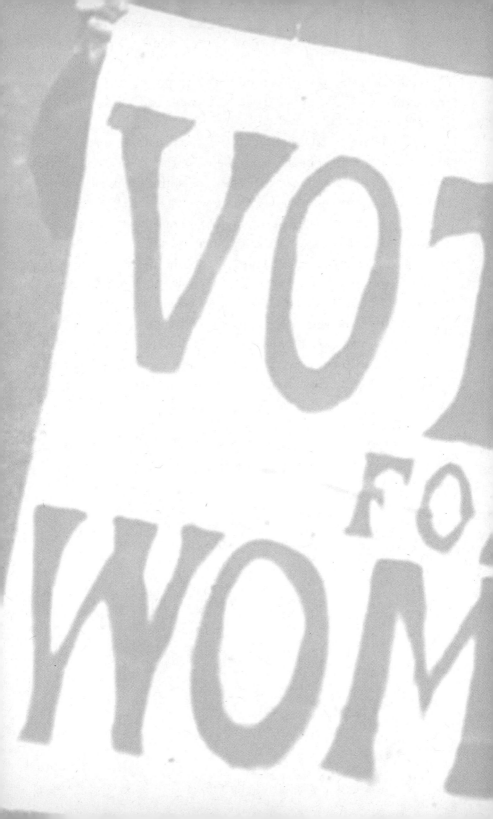

Part Six

LILY
1894–1895

CHAPTER THIRTY-ONE

$\mathscr{S}$HE PROMISED HERSELF she would wait a week before she started to worry. Her monthly visitor was due late in July, a week after David sailed for New York. Three weeks since she had said goodbye to him. Three long, lonely weeks. Most days had been grey, chilly, rain-soaked. Lily tried to read or write, but paced the floor of her room more often than not. There was no Abby to call and visit with, no hope of notes passed through the fence from David, nothing outside the house to distract her since she had been banned from everything but church.

She had come home at half-past seven in the evening the night she rejected Reverend Collins's proposal. When she walked into the house that night only her mother was there: her father and Reverend Collins were still out looking for her. The fact that she could, or would, give no account of herself for three missing hours made Papa's rage even greater.

"I was confused. I needed to think. I went for a walk by myself."

"For three hours? In the middle of the city?"

"I walked downtown, by the harbour."

Lectures, shouts, threats. It went on 'til nearly midnight. Reverend Collins politely excused himself. The fact that she had told him she wouldn't marry him somehow got rolled into the whole business of her disappearance, more evidence that her behaviour was entirely inappropriate for a Christian young woman.

"And the worst part of it," her father said, about ten o'clock in the evening as he warmed to his theme, "is that this fine young man of God, who made you an excellent offer of marriage, has now seen what kind of girl you are, and when you've had time to think better of it and realize what a good offer it is, he will be unlikely to make it again."

Lily felt as if her entire body were filled with shattered glass. She could make no sense of the fact that Obadiah Collins had offered to marry her, that David Reid was going away and had asked her to come away with him, that she had once again succumbed to temptation and lain with him, and worst of all, that it would be the last time ever.

The Reverend dropped by the following day to see if she was well after her "misadventure." Lily refused to see him. He went back, presumably, to Greenspond, and Lily went back to pacing the floor. She did not leave the house again until it was time for church on Sunday.

Over the next week she read *Bleak House*, the only Dickens novel she hadn't yet read, and went no further than the back garden. Only once did she see Johnny with a note from David, which turned out to say "Leaving on Friday the 14th. Will you reconsider?"

She burned the note.

Friday the 14th dawned with a hard rain. Lily had not sent a return note to David. He was leaving. Unless he had changed his mind, decided to stay. He could stay in St. John's, keep on working away at the *Evening Herald*, start going to church. He could come to the front door, meet her father, ask for her hand in marriage. Papa would say no, but Lily would defy him, head held high, and marry David anyway. And in a little while, three months or six months or a year, her parents would see what a fine young man David was. There would be a grandchild someday, and Lily would be forgiven for being a headstrong girl who got married without her parents' permission. It would all be so easy: why wouldn't David do it?

By the beginning of August it looked like there might well be a grandchild, after all, without the benefit of even a secret wedding. Lily wished she could read that medical book again, the one she had seen in Abby's parents' library, but she had no way of getting to that or any other book, and there were no useful volumes on her parents' shelves. Perhaps she had misunderstood it. Perhaps if you missed your monthly visitor only once, it didn't mean anything. Surely it had said a woman couldn't be certain until she had missed twice? She would have to wait all of August to be sure.

The calm thoughts, the thoughts assuring her that she must be mistaken—those thoughts came during the day. She rehearsed them, repeated them soothingly to herself during the times when *Bleak House* slipped from her hands and she couldn't focus on the words. In the daytime, she could convince herself of anything. That she wasn't going to have a baby. That David would go to New York, realize he couldn't live there without her, and come home to marry her. That God could forgive her sins.

But at night all those careful defenses fell away. She drifted into a troubled sleep and woke in the dark, knowing she was going to have a baby whose father was far away, that she was going to be shamed and cast out. She would have to go to a home for unwed girls, or no, worse, they would send her to Harbour Grace, to her grandparents, and she would have the baby in seclusion and then it would be taken from her, given up for adoption. She would never even see David again and he would never know about his child, and she would be farmed out to some relative around the bay and become the spinster

319

Trudy J. Morgan-Cole

cousin, never to marry or return to the city of her shame.

When those thoughts crowded into her head she felt snakes of terror twist in her gut. And then she would convince herself that those were cramping pains and that her period was coming after all, and she would lie there believing she had been given a reprieve.

August grew hot and muggy, despite the general rule that summer was over after Regatta Day. In mid-August a letter arrived from New York.

> *Dearest Lily,*
> *I got my landlady, who has rather pretty girlish handwriting, to address the envelope in hopes that if your parents question the sender, you can claim this is from Abby. When I think that such tricks are necessary to write to you it makes me angry, but I see no other way. The thought of never hearing from you again shatters me.*
> *It's a great city here, my love. So different from old St. John's—and not just because it's bigger. There's a kind of life pulsing through the streets here. Even knowing I've left you behind and that you may never follow me— missing you every hour—still I'm glad to be here. I probably shouldn't confess that but I can't lie to you. I only wish there was a place we could both feel this way together.*

Lily locked herself in her room, read the letter, cried for an hour, reread the letter and burned it. It would have been better if he hadn't written. Better for him to have just sailed silently out of her life. She could pretend the whole affair had never happened. Only she couldn't. Not if she were pregnant.

August ended. By mid-September there could be no further denying it. Two months had passed without her monthly visitor. She looked at herself in the mirror and wondered how soon women started to grow large. She looked no different, but her breasts felt sore

and she was often sick to her stomach, which she knew were signs she was carrying a child.

The night she finally admitted the truth to herself, she prayed for the first time since July. She confessed her sins fully and with an open heart. She knew now that no love, no pleasure, no moments of delight in each other's arms could ever be worth the agony, the torment she was now suffering. A man could walk away from a love affair, could go on to a new life in a new city and write about how happy he was there. He could cherish her like a sad and lovely memory that would grow smaller and sweeter with the years. But Lily had no such luxury.

She prayed for the baby too, knowing the only half-way respectable solution was to go away and bear the child in private and then give him away. Him, or her. A son or a daughter. David's and hers. Lily tried to place it all in God's hands but she could not imagine leaving the child with someone else. For the rest of her life that child would stamp her with the stigma of her sin, but also with the only tangible memory of love. How could she give up such a child?

She wrote two letters, finally. She was still virtually a prisoner in the house and garden. During the times when her father was at work and her mother was lying down in her room, Sally was nearby, doing her work with watchful eyes. Only in her bedroom or in the garden did Lily have any privacy. She gave the two letters to Johnny Murphy with some money for postage and prayed that the boy was trustworthy enough to take them to the post office rather than spending the money on candy or tobacco and tossing the letters in the gutter.

People at church began to ask how she was, why she didn't come to the Sunday School outing or that wonderful concert last week. Mrs. Ohman dropped by three times to try to visit, but was turned away, once by Mother and twice by the efficient Sally. The third time

Trudy J. Morgan-Cole

Lily was actually on the stairs to hear her say, "No, sorry Ma'am, Miss Lily isn't seeing nobody."

"Are those her orders or Mr. Hunt's orders?" Mrs. Ohman's rich voice rang out.

Lily thought of running down the stairs, racing into Mrs. Ohman's arms, begging for rescue.

"Don't make no difference, Ma'am, she won't see you either way."

"Can I leave a note?"

"Probably best not to, Ma'am. Miss Lily haven't been very well and I've been told over and over she's not to be disturbed."

Lily turned and went upstairs. Mrs. Ohman was still bickering with Sally, their voices mingling into a single high-pitched chitter as Lily continued up to the third floor.

For a fortnight it seemed there would be no reply to either of her letters and she fell further into despair. She really was all alone, then, in the world. Nobody would help her, no one would rescue her. Then Abby's reply, a postcard enclosed in an envelope for privacy, arrived.

It's a pickle and no mistake. She could hear Abby saying the words, her pretty mouth curving downward with shock even as she couldn't resist thinking what a delightful melodrama she'd been caught up in. But her offer of help was immediate, even though Abby was still a guest in her aunt's house and was not really at liberty to offer house-room to Lily. She had said they could "puzzle out what to do" but there was no solution to this puzzle. Even God could not change what had happened. Unless...

Lily knew that not every woman who conceived a baby went on to give birth. She had heard of miscarriages though she was vague about what was actually involved. Would it be a sin to pray for a miscarriage? Was there something one could do to make one happen? That in itself would surely be a sin—although any stain of guilt might be worth it if she could go back and erase the past, erase the child she now knew was growing in her womb.

She did not burn Abby's letter but stuck it in a drawer with some old issues of the *Water Lily* and WCTU handbills. How strange, that all that had once seemed so important to her, that she had slaved over little essays and poems in hopes they would be published. That she had handed out leaflets to invite women to meetings. She thought of that Lily, the Lily of just a few months ago, as an alien creature, strutting the streets like a peacock spreading its tail, drawing attention, opening herself out to the larger world. Now she was a snail curling into its shell, drawing more and more of herself inside.

While she thought about Abby's letter and whether she could really go to New York, the first week of October came and went. Another week in which she should have had her monthly visitor but didn't. Three months. She studied herself in the mirror again and thought she could detect a slight thickening of the waist, though everywhere else—arms, face, legs—she looked thinner, because the combination of nausea and distress was making it hard to eat much.

Then the second letter came, in the same pained careful handwriting as before, the handwriting of David's New York land-lady. "Another letter from Abigail?" Papa said, scanning the New York postmark as he handed over the letter. "I hear she's engaged to be married."

"I hadn't heard that. Perhaps that's what she's writing me about," Lily said, taking the envelope.

She opened it upstairs. Inside, David's familiar scrawl, a few lines inviting her to come to him. *Soon it will be too late—for you, that is.*

She could do it, she thought. Go to New York. Stay with Abby. At worst it would offer a more comfortable spot than Harbour Grace to live out her months of shame and then come back. Perhaps even her parents would not be any the wiser. At best, well, she would see David. They could talk, decide what to do. He had, after all, said he

Trudy J. Morgan-Cole

would marry her, though neither of them could imagine a life together that would make them both happy.

But now Lily couldn't imagine a life anywhere, with anyone, that she could be happy in.

She went to her father three days after getting David's letter. "The letters I had from Abigail? She wants me to come visit her in New York."

"She does? I'd have thought she'd be busy preparing for married life. I spoke to her father just the other day. The wedding's to be in the spring, in New York."

"Yes, yes I know." There had been nothing in Abby's brief note about a wedding, but it was easy to improvise. "She wants me there for the winter, to help her plan and prepare, and then to stay for the wedding." Six months. She counted ahead. April. The baby would come in April, about the time Abby would be getting married to some rich American. "I could stay 'til she's married and come home in the summer. She might—she may want to ask me to be a bridesmaid, Papa." Though not likely, if Lily was a big as the broad side of a barn. "To tell the truth I feel the need of a change. You know I haven't been feeling well."

Papa nodded slowly. "Yes, I've noticed, and your mother has told me you've lost your energy and your appetite. Lily, you know I did what I had to do. If nothing else, your reputation would suffer, if I allowed you to walk the streets unchaperoned, to go out to radical meetings, to keep unsuitable company. I know you're a good girl—I know you always have been—but a girl needs her father's protection until it's time to pass into her husband's care. When you have a daughter of your own someday, you'll understand why I had to act as I did."

When I have a daughter of my own, which may be sooner than you think, Lily thought. *When my daughter has grown up, perhaps we will live in a different world. Where a girl can love whom she chooses, and go where she wants, and make her own choices.* It seemed like a fairy tale she was telling herself, an enchanted land where the princess could become heir to the kingdom.

"I think a winter in New York would do me a world of good, Papa."

"No. No, I can't allow it."

"Won't you please think about it, at least?"

"Absolutely not. Lily, you know I've never thought Abigail Hayward was a good influence. I've only allowed you to be friends with her because I respect her parents. But I don't agree with their choice to send her off to New York. Apparently it fits with the life they want for their daughter, but it has nothing to do with the kind of life we're preparing you for. Your problem has been too much freedom, and that certainly won't be remedied by sending you off to stay in a foreign city with a flighty and reckless girl, under the chaperonage of an aunt we don't know. If I fear for your safety and good judgement here on the streets of St. John's, why on earth would I ever let you go to New York?"

Tears welled up, but Lily fought them back. It was, after all, only to be expected. She had made the best case she could but she had always known he must say no. She dabbed at her eyes with her handkerchief.

Papa's voice was gentle and low. "Lily, I agree that the existence you've been leading these past months is not good for you— moping about the house, being always alone. I miss your spark, your spirit. You are the only thing that keeps this house from turning into a mausoleum. But running away to New York, trying to copy Abby Hayward's life, which can never be yours, is not the answer. The answer is to turn your thoughts to your own future, to the kind of life we have always prepared you for. Marriage to a good, godly man. It's time to think of being a wife and mother, Lily." He waited but Lily said nothing to fill the silence for him. The mantel clock ticked, ticked away the moments. How little time she had left before the whole mess was out in the open!

"Reverend Collins is coming to town again in November, while the steamers are still running," Papa said.

"He seems to make a great many trips to town," Lily sniffled, reaching for the handkerchief again. "Are you sure he's not neglecting his parish?"

Papa smiled but said, "He is a very conscientious young clergyman. He is coming to town because he hopes you will have a different answer to his question. I understand that you didn't feel ready, the last time he asked. You weren't prepared. But you have had time to think. Think and pray about it, Lily. It is time to move ahead."

She thought. She prayed. She wondered if there was a plan that would somehow get her to New York with no money for a steamer ticket. She prayed by the hour, looking for signs, reading the Bible, waiting for anything that might tell her where to turn.

She took out David's postcard, tucked away in the same drawer with Abby's. He loved her. He wanted to help. He wanted to be with her. But he hadn't said the one thing she most needed to hear. He hadn't said, "I'm coming home at once."

That was what it came down to. What she needed from him was so simple. Not an invitation to come to a faraway city when she had no means or money to get there. What she needed was for the father of her child to come home and take care of her.

She would not write to beg him to return. What kind of basis for a marriage would it be, if she asked him to make a great sacrifice, unwilling? The marriage would begin with Lily always under a great burden of debt.

One could begin a marriage that way, but it would not be, never could be, a love match. Sometimes it might be the only choice.

As promised—or threatened—Reverend Collins came to town

in November. The air was raw with northeast winds by then, the sky a perpetual ceiling of grey. Lily had begun to choose looser, high-waisted dresses: no-one could yet have guessed, glancing at her, but she could see it herself, feel it in the tightening of her waistbands. More than four months along, now.

Reverend Collins took her to a choir concert at St. Thomas's Church. It was the first time she had been out of the house, except for church, since that day in July. But Papa didn't seem to mind trusting her reputation, her girlish purity, to the Reverend Collins.

They went for a drive after the concert, though it was chilly and Lily huddled inside her fur coat. "Thank you for that," she said, with at least a little sincerity. "I haven't been out much at all these past months. It's been quite dull."

"It's lovely to see you enjoy yourself again, my dear," the Reverend said. "How I'd like to see roses bloom in those pale cheeks! I know a life in Greenspond would not offer you much in the way of diversion, but it would be a life of useful work and companionship. Have you given anymore thought to my offer?"

"I have," said Lily. She shivered, possibly from the cold, but she did not want to have this conversation in her parents' parlour.

She told him everything. Everything, except David's name. She did not try to colour the truth, or not very much. She told him that she had fallen in love with someone else, a young man who was kind to her but whom her parents would have considered an unsuitable husband. She had been tempted, and fallen into sin. "And now I am going to have a child," she said. "A child with no father. I am a sinful woman, Reverend Collins. I want a new start, and a father for my child, but I cannot ask you to take on such a burden, especially since it will seem to others that the child is yours." She had rehearsed the words over and over, like a part in a play.

She watched his face change as she told her story. His eyes widened. A frown creased his brow. The corners of his mouth,

Trudy J. Morgan-Cole

upturned in what he must have thought an appealing smile when he started to speak, turned down, and his eyes faltered away from hers when she finished speaking.

"I ought to take you home," he said after a moment. "I should speak with your father."

"Mr. Collins, I beg you—my father and mother know nothing of this. I have kept it a closely guarded secret, and I have trusted only you with it."

"No one else? Not even this—this man? The father of your child?" The word "father" seemed distasteful on his tongue.

"Of course I did tell him. But he isn't—I can't marry him. He has gone away, and he won't return home to care for me and for his child." She felt disloyal as she said it, painting David as a man who would shirk his responsibility. But at bottom it was nothing more or less than the truth.

It was likely that Reverend Collins would withdraw his offer of marriage and tell her father at once. She was surprised when he said, "It would be like Joseph."

Lily knew what he was thinking immediately, but prompted him. "Like Joseph?"

"Joseph, the earthly father of Jesus, had to take on not only the responsibility of Mary and her baby, but the shame of having people think he was the father—that he was the one who had sinned in having relations with her before they were married. But he bore it all with grace."

"But I am not the Virgin Mary," Lily said. "Only a girl who has sinned."

"Yes, yes," he said, his eyes still on the road and not on her. "So in a way it would be more like Hosea and Gomer." He turned to her. "Lily, I won't speak to your father tonight. I won't deny to you that I'm deeply disappointed, that you're not the girl I thought you were. It's a heavy blow, to be sure. But I must go home and think and pray on this—be sure of what God is calling me to do."

Lily had always disliked the book of Hosea—or 'Osea, as Mr. Collins pronounced it—and thinking of it now she felt sorry for Gomer. Hosea's sinful wife had run away from her husband and become a harlot, and he took her back. But for the rest of her life Gomer would have had to live with that burden of gratitude, of knowing that he had stooped into the gutter to lift her up.

He came the next day. Lily had not slept all night. In the morning she stood at the window and thought, *David could come home.* He might return on a steamer, without sending a letter or a cable because he knew it might not be safe, and at any moment he might walk up to her front door and rescue her. He might say, "You must marry me" and she would have to say yes. It would be so wonderful, not only to see him again but to have someone else take away the awful burden of deciding what to do.

Instead it was Reverend Obadiah Collins who came to the door at eleven o'clock in the morning. Lily had touched nothing except tea on the breakfast tray that Sally brought up. He walked up the street with his head down and his hands clasped behind his back, like a man going to do something serious and important.

Lily took out the contents of her dressing-table drawer and looked through them: not just David's postcard and Abby's but the copies of the *Water Lily*, the leaflets, the scraps and pieces of a life she had almost lived but then abandoned. Then a knock came. Sally said, "Your Papa would like to see you in his study," and he was down there with the Reverend, the two of them on either side of the desk, and neither of them looked happy. But the Reverend was there. Happy or not, he was there.

"Sit down, Lily," her father said, indicating a chair. "Reverend Collins and I have been having a long talk, heart to heart." Lily sat in the chair next to Reverend Collins, which made it feel like they were two naughty children called into the headmaster's office in school.

Trudy J. Morgan-Cole

"He has confessed something that surprised me greatly, that seems entirely out of character with what I know of him, and of you too. You have been headstrong, Lily, but I never thought you wicked. However, I understand that you are an innocent young girl, easily led astray, and the greater blame rests on Reverend Collins' shoulders."

Lily looked from her father to the Reverend, waiting. The Reverend reached over and took her hand. "Lily, my dear, I've confessed to your father that when I came to town in July, that you and I—that we were indiscreet, and did what we should not have done, when our engagement was not yet even settled, much less our marriage. That we want to be married very quietly and quickly, before the baby comes, and that I will endeavour to do all I can before God to atone for this error by taking care of you, and of our child."

It was the most natural thing in the world that Lily should burst into tears at that moment. There could be any number of reasons for it.

"I need not say again how disappointed and surprised I am," Papa said, "especially as you are a clergyman, Mr. Collins. But I think it is a failing that people are apt to forgive and forget if the marriage is made promptly afterwards."

When she was alone with the Reverend, Lily said, "I suppose I ought to thank you."

The Reverend looked a bit taken aback. "I…I had thought you would be grateful."

I am, Lily thought. *I have to be. And I will have to be, every day of my life.*

The word was out in church the next day. "Oh, you should have a Christmas wedding!" cried Daisy Gill, when Lily said only that they would be married "Quite soon."

But it was not a Christmas wedding. It was a twenty-fourth of

November wedding in the parlour of the bride's parents' home. A week had passed since the marriage proposal; Reverend Collins wanted to be married and back in Greenspond while it was still possible for a boat to travel there, before the weather closed in. He had cabled home to tell them he would be away an extra week, but would bring his bride when he returned. Lily's father and mother were present. There were no other guests, no wedding supper, no celebration.

Before the wedding she had written a long letter to Abby, explaining what she was doing.

> ... *Thank you for offering, but there was no way I could come to you: Papa wouldn't allow it. D said the same— that I could come to him in New York—but what good it does me to have him, or you, or anyone who cares for me in New York when I am here, I don't know. I have been forced to turn to the only person I thought might help me, and he did help, though God alone knows how he will make me pay for it.*
>
> *Anyway it will all be over very soon. And I will be married before you after all. What fun.*

Her note to David was much shorter. She sent a telegram.

MARRYING REVEREND COLLINS NOVEMBER 24 STOP IT'S FOR THE BEST STOP NO NEED TO WRITE AGAIN STOP

She could, of course, have written to him after it was all done. But she cherished that thread of hope that there was in David Reid some spark of Young Lochinvar, that he would batter at the door and tear her from the arms of Obadiah Collins even as the vows were being said. He could claim Lily and his child and carry her off to— where? It hardly mattered anymore.

Trudy J. Morgan-Cole

CHAPTER THIRTY-TWO

*I*T BEGAN TO snow almost the minute they landed in Greenspond, or so it seemed to Lily. The parsonage was small but it felt cold, bare, and empty. She knew that her job was to make a home of it, to grace it with a woman's touch, but a weight of lassitude had fallen on her as soon as she stepped off the steamer. When she accompanied the Reverend to church on Sunday, people crowded round to shake her hand and welcome her. Nobody seemed to feel there was anything hasty about the wedding: they knew their young minister had been going into town to court a girl there. Lily caught no covert glances at her waistline, even from the older women. There was nothing to see anyway. Unclothed, she could see a slight roundness to her belly, but under a corset, petticoat and dress there was no hint at all.

She got a keener glance from the Reverend's mother when they went over to Wesleyville to visit his parents. They presented their son and his wife with a handsome set of china that must have been ordered long before the wedding was confirmed. Mrs. Collins was nothing like Lily's own mother. She reminded Lily more of

Abby's mother or of Mrs. Ohman, women filled with an alarming energy. But where Mrs. Hayward's energy was dedicated to moving in the right society, and Mrs. Ohman's to bettering the world, Mrs. Collins's energy appeared to be directed towards setting other people straight and pointing out the errors of their ways. In a three-hour visit Lily heard from her all about what was wrong with the Ladies' Aid, why the Sunday School was being run improperly, and who was wearing inappropriate hats to church. What would this woman do when she discovered a real sinner, right under her nose, in her son's house?

December. Snow, rain, sleet, snow again. Visits from parishioners with small wedding gifts. At night Lily slept in the master bedroom alone; the Reverend slept, as he had done before marriage, in a little closet of a bedroom off his study. "Of course, when your child is born," he had said, looking down at his feet, "we shall, ah, be together as man and wife. I hope we will have more children. I want children of my own, you understand."

Christmas Eve. One month since her marriage. Lily woke while it was still dark. She had had trouble sleeping for months now, but usually managed to fall into an exhausted sleep sometime in the early hours of the morning. Now she was awake at five, cramps twisting in her stomach. The pain was sharp and red-hot. She cried out, then muffled her face in the pillow.

August, September, October, November, December. Five months, nearly six. Was the baby coming already? She almost laughed—even in April there would have been no hope of convincing people it was so very premature. But now? It was a joke, another of God's little jokes.

By the time the sky lightened, Lily knew she had to call the Reverend. She gritted her teeth to keep from screaming. She didn't want the housemaid to know. Then she remembered they had given the girl Christmas Eve and Christmas Day off to spend with her

Trudy J. Morgan-Cole

family. Maybe the baby was coming, or maybe something else terrible was happening. She had never seen a doctor or a midwife. It struck her for the first time that she had entered upon this whole marriage on the grounds that she was expecting a baby and no one had ever told her for certain that was the case. Maybe there was no baby. Maybe she was dying.

She dragged herself to the door, doubling over as another wave of pain rolled over her. "Reverend Collins!" she called. She had never yet called him Obadiah.

He came and told her to get back in bed, then went himself to fetch the midwife. Lily lost track of time under waves of pain. Then the midwife was there, an old woman who muttered and shook her head. "This don't look good," she said. "How far along do you say you are, Missus?"

"July 8," Lily said through gritted teeth. That one thing she knew for certain. On the eighth of July she had lain down in a bed with her lover and conceived this child. She tried to lock her jaws against the screams but the midwife said, "Have a good holler, my love, it'll do you good. Not much else will, now."

She had thought the wedding day was the worst of her life but that was only because she was a little fool, an ignoramus. An innocent girl, as her father had said. Could she be a fallen woman and an innocent girl at the same time? Now she was innocent no longer, but still falling, falling through pain and darkness and horror, screaming and pushing like a barnyard animal to give birth to something the midwife had told her would not, could not live. No one had even guessed she was having a baby. She had sold her life away for nothing. If this had happened a month earlier, on the morning of the twenty-fourth of November instead of December, everything would have been different—no wedding, no husband, no chilly parsonage in Greenspond.

It wasn't over 'til midnight, as Christmas Eve turned to

Christmas Day. Her whole day, her child's whole life, had been bordered by this one room, this bloody bed, this square of streaky window glass that grew light and then rain-covered and then dark again.

"'Tis all over now, Missus," said the midwife. She had taken the thing away to dispose of—Lily didn't ask where or how—got Lily out of bed when she was able and scrubbed up, changed the sheets, changed Lily's bedclothes. The room looked tidy again; a fire burned in the grate, and the midwife sat next to Lily with a bowl of beef broth, spooning it into her mouth.

"You'll need to rest now, a good few days. Don't be up and about too soon. I'll drop back Saturday or Sunday. And don't worry—the Reverend give me extra money, but he didn't need to, I been at this business long enough to know when to hold my tongue. Nobody will know nothing but what the minister's wife was laid up with some female trouble. The Reverend thinks we can make it like nothing ever happened." Another spoonful of broth. The midwife wasn't really as old as Lily had thought. Middle-aged at best. Her dark eyes were shrewd. "There's no better skill than learning when to keep your mouth shut and I knows it better than most. All the same, you can't really make it like a thing never happened, especially if the thing is a baby. Whatever you does after this, however many more you has, it always happened."

"Yes," Lily said. She had hoped for so long that some miracle would come along and make it un-happen. But the miracle had come too late.

Her husband came in when the midwife had gone. He stood by the window, hands in his pockets, bouncing slightly on the balls of his feet.

"How are you feeling?"

"Tired. Sore. Exhausted." Did it feel the same, Lily wondered,

Trudy J. Morgan-Cole

to birth a living child? But then you would feel full instead of empty, surely.

"It's a great pity. But it may prove to be for the best in the end. God moves in mysterious ways."

The cup that had held the beef broth was still on the side table. Lily had her hand around it before she stopped to think. She hurled it straight at his head, but he dodged aside and it shattered on the wall, shards of white crockery splintering around the room.

"You're very upset," he said. His tone had not changed at all. After a moment he said, "I told Mrs. Cuff—no one needs to know about this. After you've recovered, it will be like a fresh start for us both. We'll begin again."

"Go away." She buried her face in the pillow. When she looked up again he was squatting on the floor, picking up pieces of the broken cup. The sight moved her for a moment, 'til she thought, *He won't want the maid to see this tomorrow, to know I'm going mad.*

CHAPTER THIRTY-THREE

*S*HE STAYED IN bed for a week. When the midwife came again she told her to get up. "You're not the first woman to miscarry and you won't be the last. It's a hard thing but there's harder things than this, you mark my words. You take to your bed and you might never get out of it again." Her words were harsh as sandpaper but Lily felt no urge to throw a cup at her head. She got up, dressed, began to move cautiously about the house.

She went back to church two Sundays afterwards. The ladies of the congregation showed a gentle mix of curiosity and sympathy. One older lady pulled her aside and said, "I used to have a terrible, terrible time at my time of the month when I was your age. The old granny, Mrs. Cuff's poor mother-in-law that was, she used to make me a lovely tea to help me get through it. It will all be better once you haves a baby—it was for me."

A baby. Because of course she would stay here, stay in Greenspond as the minister's wife, bear him children. She had made a vow before God.

After dinner the Reverend went back to the church to teach

Sunday School. He wanted Lily to help with that when she felt better, to take a children's class. These were things the minister's wife was meant to do. He wasn't merely taking a bride, he was hiring the other member of his team. They were to be like a pair of oxen yoked together, for what church—other than a papist one—could function without the minister's wife?

When he was gone Lily went to his study and took down his strongbox. She searched through his desk 'til she found the key. He was not very good at hiding things, perhaps because it had never occurred to him that his wife might steal his money.

She counted out banknotes. Her passport was here in the strongbox along with his. She had never carried it herself; her father had given it to the Reverend with her other important papers, in case they travelled together someday. But how much did a steamer ticket to St. John's cost? How much more, then, a ticket to New York? She had no idea. She counted out the money and sat with it in her hand, awash in the vast ocean of her own ignorance. She could not even run away because she did not know how much a steamer ticket cost, had never been on a journey on her own before.

And how could she sneak aboard the steamer, when everyone came out to see the passengers board, to put their mail and packages on board, to wish the travellers well? Who could ignore the minister's wife setting foot on the boat? It was a long and tiresome journey: off the island of Greenspond itself, then on down the coast, stopping at every little port; everyone in Bonavista Bay would know that the Greenspond minister's wife was leaving home. And on top of everything—oh, she had forgotten—it was January. No steamer service, no hope of escape, 'til spring.

She would not live until spring.

And yet she did. Her body, that resilient animal thing, recovered. She kept the door of her bedroom closed to him, telling him she wasn't ready yet. She had read once, in a book, that until a man and woman came together in the marriage bed it was not really a marriage, and could be annulled. Could that be true? And if it were, who would vouch for her, when her own father believed she and the Reverend had been like man and wife long before the wedding ever took place?

There was no one here to help her. No one in St. John's either, yet when spring came—April, when the baby should have been born—she begged the Reverend to allow her to go home. "To visit," she said. "I need to see my parents." She did not even know if they would welcome her in the house, if she really were going home for a visit. She had written on the first mail-boat to tell them the baby had come early, and did not live. She had never seen it— did it even look like a baby? She pictured it with skin made of glass, so that everything inside could be seen.

"How long will you stay?"

"A week or two. Is that all right?"

"I don't want you to be away too long. I feel you haven't really settled here, Lily, and I need your help and support—around the house, and in the church. I feel you're not happy here."

She thought of throwing something at him again but she had been so good, so docile, all winter that he had surely written off that one incident as a moment of madness brought on by the strange mystery of a woman's body.

He agreed to a fortnight in St. John's. She waited 'til the morning the steamer left, when he was down at the church meeting with the Vestry, to steal the money from the strongbox and take her passport. She had asked around, in casual conversation, to try to get an idea from people of how much it cost to travel; she took more than she thought she would need.

When she got to St. John's, she inquired about tickets to New York before she ever left the docks. She counted out her money there in the Furness-Withy office. She had only enough to go to Halifax,

Trudy J. Morgan-Cole

with a little left over to hire a room for the night. The steamer left the next morning.

What was the good of going to Halifax, with hardly a cent to keep her when she got there? Not enough to stay for more than a night, nor to go further on the steamer, nor to buy a train ticket. Enough, perhaps, for a meal and room—and enough to send a cable.

The next day she stood on the deck of the ship, watching St. John's slip away. She had spent the night in a room at the Crosbie hotel where the desk man had looked at her strangely, a young woman travelling alone. She kept her wedding band firmly on display, though she meant to drop it overboard into the sea on her way to Halifax.

The crossing was rough and Lily was sick as she hadn't been sick since the earliest days of her pregnancy. It was hard to believe, now, that she had really been pregnant, had carried David's child inside her for nearly six months before letting it slip away. Maybe her husband was right. It would be like it had never happened. She could have the new start he had talked about. Not with him, of course, and not in Greenspond.

"Lily! Is that you, Lily dear!"

The one thing she had gambled on was that she would not know anyone on the steamer. She had gotten from the harbour to the hotel and back again this morning without seeing anyone she recognized, and that was miracle enough, St. John's being the town it was. But here was Jessie Ohman, of all people, under a magnificent feathered hat with her hands shoved into a fur muff, strolling about the deck. She was on her way to Montreal, where her husband had already settled and opened a business.

"And truth to tell, I'm not sorry to be leaving," she confided to Lily as they stood in the bracing sea wind watching the grey waves roll past. "Newfoundland will always be home, but after the barriers we've faced these last few years I'll be glad to be moving to a more enlightened place. The women's cause is much more advanced in Canada."

Lily nodded, wondering what story she should spin for Mrs. Ohman about her presence on the ship. But Mrs. Ohman was doing her work for her: "Going to New York? Oh, you must be going down for Miss Hayward's wedding, are you? How nice that you're able to go. Did you get the card I sent for your marriage?"

"Yes, I'm sorry, I didn't send out thank-you cards," Lily said, aware of the enormous breach of etiquette she had committed.

"Ah well, I thought you must be very busy out there. It's not an easy life, you know, my dear, but a minister's wife can do so much good. It's every bit as much a calling for her as for the minister himself. And I'm so glad, Lily, that you made a wise choice. I know it's easy for young girls to get distracted by romantic notions, but in the end, nothing matters more than choosing a godly man."

It was like the moment when she had thrown the cup at the Reverend—Lily's hand moved as if it were its own creature, darting through the icy air to slap Mrs. Ohman's smug round cheek.

Mrs. Ohman gasped, put her own hand to her cheek. "Lily! Whatever do you—are you all right, my dear?" Lily turned to go but Mrs. Ohman reached out and grabbed her upper arm. "Has something happened? Talk to me, Lily. Clearly you're upset, your mind is unbalanced."

"If it is, it's all your fault!" Lily said, finding her voice, feeling as if she had been silent for months, for nearly a year, perhaps for her whole life. "What lies, what lies you told me! You told me a woman was the equal of any man, that we had the same rights as men, that all we had to do was stand up and demand those rights and that when we did so the Lord would bless us for doing His will! You told me those lies and made me believe them and you don't even believe them yourself! Why did you let me believe they were true?"

Trudy J. Morgan-Cole

She was howling now, crying all the tears she had locked inside since the night her child was born and died, or perhaps since the day she sold herself to Reverend Collins in return for respectability. Tears dried on her face in the wind before they had a chance to fall.

"My dear—you're overwrought—you need to get down to your cabin, have a nice cup of tea, can we do that? Come, let's go below." Mrs. Ohman took Lily's arm, steered her inside. "You mustn't confuse these things—I do believe in the rights of women, but I also believe in the sanctity of Christian marriage. You mustn't think, as some misguided women do, that if we assert our rights under the law, we throw off that Higher Law."

Lily wrenched her arm from Mrs. Ohman's and turned to face her. They were in a corridor now, a narrow passage leading to the cabins, and without the howling of the wind on deck it was likely people could hear her shouting, but Lily did not care. "They are right—they are, and you are wrong! Everything you taught me, everything you said about freedom and equality—of course it leads to all the rest. Free love and fallen women. If you don't see that then you're blind and short-sighted! Oh, what a fool I was. I believed it all, and now I'm paying the price, and God help me, I'll be paying it every day of my life 'til I die!" She turned to run and this time Mrs. Ohman did not grab her arm or run after her. Lily found her cabin and locked herself inside and cried 'til her eyes and throat and chest burned, and she felt scooped-out and hollow. She heard a tap-tap at her door, but ignored it, and did not see Mrs. Ohman when the ship docked at Halifax.

When the porter had taken off her case and she had finished with the customs shed, Lily stood on the pier, watching the crowds of passengers depart. Everyone had some place to go, it seemed. Everyone had a place in the world except Lily Hunt. Lily Collins. *I am all alone*, Lily thought.

"Ma'am? Do you want me to call a cab for you?"

She had no money for a cab. She walked with her little case to a hotel near the station that didn't look too expensive. Halifax— a different world, a foreign city. One that had not had to burn down and reinvent itself but had grown here solidly, uninterrupted by fire and disaster. She wondered what New York was like, or for that matter the rest of the world. Wondered if she would ever know.

She took a piece of paper from the hotel desk and wrote out the two messages she would bring to the cable station. She wrote and rewrote each of them, crossing out words, not just to save money but to find the right thing to say. Finally she finished them and read over both messages.

> *Have left the Reverend. Am in Halifax. No money to go*
> *further. Cable with instructions or money or come for*
> *me please.*
>
> *Sorry. Took money and ran away. Am in Halifax. If you*
> *send money for me to come home I promise to try*
> *harder.*

She sat with the two messages on the desk. She had no idea which one to send. Perhaps in the morning it would be clear.

Trudy J. Morgan-Cole

Part Seven

1923–1925

Grace

CHAPTER THIRTY-FOUR

HE PROW OF the steamer pushed a clean line through the dark grey water, foam falling away on either side. They were far enough out to sea that no land was visible anywhere; the illusion was of being on a ship headed on an endless journey. Grace stood on deck wrapped in a sweater and a blanket. Rome had been blistering hot and New York barely cooler. She had no winter coat with her.

"She wrote to tell me she was having a baby." Grace could still hear David Reid's words, see his hands laid flat on the table in front of her. A baby. Whatever she had imagined about her mother loving and leaving another man, she had never imagined this. Never imagined that Lily Hunt, thirty years ago living in her father's house in St. John's, had conceived a child out of wedlock.

She had been silent for a minute, then, more breath than speech, had said "Charley?" Her brother had been born in 1897, nearly three years after her parents' marriage. He had been just short of his twentieth birthday when he died at Monchy. Which part of that was a lie—Charley's birthdate or her parents' marriage date?

But David Reid shook his head. "The baby died. A miscarriage,

I guess you'd say, or a stillbirth."

"You—my mother—she was going to have a baby, and she miscarried?"

"That's what Abby Hayward told me. The last I ever heard from your mother, after she told me she was pregnant, was that she was going to marry your father. I never got another letter, not a postcard nor a cable. It drove me crazy, wondering what had happened, so finally I looked up Abby and she told me."

They had stayed another hour in the little restaurant. The waiter, who was also perhaps the owner, had brought them some sweet rolls, more discreet whisky for Mr. Reid and a cup of proper English tea for Grace, to banish the taste of the Turkish coffee. Stayed talking, even though immediately after Mr. Reid's revelation Grace had thought she would get up and leave, that she couldn't talk with him further. But it turned out that she could.

"She was right, you know, your mother," David Reid told her. "She wouldn't have been happy with the life I've led. And if I'd done what she wanted—stayed home in St. John's, changed myself all around to be a good husband and father—well, I'd have felt stifled. Trapped. All that business about true love conquering all—I don't believe that."

"So—have you been happy?"

He smiled a half-smile and stared down into his glass. "Happy's not the word I'd use. I've lived the kind of life I wanted to live. I've done at least some of the things I meant to do. I doubt when I die anyone's going to say, *There goes old Reid, God rest his soul, he lived a happy life.*"

Grace played his words over and over like a gramophone record in her mind as she watched the steamer push through the waves. She imagined docking in St. John's and getting on the train at once for Catalina, walking to the manse and sitting down with Lily at the table. Telling her everything. Asking for the truth, at last.

Instead, she returned to St. John's, to church work, and to the Women's Franchise League. The general election had returned the Squires government to office, but one of Squires's defeated ministers had made sweeping allegations about corruption in the government and there were talks of the prime minister resigning. "When that sleveen is gone for good," Mrs. Salter Earle said at the one meeting she attended, "then we'll finally see some real progress."

"Progress on the women's vote, certainly," said Mrs. Gosling. "And high time, too. Squires has been stalling and delaying for two years on the issue. They say he'll be out by the end of June, and it'll likely be Warren who replaces him."

"Changing one bad leader for another," said Mrs. McNeil. "The party's still the same. I don't say we'll see any real progress until there's another election."

"We're not prepared to wait another four years!" Grace burst out. "You should have been there—in Rome—you can't imagine how it felt to be like the poor sisters at the table. Almost every other woman in the English-speaking world, every white woman in the British Empire, can vote. Do we have to wait another four years before we get our chance?"

"It won't be four years—without Squires that crowd won't hold together more than a few months," said Mrs. Earle. "We'll be back at the polls within a year, you mark my words. Well, the men will be. Now, whatever coalition they come up with is going to have Reform or Progressive in its name, they all do that. What we need to know is who's going to be really progressive—who's going to give us the vote."

In the aftermath of the Congress and the election, the League met more often, and her job at Gower Street kept Grace busy as well, dealing with problems that had arisen during her extended break. Rome and New York—the conference, and her meeting with David Reid—were two huge things that she had to somehow examine and

Trudy J. Morgan-Cole

make sense of, but all around her life went on like a rushing stream, with no intention of giving her time to pause and think about it all.

The mail piled up for the weeks she had been away included a thick letter from Jack. He had been away nearly a year now and had committed to another year with Dr. Grenfell's mission. He hoped to come home for a visit this fall, to see his parents and Grace, before returning for another long, dark northern winter.

Grace laid down his letter and tried to remember David Reid's words about love and happiness. Could she be happy, married to Jack and living in Labrador? Could she be happy in St. John's without him? And was it even her choice? In all the letters he'd written from Labrador, he had never mentioned marriage. Perhaps they really were nothing more than friends now.

She wrote to Jack about meeting David Reid: even if he was only a friend, he was the only person she could tell about the encounter and even having someone to confide in on paper was better than telling no one at all. She did not include any of Mr. Reid's comments on love and marriage or any speculations as to how those might apply to her own situation and Jack's.

One hot day in late August, Grace was making her usual round of hospital visits when the head nurse pulled her aside. "Miss Collins? We have a patient here who is asking to see you."

"Oh, of course—which ward?" Grace said.

"He's in a private room upstairs. And I should warn you, Miss Collins, he's not one of your parishioners. He says he knows you from years ago—from the veterans' hospital. A Mr. Barry?" The nurse looked for recognition in Grace's face and Grace knew at once what she was worried about: that Grace would recoil from visiting a man so badly disfigured.

But she was delighted to hear the name. Ivan Barry! Grace had lost track of him in the years after she left the Empire Hospital, and often wondered what had happened to him. As she climbed the stairs to his private room she thought of all the time she had included his name in her morning prayers. Grace tried to keep up a practice of praying by name for people she had worked with over the years, as specifically as memory would allow, and Ivan Barry's name was on the list in the back of her Bible. Grace might pray, on a given morning, that her old Social Work classmate Miss DeWitt, to whom she still wrote regularly, would be given grace and strength and perhaps a bit of extra cash to help run that orphanage in the Appalachians where she worked. She might pray that Effie Butler, married at sixteen, would be better able to provide for her own children than she had for the four little siblings in the orphanage—for whom Grace also prayed, by name. But when Ivan Barry's name arose on her prayer list Grace was at a loss, and prayed only that the Holy Spirit would comfort him. "And when the time comes, may he have an easy death and be taken to Your arms," she would pray, wondering if this had already happened. She had not forgotten the hours spent with him in the old hospital and her firm belief that Charley had met a better fate by dying in France. It would be a mercy, Grace often thought, if God had taken Mr. Barry home by now.

But here he was in the General Hospital. Perhaps he was dying now? And she just happened to be here, and could perhaps share a few words of comfort at the last.

She found Ivan Barry sitting up in a chair by the window, not looking at all as if he were dying. He wore a cloth mask that covered the missing parts of his face; he could not smile at her, but lifted a hand in greeting. Grace sat on the edge of the bed opposite him and asked how he was.

"Well enough...touch of—trouble in the lungs. Bothers me from—time to time." Of course his words did not come out crisp and clean like that: there was the usual garbled wheeze, though Grace imagined his speech was a little clearer than it had been years ago. No

Trudy J. Morgan-Cole

doubt, being the kind of man he was, he practiced to get it right. She had to strain to understand, but as always, the longer she listened the more she could hear his words and not just his tortured voice.

"But otherwise you're well? How—where do you live?"

She thought she saw a gleam like laughter in his one good eye. "I found—ways. Boarding house, here in town. Tried to go home but—hard. For the family."

Hard for you too, no doubt, Grace thought. She gestured at the mask. "You wear this now?"

"Yes—easier. For people." When Grace nodded, she saw his eye-smile again and he said, "Like—Phantom of the Opera? You read that?"

"I've heard of it," Grace laughed. "I can't imagine you kidnapping young girls and holding them captive, though."

"No. I do have—a captive. My cousin. Nice girl. Only one in the family can—be with me, much. She wanted to live in town and—like you. Doesn't mind—seeing me. Helping. I have—my pension. Not much but—enough for room and board, a little pay for her."

So he had found someone to help him, found a way to make a life, Grace thought. And he had been here in town all along, living in a boarding house. She ought to have looked him up. Of course he was Church of England; the poor relief people in his own church probably knew about him and helped where they could, just as she did with a few badly wounded veterans in her own congregation who were unable to work. His meagre veteran's pension couldn't have paid for a private hospital room, Grace thought—and then realized the hospital had probably chosen to put him here, to spare others the sight of him.

Mr. Barry picked something up off the window ledge and passed it to her—the veteran's newspaper, opened to a page with an article circled. "This is—what I do now. When I can," he said, and Grace began to read, seeing the by-line I. Barry, Royal Newfoundland Regiment, at the bottom of the column.

It was a simple little piece, a letter to the editor, but it was lyrical and even beautiful. She remembered he had wanted to be a minister. "So now you write the sermons you won't get to preach?" Grace said, after she had read it.

"I—try. Essays, here and there. A few published, some others— maybe one day." Speech was still a great effort for him but his pen flowed freely. "Letters, little sketches—you know about the poets? Owen, Sassoon—the poets of the war?"

Grace nodded.

"I'm—no poet. But—can write, a little. Someday—maybe more."

"Maybe a book?" Grace suggested, and he too nodded. "You should write it," she said. "A story like yours—there must be hundreds of other men who've suffered what you have, and don't have your skill at putting it into words. Keep writing."

"Oh—I will. No fear—about that."

She could see he was tiring and she said goodbye then, promising to visit again. How strange, she thought, when she had been picturing, even praying for his peaceful death these past few years, to see Ivan Barry still so stubbornly alive. She had always pitied the man but pity, she saw now, was an insult to such a passionate desire for life.

When Grace arrived home that day a telegram was waiting. ARRIVING CATALINA ON *HOME* SEPTEMBER 1 TO VISIT FAMILY FOR A FEW WEEKS THEN BACK TO LABRADOR FOR WINTER SEASON STOP CAN YOU MEET ME IN CATALINA.

Jack knew she had not been home for nearly a year. She had told him, finally, the story of her mother burning the petitions. "It's not that I'm refusing to go home out of spite," she had written him, "but somehow it's easier to stay away. I will go home again—perhaps when you come for a visit?" Now he was coming home. Grace could only spare a day or two from work, having taken so much time away in the spring for the Rome congress. Jack had not mentioned coming to St. John's; if she wanted to see him she was going to have to go home. Seeing her mother again and seeing Jack would both be difficult, for such different reasons. It might be easier to stay in town and set her face firmly towards the future, putting the past behind her.

But she took the train out home on a Friday morning. Jack was waiting for her on the station platform. It seemed they were always meeting at train stations and she was always sizing him up, evaluating the changes in him since she had seen him last. Did Jack do the same with her? And what did he see?

He stepped toward her, then hesitated. They stopped a few feet from each other, then Jack reached to take her train case. When his hand closed over hers on the handle, she moved closer, and Jack pulled her into his arms, right there on the platform for all of Catalina and Port Union to see.

"I told your parents I'd drive you to the manse," he said.

She sat next to him on the seat of his father's gig, and the knot of tension that had been in her stomach the whole train ride, the fear of what she'd find when she saw him again, dissolved as soon as Jack smiled at her. He seemed like his old self—not the Jack she had known before he went to Labrador, but the Jack who had come home from overseas and won her heart.

But if the barrier between Grace and Jack seemed to have crumbled, the barrier that separated her from Lily seemed as impenetrable as ever. When she walked into the manse and said hello to her parents, Grace saw, as she'd been seeing in her mind's eye since New York, a different Lily—a young Lily, brave and frightened and alone, carrying a child whose father was far away, marrying a man she hoped would shield her secret. But that younger, vulnerable Lily disappeared almost at once behind the thin, stern, greying woman who had burned the suffrage petitions, who had not given her blessing for Grace to go to Rome.

They embraced, coolly, pressed their cheeks against each other and stepped back. Grace had imagined all kinds of conversations, tearful confrontations with her mother in which she confessed the visit to New York, confronted Lily with what she knew, forgave her for burning the papers. Instead there was only this wary politeness. Nothing was said about Rome, or about suffrage, or about why it had been so long since Grace had been home. Getting out of the house to be with Jack was a double pleasure, first for Jack's sake and second as an escape from all the things unsaid between herself and Lily.

On Saturday evening Grace and Jack walked over to Port Union to watch *Nanook of the North* at Congress Hall, the latest of the town's impressive new edifices. Moving pictures were a rare treat outside St. John's: another of the blessings Mr. Coaker had bestowed on the Union faithful. "Do you think the film will be anything like life in Labrador?" Grace asked Jack as they walked.

"I don't know how a film could capture it," Jack said, "but I'll be interested to see someone try. Even if it only shows a little of what life's like up there, it's a world most people never imagine, much less see."

"You really like it there, don't you?"

"Even I find it hard to believe sometimes, but yes, I do. People keep asking—Dr. Grenfell himself asked me, when he visited this summer—if I'll go back to medical school," he added as they walked across the bridge. "The way they look at it, I'm doing good and useful work, and I could do so much more if I qualified with my M.D. But I have to tell them I can't. I don't really understand it myself, but I know there's a balance I have to hang onto, and going back to school would destroy that balance, somehow. I don't suppose you can understand that anymore than the rest of them can."

Trudy J. Morgan-Cole

"I don't, fully," Grace admitted. "But I know how unhappy you were in Montreal. I wouldn't wish that on you again."

"It's not just unhappiness," Jack said. "It's a kind of...desperation, I suppose. I believe now I can fight it as long as I'm doing work I believe in. It's not as if everything's wonderful all the time, it's just that I can keep my head above water. There's been reports on this kind of thing, you know—men who came back from the Front and broke down months, even years later, but I think the simplest thing, the thing the old folks would say, is that if I went back to school my nerves wouldn't stand the strain." He took her hand. "We said when I went away that there were no strings binding us. All this time, I've been reminding myself of that, afraid every letter I got from you would say you were engaged to marry someone else."

"I used to imagine I'd get a letter from you telling me you'd fallen in love with an English nurse and got married, or that you were going native and moving into a tilt with an Esquimo woman." Grace stopped to lean over the bridge rail, watching the water tumble over the rocks below, the river widening at its mouth to open into the broad harbour beyond.

Jack laughed. "No, there's no one else for me. Sometimes I can't imagine sharing my life with anyone else. What do I have to offer, really? I'll never be a doctor. I might live out the rest of my life on the Labrador coast, and that's not much of a place to raise a family. And I can't even promise a woman that I'll be sane or stable from one day to the next. I feel fine now, but I remind myself of Sol Sweetapple's old fish store—something that's been patched and propped up so many times, so many different ways, you have to worry that the next strong wind might blow it down."

They were walking again, into Port Union now. Grace could see, on the flat roof of the Union Store, the white triangles of codfish laid out to dry: fishermen were using the store roof as a flake. Nothing was wasted in Port Union. As always, the optimism of the place infected her, and she took a deep breath, trying to find words to match her thoughts.

But Jack spoke first, still gripping her hand in his. "I say I can't imagine sharing this life with anyone, but the truth is, I can't imagine a life without you in it, either. I love you as much as I ever did, Grace—maybe more, after the way you've written to me and kept believing in me. I don't know if it's fair to you, loving you when I've got so little to offer. But I can't change how I feel."

Then Grace had the words she needed. "I don't know what's fair and what isn't, or if that even matters when it comes to love. I know this much—I'll marry you, Jack Perry, if you ever get around to asking me. If you don't ask, then I'll do all right by myself. I'm a New Woman, or so my mother tells people, in a tone that makes it clear she doesn't approve. I can get by on my own—but I'd rather get by with you."

"Somewhere in that speech I think you proposed to me, Miss Collins."

They were at the steps of Congress Hall. The good people of Port Union were crowding into the yard, drawn by the unusual promise of moving pictures. It was hardly the place to kiss or embrace, but Jack took both Grace's hands in his and held tightly. She thought of David Reid saying that he and Lily had been better off without each other. She thought of Ivan Barry alone in his boarding house, writing essays. *We live the lives we make for ourselves*, Grace thought, *as best as we can.*

"I don't want to be sitting alone at a restaurant table in thirty years, wondering about the life we might have had together," she said. "Even Battle Harbour would be better than that."

Trudy J. Morgan-Cole

CHAPTER THIRTY-FIVE

LILY HATED WINTERS around the bay. Her girlhood memories of winters in town were pleasant—sleigh bells in the streets, walking through crisp snow, church bells ringing out through chilly night air. Had it always been so bright and cold and clean? Or had memory transformed twenty winters into a series of Christmas cards?

Before her marriage she had spent one winter outside town: that winter after the fire, when she and her mother lived in her grandparents' house in Harbour Grace. The day of the fire she remembered feeling aflame herself, as if she were incandescent. Then came that dull indoor winter in Harbour Grace, reading books by the fire and waiting for spring. It was tedious, but did not match the crushing despair of that first Greenspond winter—the worst winter of her life, Lily thought. Then she wondered about the winter after Charley died. No, the first winter of her marriage was the worst, the winter when she lived in that cold godforsaken parsonage on a barren island with a man she could never love. The winter she lost David's child, and lay in her lonely bed plotting escape.

In the spring that followed that endless winter she did escape. Then she cabled the Reverend from Halifax and he sent the money for her to return. He even came to Port aux Basques to meet her steamer, though whether that was to help her or to make sure she really came back, Lily never knew. He said that he knew her mind must still be unbalanced over the loss of the baby. He said, "I forgive you. Only you mustn't try to run away again; you must learn to be content."

She did not run away again but she did not learn to be content either. She learned other things. She learned to be the minister's wife, to rule the manse and the Sunday School and the Ladies' Aid with an iron fist inside a velvet glove. She learned to take pleasure in a well-run household, in a well-organized parish. She learned to admire newly hooked rugs and rows of jelly preserves on her pantry shelf.

She learned to share a bed with her husband and to banish all thoughts of David Reid. She learned how very much her husband enjoyed playing the role of Hosea, the godly man who took back the wayward wife. She learned there was a kind of power in being Gomer, too, in being the wife of a man who knew she wanted to leave. She learned that he had changed the key to his strongbox, and hidden the new key where she could not find it.

Never once, in all that time, did Lily feel content. Resigned, perhaps. Not content. Then Charley was born. Lily held him in her arms and thought, *This is my reward.* And again, three years and two miscarriages later, Grace. She had her son and her daughter, and she loved them with a love more fierce than she had ever felt for David Reid. From the moment each of them left her body, her only fear was that she would lose them.

Her children were her consolation, but she didn't want to raise them in godforsaken fishing villages. They deserved better than that. Lily waited out those first years in Greenspond and thought that

Trudy J. Morgan-Cole

if her husband were more ambitious they might get back to St. John's someday. Instead they moved from one outport to another, each as barren and poverty-stricken as the last.

Since William Coaker had moved to Port Union people said it was as good as being in town, that Port Union had everything St. John's had. Lily laughed at them—to herself, of course. Port Union was a freak, an American town built on top of a Newfoundland outport, with the skeleton showing through. It was nothing like St. John's, the city she loved and almost never returned to. Once every year or two, with the Reverend, who did not let her travel alone now. She saw her parents, returned for her mother's funeral but not for her father's remarriage to the entirely inappropriate Daisy Gill, her old Sunday School teacher. She wrote Abby Hayward Parker one letter a year at Christmas. She knew every woman in every town they lived in; she drank tea in the kitchens of fisherwomen just come in from making fish on the flakes and she sat on committees with the wives of merchants who sent their children to school in England. She never made another close woman friend, not after Abby Hayward and Jessie Ohman had both led her astray. She would never again love anyone but her children, Lily promised herself.

Now the children were gone—Charley dead and Grace gone away. She had fought with all the strength she had to protect them, to spare them suffering, and to keep Grace, at least, safe by her side. You couldn't do that to a son, but a daughter, surely, you could shelter from the world. But not Grace. She was as headstrong and eager for the world as young Lily had been years ago. Lily had lost her children after all; she had not been able to keep them safe, any more than Lily's own parents had kept her safe.

Lily had seen it when Grace came home for a few days in the fall—her first visit home in ages, and she had barely pitched long enough to look around. She was off out the door with young Jack Perry, that useless know-nothing, as soon as she had her bags laid down. He had been down on the Labrador for, what, a year or more? Lily thought the whole business of Jack going off to work for that Grenfell man was foolishness, but all the same at least while he was in Battle Harbour he wasn't in St. John's getting Grace into trouble. The few days they'd spent together here in Catalina—well, Lily was nervous about that. The two of them roamed all over Catalina and Port Union those warm summer days and evenings. Grace was all full of high ideals and as righteous as a preacher, but then Lily herself had been that way once, and her high ideals had not stopped her from getting up to what she shouldn't. What would become of Grace if she were in the family way and young Perry was off on the Labrador coast with the Esquimos?

Now Grace was back in St. John's and Lily was alone again with the Reverend. He was busy with parish meetings and visiting the sick, reading books and writing sermons, and jawing with William Coaker whenever the old man was in Port Union. Lily had her own kind of busy-ness, organizing the fall sale of work and making sure the new schoolteacher didn't fool up the Christmas pageant, but what pleasure she took in such things had paled in these last few years. More and more she found herself laying aside work to sit alone with her thoughts, which seemed to grow darker along with the skies of late November.

She sat in the parlour one chilly morning, crocheting lace edging on a pillowcase for the sale, when the front door opened. Her husband never came home at midmorning; he came for his dinner at twelve o'clock sharp. He stayed in the office at church and wrote his sermons there, and made himself available for parishioners if they needed to drop by with a question or a problem, which they generally did.

But he was here, at ten-thirty in the morning. He explained he hadn't been feeling well, was overcome with weakness and—he was going to go on, something about his stomach, but Lily didn't want

Trudy J. Morgan-Cole

to hear indelicate details and told him he should go lie down. He went up to his study, reappeared at lunchtime but ate only a little. Then he had to go again, because he was meeting with someone at the church—some workmen coming to do something to the church, something that needed to be done before winter. The roof? Windows? She wasn't sure. Apparently it couldn't be done in summer because the workmen were also fishermen; nothing could be done 'til the fishing was done. At any rate the Reverend went to his meeting and by suppertime seemed quite himself again.

Lily might have forgotten the odd incident but for what happened later. At the time it was only an interruption between trimming pillowcases and going to play piano for the Christmas concert rehearsal. But later it was from that day, the day of coming home early, that she dated the beginning of what people referred to as All the Reverend's Trouble.

The Reverend's Trouble was a private matter for the first little while—a collection of complaints and ailments that he kept mostly to himself. But there were further interruptions to the routine: a day's work he could no longer complete, meals he could not eat. "Dyspepsia," he said. "Indigestion." It happened often enough that for the first time since she had known him the portly Reverend began to lose weight: his suits hung loose off a diminished frame. When Elizabeth Perry pulled Lily aside after church and said they were all praying for the poor Reverend, Lily adjusted her vision and looked closely at her husband. The man was ill; something would have to be done.

There was a doctor in Bonavista, but the Reverend would not go to see him, even after the Sunday when he was so ill he could not give the sermon. One of the deacons—a kind and sincere man chosen for his piety and not for his ability to speak in public—had to get up into the pulpit and read out the sermon the Reverend had penned, stumbling over words like "justification" and "sanctification." Lily sat through the hesitant reading and the concerned questions of the congregation afterwards. She went home to find that her husband had spent the morning vomiting into a chamber pot, and the maid was in tears.

They were locked hard into winter then. It was January, and hard to go anywhere, much less all the way to Bonavista for the doctor. The Reverend rallied and felt a little better. He preached the next Sunday and thanked everyone for their prayers. But he continued to lose weight. Lily had to take in all his trousers. As she did so she thought, *If he really is ill, seriously ill, I will have to care for him, I will have to wipe drops of sweat from his brow and likely far worse.* Even adjusting his pants seemed too intimate.

For five years, early in her married life—from the time she returned from Halifax to the day she knew she was carrying Grace—Lily had submitted to her husband in the marriage bed, endured his touch frequently enough to conceive four times. After Grace, her second surviving child, was born, she told the Reverend there would be no more. She had the two children, a boy and a girl, and henceforth she would sleep alone.

He had not been happy about this, had told her it was part of her duty as a wife. He said a man had needs and that as a man of God he was not free to satisfy them elsewhere, so she must save him from sin and allow him back into their bed. She had gambled on the fact that he wasn't the kind of man to force her, and she was right.

Now Lily found herself having to go into his bedroom, then switching rooms to give him the more comfortable bed because he so rarely got a good night's sleep. In February she finally wrote to the Bonavista doctor and asked him to come.

Lily thought afterwards—she should have realized it before-hand, really—that all her husband's hesitation, his refusal to call a doctor, had been because he already knew something was far more

363

Trudy J. Morgan-Cole

wrong than dyspepsia. He had wanted to put off the evil day, to avoid having the truth confirmed.

But it was confirmed, and there was to be a journey to St. John's for an operation. Much as she hated Catalina, Lily did not enjoy travelling to town. She loved walking through St. John's shops, fingering lovely bolts of fabric and picking up bone-thin teacups and leafing through brightly coloured magazines, but in the end it only reminded her that such luxuries were not to be had in her everyday life. She came away from a stroll down Water Street more discontented than before. Lily believed, and told others, that everyone should accept her lot in life and make the best of it, but it was harder when she was inSt. John's.

What she didn't want was to come to town this way—as the poor relative, the outport minister's wife, in need of help and pity. She always hoped that when she came her father would feel pleased, would think that this match he had brokered so long ago with had worked out very well. She liked to imagine that Daisy would look at her and think, "Now there's a real lady," and that Grace would think, "I wish I could be like my mother—so graceful and composed." She wanted people to greet her in church and afterwards say to each other, "Ah, Lily Hunt—Lily Collins she is now—she's done well for herself, hasn't she?"

Lily had never admitted these thoughts to herself before but the first night that she spent in the guest-room in her father's house they all came out and paraded themselves before her. This visit was everything she dreaded: she came to town as a woman in need. Everyone was kind and helpful; Grace and Daisy took turns going to the hospital to sit with the Reverend so that Lily could rest. On the day of the operation Grace sat with Lily all morning in the hospital waiting room.

"Will you both stay in town while Papa's convalescing?" Grace asked. "Grandfather and Daisy would be glad to have you."

"We'll stay until your father is well enough to travel. After that, I'm sure he would be more comfortable in his own house."

"Then let me come back with you. You'll need help—more help than a housemaid can give."

"What about this precious job of yours? I thought it was so important, you couldn't leave it to come home for a holiday."

"This would be…different. It's not a holiday. I'm sure the church would understand."

"Either your job is important or it's not; you can't have it both ways."

"Let's not quarrel, Mama, not while Papa's in the operating theatre."

"It's good of you to offer, but I'll manage just fine at home with your father. No need to change any of your…plans."

It was a very long operation but the doctor came out afterwards to tell them that he thought it was a success, that he believed they had "got it all." Then there were days of recovering in hospital and another fortnight at the house on Queen's Road while the Reverend got back on his feet.

"On his feet" meant shuffling around the house leaning heavily on a cane, but at least he was getting dressed in suits again instead of wearing a bed-jacket. And his spirits were good: he told everyone that he felt much better, although he still could not eat properly—only thin porridge and custard, and not much of that.

When they boarded the train for Catalina, Grace again offered to come with them but Lily refused. "Your father is on the mend and it's not as if I'm alone in the house—I have help. There'd be hardly anything for you to do." Lily couldn't help thinking that another sort of daughter—a girl like Camilla Coaker, perhaps—would not have accepted the refusal so easily.

Later she thought they had returned home too soon. The Reverend could walk, and he no longer needed dressings changed, but

Trudy J. Morgan-Cole

he was weak and found it hard to get around the house: once he was upstairs in the bedroom he didn't like to come downstairs only to climb up again. So his meals had to be brought up on trays. The girl, Hannah, had to clean the house and cook light meals for Lily, while making custards and cream of wheat and porridge for the Reverend, toting them upstairs on trays and then bringing the crockery back down to be washed. It was more than one girl could cope with, so Lily took over making and delivering her husband's food herself.

Parishioners and neighbours dropped by the house every day. The Reverend did not always feel well enough to see them so Lily was required to sit and visit with each one, and carry up their good wishes. It wasn't only good wishes they brought: the church, after all, kept meeting every Sunday and business had to be taken care of. The Reverend made an effort to get up to meet with the deacons when they came, but he was exhausted afterwards.

If Lily insisted he rest and not be disturbed then she found herself dealing with not only the church business that had always been hers—the Women's Guild and the Sunday School and the Missionary Society—but also chasing down the workmen who had not, after all, put the new roof on properly, for it leaked in the spring rains. Betty Bursey came, shamefaced and hardly speaking above a whisper, to ask could the church help her out, for with Heber not able to work since his accident she couldn't feed the children. Olivia Edwards died in childbirth and Lily had to send a message to the Methodist minister in Elliston to come and conduct the funeral service, and gravediggers had to be arranged, and all the little Edwards children packed up and sent on the train to a great-aunt in Bonavista who would look after them, for their father was nearly helpless in his grief.

One cold night Lily came down to answer a knock at the door after tending to her husband who had been throwing up 'til he had nothing left in his stomach and was reduced to the dry heaves. She found Solomon Sweetapple there to say that old Sarah Gullage was dying. Sarah wanted the minister at her deathbed and if the minister couldn't be there, Solomon could go because he was a deacon, but he couldn't bear to go alone. Surely the minister's wife would be some comfort? Lily ended up asking Hannah, the maid, to come back for a few hours to keep an eye on the Reverend while she herself hiked up over the road in the dark with Sol Sweetapple, and sat for two hours with a dying woman who was more certain to see the face of Jesus when she closed her eyes, Lily thought, than either Lily herself or poor Sol, who could barely stammer out a prayer. It was nearly dawn when Lily got home.She paid the maid extra for staying there all night and never mentioning a word to the Reverend, so that he wouldn't worry.

It was astonishing, to think of all the work he did, all the troubles people brought to his door. All these years Lily had thought of herself as a model minister's wife, a perfect helpmeet, but her work had been committee meetings and sales of work and fund-raising concerts. People did not pour out their hearts or ask her for help: she was surprised they did so to her husband. She had never thought of him as a particularly tender soul—not like Grace, always looking for hard-luck cases—but perhaps once the clerical collar was on, the hard cases sought him out naturally.

The only blessing Lily could count that spring was that she was sleeping better now; she was so exhausted when she fell into bed every night—the hard narrow bed off the study where her husband had slept most of his married life—she slept for four or five hours before she woke to look at the dark sky outside the window and wonder how she would get through another day.

One afternoon she came downstairs balancing a tray with a teacup, a bowl of custard, and a plate of bread crusts. She was trying him with a little toast now, hoping to tempt him towards solid food, though he could only nibble it if he soaked it well in tea

Trudy J. Morgan-Cole

first. He had gotten through half a slice of toast and Lily wanted to believe that meant he was getting better, that things would soon be back to normal. How little she had appreciated normal, when she had it.

"Mother. Can I take that?"

Grace stood in the hall, with her trunk at her feet. Lily stopped on the stairs, holding the tray before her.

"Mrs. Perry wrote me," Grace said. "She wrote to say you looked completely worn out, that Papa was still bedridden most of the time, and that she thought you wouldn't ask for help but needed it. So here I am."

"How long for?"

"As long as you need me. I resigned my position at Gower Street. Now, let me take that tray." She took it out of Lily's hands, and went to the kitchen, and Lily followed her.

CHAPTER THIRTY-SIX

HEY FOUND A rhythm of working together that summer: Lily, Grace, and Hannah. Hannah cooked dinner for Lily and Grace, and cleaned the house, which included cleaning the sick room. Lily made the Reverend's meals, bland dishes he could tolerate, and brought them up to him. She also did a little cooking for herself and Grace on Hannah's day off. Grace did little in the kitchen, except to pitch in when asked, but she met with the deacons and told them when questions were too petty to disturb her father, then referred church members back to those same deacons when they had problems. Visitors who came with kindly intent had to visit with Grace first before she decided whether the Reverend felt up to seeing them that day. She also sat with her father for hours, reading to him when he was too tired to read for himself.

This was, Lily thought, the greatest advantage to having Grace at home, both for herself and for the Reverend. Before Grace came, he had complained that Lily was so busy, she had no time to keep him company. As if she ever had! Keeping each other company had not been a feature of their marriage, but now that he suffered enforced idleness he was desperate for a companion. Grace was the perfect person to fill that role.

When they first came back from St. John's after the operation, Lily had imagined her husband back to his usual routine within a few weeks. The reality was different. By midsummer, in the warm muggy days of July, he was able to get up during the day for longer periods, to sit in a chair on the front porch and watch the busy activity of an outport at the height of the fishing season. Grace often sat with him and they watched the small boats, which had put out to sea in the predawn hours, coming back to shore at midday. The Reverend recognized the different boats and could name the men in them even from a distance. From the porch of the manse they could see the men at the wharves unloading the fish, then joining the women at the flakes, gutting and splitting and laying the fish out to dry, acres of white cod open to the sun. These were the fishing families who stayed and fished Trinity Bay over the summer; many more went off to the Labrador and the Reverend was always accustomed to his smaller congregation during the summer months.

He said he was writing a sermon, that he would preach again soon, but in July the deacons were still taking turns at preaching. One hot afternoon Lily stood in the kitchen making raspberry jam, listening as her husband and daughter talked on the porch. Grace had been reading him one of John Wesley's sermons and they ended up talking about heaven.

"You can't say it in the pulpit at a funeral of course, but I've always had my doubts that our ideas about heaven are very Biblical," the Reverend said. "You know, floating about on clouds, becoming guardian angels…"

"Playing golden harps?" Grace suggested.

"Yes, all that—it comes from bad hymns and worse religious literature, not from the Scriptures. Jesus called death a sleep, and the Bible talks about a resurrection at the end of time, not about floating off to heaven—I do wonder about it sometimes—read an interesting sermon on the topic years ago...I wish I remembered who it was by."

"But I suppose people would be very shocked if the minister suggested poor Nan wasn't in heaven right at the moment," Grace said.

"Oh, shocked indeed—keeping your more troublesome questions to yourself is part of being a clergyman. So good to have someone as intelligent as yourself to discuss it all with," he said. "You know, you'd be a better preacher than either Abel Courage or Solomon Sweetapple. I ought to get you up in the pulpit on Sunday morning!" He laughed a faint, wheezy laugh.

Lily poured her jam into jars, hearing in that laughter a faint echo down the years. Young Obadiah Collins, chuckling at the thought that if women were allowed at the ballot-box, they might someday dream of standing in the pulpit. And young Lily Hunt disdaining him for his backward views, though never brave enough to say it to his face.

She laid the jam jars aside, each one a dark red jewel in the sun that slanted through the window. She wiped down the counter, then dried her hands on her apron and took it off. Outside, Grace's voice and the Reverend's rose and fell out on the porch, as steady a background as the surf on the beach. Lily had heard tell that the round beach rocks down by the shore had not always looked like that: it was the effect of thousands of years of the ocean wearing away at them that had smoothed their edges and made them what they were. So decades of life seemed to have done to the Reverend: smoothed the edges of his opinions to the point where he could chuckle about his daughter preaching sermons.

She went to the front door and hesitated before pushing it open, not wanting to interrupt them. The Reverend seemed well and happy when he was talking theology with Grace. The two of them were a small world unto themselves, and Lily had nothing to say about theology, about the Biblical concept of heaven. For many years now

Trudy J. Morgan-Cole

her concerns had been entirely earthly. But she went out onto the porch and sat on a chair a few feet away from them, listening to their talk, thinking about waves wearing away at beach rocks.

She wondered if it was possible that her husband had actually forgotten, after all these years, how he and Lily had first come together? He had never known David Reid's name; only that Lily had kept the company of suffragists and been friends with frivolous Abby Hayward. He knew that Lily had been unchaste with some nameless man who left her with child and did not marry her. Surely he had not forgotten! Surely he knew how the wrong associations could lead a girl down the wrong path. And not every girl would have an Obadiah Collins to rescue her. Grace had only shiftless Jack Perry, no use to any woman.

But his little jest about Grace preaching a sermon had been ten minutes ago and Lily could not drag it up again only to point out that it was a mistake to put such thoughts in a girl's head. They were talking about heaven again, and Lily willed herself to sit and listen, and not interfere.

"Still, I do want to preach about heaven if I can do it without treading on too many toes," the Reverend said. "At least, I want to preach about the hope of the resurrection. I tried to preach something of the sort after our Charley was killed but—I don't think my heart was in it, then. I couldn't persuade even myself. Now that I've had my own brush with mortality—well, perhaps I have a new perspective. But I don't find I have the strength to write for more than half an hour or so at a time."

"You could dictate to me," Grace offered. "That would save your strength."

"Well now my dear, that's a fine offer, I may just do that. I may just." And something else in his words gave Lily a little heartfall then, to hear how easily he accepted his status as an invalid.

Yet he did climb into the pulpit and preach on the last Sunday in

August, and again for the next two Sundays, each sermon dictated by him and written out by Grace. His voice lacked the volume of his old pulpit delivery. But the congregation were so glad to have him back preaching again they would have forgiven him anything, and as these post-illness sermons were shorter than his standard forty-five minutes, perhaps they were glad for other reasons too.

On the third Sunday that the Reverend preached, Jack Perry sat with Grace and Lily in the Collins family pew. He had arrived two days earlier on the Labrador steamer, and that evening Grace sat down with her mother at the kitchen table over a cup of tea.

"Mother, Jack and I are going to get married. We'd like Papa to perform the ceremony, if he feels up to it."

"Is that how it's done now? 'Jack and I are getting married'? When your father proposed to me he went to speak to my father about it; we didn't sit my parents down and announce it was happening. Times have changed." Lily wished there were a way to take back words once spoken: she hadn't meant to sound bitter. She ought to be wishing Grace happiness, however slim she thought the chances were. And she ought not to lie about her own marriage. She and the Reverend had, after all, discussed the plan before he ever went to her father with a proposal.

"Yes, times have changed." Grace's tone, too, was sharp. Then she drew a deep breath and added, "Of course Jack will still speak to Papa. Only I wanted to talk to you first, not about the wedding, but about what happens afterwards."

For a terrifying moment Lily thought Grace meant to ask her about the marital act. To deflect that possibility she said, "I suppose you're going off to the wilds of Labrador after him, are you? Going to live life in a tilt like a trapper?"

"Right now we both feel—well, we want to stay here. I don't want to leave you to care for Papa alone."

"Your father is getting better. He won't need much care, soon."

Trudy J. Morgan-Cole

Grace looked down into her teacup. "I know you want to believe that, Mother, and so do I, but I really don't think it's true. Cancer is a difficult thing. With winter coming on, I'd feel better if Jack and I were here to help you. Jack can find work with his father or with Mr. Coaker in Port Union. He agrees I need to be close to you and Papa until—well, while Papa's so ill."

She had been going to say, *Until Papa dies.* Those words, even left unspoken, hanging in the air of the room, took the heart from Lily. She wanted to be strong, to need no one, but she nodded. "Of course you and Jack are welcome to stay," she said. "I would be—I'd be glad to have you."

Grace and Jack's wedding was as simple as Lily's own had been. The Reverend, his voice a bit thready and his hands trembling, pronounced them man and wife in the parlour of the manse with only the two sets of parents present. It was the Reverend who suggested that Jack move into their house with Grace rather than the both of them moving over to the Perry house. They moved the big double bed into Grace's room. Lily kept her old bedroom, but with the narrow single bed from Grace's room. They moved the Reverend's bed down to what used to be the good parlour on the main floor, nearer the lavatory. Lily watched him walk down over the stairs to his new room and thought, *He'll never go up those stairs again.*

That week after the wedding was a great upheaval, everyone moving things about and trying to let the Reverend rest as much as possible. Late one night Lily went up to the attic with a box of old clothes too worn out even to give to the poor. After Christmas, perhaps, she'd start on some rag rugs. Grace and Jack were unpacking boxes in Grace's old room.

"Are you ready to pack your dolls away now that you're a married woman?" Lily heard Jack say. There was teasing laughter in his tone; Lily thought of how long it had been since she had heard that note in a man's voice.

"Not that one!" Grace protested. "That's Henrietta, she was my favourite toy. Mother bought her for me in Toronto and I thought she was the most beautiful thing ever. I was afraid to play with her because I thought she'd get broken, but I'd lie here in bed looking at her up on her shelf and make up the most fantastic stories about her adventures—I had her travelling the world, climbing the Himalayas— I even wrote a little book about her, *The Adventures of Henrietta*, in one of my old scribblers. It's probably still around here somewhere."

"I wouldn't be surprised—everything else seems to be here somewhere," Jack said, and there was the laughing, scuttling sound of two young people in love mock-fighting, a sound Lily knew would end with a kiss. Ashamed to be eavesdropping she hurried off to the attic stair as Jack said, "All right, Henrietta can stay!" And up in the attic, above the muffled sound of the newlyweds making love under Henrietta's glassy eyes, Lily sat on the lid of a trunk and put her face in her hands and cried 'til sobs shook her whole body.

At the end of October the last Labrador steamer left port. Jack had given his notice at the Battle Harbour hospital and they had someone else to replace him. So he and Grace would stay, for the winter anyway. That was the morning Lily went to the Reverend's room to bring in his cream of wheat and found that he had soiled his sheets, not being able to get up to get to the lavatory or even the chamber pot. He lay there like a child, without shame, only wanting to be helped and cleaned up.

Lily set to the work, lifting him to his feet and putting him in a chair while she called Grace down to help her clean up the bed. As she helped him over to the chair she felt how light his once stout body had gotten. It was Jack who, when the bed and the Reverend had both been cleaned up, picked him up like a child and carried him back to bed.

Throughout the fall, the deacons continued to take the sermons; once or twice Jack preached, and he was better than the deacons but not as good, Lily thought, as Grace would have been. Then the circuit

Trudy J. Morgan-Cole

wrote to say they were sending a supply minister to fill in as long as needed. The new supply minister and the deacons managed things: there was no longer a need for anyone to ask the Reverend to make decisions or give advice. Mr. Coaker—Sir William Coaker, now, the King had given him a knighthood—came by to visit two or three times before he went to his winter home in Jamaica. The visits were short ones; Obadiah Collins had no more strength for long conversations.

On Christmas morning Jack and Grace got the Reverend up in his chair after breakfast. Lily had ordered gifts from the Eaton's catalogue earlier in the fall: a handsome new watch for Jack; a gold locket for Grace. Grace's wedding band was the plainest gold circlet and she had no other jewellery. Lily wanted to see her in something lovely, for her to have at least one nice piece to wear.

"Oh, Mother, how pretty," Grace said, and Lily felt at once that the word *pretty* was a reproach, that the gift was frivolous. Grace was such a serious girl, but what should she have gotten her? Jack had given Grace a book, a big heavy thing of essays or something, which seemed to please her more than the locket, though later in the day, when the young couple went out to have dinner with Jack's parents, Grace wore the locket.

Early in the new year, the Reverend could no longer get out of bed. That meant he had to be lifted to a chamber pot. There were chores of cleaning and washing and taking away full pots and soiled sheets—things Lily had never imagined herself doing. There was Grace and Jack and Hannah, still, but so much of it fell to Lily; so much of it she felt shouldn't have to be done by anyone but a wife. She had, after all, vowed for better or for worse, in sickness and in health, no matter how unwillingly.

One day she washed him in bed and helped him into clean underwear and a fresh nightshirt, averting her eyes from the most intimate parts of the task as she generally did. When she settled his now-thin body back onto the pillows he reached out and grabbed her wrist with a hand that had become claw-like. "Thank you, Lily. You're a good woman. A good wife."

Though she hated looking at his loose-hanging private parts or the skin that was yellowish and soiled, she hated meeting his eyes most of all. But she met them now, and forced herself to see that this was the face of a dying man.

"I haven't been, not really," she said. It was no more than the truth.

Obadiah—she could not think of him as the Reverend anymore, it was like an identity he had shed along with day clothes and excess flesh—sighed. "Neither of us has done all we could have done. But you're here now when I need you, doing for me—doing more than you should, really."

"I guess this puts us even, then."

He shook his head. "No. I never thought of it that way. Never thought you owed me anything."

He closed his eyes; that much conversation had tired him. She knew with certainty that what he said was not true. There was a time when he did keep score, when he did think of Lily as being in his debt. It couldn't all have been in her mind, could it?

Lily sat in the chair by his bed, going over the years like she would go over a piece of knitting, counting back to the dropped stitch. In life you could never unravel, go back and knit up what had gone wrong. For thirty years she had felt she was paying back a debt and she was pleased with idea that these last few months' work, caring for her dying husband, had settled the score. The idea that there had never been a score to settle was more difficult to wrap her mind around.

"You were good to me long ago, when I needed it," she said finally, her voice quiet among the dust-motes that danced in the light from the window. "I don't mind doing for you, now."

She looked down to see if that satisfied him, but his eyes were closed. He had drifted off to sleep.

Trudy J. Morgan-Cole

In March, Grace announced that she was going to St. John's to stay with her grandfather and Daisy for three weeks. "I'll be here to help you with the Reverend," Jack assured Lily.

"I can manage—you go on with Grace."

"No, I want to stay. And Grace ought to go alone. This trip means a lot to her."

"Why?"

Jack excused himself to go see to Obadiah while Grace and Lily stayed at the table finishing their tea. "The bill for the women's franchise is going to come before the house on the tenth of March," Grace said. "This time, it's going to pass. Prime Minster Monroe is bringing it in as a government bill, and Mrs. McNeil writes that the Women's Franchise League has no doubt of it this time. I want to be there. It's history in the making."

Lily smiled. "If you know it's going to pass it's hardly history in the making. What's the point of going to see it if you know how it will turn out?"

"To be there. To bear witness." Grace looked up from her cup. "Like you and the others did back in '93 when you sat in the gallery and watched the motion defeated."

"That busybody Abby Hayward told you that story, did she? We were ignorant young girls and we didn't know what we were doing."

"You were fighting for a cause that's finally going to win. Are you so sure you were wrong?"

Lily sighed. "I'm so worn out, Grace, I'm not sure of anything anymore. I used to worry—I still do—about what will happen when nobody knows their proper place. Men and women, husbands and wives. Everything will fall apart."

"Perhaps it won't, though. Perhaps it will just change. You said yourself things are different now than they were thirty years ago. In another thirty years they'll be different again. Today women are getting the vote; maybe in thirty years a woman will be prime minister."

"I doubt it. Though I suppose a woman would be no worse than the crowd they've got in there now."

Grace got up and began to clear away the table. They all did so many things now that had once been clearly the maid's job. All of them in the manse were like people living near a battlefront or through some natural disaster, Lily thought—all roles were renegotiated and everyone worked together in such amity that she and Grace could even sit down and have a half-ways civil discussion about the franchise.

"That petition of yours," Lily said. "All those years ago."

"It's all right, Mother. It doesn't matter." Grace was at the sink, stacking dishes, her back to Lily.

Lily remembered as vividly as yesterday that night nearly three years ago when she'd stood by the stove holding those papers, those signatures Grace had traipsed over Catalina and Port Union getting the women to write out. That night she had thought for the first time in years of her own petition, the one only Abby had signed. She thought, too, of everything else she'd burned, all David's letters. How easy it was to let the flames eat a mistake, to leave nothing but ash. On that memory Lily had lifted the burner of the stove and dropped Grace's pages onto the smoldering embers. There was a moment, before they caught, when she could still have snatched them back. She stuck her hand into the stove to grab the paper out, thinking how Grace would feel. Then she drew her hand back, stinging from the heat. If her own mother had burned that foolish suffrage petition back in 1893—if Eleanor had ever paid enough attention, or been brave enough—what pain, what heartbreak she might have spared Lily! And now Lily might spare Grace.

So Lily had thought, that night standing over the stove, watching the paper burn away to ash, women's names winking out at her through the flames before they vanished. It was hard to believe, now, that she had done that to her daughter. Lily knew she couldn't have coped these last months without Grace and Jack. The little

Trudy J. Morgan-Cole

matter of Grace gallivanting off to St. John's to see the bill for women's votes pass the house was a small thing by comparison.

"Maybe it doesn't matter now," Lily said. "But it was—a harsh thing to do." She picked up the knives and forks, took them over to the sink where Grace was stacking dishes for Hannah to wash in the morning. "Too harsh. I knew it even then."

"About the things Mrs. Parker told me," Grace said. She sounded like she was saying words she'd been struggling with for a long time but finally had to say out loud—just as Lily had felt a moment ago. "About you being a suffragette."

"That's not what they—we. Not what we called ourselves."

"I know, I'm sorry. But what I've been meaning to tell you for a long time is—I didn't hear all that just from Mrs. Parker. I—I met David Reid in New York."

Lily could not have been more shocked if Grace had hauled off and slapped her. Here she had just been thinking how nice it was to work side by side with her daughter, the two of them getting along so well, and then Grace said that name. The platter Lily was holding, her big china one with the rose border, slipped from her fingers and crashed to the floor.

Grace knelt at once to get it. "I'm sorry, that's my fault—I know that was a shock. Look, it's all right, it's not broken."

Lily took the plate from her. "Yes it is," she said, tracing with her fingertip the long line of a crack that had appeared in the plate's surface. Well. It wasn't an heirloom or anything. "I suppose that's Abby's doing too, is it, telling you about...him? About Mr. Reid."

Grace carried the platter to the sink and began rinsing off the plates. "Mrs. Parker told me his name, but only after I badgered her. I'd already figured out a good deal for myself. Mr. Reid told me the rest of the story. He's alive and well, by the way, and he remembers you kindly. I'm—I'm sorry, Mother."

"Sorry—for what? For digging up my private business, for

poking into matters that were dead and buried before you were ever born?"

"I'm sorry about ... about the baby you lost."

"You should never have brought any of this up. The past should stay buried." *Buried, like that tiny grave in the Greenspond cemetery. Buried, like Charley's bones on a battlefield in France.*

"He writes to me sometimes—Mr. Reid does. And I write to Mrs. Ohman too, since that time I stayed with her in Montreal. And Mrs. Parker, of course." Grace did keep up a voluminous flow of correspondence; Lily had not realized that so many people from her own past wrote to her daughter. "They are all concerned for you, with Papa's illness."

"Those people—they're all ghosts to me," Lily said. She picked up the cracked rose platter, traced the broken line with her fingertip.

Upstairs in her room Lily tried not to imagine this meeting in New York between her daughter and David Reid—what they talked about, how they met, what he looked like now. Was he married? Did he have children? Had he become the successful reporter he'd dreamed of being?

Instead of playing out that scene, she tried to remember the girl she had been, the Lily who had fallen in love with David Reid and sinned with him. Years ago, the Reverend's mother had kept in her house a set of those wooden Russian dolls that nested inside one another. Was a person like that, Lily wondered, all her past selves nested neatly inside, each new layer of life built over the next, protecting as well as concealing what had gone before? That was what Grace wanted, to break her mother apart, to find inside a Lily that had lived and died long ago, tiny and preserved and perfect. But Lily thought the only way she resembled the Russian dolls was that she, too, was hollow inside.

Trudy J. Morgan-Cole

Grace

CHAPTER THIRTY-SEVEN

T HE GALLERY WAS crowded with women. All the Women's Franchise League were there, along with women Grace knew from Gower Street Church. There were even a few working women— factory girls in cotton dresses, sitting among the ladies in silks and feathered hats. Mrs. Salter Earle had brought a contingent from the NIWA.

There was, as Grace had told her mother, no real suspense about the outcome. Still there was something thrilling about seeing the men rise one after another to say, "Aye," "Aye," "Aye." When the last vote was registered a burst of applause filled the room. Grace jumped to her feet with the rest, waving her hat in the air.

On the way out of the Colonial Building, Grace found herself walking alongside Julia Salter Earle. The woman had always intimidated her, but she had greeted Grace like an old friend tonight in the House, and now took her arm as they walked down Military Road. "The real test," the older woman said, "is how long will it be before we're out of the gallery and down there on the floor along with them?"

"Perhaps you'll have to run in the next election," Grace said, thinking that if any woman could do such an unlikely thing, it would be this tough old warrior.

"Oh, there won't be another general election for years. Monroe's got a solid grip on power. But we won't have to wait that long. I intend to run in the city election this fall. If you're living in town by then you can vote for me—maybe even work for the campaign!"

"I will, if I'm here." Grace felt light-hearted, almost light-headed with the excitement of the evening. Groups of women pushed past each other, arms linked, talking and laughing. But thinking of where she might be in the fall made her grow serious. "I don't know what will happen with Papa—or, for that matter, what will happen to Mother after he dies." Jack had a job at the *Advocate* office—it wasn't work he loved, but he was willing to do it so that Grace could help her parents. The nurse at the clinic in Port Union called on Jack when she needed to set a broken leg or do some other job where she needed a second set of hands. "We'll get back to St. John's sometime, I'm sure," Grace told Mrs. Salter Earle, "but when that will be I can't say."

"Well, you should arrange to come in for a while before the election if you possibly can," Mrs. Earle said. "Fannie McNeil and May Kennedy are talking about running too—imagine that, three women in an election!"

"What if you all ran and won? The council would be half women!"

"It'll be a miracle if even one woman gets elected, but if only one does, it will be I. I'm not running merely for the novelty of having a Mrs. on the ballot—I'm running for the causes I've always fought for, for the good of the working man and woman."

"And all those working women can vote for you now!"

"Only if they own property," Mrs. Earle reminded her. While the new Franchise Act for Newfoundland had no property requirements for either men or women, the city of St. John's still required voters to own property in the city. "Don't you remember last city election, some of the Franchise League women had their husbands put outbuildings and sheds in the wives' names so they'd will be listed as property owners? If you move back to town you'll have to get yourself a little henhouse so you can vote for me. You are twenty-five, aren't you?"

"Just this year," Grace said. The law still was not truly equal between men and women, for men could vote at twenty-one and women not until they were twenty-five, which, she thought, was entirely ridiculous, for anyone who had ever met a man and a woman of twenty-one would have no difficulty saying which was the more sober, mature, and sensible.

She thought she would stay in town for a fortnight after the vote in the House: she could do some shopping on Water Street, pick up things the FPU store in Port Union couldn't supply. She could visit with friends as well as with Daisy and Grandfather, go see Ivan Barry and a few other people she wanted to look up. She could attend the first meeting of the Women's Franchise League under its new name, the League of Women Voters. To be back in town and free of the manse, dominated as it was by her father's illness, was as heady as an intoxicant.

But the next morning a cable came from Jack: REVEREND FAILING STOP COME AT ONCE STOP.

As the train wheels unrolled the miles below her, Grace wondered if she ought to have left Catalina at all. She had not thought her father was close to death, but Jack would not have called her home for any lesser reason. She did not want to be away when he died.

She felt closer to her father in these last months than she ever had. It would not change his feeling towards her or hers toward him, if she were gone when he died. The person she really thought of was Lily. In the months Grace had been back home, everything she had done—every book she had read to her father, every tray of custard she had carried to the sickroom, every time she had helped Jack turn him in bed and change the sheets—some part of it had always been a performance for which Lily was the audience. At long last, Grace thought, Lily was grateful to her. Their shared effort created a bond, however fragile, between them. What would Lily think if Grace was in St. John's celebrating the passage of the women's suffrage bill when the Reverend died?

The wait to change trains in Shoal Harbour seemed impossibly long, with no way to find out what was happening at home. *He could be dead already*, Grace thought. She wondered what her mother would do in the Reverend's absence. The manse belonged to the Methodist church—or rather, she corrected herself, to the United Church, as it was now called, though church union made no practical difference in a place like Catalina where there were no Congregationalists to unite with. The circuit would likely want either to install Reverend Kenny, the supply preacher, as a permanent minister, or bring in someone more experienced. Either way, they were letting the Collins family stay in the manse now only as an act of kindness: they would require it again from Lily when the Reverend was dead. And what then?

Jack met her at the station. "The doctor was in town just after you left," he said. "He took a look at your father and felt he couldn't last out the week. He's not eating at all now, and we're trying to give him water, but he can't even keep that down."

She was too late, in all but the strictest sense, for her father was beyond recognizing her. Lily sat in a straight-backed chair by the window. "Grace is here now, Mother Collins. Why don't you go get some rest," Jack said.

"I don't need to rest," Lily said. She had the unbending air of a sentry at her post, afraid she would be charged with desertion if she wavered.

Trudy J. Morgan-Cole

So they all kept vigil, Grace and Lily in the sickroom, Jack doing what needed to be done around the house and keeping visitors appraised of the Reverend's condition. Grace read from the Psalms from time to time; she couldn't tell if her father heard her.

In the middle of the night, after Grace had dozed in her chair and startled awake, Lily said, as if continuing a conversation, "Your father owns a piece of land over in Port Union."

"He—I beg your pardon?" Grace had to rearrange the words in her tired brain before they made sense.

"He bought a parcel of land over there, out past the FPU property, about five years ago. I think he might have thought of building on it for his retirement, or maybe as an investment. I had a look at his will the other day—he's left two thirds of the land to me, and one-third to you."

Grace was surprised: she had not really expected any legacy except perhaps her father's collection of theology books, which he had said she could have her pick from before donating the rest to the church. "What will you do with the land?" she asked her mother.

"Sell my bit of it, I suppose. I don't see anything to hold me to Port Union now your father's—that is, when your father's gone."

But she was almost right: he was nearly gone. His breathing grew more and more shallow; there was a rattle in his throat, and by morning he had stopped breathing altogether. Grace was holding his hand when the tiny wisps of breath disappeared from between his lips. She was amazed that his hand felt no sudden difference. He was a dying man; then he was a dead one. Ashes to ashes, dust to dust.

He had been doubtful, she knew, about the soul flying off to heaven after death, and when he preached funeral sermons he liked to emphasize instead the resurrection on the Judgement Day. He had told Grace once he would trust the Lord to take care of what might happen to him until then. Grace, who had her own questions about the sweet by and by, found it easier to believe that he was sleeping peacefully than that he was hovering somewhere above, looking down as she and Jack made funeral arrangements and Lily moved between the kitchen and the parlour, accepting the condolences of a steady stream of visitors and advising the maid on what to do with the cakes and pies and cooked dishes they brought.

Grace surprised herself by bursting into wild sobs as her father's coffin was lowered into the grave on the hillside looking down over Catalina Harbour. It was a sunny day, though the March wind was biting, and sunlight danced like diamonds on the water. Grace clung to Jack, but Lily stood a little apart, her arms wrapped around her own body as if holding herself together.

The minister said the words of committal and Jack moved forward with the other pallbearers to lower the coffin into the ground. Grace moved closer to Lily. She could not remember a time when she and her mother had shared the easy affection of so many mothers and daughters, arms around each other, hands entwined. Lily seemed to forever want to pick at Grace's thoughts and behaviour but she kept her body apart, guarded like a citadel. For a moment it felt like a strange thing for Grace to do, to lift her arm and put it around her mother's shoulders. She felt her mother's slender body stiffen, then melt towards her, 'til Lily's head was resting against Grace's shoulder. Only then, for the first time since the Reverend had stopped breathing, did Grace see tears on her mother's face.

The next day, Reverend Kenny told Lily the church would give her a month to pack her things before he moved into the manse. It would have been time anyway. Catalina had had the same minister for over ten years, which was nearly unheard of. Reverend Kenny himself had gotten the word that the pulpit would be his: he disappeared on the train to St. John's for a week and came back with a new bride, as fresh and pretty and unexpected as if he had gone to Ayre's and bought her for the occasion. Grace and Jack moved their things into Jack's parents' house, and Mrs. Perry told them they could stay

Trudy J. Morgan-Cole

as long as they liked. "But maybe you'll be wanting to build a house on your piece of land over in Port Union?" she suggested. It was almost palpable, her desire to have them stay—she, who had once wanted to send Jack off to India to doctor the heathen.

But Grace and Jack were not going to stay. They would keep the land—not just Grace's third but Lily's two-thirds, which Jack bought from her with money his father had given them for a wedding gift. They would build a house there eventually, they agreed: this would be the home they came back to. Someday.

Grace walked home from Port Union to Catalina one day after visiting her plot of land. It was raised up on a little height of land above the water, to the west of Mr. Coaker's Bungalow, and she pictured the modest house she and Jack would build there someday. She stopped at the Union store to buy a few things and walked on past the bustle of the town: women going in and out of the store, men at work in the wood shop and the printshop and the bottling factory, boats at the wharves getting ready for the fishing season. Spring was coming to the harbour. *When we have children*, Grace thought, *then we'll come back. This will be the place to raise our family.*

She imagined how the town would grow in the coming years. Mr. Coaker was in poor health and spent his winters in Jamaica now; a few cynics said he had made his money in Newfoundland and gone off to retire in the sun. But Grace remained loyal, if not to the man himself, at least to his dream. *None of this*, she thought, *would exist without him.* People had grand dreams, and a few actually tried to put their dreams in practice, and invariably they fell short. Trying to change all Newfoundland, Mr. Coaker had changed only a tiny piece of it. But surely it was better to try?

She and Jack were going to St. John's. Jack had a job as a hospital orderly; Grace was going to be assistant matron of a new home for unwed mothers. She would be there when the city election was held;

she could vote for Mrs. Salter Earle and Mrs. McNeil and Miss Kennedy. She and Jack might go back down on the Labrador sometime, and they would travel, and they had their piece of land and someday their house in Port Union. And they, too, might find little pieces of the world they could change. Life was open and broad as a spring day, full of plans and possibilities.

Those thoughts carried Grace all the way over the path that joined Port Union to Catalina, over the bridge that spanned the droke and down to the manse. At the door of the manse Grace paused. She thought of her mother inside, packing up or giving away the remnants of her married life. Lily was ruthless about getting rid of things, paring down her belongings. Just as Grace's own future opened up before her, Lily's life was narrowing, like a long hallway with doors being shut all around. Wife, minister's wife, even mother, really, with Charley gone and Grace grown and married— all those roles were over for Lily now, Grace thought. Lily had said nothing about where she planned to live, what she would do with the remaining years of widowhood.

Inside she found Lily writing labels to stick on trunks. "Ask Jack to come down this evening with a cart and find a boy to load these trunks up for me. I want to take them to the train station tomorrow— I'm going to ship them to Papa's house in town." She stood up, brushing off her hands. "There are only three. I've gotten rid of most everything else. I never liked most of this furniture; Joe Kenny and his new wife are going to buy it off me, and they're welcome to it."

"Then—you're sure you won't stay in Catalina?"

Lily looked surprised. "What would I stay here for? I never liked the place. I never liked being around the bay at all. I used to always hope your father would get a call to a church in St. John's. The Lord knows ambition is more important than piety if you want to get ahead in the church."

Trudy J. Morgan-Cole

"I never heard you say that—that you didn't like it around the bay," Grace said.

"Well, it didn't seem right to say it when he was alive. It would have seemed—ungrateful. Your father, God rest his soul, took good care of me. In his own way."

"So—will you go back to town? To Grandfather's house?"

"Under Daisy's roof? Not likely. My trunks will be all right there." She turned to look over her shoulder at Grace. "Are you worried I'll want to live with you and Jack? I won't, you know. I'd rather have a few rooms of my own—and I can afford it. Your father left us better provided than I thought, putting his money into that piece of land when land was cheap over in Port Union. And I'll say this for Jack and his father: they gave me a decent price for my piece of it. You don't have to trouble yourself about me."

"You make it sound like you might just walk off into the sunset and I'll never hear from you again."

Lily gave her an odd look. "And that would bother you, would it?"

"Of course it would! You're my mother." Grace was so accustomed to Lily wanting to know about—and pass judgement on—Grace's every move, every plan. Now, it seemed, she was absorbed for the first time with plans of her own.

"Well, I am going away for a little while," Lily said. "I'm going to follow my trunks into town next week, spend a night or two at Papa's house, and book passage on a steamer. I have it in mind to take a little trip."

"Where?"

"To Canada or the States, or both—I'm not entirely sure yet. I have some invitations to reply to, some old friends to see."

Grace left her mother's house that afternoon—remembering to send Jack back later in the day with a boy and a cart—thinking how little one ever knew of another person. Or maybe it was just how little she knew of Lily. Her image of a corridor with doors closing all around had been so wrong. Lily planned to turn a corner, walk through an entirely new door—or perhaps re-enter an old one.

"She must be going to New York," Grace said to Jack in bed that night. "To stay with Mrs. Parker, I suppose, but I think she plans to look up Mr. Reid."

"Do you really think she'd do that? After all these years?"

"Why else would she be so secretive about where she's going?"

All Lily had been willing to reveal about her own plans was, "When I get to where I'm going, I'll send you a letter so you'll know where to reach me. Will that do?"

"I suppose it'll have to," Grace had said.

She imagined her mother going off on the train—she had never seen Lily travel alone—to St. John's, then on the steamer to New York. Imagined a letter coming with a New York postmark and an American stamp. Tried—and failed—to imagine what her mother might do next, after showing up in New York and telling David Reid she was alive, well, and widowed.

Grace thought of David Reid's words, that living the life you wanted meant more than being with the person you loved. Did he really believe that, or was it only the thing he told himself to get him through the long and lonely days? Grace thought of their piece of land in Port Union, of two rooms on a St. John's street, of a place on the Labrador coast she'd never seen. She nestled her head into Jack's shoulder and he moved a sleepy arm around her. She hadn't lived long enough to be sure, but she thought David Reid was probably wrong.

Trudy J. Morgan-Cole

Lily

CHAPTER THIRTY-EIGHT

$\mathscr{S}$HE STANDS ON deck as near the bow of the *Bruce* as she can, wrapped up in her tatty old fur, the harsh northeaster blowing straight off the waves into her face. Lily is the only passenger out on deck on this fierce day. She had been huddled in her cabin like all the rest but she could not resist the urge to be outdoors, to watch the ship slicing through the water, to know that Newfoundland was falling behind her and the rest of the world drawing closer.

She has crossed the Gulf of St. Lawrence twice before in her life: twenty years ago with the Reverend when they went to that conference in Toronto, and ten years before that—the time she ran away.

For years Lily used to think about that journey, wonder what would have happened had she sent the cable to David Reid instead to Obadiah Collins. She can't even really remember, now, why she made the choice she did. She only remembers sitting in the hotel room looking at the two handwritten messages and knowing she would send one of them. She had not decided until she was dressed to go to the cable station. She remembers the slips of paper in her gloved hands. Maybe she had actually carried both pieces of paper as far as the cable office, reserving decision until the very last minute. But why one and not the other? Had she been driven by a sense of what was right, by the vows she had taken to her husband?

She dimly recalls debating in her head whether her marriage, at that time not consummated, was a real marriage at all. She could have easily convinced herself that David, the man she had slept with, was her real husband in the eyes of God. It wasn't morality, then. It must have been that she chose what was safe, what she knew. Going with David, going to New York and into whatever unimaginable life he was living there, would have placed her forever beyond the reach of the world she had known.

She cannot trace now what might have been in the mind of that young girl thirty years ago, but maybe, in the end, she sent the cable to the one man she was certain would come for her. Not out of love: David loved her in a way Obadiah never did. Duty, in the end, is stronger than love. Perhaps that was what she gambled on. And she lived thirty years with the consequences of that gamble.

Lily was so shocked to hear Grace talk of meeting David, sitting across from him at a restaurant table. He must be an old man now, as Lily herself is old, while in her mind he is preserved like a butterfly pinned on a board, forever young and handsome.

She cannot imagine what his life has contained all these years in New York. Hers has been as predictable and safe as she knew it would be when she chose to stay with the Reverend. The only thing she could not have predicted was the war that had taken Charley from her. That was not part of the pattern. But if she had cabled David Reid that day in Halifax, instead of cabling her husband, then she would never have conceived Charley at all. She would not have had—Charley himself would not have had—those twenty good years of young life that he laid down on the soil of France. And there would have been no Grace. One cannot wish one's children unmade.

Now it is over. The Reverend is dead. Charley is dead. Grace will go on into her own life with Jack. Lily wanted Grace by her side all those years, doing fancywork on the porch of the manse in Catalina, and instead Grace blew about like a kite on the breeze. But she came home in the end, when she was needed. "You're here now and that's what matters." Lily ought to have said those words to Grace, as the Reverend said something of the sort to her: a kind of absolution.

It is too cold to stay outside; she goes below to her cabin and sleeps until the ship docks in Nova Scotia. This time she knows which train to take and where she is going: no hard decisions to make, no cables to send. She has money in her wallet and a letter of invitation in her purse.

Is it a mistake to think you can revisit the past? For thirty years Lily has set her face against the past, or at least against that year or two after the fire when she was growing into an entirely different kind of Lily. She has tried to forget not only the people she knew and loved in those years, but also the books she read, the articles she wrote, the meetings she attended—everything that made up her life in those years. There was so much more to it than lying down on a bed with David Reid. She made herself believe that if that was a mistake, then all the rest must have been a mistake too. Grace became a suffragist and Lily was terrified, frightened as much by her own past as by Grace's future, frightened of the demons hidden in Pandora's box.

You can't change the past, she thinks. But you can, perhaps, make amends for what went wrong the last time you saw someone. You might try to weave the past into your present life before you go on into the future. Lily has been feeling old for a long, long time, but today, with the train wheels clicking away the miles of the Maritimes beneath her, she feels that perhaps fifty-one is not that old. She knows women who were widowed at fifty and lived to be nearly ninety; they were widows longer than they were wives.

As dusk falls the porter comes around to pull down the sleeper berths. Lily, who sat up on the long train ride to Port-aux-Basques and slept little on the steamer, relaxes gratefully into her berth, lulled by the gentle rocking of the train. She makes a mental note that it is always worth the extra money to pay for a sleeper. She must remember that for the journey home, or wherever she goes next.

That night, and the next day as the train clicks away the miles, Lily reads *The Age of Innocence*, a novel she filched from Grace's shelves. She reads the whole book, from beginning to end: there is plenty of time. And then she wishes there was someone to talk with about what she has just read. She hopes that her future, whatever it contains, will include conversations about books. For so many years she has read nothing but church papers and ladies' magazines.

Now the train is rolling into the final station, the big city with its towers and streets emerging out of the countryside all around, everything becoming closer and greyer. Lily is not surprised to find her heart pounding a little. She hears the conductor's voice call out the stop, and the other travellers get their cases down. A man hands Lily's cases to her. She has two: a big one and a small. She will need a porter.

She steps off the train: the platform swirls with people, with faces, with voices. For a moment she feels overwhelmed and wishes she were back in the silent manse. But that is no longer her home. What a gift, to live so many years in a house that wasn't hers, so that upon her husband's death she is forced out into the world.

"Lily! Lily Hunt, is that really you?"

Years pass, everything changes, but she would know that voice anywhere. Lily turns, straining to see through the crowds on the Montreal platform, looking for the face that matches that voice.

Trudy J. Morgan-Cole

But the face, of course, has been changed by time just as her own has. It is an old face now, plump and wrinkled, but the eyes still keen and sharp as ever. She opens her arms: just as in her letters, it is as if the years in between and the harshness of their last meeting never happened.

"Dear Lily," says Jessie Ohman, "I am so glad you have come." And Lily steps forward.

A Sudden Sun

AUTHOR'S NOTE AND ACKNOWLEDGEMENTS

A SUDDEN SUN is a work of fiction, and my main characters—Lily, Obadiah and Grace Collins, David Reid, Jack Perry, and all their families—are entirely products of my imagination. However, the world in which they live—which consists mainly of St. John's, Catalina and Port Union, Newfoundland, in the 1890s and 1920s—is real, as are many of the minor characters in the story.

Real people who make an appearance in these pages include Jessie Murray Ohman, Julia Salter Earle, May Kennedy, Fannie McNeil, and Sir William Coaker. In all cases, while I have incorporated as much as I can of the known biographies of these historical individuals, they are used as fictional characters, and dialogue attributed to them is my own invention.

Not nearly enough has been written about the movement for women's suffrage in Newfoundland. I am indebted to two sources in particular: Margot I. Duley's book *Where Once Our Mothers Stood We Stand: Women's Suffrage in Newfoundland, 1890-1925*, and Marian Frances White's film *The Untold Story of the Suffragists of Newfoundland*. White's film was what first aroused my interest in the story of Newfoundland suffragists, and among the many primary and secondary sources I read in preparing for the novel, that film and Duley's book were the guideposts to which I returned over and over.

As much as possible, I have tried to keep the adventures of my fictional characters within the boundaries of known history, but I have taken creative license in filling in some of the gaps. For example, Jessie Ohman's career as temperance crusader, suffragist, and editor of the *Water Lily* can be traced through her writings in that paper. But some of her later activities I've depicted here, such as her conflicts with other WCTU leaders or her attempts to start a Woman Suffrage League, are the products of my imagination as little is known about her career outside the pages of the *Water Lily*. In 1923, May Kennedy travelled alone to the International Woman Suffrage Congress in Rome as Newfoundland's sole delegate, but I did not think history would be too severely damaged by allowing Grace Collins, a fictional character, to travel with her.

I am thankful to the many people who answered questions or helped me in my research, including but not limited to: the wonderful staff at the Centre for Newfoundland Studies and the City of St. John's Archives; the aforementioned Marian Frances White; Janet McNaughton, who was very helpful in directing me to sources on the 1892 St. John's fire; and the staff at the various historic properties in the town of Port Union.

Thanks to everyone at Breakwater Books, a team of people who are truly committed to producing great Newfoundland literature, and to my keen-eyed editor, Marnie Parsons, who made many helpful suggestions. I always owe thanks to my friends the Strident Women for their encouragement, particularly, in the case of this book, to Tina Chaulk and Jennifer Morgan who gave the manuscript a thorough reading and made several insightful critiques.

I was privileged to have been able to spend a week at the Independent Writers' Retreat at the Tatamagouche Centre in Tatamagouche, Nova Scotia, working on a draft of this manuscript in a beautiful and serene environment. I'm grateful to facilitators Gwen Davies and Chris Benjamin, and to my fellow workshop participants, particularly Katrina Stonoff, for being part of that wonderful experience.

Thanks to readers of my blog and viewers of my vlog who have followed my "Writing Wednesday" series of YouTube videos through the writing of this novel. I continue to be grateful to the good people of Starbucks/Chapters in St. John's for providing me with my "office space" and a steady stream of raspberry mochas.

As many readers know and others might guess from the dedication, my mother, Joan (Sue) Morgan died suddenly while I was in the middle of writing this book about mothers and daughters. This is the first book I've ever written that has not been copyedited by her keen eyes, and I missed her input more than words can tell. I am deeply grateful to my dad, Don Morgan, who was, with this as other books, one of my very first readers and read it not only with an editor's eye but with the eye of someone who remembers a version of St. John's that has long passed away, and was often able to suggest corrections or additions to the historical details in these pages. I have been blessed from the very beginning to have parents who believed that writing books was a perfectly sensible thing to do, and have always supported me in that endeavour. Likewise, my husband, Jason, and my teenagers, Chris and Emma, have provided more love and support than I can ever thank them for.

Despite all the editorial eyes that have gone over these pages, any historical errors that remain, intentional or unintentional, are entirely my own.

$\mathcal{T}$RUDY J. MORGAN-COLE is a writer and teacher who lives in St. John's, Newfoundland. Her previous books include *By the Rivers of Brooklyn* (2009) and *That Forgetful Shore* (2011), winner of the Newfoundland and Labrador Heritage and History Prize.